C000050222

Library of Congress Number: 2022951719
ISBN (paperback): 978-1-956450-60-6
ISBN (eBook): 978-1-956450-61-3

For further information, contact:

Thousand Acres Press
825 Wildlife
Estes Park, CO 80517

CHANTZ

Tim Rayborn

CHAPTER ONE

"Now, they'll see. We'll show them all."

She felt the power rising inside her, returning. She was strong and it was good, very good. Her mind retreated into the grey, as if submerged under a thick fog, but she wasn't fully gone. It was like that when it flowed through her, but that was a small price to pay for the thrill.

In the body that was hers but now not totally hers, she opened her mouth to let the power out, an ancient, primal energy. Where did it come from? What did it want? Who knew? Who cared? In the moment, she reveled in it.

And out in front of her, they were there, just for her. They hung on her every word, gesture, and expression. They were hers for the taking or the leaving, all come to adore her. She could raise them up to the heights of bliss, or destroy their hearts utterly, and she knew it. Maybe she could even give them life, or the opposite.

This power was some ancient force that bound her to it and

itself to the world around her. And she welcomed it. Let all love her and fear her in equal measure.

She stepped back into the light, where they could see her, and began her song.

"I am strong," she sang.

We are strong, the power answered.

* * *

Reality wasn't what it used to be.

One moment, everything was fine. Just a normal, run-of-the-mill indie goth alternative rock show at the Leeds University Union on a Sunday afternoon in late April. Just a young band singing about the most angsty issues of the moment, playing less-than-commercial music that was a cut above the usual pop twaddle. Nothing out of the ordinary, really.

But then, things got decidedly odd, downright bizarre. Up was down, or maybe it was just an inverted up? The walls were closing in, or were they falling away very close by? It got very dark, almost brightly so. And the intense volume of the music was almost inaudible. If this was a part of the show, it was damned strange, but strangely appealing.

The band in question, the Mystic Wedding Weasels, was making something of a splash recently, and the hall was packed with young fans eager to soak up their particular brand of musical peculiarity, most notably in the figure of their enigmatic singer. And she seemed to be the source of this sudden oddness. At least, twelve-year-old witch Jilly Pleeth thought so.

Jilly couldn't pass up the opportunity to see her favorite new band live, and she'd invited her friend Lluck along for the experience. He was half-human, half Indian Fae, all teenage attitude, and could affect the laws of probability in his favor. So, not your typical fourteen-year-old. She'd met him last winter during a rather crazy adventure involving an ancient Germanic forest spirit that wanted to eat his heart; as one does. Also, his long-lost mum was now dating Jilly's best friend, a shadow with glowing red eyes; it's a rather long and strange story.

In any case, returning to the matter at hand, everything had been as expected for the first few songs, when things shifted into all sorts of odd and back, but what was happening?

"Did you see that?" Jilly asked Lluck over the din of the current song, something about feeling dreadful in the face of ultimate despair.

"See what?" he half-shouted back at her.

"You didn't notice how everything just went all... funny for a bit?"

"What are you talking about?"

"Everything just changed!"

"Changed how? What are you on about?"

"Something crazy strange is going on. It doesn't feel normal."

"All right, Ms. Witchy, I'll take your word for it. But strange is the new normal these days, anyway, so who cares? Can we just watch the show, please?"

Jilly didn't answer, but she remained unsettled. She turned her attention back to the singer, Chantz, at least that's what she called herself. Jilly didn't know her real name, if she had one. She looked to be in her early twenties, sported long black hair (with a streak of green-dyed tresses cascading down the right side of her head) and the obligatory black vestments: black dress, fishnets, black Doc Marten boots, long and wispy black shirt, open and trailing about her. But her voice was the real draw. It was enchanting, captivating;

it drew in Jilly like a... spell. Jilly scrunched up her nose in that way that she always did when alarm bells went off in her head. Well, perhaps they were more like wind chimes.

Over the past several months, she'd been studying magic after learning she was a witch, a descendent of the greatest mystic the north of England had ever known, who also happened to be alive and well, and currently acting as her mentor. Another long story. Jilly was learning to detect magic in her surroundings and in others, and this was magical, some kind of audible enchantment.

She grabbed Lluck by the arm and yelled into his ear. "It's magic!"

"Yeah, it's all right isn't it?" He bobbed his head up and down in time with the song.

She rolled her eyes. "No, you nitwit! Not the show, the singer."

"Well, yeah, she sounds good, and she's fit, if you're into goth birds."

Jilly smacked him on the arm. "Her voice! She's casting some kind of a spell as she's singing!"

"What? That's daft!"

"Any more daft than what you can do? Or me?"

Lluck shook his head and went back to bobbing it and watching the show.

Jilly remained unsettled, quite sure she'd just experienced something very out of the ordinary. And in the next moment, she was proven right.

Things got very odd again, even more so. Everything shifted and the real world seemed to fall away. Time ran backwards, or maybe it sped up. Everyone disappeared except her, or maybe they were all still there and she'd gone somewhere else. Visions of night skies and stars swam in her head, followed by radiant pools of water and pits of darkness that oozed despair. She was upside down and then right side up, enclosed in a tiny box and then standing in a field in a large, if small, stone circle and a host of lights dancing about it. Walls appeared and started to melt, rainbow colors turned to grey, spinning like vortices. And through it all she heard that voice: singing, inviting, captivating, and maybe just a bit dangerous.

And then she was back, but the room had gone dark and the music had stopped, or had it? There was an uncomfortable mumbling in the crowd, as if a record was being played too slowly. Fear rushed through her. She knew she needed to leave the hall right away. She grabbed Lluck's arm.

"I don't like this. Something's wrong."

But he didn't respond or even seem to hear her. She tugged at his arm, forcing him to move with her as she made for an open exit door. Her sense of dread became stronger as she walked, but she didn't know why Lluck seemed oblivious to it.

Something was watching her. She knew it. Something from that fantastical world she'd just been dragged through seemed to have hitched a ride back and was keeping a keen and unwelcome eye on her. She clutched at Lluck's arm and broke into a run toward the door. She had to get out.

"Come on!" she yelled as the path seemed to recede away from her and she realized that maybe she was still trapped in whatever reality shift Chantz might have conjured up. If she could just make it to the doorway before it vanished. Something—an old woman's voice?—laughed. The exit slammed shut.

"Sorry! Um, terribly sorry, everyone!" A young woman's voice with an Irish accent sounded over the PA. It was Chantz. "Looks like we've blown out the speakers. I don't think we'll be able to get them working again today. This is bollocks, but the show's over, sad to say."

There was a collective groan, and Jilly stopped to look around her. Everything was fine. She stood, holding Lluck's arm, right where they'd been standing the whole time. The hall lights were on, and the band looked apologetic.

"Um, we'll try to make it up to you all," Chantz continued, "see if we can reschedule another gig in the near future. I think that's all we can do. Again, we're so sorry! Thanks for coming out! We have some merch for sale at the tables. Cheers!"

There was a disappointed commotion in the audience, but some people headed to said tables, or began to make their way to the exits, which now looked entirely normal in the artificial light of the hall.

"That was really bizarre," Jilly said, still holding Lluck's arm.

"What? They blew the sound system out, or something." He shook his arm free. "It's a pisser, but it happens."

"You didn't see anything?"

"See what? What are you on about? Are you still thinking about magic or spells, or whatever?" He waved a dismissive hand.

She sighed. "No. Never mind. We should just go." She looked over to see the band taking away their gear. Chantz glanced around, like she was nervous, even afraid. Soon, they all disappeared backstage.

No one else seemed to have seen what Jilly did. She left the union feeling confused and disturbed.

"So, do you want to hang out for bit, or something?" she asked Lluck once they were outside, trying to lighten her mood. She squinted in the sunny afternoon light that hurt her eyes after being in the dark and realized this probably made her look angry.

"Thanks, but I should probably just get on home. Dad wanted to do some training later on, and he'll be waiting for me."

"Fine. How's that all going, by the way?"

"All right. He's getting better at it. He seems to understand how my luck powers work now and knows how to respond when I use them. He's not a full-blown superhero, or anything, but he's way better than he was last winter!"

"That's a relief," Jilly said. "I guess I'll wander on back toward the train station; want to walk with me?"

"Yeah, all right. I can get a bus from the city center."

They traversed in relative silence down the long, gradual hill that led from the university into central Leeds. Everything seemed normal, a bit too normal. Jilly thought to bring up the whole reality shifting thing again, but decided that he either really didn't see anything, or didn't want to talk about it, so she let it go.

"Right," he said as they reached a queue of bus stops several minutes later. "I can get home from here. You all right getting to the station?"

"Yes, I can walk back to the train station of a busy city in broad daylight." She rolled her eyes.

"Yeah, all right, all right. I know you can take care of yourself. Probably just turn an enemy into a toad, or something, anyway."

"Yeah something like that. So..." She fidgeted.

"So." He looked everywhere but at her.

"See you 'round sometime?"

"Yeah, that'd be all right. We'll catch another show, or something."

"Sounds good. Um... say hi to your dad for me."

"Shall do."

"And your mum."

He nodded. "She's coming round tonight, actually."

"Brilliant! How is she?"

"Good. Been spending time with Qwyrk, I think. They seem to be getting on well. I mean, I guess."

Jilly suppressed a grin but was also annoyed that she knew almost nothing about how her favorite relationship was progressing, and was only hearing about it third-hand. She let it go without asking for any more details, not that he would have them, anyway.

"Right then, I'm off," she announced.

"Good. I mean not good, I mean, you know."

"Yeah, I do. Hug?"

"Yeah, go on."

She smiled and threw her arms around him, not sure until now if he wanted her to or not. But really, she knew he wanted her to. "Let's chat soon. I've learned some new magical stuff that I'd love to tell you about. Pretty cool."

"Like being able to detect reality shifts?"

She stood back. "I thought you didn't see anything?"

"I didn't. But if you said it happened, I reckon it probably did, so, you can tell me about it if you want. Later, I mean, by text or email, or whatever."

She smiled again, relieved and a bit grateful that he trusted her. "Thanks, I'll do that."

She turned and walked away. Honestly, he could be annoying, but she did rather like him, only not really. Of course not. But maybe just a bit.

* * *

Far away, in a place of darkness and stillness, the ancient one heard the call from this young singer, reaching out across dimensions to tap into the ancient, primordial power that was her birthright. The calls were becoming more frequent, and the ancient one answered.

Good, good.

"Sing to me, child," this elder being whispered. "Bring forth your fury and your rage. Sing for me and sweep all before you into oblivion. In time, you will learn to sing of their deaths, and force all who hear your song to despair. You will be feared by those little wretched mortal creatures."

She closed her weary eyes.

"Sing now, let your voice be heard, let it become one with the past. The ancient bond that ties you to us grows ever stronger as you come into your power. Soon, you will do great things. Soon, you will do terrible things, as the prophecy of the return comes to fruition. Take my power—our power— and do with it what you will. We are strong."

Magic flowed from her and toward the young singer, but something happened. Something interrupted it. Perhaps it was the girl's own fear or inexperience. Perhaps it was... another? Something, or someone, else was there, a disruption. The flow waned, and then it was gone again, like a stream after too little rain.

She cursed and with some effort, stood. She hobbled out of her cave into a grey and misty landscape and looked around in frustration. This twilight world where so many of her kinfolk dwelled would soon be cast aside, for while she could leave and return to it more freely, most among her folk could not. But that would change, and this young one would help toward that purpose. Soon, the world of mortals would be afraid again, which was as it should be.

* * *

She sat alone backstage, now that most of their equipment had been packed away. Something odd had happened. That strange sensation had come over her again. But she could barely remember any of it now. It was always that way when the power—whatever it was— came to her, flowed through her.

"All right?"

She glanced up to see a thin, pale young man with stringy brown hair standing over her. "Yeah, I suppose." She focused on packing her bag, trying to ignore him.

"I'm Oliver. I'm a musician, too."

"How nice for you." She looked back down.

"They call me 'Liver,' 'cause it's part of me name, and I'm from Liverpool, see?"

"How clever."

"I'm a student here at uni."

"Imagine my surprise."

"Brilliant show, by the way."

"Thanks. Could've been better, I think." She gave him a quick glance.

"Nah, it were brilliant. You been to Liverpool?"

"Once." She really wished he'd just leave her alone.

"You ever hear of a band called 'Wizard Lizard'? Yeah, that was me and me mates."

She shook her head.

"Ah well, they were brilliant back in the day."

"That long ago, eh?"

"You ever hear of another band called 'Out of Thyme'? Yeah, that was me and me mates."

"I have no doubt."

"Moirin!" a familiar voice sounded, to her relief.

"Great to chat with you, um, 'Liver.' Sorry I have to go... bye!"

She got up and left the clueless young man there to reminisce about past rock and roll glories and maybe find someone else to tell about them.

"Great show, Moirin. I think it could have been one of our best." Sam, the Weasels' drummer, strolled up to her, as he stuffed a cymbal into a bag and zipped it up. "Shame about the electricity getting all bollocked."

She nodded. "I know. Too bad about that. We were on and the crowd was really into it. Shite happens, I guess."

"Yeah. But they'll likely have us back. We drew a good number of folks. We've really got something here."

She shrugged. "Maybe. Don't want to get my hopes up yet, though."

"Anyway, the rest of the lads are off to the uni pub. I could use a pint after that mess. You in?"

"Cheers, but I think I might just go for a walk or something. I've a bit of a headache, and I want to get some fresh air."

"Fair enough. See you back at the hostel later?"

"Yeah, I'll be along then. I'll text you about food or something?"

Sam nodded and walked out to the tour van.

Moirin sighed, stood up, threw on her long black coat, and wandered off from the union. She craved solitude and natural surroundings, and not just of the human-made park variety in the near vicinity.

"Those places are so fake," she sighed to herself. "And even worse, they're filled with people. No chance of being alone today, though." She felt a bit sulky about it.

After a few minutes of meandering on campus, she found a rather expansive and tree-filled enclosure marked by a sign reading "Welcome to St. George's Field." Seeing as she could lose herself in its trees, this place would suffice. Wandering in, she found herself strolling through a historic cemetery, which appealed to her gothy aesthetic sensibilities. She sat herself down on a stone bench not far from some centuries-old headstones and tried to focus, to think, to something.

She closed her eyes, trying to recall the feeling of the power flowing through her.

"What are you?" she whispered.

For a time, she felt nothing. Sighing in frustration, she opened her eyes. The field was mercifully unpopulated today, so she decided to risk singing a little tune, an old Irish folk song. She couldn't remember where she'd learned it. She couldn't remember much of anything before the last couple of years, to be honest. But there it was, stuck in her head, so she called on it.

It was a simple melody with a short verse and a chorus. She didn't even know all the words, but that didn't matter. She just sang the bit she knew over and over. It was soothing, comforting, and connected her to something, as if stirring a memory. She closed her eyes again, allowing it to wash over her. For the first time in a while, she formed a genuine smile. Not a big smile, mind you, she did have her reputation to think of, after all.

As she neared the third repeat, something happened. She heard a voice in her head, one that contrasted with her own. It was more like a momentary flash of sound, in a language she didn't recognize. It didn't make her stop singing; in fact, she wanted to continue. After she sang another verse or two, and she heard it again, like a call across some great gap. But was it far away in the distance? Or maybe in time?

How does that even make any sense?

Intrigued, she kept singing, but lowered her voice so as not to attract any onlookers. It would be just like someone to come up in the middle of it and ruin the whole experience, with their chattiness and insipid curiosity.

As it turned out, she was indeed interrupted, but not by any passersby who should have been minding their own business. In her mind's eye, she saw a face. The face of an old woman. She had long, disheveled grey-streaked hair, and her complexion was wan and weathered, with dark shadows under her eyes. There was almost something cool about her. The face was obscured, as if peering through a fog, and Moirin couldn't gauge its intent. She wasn't imagining it; her imagination was good, but not this good. The woman opened her mouth as if to say something, but no words emerged, and if she were the one speaking those foreign words, Moirin wouldn't have understood her, anyway.

The old woman smiled, but it was an odd smile, and not really a happy one, more like sinister grin. She seemed to want something from Moirin. The smile grew bigger and stretched to unnatural proportions. Her eyes began to lighten, not just the pupils, but the whole of her eyes, greying at first and then fading into a milky white.

Moirin's heart raced. She stopped singing and gasped. Whatever this thing was, she wanted nothing to do with it. She tried to open her eyes, but they were heavy, almost as if she'd been drugged. Her ears seemed to close up, and the world around her disappeared. She shook her head and tried to stand up, but just like her eyes, her legs no longer worked. She started to panic and opened her mouth again, not to sing but to scream, shout for help, something. But no sound escaped.

The face sneered at her, perhaps enjoying her helplessness. It became ever more twisted and grotesque and opened its mouth again, almost in mockery of Moirin's inability to do so. A low-pitched wailing sounded from the old woman, a mournful call that seemed to portend something awful. It rose in pitch and volume to a full-on cry, a tuneless and wordless plaint that sounded like something out of an older time. It shook Moirin to the core, but the more she heard it, the more it seemed to invite her, to draw her in, even to tempt her. Whatever the ill intent of this creature invading her mind, and however frightening its call, Moirin felt oddly at home. She began to surrender to its lure, to its awful and seductive pull.

But something in her resisted. Something told her not to yield. She heard another voice, one that couldn't be real. Not here, not now. *Remember who you are*, it suggested, *remember who you can still be, despite of all the terrible things that've happened to you since you were a child.*

"Who are you?" she managed to whisper. "What are you talking about?"

The face in front of her grew angry at this intrusion. Its wailing intensified, as if it could block out Moirin's thoughts, simply by being the louder voice in her head. But Moirin knew she had to push back, and her anger at being confronted with this macabre spectacle gave her the strength to do it.

"Get out of my head! Whatever you are, I don't want you here, and if you're the source of the power, I don't want it! Go away!"

The woman's grip on her mind weakened and dissipated, as if blown away by the wind. The force of its departure knocked Moirin backwards, straight off the bench on to the grassy ground.

She grunted as she hit the earth. She was sure she heard the faint sound of laughter as her senses recovered. Everything had returned to normal, whatever that was. A few people loitered in the distance, though none took notice of her. For once, she was glad to see others around.

"Gods, that was terrifying!" She picked herself up and debated staying among these sylvan yet sweetly sepulchral surroundings or getting out of there as soon as possible. She sighed an indecisive sigh. "Maybe I should have gone for that pint."

* * *

"Most peculiar, very odd, indeed!" Blip proclaimed as he sat on Jilly's bed. He was her self-appointed imaginary friend, only he wasn't so imaginary. And he strongly resembled a two-foot-tall bipedal frog. With a terribly posh accent. And a handlebar mustache with mutton chops. He wore a monocle on occasion, though not at the moment. Jilly had long ago given up questioning the whole business and just accepted that he liked to spend time at her home. And to instruct her in the intricacies of European philosophy, among other things.

A few hours ago, she'd returned to her little town, Knettles-on-Nidd, north of Leeds and not far from the southern part of the Yorkshire Dales. Knettles itself was a bit of an unusual place, with a strange and mystical history, which explained some of the extraordinary things she'd encountered over the past year, like philosophizing imaginary-friend posh bullfrogs.

Happily, her walk to the Leeds station after bidding adieu to Lluck was uneventful, and she hadn't had to turn anyone into a toad. Not that she could do that, anyway. Still, the trip home had been ordinary enough, and now she was eager to talk with Blip about what happened. Since her witch mentor, Granny Boatford, seemed to be out of town again, he was the magical being she saw most often and who could offer at least some insight, Goddess help her.

"So, it was a musical concert, you say?" Blip questioned.

Jilly nodded.

"And what was the name of the ensemble?"

"The Mystic Wedding Weasels."

"How odd. They sound rather experimental. Do they mainly perform at marital ceremonies? Are they a modern string quartet? Oh heavens, you're not dipping your toe into the stagnant pool of atonalism, are you? Ghastly stuff, that!"

"Um, no," she said, not quite sure what atonalism was, but quite sure that she didn't want to hear one of his lengthy explanations about it. "They're an indie band."

"Indie? As in, from the West Indies? That's a most unusual designation for a musical genre."

"No, indie, like 'independent' from the big record companies. They're not a popular commercial band, more like a club band. They've got quite a good goth vibe."

"Visigoth or Ostrogoth?"

"What?"

"You said they were a band of club-carrying Goths, so I was wondering which faction they are. Are they planning on raiding the city? We may have to look into it, if they start congregating in larger numbers. This could be their reconnaissance for a future invasion."

"No, not that kind of Goth. You know, *goth*. Black clothes and skulls and candles and personal anguish, and all that."

"I'm not following. Are you saying they wear black and cause anguish with their clubs and carry the skulls of their enemies? If they're also using magic, we'll definitely need to look into it. A new wave of barbarian attacks would be catastrophic."

Jilly sighed. "No, they're a rock band. Rock music. They mainly play in clubs, you know, small places you go to and listen to live music?"

"Ah, yes, of course! They're one of those newfangled rock and roll musical collectives I've been hearing about: Charles Berry, the Bottles, Queen Crimson, Deep Floyd, Jethro Troll. Not to my taste, I must say—I prefer Johann Sebastian Bach, as you know—but the young folks seem to find it 'groovy,' as they say. I suppose every generation must have a way to let off a bit of steam, however vulgar it might be. No matter. You're certain there's something off about the vocalist?"

"I don't know. Like I said, it was sort of like reality went haywire and nothing made any sense. But I'm quite sure it was coming from her, when she sang, I mean. It was all very confusing. When did Qwyrk say she'd be back? I think I need to tell her about it."

"Soon, I should think. Shadows are rather busy at this time of year, but she did promise to stop by before Beltane."

"Why do they get busy?"

"It's to do with the charged magical energies of the time. It happens at all of the magical moments in the annual cycle, though Beltane and Hallow's Eve are particularly potent."

"I don't know, it seems like the summer and winter solstices were crazy, if the past year is anything to go on."

"Yes, quite. We haven't had two of those kinds of aberrations so close to one another in some time."

"Do you think there might be a reason for it?"

"Possibly. Two major supernatural dangers to the world in the space of a half-year is potentially quite the cause for concern. But as far as I know, no connection has yet been found between William de Soulis and the Erlking. They seem to be entirely random occurrences. Oddly coincidental, though."

"Yeah, and now there's this. It was pretty scary. It was all around us, like the real world was just falling apart, and nonsense was taking its place, and time wasn't working. What if it's some new danger?"

"I wouldn't worry overly, child. The nature of this manifestation seems markedly different from our previous encounters. I suspect it's all rather more mundane, and certainly not the same kind of threat, if threat it be at all."

"I hope so, but I wish Qwyrk would get back soon."

"Not to worry, my dear. I suspect we'll be hearing from her in due course. It would not surprise me if, any day now, we receive a missive from her indicating that she will be returning several days hence to..."

"Jilly! Blip!"

A face surrounded by swirling violet mists and lights appeared in mid-air above Jilly's bed. It was that of a young woman with short blonde hair in a pixie cut, elfin features, and pointed ears.

"Qwyrk!" Jilly belted out with glee.

CHAPTER TWO

"Great gobsmacked groats of Gwydion, girl!" Blip clutched at his chest. "I told you not to do that!"

"Yeah, but it makes me laugh every time!" Qwyrk declared with mischief. "Hang on a second."

Her face vanished in a puff of light and lavender scented vapor. A moment later, she materialized in her full form at the foot of Jilly's bed, wearing blue jeans, short brown boots, and a long-sleeved, white, collared shirt. Her usual sartorial ensemble.

Jilly ran to her and practically leaped into her arms; Qwyrk hugs were second-to-none.

"How have you been? *Where* have you been?" Jilly asked, delighted and a little annoyed at the same time.

"I've been fine. And yeah, I'm so sorry; things get rather busy in springtime, so I've kind of been all over the place for the past six weeks."

"I told you so," Blip mumbled.

"What have you been telling her now, Blip?" Qwyrk glared at him, still holding her young friend.

"What do you mean, what have *I* been telling her?" he groused, still clutching himself, presumably for dramatic effect. "I've been continuing with my duties to instruct her in the great minds of philosophy and serve as an endearing and highly amusing childhood companion, if I do say so myself, while you are gallivanting around on missions you don't tell us about and presumably indulging in romantic trysts with that Yakshi sweetheart of yours."

"I wish..." Qwyrk mumbled with a sigh. Jilly shot her an alarmed glance. Things had to be going well. They just had to be.

"So, what brings you back now?" Jilly asked instead, determined not to bring up Qwyrk's romantic life unless she volunteered the information, even if Jilly was fairly bursting to find out more.

"Well, we have a bit of a break. Things get crazy around this time of year..."

"As I said," Blip interjected.

"Why?" Jilly asked, sitting down on the floor, where Qwyrk joined her.

"It's like the magic goes a bit bonkers. All that spring life energy and such just blasts out, and it can make magical creatures a bit stir crazy. There're more fights, more challenges, more drama, more hanky-panky, more romance..."

"Oh really?" Jilly said eagerly. "Do tell."

"And we have to police it all, it seems." Qwyrk ignored her. "Just this week I had to break up a fight between a totally pissed pixie and a completely blitzed brownie in Bradford. Yeah, drunk faery fights are a thing, and they are not for the timid, I can promise you."

"I thought you lot couldn't get drunk," Jilly objected.

"Well, that's true for me and for Holly and her folk," Qwyrk answered.

Jilly delighted in Qwyrk mentioning her special friend, who was really her girlfriend, even if Qwyrk wouldn't admit it.

"But different orders of Fae have different qualities," Qwyrk continued. "So yeah, it's quite possible for some of them to get completely snockered and cause no end of problems, which makes our job of watching over kids even more annoying than usual. And these two, hoo boy, let me tell you..."

"Scaring the young ones, were they?" Blip asked with a hint of disdain that Jilly knew was his disapproval at their no doubt reprehensible behavior.

"Squabbling over squatting rights, actually," Qwyrk answered. "They both invited over a bunch of their mates, and all of a sudden it was Fae Fight Club in this poor family's living room. Now everyone's talking about it, which they're not supposed to do. And one of the children saw the whole thing and is probably scarred for life. Anyway, that's the sort of crap I've been dealing with recently, so yeah, sorry again for being away longer than I wanted to."

"Oh, it's all right, you know that." Jilly put a hand on her shoulder. "I just miss having you around, but that's me being selfish. You can't always be here. You have your own life, your own friends, your own... special someone?" Jilly gave her a teasing nudge, but Qwyrk ignored her again, which made her even more irritated.

"Young Jilly has had a bit of an adventure herself today," Blip interjected, which only annoyed Jilly further by changing the subject.

"Really?" Qwyrk's face brightened. "Seems like every time I pop back here, you're getting yourself in more trouble! What's up now? Or do I even want to know?"

"Young Miss Pleeth can tell you all about it," Blip said. "I admit it's rather strange. Like nothing I've heard of, at least not recently."

Jilly sighed, knowing that news about Qwyrk's love life would have to wait for a bit, so she relayed what happened, keeping it brief.

"Well, that's more than a little bizarre," Qwyrk said afterward.

"As was my thought," Blip said.

"Yeah, I don't know what to make of it," Jilly added. "It kind of feels like I just imagined it, especially since no one else seemed to notice, not even Lluck."

"How's he doing, by the way?"

"Doesn't his mum tell you?"

Qwyrk squirmed a bit.

"Something you're not telling me?" Jilly inquired with a raised eyebrow, feeling bolder and wanting to get to the point.

As if taking the cue that she wanted to speak with her friend alone, Blip hopped off the bed. "Right then, I'm off. Good to see you. I suppose you two have some catching up to do, women-talk and all that. I should go and train at the dojo. Cheerio!" With that, he strode toward a bedroom wall and just faded away into it.

"I'll never quite get used to that," Jilly said, after he'd vanished.

"Yeah it's an odd one," Qwyrk agreed.

"But... you enjoy showing just your face first before you blink yourself in here."

"I only did that to see if you were home. The fact that you are, and that it still spooks Blip so much is an unexpected bonus!"

They shared an overdue laugh. But Jilly was impatient for news about one thing in particular.

"So?"

"So, what?" Qwyrk looked at the floor, hands clasped in front of her.

Jilly shot Qwyrk her trademarked glare. "How is she?"

"Who?"

"Oh come on, Qwyrk. How are things going with Holly? You've been gone almost two months, and all I get are what little bits Lluck knows and obviously, he doesn't know much! I need news. I haven't heard anything about it in ages, and it's killing me! Details! Stories of romance and true love. Come on, give me something!"

"Um... things are good. They're really good, actually. Nice, even."

"Nice? That's it?"

"Well, what do you want me to say?" Qwyrk raised up her palms. "Things are lovely and it's all really... fine. Fine and nice. And good."

"Okay, so?"

"So, what?"

"There must be more than that. Have you even kissed her? Properly? Since December, I mean?"

"Yes! Of course! Sort of..."

"What's that supposed to mean?"

"Well, um... just the other night we were taking in the aurora up in Scotland, and I put my arm around her and we stayed there for ages watching those amazing green curtains light up the sky before going back to Symphinity."

"And?"

"And it was brilliant. Then, we said good night and I... I kissed her..."

"On the lips?"

"Sort of. On the cheek, I suppose."

"On the cheek? Are you honestly kidding me?"

"What's wrong with that?"

"Well, it's *something*, I suppose. If you're really bold, maybe next time you can shake her hand."

"All right, so when did you become the romantic agony aunt of Knettles-on-Nidd, eh?"

"When my honorary big sister fell head-over-heels for the faery woman of her dreams and then proceeded to start cocking it up!"

"I'm not cocking it up! We're just... taking our time. At our ages, we don't want to rush into anything."

"It's been four months, how is that possibly rushing into anything? You adore her, she obviously adores you, so what's the problem?"

"It's just... I don't know, it's complicated." Qwyrk sighed, stood up, paced for a moment, and sat down on the bed, sighed again, and slumped forward, putting a hand on her forehead. "She's only just reconnected with Lluck, and that's a big deal for her. Huge. I completely get it. She needs time with him, and I'm not sure how I fit into that yet. Even though it's a big part of my job, I'm not all that good with kids, as you may have noticed."

"Um, hello? Kid here, remember?" Jilly pointed to herself in an exaggerated motion.

"That's completely different. You're sort of twelve going on twenty-five, and besides, like you said, we're practically sisters. I don't relate to you in the same way I do to other young people. I don't know if I could even be a like a parent to Lluck."

"But you don't have to be. He's already got a mum *and* a dad. It's fine for you just to be his mum's girlfriend. I think he'd be all right with that. I think she is, too."

Qwyrk sighed again, running a hand through her short hair. "I know, you're right. Part of it's just me making excuses. Fear of getting hurt and all that. And Holly's the same way, I think. So we dance around each other—well, not literally, that would actually be progress—and we don't talk about our past hurts and failures and fears and such. It's all really comfortable and easy, and we just go sight-seeing and hang out and it's lovely, but nothing much happens. I'm completely besotted with her, and it's driving me crazy. If I actually needed to sleep, I'd be lying awake at night thinking about her."

"Then just tell her, and don't worry about it!" Jilly put a sympathetic hand on Qwyrk's shoulder. "This is a big deal, maybe a once-in-a-long-lifetime big deal, and you'll hate yourself forever if you let her slip away. She's still around, which means she's just as keen on you, and she's probably waiting for you to take things up a notch. So, tell her how much you fancy her, tell her you want to kiss her again, and just let it happen."

Qwyrk reached up and took Jilly's hand. "You're right, but it makes me ill even thinking about it."

"Well, if you don't do it, and soon, I'll tell Lluck everything you just said, and he'll tell her, and we'll both embarrass the crap out of you!"

"Gosh, thanks for the support."

"It's called tough love, sis!" Jilly patted Qwyrk's hand. "And yeah, you'll thank me for it!"

"Fine. I'll do it."

"Excellent!" Jilly said in satisfied triumph.

"Can we talk about something else now?" Qwyrk pleaded. "Like, more about what the hell happened at that concert?"

"It was so strange. Chantz—she's their singer—is amazing, and at first, I just thought it was something about the place, the music, the band, whatever. But after a bit, it felt, I don't know, really weird. Like there was something magical coming from inside her voice, if that makes any sense. Like, every word she sang was part of something bigger..."

"You mean like some kind of a magic spell?"

"Yeah. I thought so at the time, but it's all a bit fuzzy now. What do you think she was she doing?"

"I don't know. I'm not even sure she knows; she might be doing it unintentionally. You said she looked surprised when it was all over?"

Jilly nodded. "She either didn't know she was making it happen, or it didn't go how she planned. She looked like she was afraid someone had noticed, and that she'd get found out. I didn't want to give myself away by staring at her, and I definitely wasn't going to go up and talk to her, even though I wanted to, so we just left. I think I was the only one there who knew about it, or at least remembered it. What *did* happen? Any ideas?"

Qwyrk shook her head. "I mean, magic can come from almost anywhere, so someone being able to sing spells isn't really surprising. Look at old Thomas the Rhymer. But using magic to warp reality is pretty rare. You should ask Granny about it; she'd know more than me. Is she around?"

Jilly shook her head. "Not right now. She comes and goes as she pleases, so my training is a bit all over the place these days."

"How's it going?"

"Not bad, but I'm frustrated, kind of stuck, you know? I don't think I'm getting any better."

"Well, these things take time, and you've only really been at it for what? Four months? Be patient. Granny knows what she's doing, and if she says you're her descendent and successor, you know it's true. However she wants to teach you must be the right way for you"

Jilly shrugged. "I keep telling myself that, but then I get impatient again."

"Well, good things come to those who wait and all that, but

sometimes giving it a push isn't a bad idea, just to move things along. Maybe try talking to her? Telling her you want to move forward a little faster?"

"Sounds like you need to take your own advice."

"Touché, love. And I'm going to pretend I didn't tell you to do that." Qwyrk folded her arms and looked away in mock defiance.

"Too late! You can't take it back." Jilly laughed. "So…"

"So what?"

"When are you seeing Holly again?"

"Um, in a bit. We're going out somewhere to see some spring-time greenery. I should be off back home soon, actually. I just wanted to stop by, since I've been absent for so long."

"Well, then," Jilly raised a teasing eyebrow.

"Well then, what?"

Jilly glared. "This is the perfect chance to take the initiative and get on with it."

Qwyrk grimaced. "You're right. Bollocks."

"And?"

"And… the thought of it terrifies me. Couldn't I just go fight de Soulis and the Erlking again instead? Hell, I'll sing every verse of Bogtrotter's bloody anthem. I'll even sit through one of Blip's philosophical lectures. Deal?"

Jilly rolled her eyes. "You're not coming back here until you've done what you need to do."

"All right, then. Nice to have known you. Good luck, have a lovely life."

"Qwyrk…"

"All right, fine! I'll do it, Ms. Naggy-trousers!"

"Naggy-trousers?"

Qwyrk shrugged. "First thing that popped into my head?"

"Yeah, well, I nag with good reason. If I recall, the last time I forced you to take action with her, it worked out quite well." Jilly enjoyed feeling smug in the moment.

Qwyrk sighed. "Fair enough. If I could just get the meteor shower of nerves in my belly to go away, I might be able to do it."

"There's a spell for that."

"Is there?"

"No."

"Fine. Liar."

"Yeah, well, no apologies. Now, woman up and deal with it. Go forth and deck the halls."

"What?" Qwyrk stared at her in confusion.

"You know. 'With boughs of... Holly?' That sounded so much less crap in my head than it did out loud."

"It was a bit shite, it must be said. And no jokes about 'donning gay apparel,' thank you very much. Maybe lay off the innuendo until you're a bit older?"

"As long as you don't cock this up, I promise not to try again for a year or two. Now off with you!" Jilly shooed her with her hands. "Your destiny awaits!"

"Huh. If it's all the same with you, can I just call in sick?"

"You don't get sick. It's a Shadow perk."

"Maybe there's a leaf on the train track? The wrong kind of snow?"

"It's spring. Go!"

Qwyrk uttered a few mildly inappropriate words and vanished in a purple flash, leaving Jilly to smile a smug and satisfied smile.

* * *

Moirin sat on the upper bunk of one of the beds in her hostel room. She was glad that no one else was there; dare she hope she might have the space all to herself tonight?

"Probably not." She exhaled and rubbed her temples. The power always gave her a headache, but this one was worse than usual.

She pulled out her phone and texted Sam: *feeling off, head hurts. think i'll pass on food tonight. see u in am.*

"Not even dark yet, and I'm already wiped out. Some rock star I am." Sleep was calling. To be more accurate, it was on constant redial. She lied down and stared up at the ceiling, which was just out of reach above her. She closed her eyes, but instead of going straight out, her mind raced. "Too tired to sleep; that's always lovely."

She rolled over to one side and happened to look down at the doorway to the room. And that's when she saw her. The woman from her vision. Standing there, all wild hair and sallow skin, all hollow eyes and grinning visage. Moirin gasped and sat up with a start.

"Are ya all right?"

"What?" Moirin shook her head with vigor and closed and reopened her eyes. Standing there instead was a young woman, nothing like at all like the creature from her vision. She was about Moirin's age, wearing traveling clothes and sporting a smallish rucksack. She had impressive long, curly red hair and piercing green eyes. Her accent placed her as being very Scottish.

"Are ya all right? You seemed quite startled when I came in. Scared me a bit, to be honest."

"Yeah, sorry about that. I just wasn't expecting anyone else in here tonight, that's all. And I'm exhausted, so I'm a bit wired and on edge. I think I'm seein' things. No problem though. Pick a bed, and make yourself at home." *So much for being alone.*

"Thanks. I'm Aileen. Aileen Douglas." She sat on the lower bunk opposite.

"Moirin. Moeran. Moirin Moeran, I mean. Yeah I know, they're weirdly similar."

"Nice to meet you."

"So, are you traveling far? On your way home? Leaving your home? Running away from home? Buying a home?" Small talk was tedious and exhausting.

"A little of everything, actually. Heading back north in a bit. Visitin' some friends down here. How about you?"

"On tour with my band."

"Brilliant! What's their name?"

"The Mystic Wedding Weasels. It's a bit crap, to be honest, and I keep bugging the lads to change it, but they're kind of set on it now."

"I like it. Sounds right alternative."

"Yeah, well, we're at the intersection of indie, goth, prog, and a bit of punk and metal. Whatever we feel like doing, I suppose."

"Great! So, where're ya off to next? For your next gig, I mean?"

"York, I think? Maybe. I'll check with the boys tomorrow and see."

"Let me know, and maybe I'll stop by and see you."

Moirin shrugged. "If you like. I can put you on the guest list."

"Brilliant, thanks!"

"Yeah, um... sorry to seem antisocial, but my head is hurting, so I'm gonna try to sleep for a bit, if you don't mind."

"Of course. I'm just storin' my bag here, and then I'm off to see me mates, anyway. I'll be quiet when I come back in."

"Cheers for that." Morin laid back down and tried facing the other direction. This time, her restless mind seemed a little bit calmer, and in a bit, the joyous oblivion of stygian slumber (now *there* was a good song lyric!) descended over her, and she barely heard her new roommate leave.

* * *

There was a knock at the door. Qwyrk jumped up in a tsunami of nerves. "Come in!"

Sure enough, Holly stepped through and into Qwyrk's sitting room. She wore a long-sleeved, nicely-fitted purple dress that ended above her knees, and she sported those stylish short, black boots that Qwyrk loved so much. Her long, black hair was worn down and flowed about her in the usual perfect manner, and there was that one purple streak of hair on the left side that somehow fit in so well, in this case matching her dress color. Qwyrk could only stare, convinced that she wouldn't survive the next few minutes.

"Hello darling!" Holly said in her posh accent with a big smile, striding up to Qwyrk, embracing her, and giving her a kiss on the cheek that was far too close to Qwyrk's lips.

"Hi!" Qwyrk said with a laugh and a goofy smile, aware of how ridiculous she must have sounded.

"So, what's the plan for the evening?" Holly asked, mercifully making nothing of Qwyrk's awkwardness. "Sunset in the Cotswolds? A walk in the Lake District? Bluebells in a Devon forest? I'm game for whatever; spring is springing and I'd love to take it all in!"

"Um, well... those sound like lovely ideas, really! But I was wondering if we could, maybe, chat a bit first?" Qwyrk's voice faltered, and she sat down on the sofa (almost falling onto it, really), fearing that her voice sounded too hesitant. Sure enough, Holly picked up on it, and furrowed her brow a little.

"All right, what do you want to talk about?"

"Oh, it's nothing bad!" Qwyrk tried to sound reassuring, thrusting up her hands. "Honest, it's all good, very good, in fact. Yes, indeed. So good that it couldn't be any more good... as far as good things go. I mean, sometimes things are just good, right? But other things are quite good, exceptionally good, gooder than good, actually (*gooder?*), and this is one of those things. Good things, that is..."

Holly sat down next to her. "When you start mangling your words, it means you're nervous about something." She added with a smile, "And it's rather adorable. So what is it?"

Qwyrk swallowed. "Well, I mean, that is to say, we've, we've been doing this... thing we've been doing for a few months, now, right? You know, seeing gorgeous places, chatting about all sorts, getting to know each other better..."

"I remember. I was there." Holly grinned that insufferably charming grinning grin that only she could grin.

"And, and so, well, I'm just wondering, thinking, really," Qwyrk stammered and continued, "no, wondering actually. About all of that and how it might mean something. I mean, of course, it *means* something; everything has meaning, right? What I'm trying to say is that in the course of us interacting over the past few months, I'm finding that I, well... I enjoy it. Quite a lot, really. And, and so... thinking about that enjoymenting has got me thinking about what that might possibly mean in the grander scheme of whatever we decide it might mean, and if that means anything that might be, well, *meaningful* to us, in a way that meaningfully has meaning... you know what I mean?"

"Umm... I'm not sure I do."

Qwyrk sighed in frustration. "Oh sod it! I'm sorry, Holly, but I just can't stand it anymore! I'm utterly crazy about you, all right? If you don't feel the same way, I'll understand, but I'm besotted to distraction, and all I can think about is how much I want to hold you and kiss you and, mmmphph!"

Before Qwyrk even knew what had happened, Holly's lips were on hers, soft, gentle, inviting. Then Holly's arms were around her, drawing her in and holding her in a warm, tender embrace. Qwyrk tensed, shocked that Holly had made the first move, but she relaxed, closed her eyes, and lost herself in it. Holly's lips tasted slightly of cinnamon, and Qwyrk gave in to her completely.

She hoped it would never end. They could just stay there, in that blissful moment, forever. Sod everything else.

But all good things must come to an end, and after another moment (or two, or three... all right, maybe seventeen), they parted. Both exhaled sharp breaths and they touched their foreheads to each other, eyes still closed.

"Bloody hell," Qwyrk managed to gasp.

"I was thinking pretty much the same thing," Holly whispered.

"So... that happened."

"It rather did." Holly gazed up at her, eyes filled with longing.

"Um... thank you?"

Holly burst out with a great guffaw. Qwyrk looked at her in shock for a moment, but then mirth burst forth and she joined in. They had a good laugh, which made the whole thing even more perfect.

"No, I mean, honestly, thank you!" Qwyrk repeated after they'd calmed down. "I've been too afraid to say anything, much less do anything. I suppose it was up to you to just jump in and go for it. But I'm made up that you did!"

"Well, you were the one that asked me to go watch that snowy sunrise at Sutton Bank—which was a lovely first date, by the way. If you hadn't, I might never have said anything at all. But I feel the same way, Qwyrk; I have for ages. I've desperately wanted more, too, but I was afraid. Afraid of moving too fast, of scaring you off; honestly... of scaring myself. And I was worried that my son might be a problem for you."

"No, he's not, honest, it's fine. He's a good lad."

"I mean, that's a separate life, and you needn't be involved in it if you don't wish to be. But when I'm not there, I can be with you. I'd really like that, if you would."

Qwyrk almost gasped in relief. "Yes, yes, I would like that very much. *Very* much. I cannot tell you just how much I'd like that, because I don't even know how much myself, but I promise you, it's a lot... oh Goddess, I'm babbling again, sorry!"

"No, it's charming!" Holly smiled, running her fingers though Qwyrk's short hair. The sensation of Holly's touch sent a shiver down Qwyrk's back.

Holly smiled. "So, is this the proper beginning of a beautiful friendship... and more?"

"Oh, I'm sure it is. Quite sure, to be honest. Absolutely sure, actually. Never been more sure of anything, really."

Holly smiled again and stroked her cheek. Qwyrk momentarily lost the ability to think.

"So, um, we should celebrate, or something," Qwyrk blurted out after a few seconds of blissful confusion. "Go somewhere in England, get some fancy drinks, maybe? I promise to lay low and not scare anyone!"

"Or, we could just stay here..." Holly leaned in and whispered softly in her ear, "No drinks needed. I promise you we won't even need single malt scotch tonight if we do..."

Qwyrk was fairly certain she was about to faint.

* * *

Moirin's dreams were dark and disturbing. She tossed and turned in a fitful and troubled slumber. Strange images tormented her weary mind, playing out like surreal horror movie scenes. She woke up often and couldn't get comfortable. She tried laying on her side. No good. Her stomach? Even worse. Her back? Everything seemed to spin. She sat up in the upper bunk she'd chosen and swore to herself. Looking around, she saw that her new roommate had yet to return, though she had no idea what time it was. Fumbling through her bag, hung on the bedpost beside her, she found her phone, squinted, and looked at it through bleary eyes: 3:33 am.

"Huh, that's odd," she whispered. "Twice this week I've woken up at this time."

She had one new message from Sam, but it was just a reply of the "no worries, see you tomorrow" variety. She looked around again and thought about getting up and going for a walk, but decided that might not be the best idea at this hour, adventurous though she was. That thought made her wonder about Aileen.

"I hope she's all right," she thought out loud. "Oh, why am I worried about someone I don't even know? It's not my problem."

Slumping back down on her miserable, lumpy mattress, she was about to make another futile attempt at sleep, when she noticed a shadow move right outside the window. Then another. They were only there for a second, just tall enough to be short people, maybe people trying to look in, or even worse, break in. Sitting back up with a start, she grabbed her bag and slipped down to the floor. Tossing on her boots and lacing them up, she crouched down and prepared to run, if necessary.

As she squinted at the window, she could hear her own breath, feel her own pounding heart. There was a bit of a shuffling sound, and then something, or two somethings, seemed to scurry away. Was there also the sound of beating wings?

Why am I acting like this? She thought after a minute of nothing else untoward whatsoever happening. *It was probably just an owl or a giant hedgehog or something.* "At the worst, it was some drunk lads stumbling back from a pub, looking for the front door," she whispered.

She relaxed her stance and sat down on the floor, but kept her bag clutched close. She wished she could summon the power when she wanted it, not just have it barge in on her when she was singing. If only she could learn to use it, make it her own, and not have that creepy woman show up again.

The sound of the bedroom door lock clicking made her nearly tumble over. She scrambled to sit up on the mattress in the lower bunk. The door opened, and Aileen crept in, closing it with care behind her. As she turned around, she stopped and looked at Moirin in the dim light afforded by the window.

"What are you doin'?" Aileen whispered.

"Nothing. Nothing, really," Moirin answered with an equally hushed voice. "I saw some shadows at the window and heard a sound. Didn't know what it was, so I thought I'd be ready in case someone was trying to break in. Did you see anything out there?"

"No. It was dead quiet. I mean, my taxi driver waited until I got in, so there was car noise and headlights, but other than that, it was fine. Are you sure you weren't dreamin', or something?"

"No, I was totally awake." She pointed at the window. "I saw a couple of shadows move right out there, but they might have just been animals, you know, some nocturnal things."

"I'm sure that's all it was. They do have those in the city, you know."

"Yeah, cheers for the nature documentary explanation."

"Anyway, I'm exhausted, so if we're not bein' invaded by wee nocturnal beasties, I'm turnin' in."

"Suit yourself." Moirin climbed back up to the top bunk and tried to settle down again. It didn't work so well at first. Open eyes.

Closed eyes. Open eyes. But little by little, the open eyes stayed open for briefer periods of time. As sleep loomed, she thought she sensed someone standing beside her bunk, but she was too drowsy to do anything about it.

CHAPTER THREE

"What time is Qwyrk coming over?" Blip asked as he sat on Jilly's living room couch perusing an old book. "It's already half past nine. I should like to make a start on our investigation before noon." Jilly dreaded that he was about to launch into a lecture on whatever philosophical topic had taken his fancy from the tome at hand.

"Should be any time now," she answered. If she could just stall him until Qwyrk arrived...

"Well then," he looked up with a satisfied smile. "While we wait, let us amuse ourselves with a delightful foray into Feuerbach's heady and exhilarating *Geschichte der neueren Philosophie*, the second edition, of course."

Jilly shuddered. *Here we go...*

"Can you imagine using the first?" Blip asked. "Ha! The Spinozistic elements are well worth one's attention, I can promise you. Are you familiar with the work?"

"Um... not really?" She had utterly no idea what he was talking about, and even coming from Blip, that took some doing.

"Well then, we shall remedy that this very morning! I daresay if we plunge right in, you should have a fair grasp of the basics by the time she arrives."

"That sounds, um, lovely, but," *think, Jilly, think.* "I did promise my mum that I'd send an email to... my cousin about... her coming to visit us soon, and I do need to do that this morning. So, maybe we could, you know, hold off on the *Gesundheit Deer Nervous Philosophy* book for today?" Jilly was quite pleased with her not-so-little fib.

"*Geschichte der neueren Philosophie.* Very well, see to your family obligations. It's odd that I haven't heard of this cousin before."

"Didn't I mention her? Sorry, I guess she just never came up."

"What is her name? Where does she live?"

"Her name?"

"Yes. Most humans have them, I find. Useful for telling them apart."

"It's... R-Rapunzel? She lives far away, in Cornwall. In a restored tower." *Crap, Jilly! Honestly?*

"A tower? Odd coincidence."

"Isn't it? I was just thinking that very thing this morning as I was about to write that email that I'm supposed to write... this morning. The one I'm writing, like now. The one my mum wants me to send. This morning. So I can't do anything else, sorry to say."

"When is she due to arrive?"

"What?"

"You said she was visiting?"

"I... did! I most certainly did!"

"So, when is it to be?"

"Um, soon, I think. Well, that's what I'm writing her about, yeah? To figure out when would be best for her to leave... her tower."

"Well, you'd best get on with it, I suppose."

"You're right! I'd best get on with it. With emailing that cousin of mine. In a tower. In Cornwall."

"Damned peculiar, all of it."

"Um, with respect, sir, look at the world you come from!"

To her surprise, Blip gave her a slight smirk. "Touché, my dear. Now, off with you and take care of that b-mail business."

"Email."

"Whatever." He waved his hand and went back to his book.

*　*　*

Moirin rolled over as the sound of a phone buzzing in her ear irritated her out of whatever excuse for sleep she was getting. She fumbled around and grabbed it, seeing a text from Sam. And that it was 9:30 am. *Hope ur up! Want to grab breakfast w/ us?*

"Bollocks!" She closed her eyes and opened them again, hoping that it was all an illusion, or that she was still dreaming. No such luck. And no sign of Aileen, either. Her bag was still there, set on her bunk, but she was already out again.

"Morning people," she sighed as she rolled onto her back and stared at the insipidly boring pale ceiling that loomed too close to her face for comfort. Something about it bothered her, more than just being insipid and boring, as ceilings often are.

"Did I dream about a flipping ceiling?" She had a faint impression of something menacing looming near her. She sighed. "Maybe I'm just goin' mad. All of this is nuts."

"What's nuts?"

She turned over to see Aileen enter the room, already dressed and presumably ready for the day, carrying snacks from the vending machine in the hall. "I mean, I've got nuts." She held up a small plastic snack bag. "But you can still get a proper breakfast in the dining area if you hurry."

"I'm not sure 'proper' is the word I'd use, but thanks."

"Are you all right? You look a wee bit off, if ya don't mind me sayin'."

"I'm not surprised. I didn't sleep all that well. Say, did you happen to notice anyone else in the room last night? Sometime after you came in?"

Aileen shook her head. "I'd have been scared out of me wits if I had. These rooms have locks for a reason. Is this something to do with whatever ya might've seen last night? Those prowlin' around things ya mentioned?"

"I don't know. I just had the sensation of being watched, I guess. Probably just my over-tired brain and various nightmares."

"Well, I wouldn't worry about it too much." Aileen tossed the snacks into her bag and threw it over one shoulder. "Maybe the ceiling was playing tricks on your eyes in the dark. Anyway, I'm off for the day. If I don't see ya back here later, we'll catch up at the York gig. Lookin' forward to it!" She smiled and left the room again.

Moirin stared after her. "Why did she mention the ceiling?"

* * *

Qwyrk appeared in Jilly's living room with her usual flash of violet light, where she was delighted to see both of them. Yes, even Blip.

"Hello, Jilly! Hello, Blip!" she said with an enormous, goofy smile. "Gorgeous spring day out, isn't it?"

"It is rather pleasant, I grant you," Blip answered.

"I mean," Qwyrk continued, "flowers are blooming, birds are flitting about, bees are... beeing, life is popping up everywhere... kind of makes you want to sing and dance, doesn't it?"

"Not especially, no," Blip answered.

"Oh come on," Qwyrk said. "Wasn't it Nietzsche who said, 'Those who were seen dancing were thought to be insane by those who could not hear the music'?"

"Precisely, and I hear no music, unless Jilly is planning on inviting over the Visigothic Mystical Nuptial Wombats, or whatever the blazes their name is. And I'm not sure I'd want to hear them, in any case. Rock and roll hooligans, I suspect."

"That would be something, wouldn't it?" Qwyrk said, fairly bouncing up and down.

"Are you all right?" Jilly asked, looking as if Qwyrk might have lost her mind.

"Brilliant! Never better! I can't wait to get stuck into this new mystery with my lovely friends, put our sleuthing caps on, and get to the bottom of it all."

Jilly gave her a squinty, suspicious look. Then, it seemed to dawn on her. Whether a lightbulb, a candle, or just a small band of wayward fireflies, something went off over her head.

"Um, excuse me, sir," Jilly said to Blip. "Can I talk with Qwyrk alone for a few minutes? It's just girl stuff that would bore you, anyway. We'll go up to my room, so we don't bother you."

"Suit yourselves," he said. "I'll be here delving into the limitless fascinations of Feuerbach." He opened up his book and dove back in.

Jilly grabbed Qwyrk's hand and almost dragged her upstairs to her bedroom.

No sooner had Jilly shut the door behind them, than she turned around and demanded, "All right. Spill the beans, what's going on?"

Qwyrk grinned. The grin turned to a smile. The smile became a giggle. In a moment she was in fits and felt like a giddy adolescent all over again.

"What?" Jilly insisted. "What's happening?"

"So," Qwyrk started. "I kind of sort of took your advice, though I guess I screwed it up a bit, but it didn't matter. Holly came over last night for our date…"

"And?"

"And I told her I needed to talk to her first about all sorts…"

"Yeah, and?"

"And I kind of made a mess of things, but then I just blurted it all out."

"What? Blurted what all out?"

"Everything we talked about me doing. I told her how much I like her and how much I wanted to kiss her and all that."

"So? Oh, for shite's sake, Qwyrk, what happened?!"

"She took the initiative and kissed *me*! Not on the cheek, but for real!"

"Oh, Qwyrk!" Jilly pumped her fists and jumped up and down. "This is brilliant, this is amazing! So then what?"

"Then we talked a bit more, and I suggested we go out and celebrate."

"Did you?"

"No, actually."

"Wait, what? Why not?"

"Well… we actually just stayed in and celebrated. Privately, if you know what I mean."

"Huh? Oh. Oh!" Jilly blushed. "Um, wow, that's, that's amazing."

"Yeah, it kind of is. I'm still not quite sure I believe it, to be honest."

"So, um, everything's good today, then?"

"Perfect. In fact, I'm going to go collect her in a bit, so she can help us with this whole singer business."

"Brilliant!" Jilly threw her arms around her friend. "Oh, Qwyrk, I'm so happy for you!" She looked up at her. "See, I told you that you just needed to be brave and bold!"

"Yeah, fair enough. You were spot on, as usual."

"Too right!" Jilly gave her a smug smile. "Come on, we should probably get back down to Blip."

"Yeah. I can't believe I'm actually looking forward to brainstorming with him."

"If she has this kind of effect on you, you and he will be best friends by this afternoon."

"Oh, Goddess, please! Don't ruin my day!"

Jilly laughed and opened the door.

* * *

Moirin felt like she was grasping for a pebble in a large bowl of custard whilst wearing a blindfold. Except, that was an absolutely asinine analogy. In any case, no answers came to her, despite thinking about it for a while after Aileen left.

"What happened last night? And why am I obsessing over it? It was just a bunch of crazy dreams. I can't even remember them!"

She stared at the ceiling for a while, but nothing untoward occurred (not that she had any idea what might occur, should something untoward, or even toward, deign to do so), and if anything strange had happened overnight, she'd already forgotten it.

She sighed. "Crap. Time to face the day, then."

She texted Sam: *10am? @ the cafe down the road we were at before?* An affirmative response a minute later gave her the push to get out of bed at last, even if she wasn't especially hungry. Or social. She wondered why the rest of the band put up with her.

Making a quick change of clothes into a black tee shirt and black jeans, she stashed her travel bag under the bed. "Not that there's any reason to hide it, especially if Aileen comes back, but she might not come back, so…"

As she knelt down to push her rucksack under the bunk bed, she noticed something on the floor. A pendant on a long leather cord. She picked it up and held it in her hands. It was a decent size, solid and rather heavy, and made of pewter or a similar dull silver metal. It was oddly warm to the touch, like it had been sitting in the sun. She traced her fingertips over an engraved triskelion, three spiral circles joined together in a triangular shape, but in the middle where they intersected, there was something that looked like…

"An eye?" She checked the other side and saw the same design.

"Odd little trinket. Probably just junk from one of those bloody New Age shops: 'Channel the Celtic energies' or some such rubbish. I wonder if Aileen dropped it?"

She stood up and stuffed it into her small handbag. "Just hang on to it for safe keeping. If it's hers, you can always give it back to her at the York gig… assuming she actually shows up, which, let's be honest, is not likely."

She threw on her long coat, cursed the fact that mornings and social obligations existed at all, and left the room.

* * *

"Are the tedious female issues properly discussed and resolved?" Blip asked, looking up from his hard-bound, slightly dusty, and decidedly philosophical tome.

"Fully sorted, and we're ready to go!" Jilly announced as she bounded down the stairs. Qwyrk followed close behind, finding herself bounding with the same enthusiasm as her young friend and not being bothered by that fact.

"Excellent. I'm glad not to have needed to be privy to them." He set the book down on the couch. "Did you send that mail that you were supposed to? To your cousin?"

"Cousin?" Qwyrk looked at Jilly in confusion.

"Yeah." Jilly fake-grinned. "You know, the one in *Cornwall?*"

Qwyrk gave her a blank, uncomprehending stare, but then understood. "Oh, right! *That* cousin. Yeah. The one in Cornwall. That you just wrote to. Which… is what we were just talking about up in your room. That whole 'girl stuff' business."

"That's the one! The cousin I've mentioned before. A lot. But you've not met her?"

"No, I have not. Definitely not. Not even once, what with her being in Cornwall and all that!"

Blip looked back and forth between them. "I'm beginning to suspect that there is no such cousin, and this whole taradiddle was a fabrication on the part of Ms. Pleeth in an attempt to stave off study of today's philosophy lesson. And if so, the loss is yours, my young friend, and yours alone."

"I'm not… taradiddling! Rapunzel's real!"

"Rapunzel?" Qwyrk said with in disbelief.

She gave Qwyrk a quick and sharp glare.

"…is your cousin's name, and how could I have forgotten that?" Qwyrk tried to fake a laugh but just ended up sounding like a hyena with hiccups.

"In any case, let us get to work." Blip seemed eager to drop the whole thing. "I have a few theories about what might be happening."

"I'm all pointed ears. I'm all lots of things this morning, actually." She beamed.

"Are you quite sure you're feeling all right?" he asked. "You seem uncharacteristically chipper today, not your usual sardonic self."

"Me? Sardonic? Ha. Ha ha ha!" That attempt at laughter was even worse, like a drunken parrot. Qwyrk waved her hand in dismissal. "I've always been up for a good laugh."

"Yes, usually at my expense."

"Oh, ppphhhthtt! You're exaggerating! We have a bit of good-natured banter from time to time, but it's all in fun!"

"Earlier this year, you called me a churlish, beetle-brained, bum-face. Among other things."

"Yeah, but I meant it in the nicest possible way."

"Be that as it may, I have some ideas as to what's going on."

"Sorry to interrupt, but shouldn't we include Holly in this?" Jilly asked. She flashed a sly look at Qwyrk. "You did say she should be here, right?"

"Oh, is your gentlewoman companion to join in these discussions?" Blip asked.

"Um, yeah, I was kind of hoping to have her here, if you don't mind. Not *have* her," Qwyrk blushed, "you know what I mean."

Blip shrugged. "Four minds are better than three, I suppose. Do you need to fetch her?"

"I probably should, yeah. She was freshening up and such after a busy night."

Jilly nudged Qwyrk with her elbow. Qwyrk pretended not to notice.

"Very fine. We shall pause the proceedings of our investigation and await your return. But do try to be efficient about it. In the meantime, I can instruct young Ms. Pleeth on what is meant by the consciousness of the infinite, since her missive to her 'cousin' who dwells in a tower in Cornwall is now completed, apparently."

Jilly looked at Qwyrk and mouthed, "Please hurry."

* * *

Moirin strolled down to the cafe, discovering that she was far hungrier than she realized. They were good lads, the rest of the band, and she knew she really had to do better, be more social, even if it pained her. She was so wrapped up in her own concerns that she nearly slammed right into someone.

"Oh gods, I'm so sorry! I wasn't looking where I was going and... Aileen?"

"Moirin! Good to see you up and about. I was a bit worried you were gonna just lie in your bunk all day. Have you eaten?"

"Just on my way to a breakfast with the band, actually. Then we're going to rehearse this afternoon, run some new songs and such."

"Sounds fun. I like to sing, but I don't think I could ever stand up in front of a big crowd of people and do it. My nerves would get the better of me."

"Well, you get used to it. I was a bit of wreck at first, too, but... oh, I almost forgot! I found this on the floor, under my bunk." She pulled out the necklace. "Is it yours? I wanted to make sure you got it back if it is."

"Well, yeah, it is, but you know what? I don't really need it. Not anymore." Aileen took it from Moirin's hand and placed it over her head. "Here, you keep it. Looks good on you, actually, fits with your rock star image."

"Thanks, but are you sure?" Moirin fingered the triskelion before looking back up. "And I'm hardly a rock star! We have a long way to go before that."

"Trust me." Aileen took her hand and kissed it. "You're destined for great things. See you in York?"

The gesture felt a little too familiar for someone she'd just met. Moirin pulled her hand away. "Uh, yeah, yeah, I suppose."

"Brilliant!" And with that, Aileen walked off, leaving Morin to wonder how on Earth anyone could be so cheerful and friendly, especially in the morning.

* * *

Qwyrk and Holly stepped into Jilly's living room with the usual lighted fanfare. Jilly was all smiles, and Qwyrk could only hope that Jilly wouldn't torment them too much. "Good morning, Jilly. Good morning, Mr. Blippingstone." Holly gave them a cheerful wave. "A lovely spring day, isn't it?"

"I don't think it could possibly be lovelier, or springier!" Jilly answered with an even bigger smile. So much for her not tormenting them too much.

"Quite," Holly said. "I'm very keen to learn more about your experience, especially since Lluck was there. It sounds fascinating, if a bit unsettling."

"It was." Jilly mercifully changed her tone. "I mean, it was just a show. And then everything flipped on its head." She recounted the details for Holly's benefit, and to refresh Qwyrk's and Blip's memories.

"The thing is," she said, "it felt like Chantz changed reality with her singing. It was so strange; scary, even."

"And Lluck couldn't sense it at all?" Holly asked.

Jilly shook her head. "He says he didn't see a thing. But he did believe me, and I appreciate his support."

Holly smiled. "He's good that way."

"If I may," Blip chimed in, "shall we reconvene at the table adjacent to the kitchen? I rather prefer to have a good solid structure at hand when ruminating on a topic of such deep interest. It encourages an air of scholarly deportment as we partake of the Socratic method."

"Um, sure," Jilly said, "come on, then."

They proceeded to reconvene in the manner to which Blip had requested, Holly and Qwyrk seated on one side, Jilly and Blip on the other.

"So," Qwyrk started, "what do we know?"

"Precious little, I'm afraid," Blip answered, "though I do have a theory."

There was a moment of silence.

Qwyrk raised an eyebrow. "And that theory would be?"

"Are you sure you want to hear it?"

"That's kind of what we're here for."

"I was waiting for the usual barrage of sarcasm, but very well: the Bolotnitsa."

"The what?" Jilly asked.

"It's a creature from Slavic lands. A young woman who accidentally dies in a swamp can become one. It is said she is attractive and has a fine magical voice that can lead the unwary astray. Some are benevolent, others less so."

"It's actually not a bad theory," Qwyrk said with surprise.

"Thank you, I am somewhat useful sometimes," Blip answered. "Though these creatures are usually localized, it's not impossible that one has been drawn away from its home for reasons we have yet to ascertain."

"That's a distinct possibility," Holly added, while casually moving one hand under the table to caress Qwyrk's knee. Qwyrk shivered, but tried to remain calm.

"So... um," Qwyrk said, "why would, why would she be over h-here?" *Damn it, Holly!*

"I'm uncertain," Blip admitted. "However, there is, I must admit, one potential flaw in my hypothesis. Ms. Pleeth." He turned to Jilly. "Did you happen to notice the young lady's feet?"

"Um, not really?" Jilly looked confused. "Why?"

"It's probably no matter."

Holly ran her fingers up Qwyrk's leg. Qwyrk shuddered and gritted her teeth. "What's probably no matter?" she managed to blurt out, growing hot and bothered.

"Well, you see, the Bolotnitsa has a peculiar physical trait," Blip answered.

"Peculiar how?" Qwyrk raised an annoyed eyebrow.

"Well, it has... the legs and feet of a goose."

"A goose." Qwyrk's annoyance intensified. As did her hot-and-botheredness. "So, they just walk around with poultry feet, singing to people, and somehow you think Jilly didn't notice this one small detail?"

"I said it was a theory!" Blip answered with his usual indignation. "And if the girl was wearing a long skirt or some such, how would anyone know?"

"Except she wasn't," Jilly countered, "she was wearing a short skirt and fishnets and Doc Marten boots."

"Why on earth would she be wearing a trap for catching fish? Is this some new ridiculous fashion trend among you young people?"

Holly trailed her fingers along the side of Qwyrk's thigh, and gave her a seductive look and lip-bite while Blip and Jilly were distracted with each other. Qwyrk shot her a glance that said both "stop it" and "please keep going" at the same time. "All right," she managed to say, "so our singer's probably not a goose-footed... whatever that thing it is. Any other ideas?"

"A siren?" Holly suggested, her fingers still secretly working their magic. "A magical creature that seduces and lures the unwary away to inevitable but very pleasurable doom?"

Qwyrk shivered.

"Possibly," Blip admitted, "though it would be highly unusual for one to be this far from the sea. Then again, she could be a Clurichaun."

"What's that?" Jilly asked.

Holly moved her hand back to Qwyrk's knee and started all over again.

"It's another singing creature, rather like a leprechaun, though they usually only sing when they're drunk," Blip explained, "and not terribly well, it must be said."

"Um, yeah, I don't think so," Jilly said. "I mean, they're an Irish band and all, but she seemed sober, and her voice is gorgeous."

"Great," Qwyrk managed to say in a way that didn't sound too ruttish. She was having a difficult time even paying attention at this point. Holly worked her hand back up Qwyrk's leg again.

"It *is* all rather frustrating," Holly said, "but at the same time, terribly interesting! And quite... stimulating, isn't it?" She looked at Qwyrk, bit her lip again, and trailed a booted foot along the back of Qwyrk's calf under the table, again out of sight, but most definitely not out of touch.

That was it. That was the last bloody straw. Qwyrk couldn't take it anymore. *Damn it!* "I just remembered," she announced. "There's um, there's something I'd like to look into, actually. Something important. Holly and I should go and check it out."

"What is it?" Jilly asked.

"It's um, the um... the thingie, you know?"

Jilly and Blip looked at her, and then at each other, then back to her. Holly seemed equally uncomprehending.

"The... thingie?" Jilly scrunched up her nose and made that skeptical "Jilly face" she was so annoyingly good at.

"Yeah, you know, the magic thingie, the... book. At Qwyzz's."

"The book?" Blip gave her a blank stare.

"Yeah, the book. The ancient *Tome of... MumbleTwaddle?*"

"The what?" Jilly scrunched up her face.

"It's an old book." Qwyrk tried to sound convincing. "It belonged to... um, Qwibble. He was a Shadow sorcerer, ages ago. Really powerful. Did amazing things."

"I've never heard of him," Blip said in a flat, skeptical tone.

"Well, he was a big deal back in the day, Mr. Philosophizer. During the Renaissance and all that."

"Where is he now?" Blip asked, in a flatter tone.

"What?"

"Where is he now? If he was important, I presume that he's still engaged in practice and scholarship."

"He's retired. Doesn't go out much these days. He prefers it that way, so we leave him alone. But his work is very important. Yeah, he wrote down a bunch of his ideas. Big ideas, magic ones, and some history in his main collection, the *Book of... PoodleMuddle.* It's in Qwyzz's library."

"Hang on, that's not what you called it before." Jilly crossed her arms.

"What?"

"It had a different name," Jilly continued. "The *Tome Mumble-Twaddle,* you said?"

"Yeah, well... that's... because it can change names when it wants to; it's sort of semi-sentient, right? So it doesn't like to keep one name for too long?"

"That makes absolutely no sense at all," Blip countered.

"Oh, look who knows so bloody much?" Qwyrk said in a mock huffy voice, waving her hands about in a defensive reflex. "Well, I happen to have studied with the great and learned Qwyzz, thank you for asking, and he has a vast library of old books, including the fabled *Account of DoubleBubble*, all right?"

"Hang on, that's a whole different name again," Jilly said, being far too clever for her own good.

"Of course it is!" Qwyrk bluffed. What the hell, at this point, she was just going with it. "I told you, it doesn't like to get stuck with one name! Why should a book have only one, anyway? Quite a few humans have three, sometimes more. J.R.R. Tolkien, for example, who incidentally made elves way less silly than they actually are in real life. I'm just saying." Now she folded her arms in defiance.

"This is approaching the absurdity of a Dadaist poem," Blip declared. "We've become players of roles in a veritable neo-Theater of the Absurd. What are you really on about, woman?"

"Nothing! Nothing out of the ordinary at all. Why would be I be on about something that I'm not really on about? That would just be silly, wouldn't it? Hey everyone! Here's me being on about something that I'm not really on about! Ha! Ppphht!" She waved her hands about again in dismissive ways. "I just think there might be some answers to be found in a special book in Qwyzz's library, and that Holly and I should go check it out, all right? We'll look it over and get back to you in a few hours if we find anything interesting. Or useful. Or odd. Whatever. Fair enough?"

She happened to catch a glimpse of Holly staring intently at her lap, trying to suppress a laugh.

"Fine, but don't make such a spectacle out of it." Blip rolled his eyes. "One might think you were actually planning to do something else entirely and trying to cover it up. There seems to be a lot of that going on this morning."

"Oh come on," Qwyrk scoffed with a mock laugh. *Yep,* she thought, *like an intoxicated hyena.* "Do something else? Really? What on Earth would I be planning on doing? Something else, hah!" More dismissive hand waving. *Goddess, get me out of here!*

"I've no idea," Blip answered. "You're the one making such a gaudy show out of going to peruse some obscure book I don't know about, allegedly written by someone I've never heard of. Damned peculiar, if you ask me!"

"I'm not making a 'gaudy show.' And there's nothing peculiar about it, Mr. Paranoid! I'm merely trying to contribute to our search for more information by taking myself to a place where I might be more useful. And... Holly can come with me. I need her help. It's really important."

She glanced over at Holly, who was now trying hard to hide her familiar smirk, but only somewhat succeeding in doing so. She looked up and nodded. Qwyrk noticed that Jilly seemed to realize what was happening and thought it prudent for her and Holly to be off as soon as possible.

"Right, we'll be back later." She stood up, taking Holly's hand and helping her up, as a signal that they should make a hasty exit. "And after we've examined the *Scroll of... BattleBottle,* we'll come back and let you know what we found out. I think it's really going to shed light on the whole mystery!"

Holly nodded in enthusiastic agreement, and looked to be trying to force away a laugh with a cough.

Qwyrk made a circle in the air with one hand, and purple lights started to swirl about the two of them. "Right then, we're off. Back later, no doubt with piles of new info. Ta for now, bye! Byeeeee!"

As they drew away from Jilly's home and onward to another plane, Qwyrk was quite sure she saw a knowing look on her young friend's face. She was happy to be making a quick getaway.

* * *

Moirin wandered back up to the youth hostel after her breakfast with the lads, which had been pleasant enough, though she was happy to have a few hours to herself before rehearsal. She noticed she was clutching the pendant that Aileen had gifted her; it felt warm and inviting somehow.

Returning to her room, she sat down on the bottom bunk, took off the necklace, and looked it over again. There was nothing fancy about it, not the kind of thing one would fawn over.

"Three spirals and an eye," she said to herself. "I wonder if it's some kind of protection charm or something? Ah well, it's all rubbish anyway, isn't it?"

She slipped it back over her head and a surge of warmth flowed through her.

"Hang on," she said, holding it and glaring at it. "Did you just do that?"

She removed it again. She waited for a minute or two, and then slipped it back on. Nothing. Not even the slightest sensation.

"Must have been the hot sauce on the baked beans coming back up for a visit," she sighed. "Oh, this is stupid! It's a gift, Moirin! Why do you have to be suspicious of everyone all the time?"

She stood up and paced about the room. As she berated herself for her mistrustful misanthropy, she went to the window where she'd seen something in the dark, and pushed back the curtain. Sure enough, a branch outside had been broken, enough to suggest that someone, or something, had pushed it out of the way to get a better view inside.

"Crap! There actually was someone here last night!"

* * *

Qwyrk and Holly manifested outside of Qwyrk's home in a flash of light and a chorus of mischievous laughter. And a kiss or two.

"The *Tome of MumbleTwaddle*?" Holly said after letting out a good guffaw.

"Oh, come on, I had to think of something, didn't I? It was all I could come up with under pressure. I don't do well under pressure, as you might have noticed! I'm a crap liar, and I mess up my words. And you were no help, missy, thank you very much! Being all... adorable and irresistible, and how the hell was I supposed to concentrate when you were distracting me under the table like that?"

"I was just trying to give you some inspiration," Holly answered in a false innocent tone.

"Yeah, well, it jolly well inspired something," Qwyrk said. Taking hold of Holly's hand, she led her toward her front door. "Come on," she invited. "We've bought ourselves a few hours. Let's make the most of them!"

"I look forward to perusing every aspect of this mystery with you, Ms. Qwyrk. That's a euphemism, by the way."

Qwyrk shot her a look as they disappeared into her home.

CHAPTER FOUR

Qwyrk and Holly lay in each other's arms, lounging on Qwyrk's bed.

"Well, I must say," Holly purred, "the *Tome of MumbleTwaddle* is very stimulating! Once you get under the cover, there's a lot to explore."

"You're a right laugh," Qwyrk said. "I think I'll keep you around for a bit."

"I should hope so."

"The thing is," Qwyrk said, beset with a rush of seriousness, "it probably wouldn't be a bad idea to call around to Qwyzz's and see what he actually *does* have in his library. We may as well try to make ourselves a bit useful, at least. All we've really done so far today is snog and shag."

"Is that a problem? Because I'm failing to see the problem. Why should that be a problem? Please tell me that's not a problem?"

"Not at all, but I'm kind of curious about what we might find."

"Do you think there might actually be something there? Some clues about this young woman or her abilities?"

Qwyrk shrugged. "It's possible. Qwyzz seems to have approximately one of everything you can possibly imagine crammed into his crazy house, so a bit of information on song magic in one of his endless shelves of books doesn't seem out of the question. Besides, you haven't met him yet, and it's well past time for me to introduce you. Come on!"

She slid out of Holly's embrace with some reluctance and hopped out of bed, throwing on a silk robe hanging nearby.

"Let me just go contact him and see if he's home. His home's nearby, and he'd probably like the company, to be honest."

"Yes, of course." Holly sat up, sadness falling across her face. "It was his wife who betrayed him, right? Locked him in their cellar? The one who was in league with de Soulis?"

Qwyrk nodded. "He says he's come to terms with it, but honestly, I don't know that I believe him. So I like to stop by from time to time and see how he's doing. I'm sure he'll be right pleased to see us."

"Then I'd be delighted for the introduction. Um..." she looked down, "we *are* getting dressed before we go over, right? I mean, I know Shadows can be rather unconcerned about such things, but it might a bit shocking if two gorgeous ladies just show up at his doorstep in the altogether, asking to see his library." She smirked that charming smirk with a smirking smirkiness that Qwyrk couldn't resist.

"Yes, darling." Qwyrk rolled her eyes. "I don't know what you've heard about Shadows, but prancing around naked isn't exactly a big priority for us."

"Oh." Holly flashed a mock frown. "That's a shame."

* * *

Outside the hostel, Moirin examined the broken tree branch and noticed fresh footprints in the dirt.

"Crap, crap, crap! Whoever was here must have been hanging out right as Aileen got back. That's creepy as hell. I'm glad she got back inside all right."

She thought to tell one of the hostel managers and went back to the office, where a young lady was on duty as the desk attendant, busy chatting on the phone in what sounded very much not like hostel business:

"Yeah, I know! I told 'im it were not on! Too right! What? Oh no, no, it weren't that much of a hassle. I just wanted 'im to stop mitherin' me, that's all..."

"Um, excuse me..." Being polite wasn't one of Moirin's favorite activities.

"He took me to this right posh place, right? Too much, if you ask me."

"Um," Moirin said with a little wave, "I noticed something outside you should probably know about—"

"But the food was all just shite with sugar on. Yeah, not a decent thing on the menu!"

"Uh, I think someone was prowling about outside last night, maybe trying to break in."

"And just cuz of that, he started expectin' things."

"Um, I could come back..."

"What did I do? I clocked 'im in the nadgers, didn't I?"

"Yeah, I'll probably just come back, then."

"And he's like rollin' about on the ground, and I told him he were on a Scarborough warnin'. Shut 'im right up. Sorry, hang on a minute... can I help you?"

But Moirin was already out the door, her lack of faith in humanity fully restored. She decided to check the other side of the building but saw no signs of other disturbances. Nothing.

A sinking feeling filled her belly.

"Whatever was out here last night was either looking for me or for Aileen, and given all the crap in my head lately, it's a sure bet it wasn't Aileen. Shite."

* * *

"Well, here it is." Qwyrk gestured at the decidedly odd construction of her mentor, hopeful that Holly wouldn't be put off.

"What a lovely and remarkable-looking home!" Holly exclaimed, to Qwyrk's immediate relief.

Qwyzz's mansion, an outstandingly ornate ode to the ramshackle, presented as a splendid three-story pile that mixed medieval castle and Tudor manor house in largely improbable and yet strangely harmonious ways. Every time Qwyrk stopped by, something looked a bit different: a new turret here, a redone crenellation there, or even just a new colorful flag waving in the breeze. But the front door always remained the same: an impressive wooden portal set in a stone gothic archway, with a large bell hanging in front of it. Well, the bell was always changing, manifesting in different sizes, shapes, types of metal, and even sounds.

"Yeah, it's a bit all over the shop, but it's oddly beautiful, somehow," Qwyrk said. "Still," she added as they reached the door, "there's one thing you have to watch out for."

Holly raised an eyebrow in a questioning glance.

Qwyrk rang the bell and stepped back. "This," she explained with a forced smile.

"Allooooooooo!" a stony voice called from above them.

"And so it begins," Qwyrk sighed as a rain of small pebbles splattered on her head and fell to the ground.

"And who do I have zee plaisir of addressing this day?" A little figure appeared over the edge of the roof far above. It looked a like a stone carving of a dog, but with devil's horns and bat wings, which flapped intermittently.

"Gargula, it's me, Qwyrk," she called up. "You've seen me Goddess-knows-how-many times over the past year. I have someone with me, and we want to speak with your master. He's expecting us, and it's important." She turned to Holly and held up one finger. "Wait for it..."

"Qwyrk?" the gargoyle answered. "I do not know zis name! How do I now you are zis 'Qwyrk' who is allegedly expected by my master? You might be anyone at all. You might be Tamerlane, come wiz his armies from Samarkand to wreak havoc on zis abode, or you might be an assassin of zee Levant, sent by zee Old Man in zee Mountain, trying to sneak into zis sanctuary and commit horrific deeds best left untold! Until I know for sure zat you are who you say you are, I will not allow a breach of... ow!"

A second little creature swatted Gargula with one of its wings, sending another spray of pebbles cascading down on Qwyrk and Holly, like the sands of an hourglass, only far more annoying and far less indicative of the time.

"Gargula!" the second gargoyle scolded, "do not be such an ass. You know very well who zis is, and that she is welcome any time. Now, go and make yourself useful!"

"And what do you suggest I do, ma dame Babewin?" Gargula sneered. "Simply hand zem zee keys to the mansion? Allow zem entry wiz no questions? How iz zat making myself useful?"

"I do not know, and I do not care what you do, but just go, or I will thump you again!"

"Bah, do your worst, you silly shrew-wife!"

"I'll do much more than that, you annoying tête carrée!"

"Oh?" Gargula snapped. "Well then, plouc, I say: Plouc! Plouc! You are nothing more, nothing less!"

"Oh? Oh?!" She whacked him again. "Take that, you moule à merde!" More pebbles flew in every direction.

"So... this is normal, I take it?" Holly asked, watching the drystone donnybrook on the rooftop with increasing bemusement.

"Oh, this is mild, actually," Qwyrk answered. "Some days, they go full-on with medieval French insults and end up sparring for ages. This is more like an abridged version; be glad."

The gargoyles' raspy little voices were still echoing in argument around the rooftop when the door opened. A Shadow gentleman with shoulder-length white hair and a thin white beard stood before them, bedecked in a black velvet robe with silver trim and embroidery that resembled constellations, each of which moved about the garment in random directions.

"Qwyrk, my dear! How lovely to see you!" he exclaimed, opening his arms.

"Qwyzz!" Qwyrk laughed and gladly embraced him, always relieved to find her master looking well and happy.

They parted and beheld each other for a moment.

"So," he started, "I received your message. Nothing is too grave, I hope?"

"No, nothing bad, I don't think," Qwyrk answered. "At least not yet. We're just looking for some information on something to be sure. I'll tell you all about it in a minute. But first things first," she stepped to one side with a smile, feeling flushed with pride. "This is Holly. She's Lluck's mum, and my, um, you know, my... girlfriend?"

Holly shot her a look of amusement mixed with fake indignation, but stepped forward with a smile and held out her hand. "It's a pleasure to meet you. I've heard all manner of lovely things about you, and now I suspect they're even truer than I've been led to believe."

She's so good at introductions and social etiquette, Qwyrk mused with admiration and a hint of envy.

"The pleasure is mine, my dear," Qwyzz responded. "If Qwyrk judges you to be worthy of her affections—which is no small thing—then you are as family to me, as well. I am ever at her disposal and now at yours. But if I'm correct, you're quite some distance from home, are you not?"

"Yes, that," Holly said. "It's a rather long story."

Qwyrk hoped that Holly wasn't feeling unintentionally put upon, given what she'd had recently learned about her family's flight from the lands of India so many centuries ago.

"Well, you can tell me all about it at your leisure if you'd like, or not," Qwyzz answered, dispelling Qwyrk's worries. "Please, do come inside, and try to ignore my gargoyles. They're a bit... spirited at times."

"Really?" Holly raised an eyebrow and smiled at Qwyrk. "I hadn't noticed, to be honest."

"It's true, I assure you," Qwyzz said. "Strange little creatures, they are, but a decent early warning system."

"I've no doubt, "Holly quipped. "In fact, I'm quite sure they could even fend off a team of assassins from the Levant."

"Eh?" Qwyzz seemed confused.

"Nothing, nothing at all." Holly nodded toward Qwyrk as they entered his enchanted abode. "Just a little joke. I make those sometimes. And sometimes, people even appreciate them."

She winked back at Qwyrk, who resisted the urge to respond to her teasing.

"Ah, good!" Qwyzz said. "I suspect we shall get along famously."

"I suspect we shall!"

* * *

Jilly and Blip wandered back into the living room.

"We're not getting very far," she said in frustration, slumping down on the sofa.

"I agree," Blip said. "I'd hoped this morning might show some more progress, but we seem to have hit a proverbial iceberg on the ocean to illumination."

"I don't think it's quite that bad," Jilly offered.

"No, I suppose not. Perhaps Qwyrk and her gentlelady will find some answers in that confounded book they're after, the *Scroll of HiggletyPiggeltyHumptyDumpty* or whatever the blazes it's called. Very peculiar that I've not heard of it, or the wizard who supposedly authored it."

"Well," Jilly tried to defend Qwyrk's behavior, quite certain what was really going on, "maybe there's only one copy, and maybe the wizard just wanted to keep to himself." She was rather proud of her creative prevarication.

"I grant that is possible, but it's still highly irregular."

"I'm sure Qwyrk and Holly are doing everything they can." Jilly forced back a giggle.

"In the meantime," Blip said, "tell me once more about the incident. There may yet be some small detail we missed."

Jilly sighed and retold the whole story. Again.

"So," he said after digesting her account, "you believed you were running for the exit when in fact, you were not moving at all?"

"Yeah, that was really odd. I was sure something was chasing after me, and I tried to get us out of there, but once the spell was broken, we were still in the same place."

"Hmmm, so not only did you perceive illusions to be real, but your sense of temporal space was disrupted as well."

"Um... yeah, all of that."

"And the only ones for whom time and space have no real meaning are the dead," he mused.

"Wait. Are you saying that I... *died* while she was singing?" Near panic gripped her.

"No, no, child, not at all." He put up his froggy hands in a gesture to calm his frightened student. "I am merely suggesting that her magic may be connected to the realm of the dead, and she may draw its power from it."

Jilly shivered. "That's... super creepy."

"Not especially. Said realm is merely another series of planes of existence, where both good and ill can exist in their own unique forms. Beings such as Qwyrk, Ms. Vishala, and myself cannot enter into them, as we are of a different substance, but since you are mortal, and magical to boot, it could be that you were able to perceive some of that connection between the realms. It might also explain why Lluck, being half-Fae, could not do so."

Jilly marveled at how smart and perceptive Blip could be sometimes, when another thought came to her. "This almost sounds like something Star Tao could help us with," she said.

"Possibly. The boy has his uses, to be sure."

"I'll text him at some point. So," she added, "if Chantz is alive, but drawing on the power of the dead, does that mean the dead are trying to work their magic through her? To do something in our world?"

"A good question. And one that raises unsettling possibilities if so."

Jilly didn't respond, but hugged herself at the thought of it all.

* * *

Qwyrk and Holly enjoyed Qwyzz's hospitality, including some of his fine home-made port, while they watched a parade of magical strangeness unfold: a suit of armor in one corner that perpetually polished itself, a game of chess that played itself (and in which the pieces swore at each other in Old French), and a small wyvern that flitted in and out of the room on little wings, leaving tiny trails of smoke in its wake. Qwyrk took pleasure in seeing Holly delight in it all.

"So, a singer with magical powers," Qwyzz said, after listening to Qwyrk's second-hand telling of the Leeds incident. "There are a number of possible candidates, of course, but it's a rare talent for a human, and the young lady seems more human than otherwise."

"Well, my son seems completely human," Holly countered, "and look what he can do."

"True enough," Qwyzz conceded. "Though he has your Fae blood, despite appearances."

"Is there anything in your library that could help us?" Qwyrk asked. "I mean, of course there is, but anything specific?"

"I have a hunch about something; excuse me for a moment." He shuffled off to one corner of his vast collection. He returned sooner than she expected.

"I think this one will be useful." He set a book down in front of them. There was nothing remarkable about it: medium-sized, dark brown cover, very old, a bit dusty. "There are several Celtic tales and histories in here that might shed some light on things; very musical people, the Celts. I'd be delighted to sit and read through them with you, but alas, I have another appointment, and I fear it shall take most of the day."

"No problem. Can we borrow it for a bit? Only because," Qwyrk glanced at Holly, "it might be easier to browse through it at my place, and not have to inconvenience you by staying here."

"Yes, yes of course! You know I fully trust you. Just make sure you return it promptly. If the book is away from the library past sundown, it emits a rather shocking alarm, I'm afraid, rather like an ancient Celtic lur horn."

"That shouldn't be a problem," Holly said, "I'm sure we can pore over it with all diligence and have it safely back here before too long. Celtic stories, you say?"

"Indeed, and what a marvel they are! I wish you happy hunting," Qwyzz said in a satisfied voice.

"Does it have a title?" Holly asked, a sly smile on her face.

"Oh, I suspect that it has several. Books like this often do."

"Really? How very interesting!" She smirked at Qwyrk.

"Right," Qwyrk announced, standing up and taking hold of the old tome, "we'll take this back to my home and tuck into it straight away!"

* * *

Moirin wandered up and down the streets of the hostel's neighborhood. She didn't want to go back to her room in case someone was still watching her, but it was too soon to meet up with the lads for rehearsal. She found herself missing Aileen's company, which was an odd sensation, to be sure. But Aileen was probably long gone, off on some travel adventure. Maybe they'd reconnect in York, maybe not. Moirin hoped so, which was another odd sensation. There was something about Aileen that felt almost familiar, but she couldn't explain it better than that.

"Oh, this is just crap!" She stomped. "So I've got some scary old lady visiting me in my head and giving me awful dreams. I've got creepers hanging around outside my hostel window. I had a weirdly familiar roommate for a night, and apparently when I sing, all kinds of strangeness happens. What the feck is going on?"

She sighed in frustration and had the urge to hit something, but sadly, there were no suitable targets (or people) nearby. She decided to go back to the hostel, grab her bag, check out, and head over to the rehearsal space early. "I can always just zone out on my phone for an hour or two."

Returning to her room, she saw that nothing had been moved, and no new people had settled in. *Thank the gods.* She reached under the lower bunk to retrieve her bag and happened to glance at the ceiling above the top bunk. Her jaw fell open and she dropped her bag. There, faint but visible, was a grey spiral, painted on the surface.

"That wasn't there this morning!" she whispered. "I don't think Aileen's been back. That means someone came in here while I was out and put it there!" A chill shot down her back.

A quick check of her bag revealed that nothing was missing, or added, so she stuffed the rest of her clothes inside it, ran out of the room, threw more cash than was needed at the same desk receptionist (who looked very confused, and didn't seem to recognize Moirin at all), and fled from the hostel without waiting another minute.

* * *

Qwyrk and Holly lay in each other's arms, lounging on Qwyrk's bed.

"We're not being very productive, you know," Holly offered.

"Hey," Qwyrk said, mustering up her defense, "we spent almost twenty minutes looking through that book!"

"I'm sure it wasn't more than ten."

"Oh, come on, it was at least fifteen."

"Fair enough," Holly said, "we'll split the difference. I suppose we should get back to it. It would be nice to have at least *something* to offer the others, no matter how small."

Qwyrk could only agree. "You're right. It'll look a bit off if we go back empty handed."

"And after all that time we spent consulting the ancient *Chronicle of DoubleTrouble*."

"See?" Qwyrk pointed at her. "You're getting the hang of it! The fine art of bluffing to avoid work is something that is greatly underappreciated, let me tell you."

"Well, you seem to have mastered it." Holly's expression turned puckish. "Actually, on second thought, you're rather rubbish at it."

"Oh, thank you very much." Qwyrk shot her a look.

"You're most welcome."

"I got us a few hours of alone time, didn't I?" Qwyrk was still proud of her fib.

"That's true. And I've quite enjoyed it."

"Glad I did something right. And we *did* do some research, so see? It was a win all around!"

"I'm not sure ten minutes qualifies as 'research.'"

"Hey, we agreed it was fifteen! But we have time to do some more before we head back." Qwyrk again slid out of Holly's embrace with some reluctance and hopped out of bed, throwing on her silk robe.

"Do you have one of those for me, too?" Holly teased. "Or do I have to be like a Shadow now and walk about *au naturel*?"

"We don't walk around naked! Honestly, what gave you that idea?"

"You've said it yourself: clothes don't matter to you, you just wear them for others' benefit."

"Yeah, but I meant that in the same way as food; we don't need them, but we wear them."

"So like, fruit hats and banana skirts?"

"What?"

"A joke, darling; goodness, no one seems to appreciate my humor, today! I think I'm losing my touch. But truth be told, the clothes you have are rather, well, limited. I could help a bit with your wardrobe, if you'd like."

Qwyrk flinched at the thought. "There's nothing wrong with my wardrobe."

"No, but a little extra sprucing up never hurt anyone."

"I spruce just fine, thank you."

"Maybe, but I wouldn't say no to a chance to add a little more variety to your look."

"I'm good, thanks."

Holly raised an eyebrow. "I'll get you into a little black dress eventually."

Qwyrk cringed. "That'll be the day."

"Just remember, if I get you into it, I can also get you out of it."

"All right, now I'm listening..."

"Let's leave that for the moment, shall we?" Holly slinked out of bed. "We have the *Book of Double, Double, Toil and Trouble* to get back to. No doubt, there are some damned spots and knock-knock jokes inside."

"That was a decent Shakespeare reference. Take a bow."

"Thank you. See? I'm rather clever and hilarious."

"Here, Ms. Hilarity, put this on, if you want." Qwyrk tossed her another robe from the same rack.

Holly took it and did so. She looked down at it and squinched. "What?"

"It's a bit sheer..."

"It's fine! For lounging about here, who cares?"

"Not Shadows, apparently."

Qwyrk shook her head, and they wandered back over to the book, still open to the same page where they'd left it before getting... distracted. She began flipping through the pages. Several accounts in several languages made reading it a much bigger problem than it needed to be.

"I'm still not quite sure what we're looking for," she said. "This book is mostly a history of Irish lore and folk tales from Britain. I don't see why it would be of much help."

"Maybe what Jilly experienced has happened before?" Holly offered.

"Yeah, I thought about that, but I was hoping we might have something like a case study, or even a spell book. Something more concrete, not just old legends."

Holly turned to the last few pages.

"What are you looking for?" asked Qwyrk.

"Books often have these things in the back called indexes," Holly quipped.

"Clever girl. And a pain in the arse."

"Aren't I just?"

Sure enough, the volume had a fairly comprehensive index that listed all manner of archaic names, places, events, curses, embarrassments, and so on, though after a few minutes of perusal, nothing about singing magic presented itself.

"Damn," Qwyrk swore. "At least we tried. We'll just have to make up some excuse about how it didn't go as we'd hoped. I mean, that's not exactly untrue."

"Wait... what about this?" Holly said, pointing to a word Qwyrk had never seen before. "The *bean chaointe*?"

"You speak Gaelic?" Qwyrk asked with a touch of incredulousness.

"A bit." Holly smiled.

"I'm impressed. Seriously." Qwyrk rested her head on Holly's shoulder.

"Well, I had quite a bit of time on my hands, and after the splendid mess I made of my mother's made-up name for me, I thought I should at least try to make it right by learning a bit of the proper language. I'm no expert, though."

"Fair enough." Qwyrk could listen to Holly go on about any topic for hours and be quite content doing so.

"So what does it mean?"

"Something like 'the keening woman', though that's not quite right, but it's close enough."

"Keening, as in singing about death?"

"That, or predicting a death that's on the way."

"Interesting, but not quite the bending of realty."

"No, but it's close enough that it may be linked. And what's death, if not a shift in one's reality? The ultimate shift, really."

"Well, we wouldn't know, obviously," Qwyrk cracked, but realized right away that Holly had indeed been through that awful experience when she lost her father to the Erlking. She raised her head and looked at Holly, now feeling terrible. "Darling, I'm so sorry. I didn't mean to make light of anything."

"It's all right." Holly put a gentle hand on hers. "You were just trying to be witty. Think nothing more of it."

Qwyrk was simultaneously relieved and smitten, even as she felt bad for mouthing off without thinking.

Holly flipped to the appropriate page. "Hm, it's the text of the *Cathreim Thoirdhealbhaigh*."

"The what, now?"

"It's an old book that tells of wars in medieval Ireland. Interestingly, though humans consider it to be mostly a historical chronicle, it does go into some detail about these keening women, three of them, actually. Their voices held powerful magic."

"Not much to go on, but it could be a clue. Maybe the singer in the band is one of these keening women." Qwyrk peered down at the writing.

"Perhaps, though it would be more than a touch unusual for one of them to just pick up, leave Ireland, and start touring with a goth-indie group around present-day England. They usually sang to warn of the deaths of noble families and kings. I doubt an uncertain, nomadic life would be a very satisfying alternative."

"True," Qwyrk said, "but when you've been around as long as they have—as *we* have—the more mundane might have a lot of appeal for a change. Still, Jilly mentioned that after the gig, Chantz looked like she was nervous, maybe even scared. That doesn't really sound like the behavior of an ancient spirit singing for the dead. I think Chantz knows she can do something, but maybe she doesn't know how or why it's happening. Maybe she's afraid of being discovered."

"Maybe she's afraid she's being watched."

"By who?"

Holly shrugged. "But if Lluck didn't notice anything out of sorts, then she might have a specific power. Maybe Jilly only saw it because she's been so immersed in studying magic for the past few months. I don't know. Perhaps Chantz has some enchantment that's not meant to be seen, except by very powerful magical beings."

"Which would explain why she looked nervous. You think these keening women are involved somehow? Is she being followed? Does the... Catherine Bird-heal-bay chronicle thingie say anything about them bending reality by singing?"

"You're really crap with Celtic words, aren't you? Honestly, what kind of faery are you, anyway?"

"That's just it, darling, I'm a Shadow, remember? We don't need food or drink, and we walk around naked all the time."

"Sadly, that's just an urban myth, or so I've recently learned. Getting back to your question, there's nothing in the book about remaking reality, as far as I can see." She flipped through several pages, scanning them. "But if that skill is something that's hard to perceive except by those who are magically-inclined, maybe no one who wrote down these stories even knew they could do it."

Qwyrk nodded. "It's not much, but it's a start. We should take the book back to Qwyzz. Then we need to pop back to Jilly and Blip. Maybe they've found out something on their own. Jilly's quite the wiz with the internet."

"Sounds like a solid plan. See? We did accomplish something!"

"We did indeed, so let's be responsible, and go right now."

"I agree," Holly said with a satisfied smile. "Lead the way!"

CHAPTER FIVE

Qwyrk and Holly lay in each other's arms, lounging on Qwyrk's bed. Yet again.

"Well, that didn't quite go to plan," Holly said.

"No," Qwyrk said, "but sometimes setting aside plans is for the best."

"We really probably definitely should go," Holly answered. "Jilly and Blip will be expecting us, and it's getting on into afternoon. Plus, we need to get the book back to Qwyzz's soon."

Qwyrk nodded. "I don't know what his alarm does exactly, but if Gargula and Babewin are any indication, the book will probably start swearing at us in Old English, or something."

"Hwaet!" Holly exclaimed, making a fist and shaking it triumphantly.

"What?"

"No, hwaet..."

Qwyrk raised herself up on one elbow and gave Holly a blank stare.

"The first word of *Beowulf*?" Holly said, looking as if she couldn't believe she had to explain. "The one no one can translate because no one remembers what it means anymore? Well, *I* know, but humans have let it slip away over the last thousand years."

"All right, so what does it mean, Ms. Linguistic Fancy-Knickers?"

"I won't tell you, just to see if you'll figure it out on your own."

"Tease."

Aren't I just?"

"Fine, I'll get right on that, just as soon as we've solved our latest mystery and saved the world again, which we maybe most definitely probably will have to."

"It does seem to happen rather often with you lot."

"Yeah," Qwyrk sighed. "The odd thing is, it's been quiet for ages, decades even, and now all of a sudden, we're getting bombarded with these crazy world-shattering crises every few months."

"In which case, we really should attend to our friends and tell them what we've found."

"You're right." Qwyrk slid once more out of Holly's embrace with great reluctance and hopped out of bed. "We really do have go this time. No more lingering, no more distractions. We have to be at least a little bit responsible."

"I can do that... for a while, anyway. But I shan't be responsible for my behavior post-responsibility." She winked.

"I'm counting on it," Qwyrk said as she exited the bedroom.

* * *

Moirin ran until she was out of breath, slowing down only from sheer necessity. She stopped, realizing she must have looked a complete idiot, running in fear from a youth hostel in broad daylight. She found the nearest bus stop and flopped down on the bench. All she wanted now was to get as far away from that room as possible and try to forget about everything. An afternoon's sing with the band would lift her spirits, depressing lyrics and all. That's what made their songs good, anyway.

A bus happened along soon after her hasty arrival, and she was glad of it, boarding and taking a seat on the upper level. She squinted as she looked out at the obnoxious, cheerful, sunny daylight that flooded the top deck. Glancing down, she noticed that her hand was cradling the pendant again, and that it still felt warm to the touch. There was something very comforting about it, something inviting, and the feeling of familiarity washed over her again.

"Who is Aileen?" she thought aloud. "How the hell did that spiral get on the ceiling?"

She closed her eyes, hoping for an answer, something, anything. But no visions wafted into her mind, unsettling or otherwise. Wherever this power was coming from—if it was coming from anywhere at all and she wasn't just going insane—it was damned inconsistent. She mused on how she'd ended up at this point. Sometimes she remembered her life one way and sometimes another, as if her past had more than one version, and she was never sure which one was true.

"Maybe I really am losing it." A longing, a sadness came over her, but she didn't know why. The sense that she'd forgotten something important, and once in a while she could remember a little, only to forget it again, haunted her. She tried to concentrate, to bring it back into her awareness. Something was there, if only she could grasp it, but it was already fading away, back into that impenetrable fog that clouded her memory so often.

"Why can't I remember? What's hiding from me? What am I hiding from myself?" Tears ran down her cheeks and, annoyed with herself, she reached up to wipe them away in a hurry, lest someone see her. With a sniff, she forced back her emotions, and after a few deep breaths, calmed herself down. Suppressing feelings came easily to her, but she knew that one day, it would all catch up with her. Not today, though.

"Just go and sing, you cow," she said. "Stop worrying about this crap! It's probably all because you're exhausted, anyway. None of it's real!"

Sure enough, her negative self-pep talk did the trick, and she had no more annoying and embarrassing emotional flare-ups for the rest of her journey.

* * *

They left Qwyrk's house, tome in hand, which for the moment at least, was not screaming at them in Old English. Qwyrk prepared to take them back to Qwyzz's.

"Huh, that's odd," she said as she happened to glance back.

"What?" Holly asked.

"Over there." Qwyrk pointed. "I don't remember that tree being so close to my house, and I'm sure it wasn't an oak."

"I don't understand."

"I don't either," Qwyrk replied, walking over to said tree for a closer look. "I swear, it was at least five, maybe seven feet farther away when we got here earlier. It always has been."

"Do trees walk about freely here? Or suddenly change into other trees?" Holly asked, following close behind. "I mean, I wouldn't at all be surprised after seeing Qwyzz's house."

"Not that I'm aware of." Qwyrk shook her head, looking at it up and down again.

"Could someone have moved it here by magic, as a joke or something?"

"Maybe, but it would be a piss-poor prank. I mean, why would they? 'Hey Qwyrk, we confess! We moved a tree a whole five feet closer to your home and changed it into another species for the hell of it... that was a right laugh wasn't it?'"

Holly shrugged. "Are you sure you're not just tired? We have had a rather exhausting day, you know." She bumped Qwyrk's hip with her own.

"Bollocks, you're probably right," Qwyrk answered. "I swear I'm losing it sometimes and right now, I can't even think straight."

"I'll take that as a compliment."

"You do that. Come on, let's get back to Qwyzz's. We've probably been gone just long enough for Gargula to claim he's forgotten who I am again. That should be a laugh riot."

* * *

The old woman opened her eyes, satisfied. All was proceeding as she planned. The young lady in the mortal realm was proving herself to be the perfect vehicle.

"Tis a true shame about the other one," she mused. "A fine pair they would have been. Most dangerous and deadly. But alas, some sacrifices must be made to attain what we strive for."

She began to hobble over the uneven terrain of this rocky, misty, twilight world where she was forced to spend so much of her time, dwelling in its obscurity, in its mundanity, in its dismal and unending mediocrity. The thought of being banished here forever had never sat well with her, and she knew that her imprisoned kin and allies were growing ever more restless, ever more enraged.

"Much remains to be done and the time grows short. There may only be one chance. One 'Chantz.'" She cackled at her word play.

"It's time to step things up, I think," she said, climbing over an abnormally shaped boulder with the help of her walking stick. "Nudge her a wee bit more. Invade her dreams a tad more deeply. Invade her waking hours a bit more brazenly. Give her that little push she needs to plunge her over the edge, open her mind with a reunion she doesn't want, give her back her memories, shock her into her destiny."

She chuckled as she made her way back to her murky cave in this dusky world, to sit and meditate, to reach out across the realms, to sow the seeds for what must be.

* * *

As luck would have it, Gargula didn't greet them, and Qwyrk was quite happy not knowing where he'd gone off to, thank you very much. So they were able to enter Qwyzz's home (which somehow looked different even in the short time they'd been away) and deposit the book on a small table by the sofa without it launching into the *Poetic Edda*, or the *Illiad*, or whatever it did.

"Brilliant!" Qwyrk took Holly's hand. "And now we'll head back on over to Jilly's..."

"And just who are you, and why are you here?"

Gargula stood inside on his hind legs, near the door, front paws folded in front of him, wings unfurled behind, all two feet of stony gargoyle intimidation. So much for avoiding him.

"Oh, for crap's sake!" Qwyrk started. "You know damned well

who we are. But what the hell are *you* doing inside your master's house, eh? I've a feeling you're not allowed in here, Monsieur Merde-Tête. Maybe Qwyzz would like to know what you get up to in his absence, hm?"

"Ack! Nooooo!" Gargula's expression fell into one of genuine fear. "Oh, please, s'il-vous-plait, non, mademoiselle Qwyrk, please do not tell zee Master zat I sometime come into his lovely, exquisite, and resplendent maison! I mean no harm, none at all, I promise you. I merely like to…"

"To what?" Qwyrk folded her own arms and gave him a withering look.

"To… well, zat is to say…"

"I'll tell him, so help me, I will," Qwyrk threatened. "What the bloody hell are you doing in here?"

"I like to dance…"

Qwyrk shot a glance at Holly, who looked back at her with a blank stare that told her this was near to the last thing either of them expected to hear.

"Dance?"

"Yes, I am learning ballet, and I need room to move freely and properly. Also, zere is a violin here that plays itself and takes requests. I can ask for anything I wish: *Giselle, Swan Lake, Daphnis et Chloé…* zee whole, how you say, shebang!"

Qwyrk had a vision of Gargula dancing in a tutu, and it was one of the more unsettling mental images to cross her mind in some time. At least this week.

"So, you come in here to practice the plié and the pas de bourrée?" Holly smiled. "I think that's quite charming!"

"Don't encourage him!" Qwyrk whispered.

"Why ever not? If Gargula wants to embrace the art, he should have all the encouragement we can give!"

Gargula bowed. "Merci madame, vous-êtes une vraie dame."

"Merci, Monsieur Gargula." Holly gave him a nod. "I admire your commitment. I wish I had time to work on my own ballet skills more."

"Wait, you're a ballet dancer, too?" Qwyrk stared at her. "What am I saying, of course you are." She turned her attention back to their rocky little interlocutor. "Look Gargula, what you do here is your business, even if you're not technically supposed to be in the house. Just don't mess up the place and knock things over, all right? You know how particular he is."

"Of course not! What do you take me for, some barbarian? I have zee utmost respect for zee master, and I always leave everything as I found it! Well, there was that one time when... never mind!" He launched into a tirade of grumping and presumed swearing in various French dialects spanning several hundred years, while stomping about and making the floor rattle, all of which made Qwyrk's mental image of him in tights seem that much more unsettling.

"We'll, leave you to it, then," she said, taking Holly's hand and making for the front door.

"I must admit, I'd rather like to see him dance!" Holly said once they were outside.

"Careful what you wish for, dear. We'll probably get an invitation to his first recital."

"I'm game!"

"How did I not know you do ballet?"

"I'm a woman of mystery, darling. You'll discover all sorts of interesting things about me eventually."

"Is there anything you don't do well?"

"I'm rubbish at cricket, rugby, and football."

"Well, that's something, I suppose. And on that note: off to Jilly's."

Qwyrk sighed as she heard a violin and Gargula back in the house, moving about in ways that she'd rather not witness.

* * *

"The keening women. Potentially very interesting," Blip mused, stroking his froggy chin after hearing Holly tell them what she'd learned. "I don't know why I'd not thought of them before, but it does make good, if undoubtedly ominous, sense."

"Who are they?" Jilly asked.

"Well," he replied, "they are very ancient and primal spirits who are said to sing to announce the deaths of those of importance in the mortal world. You see, Ms. Pleeth? We were correct in our death hypothesis, though said singing is only one activity among the great many that they are known to enact. Their stories are legendary. You know them better as banshees."

"Crap! Of course, the sodding banshees!" Qwyrk swore as she leaned forward from where she sat on Jilly's couch and put a hand over her face. "Why didn't I make that connection when you mentioned them?" She looked at Holly and felt ignorant and frustrated. Again.

"I'm sorry, darling." Holly rubbed her back. "I assumed you knew it or I certainly would have said something."

"No, it's not your fault. I'm just thick."

"You're anything but that."

But Qwyrk didn't believe her.

"So, banshees," Jilly interjected. "Like wailing, howling, screaming banshees?"

"The very same," Blip confirmed. "They have struck terror into the hearts and minds of mortals for thousands of years. It's believed that if a mortal hears one's fell voice, they are doomed to die shortly after."

"But... I heard her sing!" Jilly looked terrified. "Does that mean..."

"No, no, honey!" Qwyrk got up and went to Jilly, her own feelings of inadequacy forgotten. She put an arm around her young friend in comfort and gave her a gentle squeeze. "Whatever Chantz is, she's *not* a banshee. But maybe a banshee is trying to do something through her, using her voice for something?"

"Such a creature would have to reach out to her from one of the realms of the dead, if that is indeed what is happening," Blip offered, "and that takes some doing. But to what end? To enrapture young and foolish mortals at a blasted rock and roll concert? It makes no sense!"

"When has not making sense ever been an issue before?" Qwyrk asked. "It just means that we don't know what this banshee's really up to yet."

"It is very unusual," Holly added. "I mean, I've had no dealings with them, but I've heard stories, and they're anything but nice. It's not like them to play games or do something just for the fun of it. Perhaps they're using this young woman as a tool for something else, something horrible."

Qwyrk nodded. "There's never a shortage of villains planning things that are definitely not good for the rest of us. Finding out what they're up to is always a priority. So if—and I must stress we don't know much yet—if something like a keening woman is trying to do something bad through Chantz, that's definitely on the radar as something I have to watch and take care of."

"Something *we* have to take care of, surely?" Holly added.

Qwyrk nodded vigorously. "Of course, absolutely." Her inadequate feelings came rushing back.

"Well, whatever we're going to do, it might have to wait till tomorrow," Jilly said. "My parents will be home soon. I know, amazing, right? They're actually coming back early, if you can believe that. And then we're going out to dinner at some posh place in Harrogate. They're probably just using it as an excuse to look at buildings or something, but at least it'll be real food. So maybe we can meet here again tomorrow? They'll be back at work by then, probably home late, as usual."

"Fair enough," Qwyrk said, giving her a final hug before sitting again next to Holly. "Actually Jilly," she continued, "why don't you get online tonight, and find out all about this rock band. I mean, you're a fan, right? There must be more on them out there than just what's on their website, like those newsgroup/discussion group things. People still use those, right?"

"Quite a lot," Jilly nodded.

"Good, brilliant. See what else you can learn about her, if anything. I'm assuming 'Chantz' is a stage name, so try to find out more about who she really is, where she comes from, that sort of thing. I mean, you said she's Irish, which gives her at least some link to the banshees and whatnot."

"I can do that." Jilly smiled and eagerly cracked her knuckles. Everyone winced. "Oh, sorry. I was trying to look all impressive, not gross everyone out."

"Oh, you're plenty impressive," Qwyrk said, "cracks and pops notwithstanding."

"I shall make a few inquiries myself," Blip said, hopping off the chair opposite. "If one of those blasted creatures is determined to make mischief, we need to know who it is, and what her agenda might be."

"Should we stop by Qwyzz's again on the way back to your home and see if he knows anything else?" Holly asked Qwyrk.

Qwyrk shook her head. "He didn't say when he'd be back, and the prospect of possibly walking in on 'The Stomping Stone Beauty' prancing about to a disembodied violin doesn't bear thinking about."

Holly suppressed a chuckle.

"I have no idea what you're talking about," Jilly said, looking at them in complete confusion, "but your world is really strange. That's all."

"And you wouldn't have it any other way, dear!" Qwyrk answered. "This is potentially big news, so we'll need to have a think about what our next move is. If a banshee is interfering in this young lady's life, we have to do something about it, try to stop it. But trust me, it's not going to be pleasant."

"Bah, we shall meet her head on and claim victory yet again." Blip drew himself up. "Onward, then, stout companions, to another battle, and to glory!" He spoke with a raised fist and as much of a rousing tone as he always displayed at the start of some new metaphysical catastrophe. But Qwyrk found herself feeling more unsettled than usual about this situation, and she didn't know why.

* * *

Moirin felt more settled after a good sing. She found it splendidly cathartic to vocalize her dark thoughts to music and to get it all out, whether that be in plaintive dark ballads or full-on agonized heavy metal screams. Today's upset had receded, especially after a good post-rehearsal Indian dinner and a couple of pints. Now, the Weasels were packing up and getting ready to move on. Time to put this city behind her. Too much weirdness had happened here in a very short time, almost as if it were accelerating. But toward what?

"Next gig's gonna to be brilliant," Sam said, interrupting her thoughts. He loaded the last bit of luggage into their van. "It's basically made for us."

"I hope so," she answered as she climbed into the back seat with him. "That whole electricity plonking out thing at the uni was a bit rubbish. Ruined a great set." She didn't say anything about her own reality-warping experiences on stage, of course, or the odd post-concert visions at the cemetery.

"Nah, the next spot's perfect. A dedicated venue with all the right sound equipment, and a built-in audience who come to all the weekly shows. We should pack them in!" Keegan, the guitarist, was the band's eternal optimist. He was also the designated driver, the band's accountant, and publicity manager, which was probably a good combination considering how rubbish everyone else was at those things.

"Sounds great to me," Moirin replied. "We could do with a hit show. If we're ever gonna make our mark, we really do need bums on seats, or feet on floors, whatever. There's something to be said for being a cult band, but when you have only a few more fans than band members, it's a bit of a problem."

"Trust me, it'll be amazing," Keegan said, as he started the van and Ronan, the bassist, jumped in the front with him. "York, here we come!"

* * *

Qwyrk loved watching Holly sleep. Reverie could wait for a while; this was too lovely a sight to miss. She lay next to her new girlfriend and smiled, allowing her mind to drift off to thoughts of the past day, how gorgeous and amazing it all had been, how this was just the beginning, how it felt like being an adolescent again, how nothing else really mattered. Even her own feelings of self-doubt and inadequacy faded in the face of the peaceful and somniative scene before her. She half-closed her eyes and reached out to stroke Holly's hair. Nothing could ruin this moment, nothing could...

"Crap!" she swore, sitting upright, a horrible realization coming to her. "Crap, shite, damn it, crap!"

"What is it? What's wrong?" Holly awoke at once and sat up next to her.

"Big problem, love. A massive cock-up on my part. We had a report of a Darkfae doing suspicious and bad-looking things up in Richmond, not just your usual NN rubbish."

"NN?"

"Sorry, Nighttime Nasty. Unlike Bogtrotter's mates, this thing's been seen snooping around outside people's homes, especially ones with children. We're not sure what it is, but it might well try to kidnap someone at the very least, and I don't want to think about what else it might do, like some sort of sacrifice or something."

"That's horrid! But how does it involve you?"

"I was supposed to patrol up there tonight, starting about two hours ago. We had word that it might come back, and it's up to me to check it out. Crap! I totally forgot. I got so wrapped up in things here that it just completely slipped my mind."

"So what do we need to do?"

Qwyrk bounded out of bed. "I have to get over there, now."

"Let me come with you."

Qwyrk experienced a sudden twinge of protectiveness about her duties, even while knowing that an extra pair of hands would be most welcome. Nevertheless, she asked: "Are you sure? Things might get ugly."

"All the more reason 1 should be there." She threw on her clothes.

"Honestly, I'd be happy for the help, thanks." And bloody hell, Qwyrk actually meant it!

She followed Holly's lead and got dressed. A few moments later, they were dressed, if a bit disheveled. Qwyrk took Holly's hand. "Ready?"

Holly brandished her elegant weapon and nodded eagerly, but Qwyrk didn't share her enthusiasm. The stress of her mistake weighed on her, and she feared what they might find, or what she might have let happen.

CHAPTER SIX

In a flash, Qwyrk and Holly materialized in a dark alley behind two rows of stone houses. The air held a chill, and the flagstone pavement was slick from a recent rain and smelled damp.

"Do we know where we're going?" Holly asked.

"I should be able to figure it out. These things usually leave a trail, kind of like a slug, but with magic."

"What a charming mental image," Holly said.

"Hey, whatever works. We know it's looking for houses to break into, and I'm willing to bet it's not just picking them at random. It might be searching for someone in particular, or at least a certain kind of someone."

"What kind?"

Qwyrk shrugged. "Depends on what it has in mind for the victim, but it's not usually dinner, a film, and drinks after."

They walked a short distance, Qwyrk looking up and all

around, scanning the rooftops as best she could from her street-level vantage point.

"There!" She pointed upwards. "That attic window is a bit ajar, and I can see the traces of magic on its edge."

"I don't see anything. What does it look like?"

"Sort of like glowing, orange slime. There's a line of it running up the side of the house."

"How utterly revolting."

"Funny thing, though. The window's not open far enough for any regular-sized creature to fit through it, unless it went to the trouble of closing it behind, but that wouldn't make any sense, unless... oh no. Oh, Goddess no!"

"What? What is it?"

"We have to get up there right now!"

She grabbed Holly around the waist and leaped into the air, aiming straight for the window. They landed on the diagonal roof right next to it, and Qwyrk pulled the window open, paying no heed to accidentally just tearing the whole thing off. She threw herself inside, and Holly followed right behind.

* * *

Moirin settled into her room in the B&B in York. It was a fair bit nicer than that hostel in Leeds. This place was warm, quiet, and she had it all to herself. The lads were good to let her have her own space; she'd thank them again in the morning. She glanced out the window onto a portion of the city's ancient wall, which towered over the narrow street. She again found herself longing for something that seemed just out of reach, just beyond her recollection.

She sighed and closed the curtains, and after a few minutes of preparations, eagerly crawled into the comfortable bed to sleep for an untold number of hours and maybe feel vaguely human again in the morning.

"No more roommates, no more weird visions, no symbols painted on the ceiling," she said to herself, as much for her own comfort as a declaration of her intentions. "Just a good, long, slightly alcohol-induced sleep, and a fresh start tomorrow. So mote it be!"

She made a little pseudo-magical gesture with her hands. Lately, she'd found herself drawn to various metaphysical ideas and philosophies, and her recent experiences with her own voice and otherworldly visions confirmed that there were more things in heaven and earth and all that. But that was a musing for another time. "When I'm not dead knackered," she whispered.

Lights out, eyes closed, this was going to be a night to remember, or better yet, not to remember at all.

*   *   *

Qwyrk and Holly found themselves in a child's bedroom, confronted with something no child should see. Looming over the bed, a misshapen creature pulsed and changed shape with each passing moment, as if it had no form of its own to hold on to. Scraps of recognizable creatures melded into each other, with other parts of its body being nothing more than shadows or lumpy, almost molten, flesh. The eyes on its otherwise featureless face burned in a hideous yellow-orange, and they glared in anger at Qwyrk and Holly. In the bed, a little girl clutched at her covers and a small teddy bear, her eyes wide with horror.

"Don't even think about it, buggane!" Qwyrk threatened, already furious. "You shape-changers are the lowest of the low. What are doing, huh? Trying to steal her form just for laughs?"

"You are not welcome here, Shadow! Nor you, Yakshi!" the

thing spat in hate. "Your time is coming to an end, and ours is rising! Leave now, and let me finish my work, lest you regret it."

"Yeah, right, that's not going to happen." Qwyrk clenched her fists, and Holly unfurled her stick, swinging it about and leaving trails of light in its path. "In fact, we're going to go way beyond kicking your arse and well along the path of putting you down permanently!"

The buggane lunged at them, shifting into an amorphous shape that hindered their attempts to attack. Qwyrk leaped over it and landed in a crouch behind, turning about in one motion to land a solid punch on what passed for the creature's back. Holly swung her stick down onto a portion of its blobby flesh, connecting but sinking into it like a repulsive foam mattress.

"Ugh, this is disgusting!" Holly drew back her weapon in haste to try again.

Qwyrk reached out and grabbed the creature by the stub of its head, pulling it back toward herself, and landing her elbow on what passed for its chest. Holly took the cue and slammed the edge of her stick straight into its almost-face. Qwyrk struggled to keep as quiet as possible while subduing this damned difficult enemy.

The buggane faltered and pulled back, as if judging whether this fight was worth it. Apparently not. It staggered away from both of them, and before they could press their attack, it shifted into a snake-like form and slithered past them and back out the window before they could stop it.

"Damn it!" Qwyrk ran to the window, turning to look back at Holly. "I'll chase it," Qwyrk whispered, realizing that she needed to lower her voice. "I can follow its trail. You stay here and look after the girl."

"Are you sure?" Holly whispered back.

"Quite. You have a knack for dealing with kids, way more than I do. She's going to need some calming down, and I don't want whoever takes care of her waking up. With a bit of luck, tomorrow she might even think the whole thing was just a bad dream. See what you can do. I'll be back as soon as I can."

"Qwyrk..."

"If I need you, I promise I'll holler. All right, not really, but you know what I mean. With this." She held up her hand to show the little gold ring set with a green stone. She blew a kiss at Holly and jumped through a portal of violet light in pursuit of their foe.

✻ ✻ ✻

Holly let out a nervous sigh and turned to look back at the child, who cowered in her bed. Holly wrestled with her mothering instinct in that moment and she thought she might cry. She eased herself toward the child, who stared up at her with what seemed like a mixture of wonder and more than a bit of fear. It occurred to her that the girl must have seen Qwyrk only as a shadow with red eyes, which would have been almost as frightening as seeing the buggane itself. She knelt down by the side of the bed, bringing herself to an equal level with the child.

"Hello," she whispered with a warm smile. "It's all right; I won't hurt you. What's your name?"

"Ashanti," the girl whispered back, her eyes wide.

"Ashanti, that's a beautiful name!" Holly smiled. "My name's Vishala, but you can call me Holly, if you like. That's my special name that only my friends know about."

"Are you an obosom?"

"A what?"

~ 103 ~

"Mama says they're spirits who protect us. They're like us, from Ghana, in Africa, far away."

"Oh, that's lovely. No, I'm not, but I suppose I'm kind of like that, actually. I'm a Yakshi."

"What's that?"

"We come from India, which is very far away from Africa. We're kind of like faeries."

Ashanti giggled and sat up a little, bear still in hand. "I like faeries!"

"I'm glad. I like them, too! We Yakshi, we keep people safe from things like that monster."

"Did it want to hurt me?"

"I don't know," Holly white-lied. "But we wouldn't have let it."

"Who was that with you? She sounded like a girl, but she looked scary." She hunched under her covers again.

"That's my... friend, Qwyrk. I know she might seem a bit scary to you, but she's actually lovely and very nice. And she doesn't really look like that; it's just a clever disguise. Most people, girls and boys and their parents, can't see her real face."

"Why not?"

"I don't really know. It's just the way things are."

"What does she look like?

Holly glanced away for a moment and beamed as her mind filled with lovely, warm thoughts. "She's beautiful. She has short golden hair, sparkling eyes of green and blue, and the prettiest smile. And believe it or not..." Holly leaned forward and lowered her voice even more, as if telling the greatest of secrets. "She has pointy ears!"

"She does?"

"Yes, and so do I! Would you like to see?"

Ashanti nodded, leaning forward, still hugging her bear tightly.

Holly smiled and pulled back her hair on one side, to reveal said pointed pinna.

Ashanti's eyes grew wide in wonder. "Ooooh!"

Holly chuckled. "You see, there *is* magic in the world. It's all around you, if you know where to look."

"Mama says so, too. She tells me that the abosom are our friends and watch over us. She can do magic. Do you want to meet her?"

"Well, she sounds very wise, and you should listen to her. But she's probably sleeping right now, and we wouldn't want to wake her. You can tell her about me in the morning, if you like." Holly realized this was not what Qwyrk wanted, but in the moment, it was the right thing to say.

Ashanti nodded and relaxed some more.

Holly pointed to her bear. "Who's your friend?"

"This is Effie. She *is* my friend, my best friend, and she keeps me safe at night."

"And I'll bet she does a very good job of it!"

Ashanti nodded. "She's like you and your friend. She chases away monsters."

Holly wanted to change the subject and divert the child's thoughts from what she'd just seen. "How about if I tell you a story, to help you go back to sleep? Would you like that?"

"Yes, very much!" The child nodded again, looking delighted.

Holly sat on the floor. "Wonderful! I know a good many stories. What kind do you like? Stories about talking animals? Enchanted places? Brave girls who save the day?"

"All of those!" Ashanti beamed.

Holly chuckled. "You shall have me here all night!"

"I'd like that!"

"Well, you need your sleep, so how about just one tale for now?"

Ashanti nodded and lay herself back down, Effie in hand.

"Now," Holly said, "close your eyes, and let's take a trip together to a magical land..."

* * *

"I'm going to kick your bloody arse on a one-way trip back to your dump of a magical land!" Qwyrk had the buggane cornered in an old alley.

"Heh!" The amorphous creature pulsed in front of her. "You can try to banish me, Shadow, but even if you succeed, you'll not stop what shall happen."

"And what pray tell is that?"

"It is not for me to know of the great plan, but I promise that you'll learn of it soon enough."

"Ah, so that's the way it's going to be, eh? You know, you villainous types always do one of two things. Either you capture us and proceed to go into painful detail about every boring, stupid part of your master plan—like, down to describing your trips to the flipping hardware store—or you just taunt us about how magnificent it all is without revealing anything. I'm honestly not sure which one's more annoying. Tell you what? Let's do Twenty Questions, and see if I can guess what it is. If I do, I get to kick your arse. If I don't... well, I'm still going to kick your arse, but it'll be more useful to me if you tell me first. Deal?"

"I detest your kind."

"Feeling's mutual, mate. You steal other's forms, and that makes you the one of worst kinds of thieves I can imagine. Now, why were you in that little girl's room? What's so special about her?"

"Has the game of questions begun?"

"Oh right, sorry. I have to phrase it as a yes-or-no question, don't I? All right: are you going to tell me why you were in that girl's room, or am I going to have to mop the alley with you?"

"Yes."

"Fine, then. I'll... wait, 'yes' what?"

"I shall tell you why I wanted the girl. There is nothing you can do about it, anyway. And it will amuse me."

"Uh, that's a new one. All right. Go on, then."

"The little one was chosen. She is perfect for... arrrghghgh!"

The buggane's fiery eyes went wide.

"Wait, perfect for what? Chosen by who? What's going on?"

The creature fell to its knees and began shifting rapidly through multiple shapes. Its pained groan turned to an agonized scream, and it began to twitch and convulse.

"Right, this is not exactly how I pictured this going." She took a few steps back, in case it exploded and showered her with buggane goo.

Instead, it collapsed to the ground and writhed, as each new shape it took on became smaller and ever more shriveled. Smoke began to stream from whatever eyes and ears it assumed with each new form. As it withered away in front of her, Qwyrk was at a loss as to what she should do.

"Um, not to sound callous, but could you, maybe at least tell me what's happening to you?"

But it gave her no answers, and soon, a final cry escaped a small, smoldering husk that afterward festered with a terrible odor on the cobblestone ground, where the thing had stood less than a minute before.

"Crap." She looked behind her to make sure that no one had seen the whole gruesome spectacle. "This is so not good."

* * *

Somewhere, far off in a dream, she wandered. Moirin looked down and saw that she wore a grey robe, roughly-spun, and a bit tattered at the edges. She found herself standing on rocky and uneven terrain, her view obscured by the dark and misty air. It could have been dusk or dawn.

"Am I lucid dreaming? Was it the Leeds beer?"

She took a few steps and noticed that her feet were bare, but that the rocky ground didn't hurt. "I mean, why would it, it's *my* dream, after all. Hey, I wonder if I can fly?"

"That talent was not given to you, I fear," a voice in the mist replied. A familiar voice, one she'd heard many times, while singing, when nodding off to sleep, but this? This was the first time the voice called to her in a dream, a dream so real it might as well have been reality.

"I know you," Moirin called out.

"Do you?" A shape emerged from the mist, a small figure adorned in a hooded cloak and holding a walking stick. A few more steps revealed it to be the woman, with her tussled hair and frightening features. She smiled a cold and unwelcoming smile.

"Who are you?" Moirin demanded.

"I thought you just said you knew me?" she replied. "Clearly, you do not."

"All right then, What do you want?"

"Ah, now, that is another matter entirely. It is not so much about what I want, but what you want, what you need."

"And you know what I need, do you?"

"I've a fairly good idea. But do you know, Moirin? Chantz? Whatever you choose to call yourself?"

"Chantz is a stage name, that's all."

"It's a good play on words."

"Yeah, well, I thought it was clever."

"Tell me, why do you need a false name to sing, when you already possess a false name?"

"What are you talking about? My name is Moirin! Moirin Moeran."

"Is it now?"

"So you're saying that I don't even know my own name?"

"Tell me: where do you come from?"

"I think that's pretty damned obvious, given my accent!"

"Yes, but where? Where exactly in Ireland do you come from?"

"D-Dublin... I suppose?"

"You suppose? Well, that's not very convincing, is it? Most folk have a good sense of where they're from. When is your birthday?"

"Um, August."

"August? That's all? What are your parents' names?"

"Look, I'm exhausted and I need sleep." Moirin tried in vain to change the subject. "I mean, I *am* asleep, or something, but... why are you doing this?"

"I'm trying to help you unlock things in your head that should never have been bound up, dear Moirin. Plant seeds that will grow into a glorious vine that will allow you to escape the prison of your own mind. You see? I'm trying to help you, dear."

"Help me how?"

"To reclaim who you really are, child! But I don't want to tax you overly, not at the start. Return to your world, and cogitate on the questions I have posed for you. See what drifts into your thoughts as you imagine answering them. You might well surprise yourself with what you come up with, though they may not be the answers you want. Go now."

She waved her hand and Moirin felt tired inside of her own dream. She was going crazy, that was all there was to it. A moment, or perhaps hours, of black came, and she opened her eyes to see something she'd not expected at all.

*　*　*

Qwyrk reappeared in the child's room to find, as she hoped, Holly sitting quietly and keeping watch over the sleeping girl. Holly placed a finger over her lips, and Qwyrk nodded in reply.

"Success?" Holly whispered as Qwyrk approached.

"Sort of?" Qwyrk whispered back. "Things got weird; weirder than usual, I mean. It's a bit of a long story. I'll tell you when we get home, but for now, she's safe." She motioned to Ashanti. "And so's everyone else in town, I'd guess."

"Good," Holly answered. "We should go before we're found out."

"You are too late for that," said a voice at the door (already open a crack). It pushed back to reveal a young African woman standing in the doorway. She wore a simple garment of white, and carried a decorated staff that could have been magical, or a weapon, or both. She wore her hair braided in long, tight plats tied back.

"You are Fae and Shadow, yes?" she asked.

Qwyrk and Holly looked at each other in surprise, and back at her; both nodded.

She motioned to them. "Come. Let her sleep."

Sensing they didn't really have a choice and not wanting to wake up the child, or rudely just vanish, Qwyrk motioned with her head to Holly that they should do as the woman asked. They followed her down a flight of stairs and into a sitting room, adorned with beautiful art, perhaps traditional works from her homeland.

"I am Adjua," she said turning to face them without expression. "You saved my daughter's life tonight; I thank you and owe you a debt."

"You don't owe us anything, and I'm so sorry we trespassed in your home," Qwyrk said. "We didn't really have a choice. That buggane was going to take her, and we don't know why."

"Buggane?" Adjua clutched her staff and looked back and forth between them, curiosity and suspicion displayed in equal measure.

"They're Darkfae," Qwyrk explained. "Shape shifters. Nasty bunch, overall. I don't normally see them around these parts. Maybe that's because I'm not usually looking. But it was trying to take her; it even said so."

"What happened to the creature?" Adjua demanded. "Is my daughter truly safe?"

"I cornered it in an alley a few streets away." Qwyrk tried to sound reassuring. "It taunted me, but then decided to tell me why it was after her. I was all ready to hear whatever horrid excuse it came up with, but then it started shrieking and burned up as it transformed through a mess of different shapes. There's nothing left but a bit of smoke and ash, and a stink like you wouldn't believe. I'm guessing something killed it by magic or a curse before it could talk."

Adjua looked at her in shock. "So you do not know what this... buggane wanted with my child?" She asked in a calmer voice than Qwyrk expected.

"No, sorry." Qwyrk shook her head. "It did say something about how we can't stop what's coming, but that's the kind of bragging those things usually like to do. I have no idea if it was telling the truth, or just messing with my head. But given its little pyrotechnic exit, I'm going out on a limb and saying it wasn't just showing off."

Adjua was silent for a moment. "I am a dream-seer. When I sleep, sometimes I have dreams that are more than dreams. I know when they are special, and they show me things. Sometimes the future, sometimes they warn me of trouble. I saw Ashanti in danger in my sleep tonight, but I should have woken up before I did. It felt like something kept me asleep, and it was not until I would have been too late that I woke and rushed to her room to find you. Thankfully, you protected her, saved her."

"So, that creature tried to kidnap her and something tried to keep you from stopping it," Holly said with a shudder. "I'm a mother myself, and the thought of that makes me ill."

"I am very worried," Adjua said. "Ashanti is no normal girl. I come from a long line of wise-women, going back centuries in our homeland, but we are only mortal, not like you two. We see, we hear, we observe, we work with spirits to help others where we can. But Ashanti, there is something different about her. There is a light in her eyes, a fire in her spirit. It tells me that she may become much more. There is great power in her; I can feel it. She may be the greatest of us."

"I have a young human friend who's recently discovered her own magical gifts. She's quite something." Qwyrk said. "Maybe she and your daughter should meet sometime."

"No," Adjua answered. "I mean no disrespect, but Ashanti is too young. She is not yet ready. I need to let her be a child for as long as I can. She deserves that."

"If something's after her, that may not be an option, I'm afraid," Qwyrk said, feeling remorseful about saying it. "But that creature's gone, and I'm not sensing anything else out there right now. Look, I have a friend who can work some protective magic around your home, make sure none of those things can get in. It won't last forever, but it should be enough to discourage any more of them from trying, a least for a while. You can decide what you want to do after he's done it. I'll go see him right after we leave and have him get on it. Sound good?"

Adjua nodded. "You are kind, Shadow woman, thank you."

"Qwyrk. My name's Qwyrk. And this is Holly."

They all exchanged handshakes and pleasantries, and Adjua seemed to warm to them a bit.

"We're going to find out more about what's happening, I promise you," Qwyrk said. "Normally, this sort of thing would be a routine seeing-off of some pillock or prankster, but what happened tonight worries me. A lot. I need to know what's going on. If... when I find out more, I'll come back and share it with you."

"Thank you," Adjua said with a nod of her head. "I will wait for your friend's protection. I also have some magic of my own that I will work tonight. Together, I pray we can keep this dwelling safe."

"I'm sure we can," Qwyrk answered.

"If you need us for anything, don't hesitate to call." Holly produced one of her golden rings set with a little green stone. "Wear this, think about me, and call my name. I'll hear and reach out to you."

"You are most kind." Adjua took the little ring and examined it, more in curiosity than in surprise.

"We should really go now," Qwyrk said. "Sorry again for all of this. It's not your fault, but we'll fix it, I promise!"

"I believe you. You are both of the good and are welcome in this home. Though, perhaps next time, you could knock first?" She raised an eyebrow and bowed her head a little. Qwyrk did the same in return.

Taking Holly's hand, Qwyrk made the circle of light and in a flash, they were gone.

* * *

Moirin opened her eyes, emerging from a deep, groggy sleep. A chill washed down her back. She looked around herself in shock. It was still dark, and she had no idea of the time. A mist hung in the air, though not as thick as the one in her lucid dream. She was standing upright, outside, on the medieval wall opposite her bedroom. Her nice, warm bedroom where she should be sleeping in until noon like a proper rock star.

"What the feck?"

She made her way off the wall and down the grassy slope it rested atop, back down to cross the street and run to the front door of her B&B. Her bare feet slapped on the icy cold pavement, which made the whole experience even worse. Teeth chattering, she fumbled about and was relieved to find that, somehow, she had the front door key and her room key in her sleep trousers' pocket. She made a quick entrance, and closed the door as quietly as she could. Still shivering, she dashed upstairs and back to her room, her lovely, warm room, where she locked the door behind her, dove back into bed and began to warm herself under the duvet.

"Great," she whispered as warmth crept back into her chilled extremities. "Now I'm a sleep-walker, too. What the hell is next? Forget I said that, I don't want to know. I just want about a hundred more hours of sleep and no more bizarre dreams."

The clock said it was nearly 2:00 am, so one hundred hours couldn't be an option, but she'd take eight. Or ten.

What had that dream been about? It seemed so real at the time, but now it was fading, like all dreams do. Was there something she was supposed to remember? If so, it was gone now. In a few more minutes, she'd relaxed and fallen back into a deep sleep of the kind she craved so much and was so fleeting lately.

* * *

After visiting Qwyzz to alert him, Qwyrk and Holly flashed back to Qwyrk's home and trudged in without saying a word. They flopped down on Qwyrk's plushy couch with a grand thud.

"Goddess, what a night!" Holly sighed, tossing aside her jacket and stretching out. "I'm exhausted, and look at you; you hardly seem winded at all."

"Was that really a good idea?" Qwyrk ignored her comment, nerves swelling inside her for what she was about to say. "Giving Adjua one of your rings?"

"What do you mean?" Holly said, sitting back up.

"Well, you barely know her, for a start. She's a human magic-worker who can see me as I am, and staying hidden from humans, especially magical ones, is one of our main priorities."

"She's a mother worried about her child, and now she might be vulnerable to attack by all sorts from outside of her world. More than anyone, I can appreciate that. And I should hope you would, too."

"I know, I know, I just..."

"What?"

"I just think... maybe you're letting personal feelings cloud your judgement a bit here? I mean, I know you spent time with her daughter, but we have to be careful about getting attached."

"So, I was supposed to let a beautiful child be terrified and traumatized by that horrid thing and do nothing?" Holly stiffened and inched away from Qwyrk.

"No! Not at all. Look, I'm glad you talked with Ashanti and told her a story and got her back to sleep, and all that. She was scared, and you did the right thing. You've got that whole motherly business going on that I sure as hell don't..."

"But?" Holly raised an annoyed eyebrow.

"But we have a bigger problem, or at least I do. I screwed up tonight. Possibly really badly. I mean, it's one thing to miss a routine patrol. That's not good... but this? This is awful. I got sloppy, I got distracted. I was so wrapped up in spending time with you that I made a mistake that could have led to humans getting hurt, even dying. That can't happen again, Holly. I won't let it."

"What are you saying, Qwyrk?" Holly looked distraught. "Is this the 'I have to break up with you' speech? Because I really can't handle that, not now. Not ever, actually."

"What? Oh no! No! Goddess no! Holly, love, believe me, that's the last thing I want to do." Qwyrk reached for her hand. "Ugh! That makes me ill just thinking about it. No, I'm saying that we have to be more careful. We've been acting like a couple of crushed-out adolescents in their seventies. I mean, I feel giddy, happy, stupid, and it's brilliant. But I worry about it distracting me to where I make more mistakes and someone really does get injured, or even killed. I can't have that. Ever."

"So what do you propose?"

Qwyrk sighed. "I don't know."

"Well, that's very helpful." Holly pulled back her hand.

"Holly..."

"What? What do you want me to do about it? I've no idea what your responsibilities are on a day-to-day basis. And honestly, it's none of my business, unless you choose to tell me, which apparently you don't."

"It's not that I don't want to tell you. We just have all these ridiculous regulations about how we're supposed to handle things. And you giving Adjua a way to contact you could create... problems."

"What kinds of problems?"

"I don't know, but if it's found out, it might come back on me. We're supposed to stay away from humans in situations like this, I mean, beyond Qwyzz working some magic for their home."

"Well, perhaps *you* are, but I'm not subject to Shadow laws, and I'm not leaving that child unprotected."

"See? That's what I'm talking about. I think..."

"What? What do you think, Qwyrk?" Holly stiffened again and sounded angry. Qwyrk's stomach twisted into knots.

"Nothing," she half-whispered and looked away.

"No, you obviously have something to say."

Qwyrk barely glanced back toward her. "Are you... are you sure this isn't about Lluck? I know how bad you feel about what happened, about leaving him behind, and missing out on so much of his childhood. I just, I don't want you to get attached to a child who's not..."

"Who's not mine? I'm very well aware of that. What you're really saying is that I already ruined one child's life, and you wouldn't want me doing it again, would you?"

"Holly, no, that's not at all what I meant!"

"For the record, I gave Adjua one of my rings to help her out of a situation that *you* created by not being there when you were needed."

"That's not fair! You were just as invested in our time together as me."

"Yes, but I didn't know you had something else important to do, or of course I would have given some of that time up."

"I'm sorry, I just... forgot, that's all."

"That's not my fault."

"I didn't say it was. Holly..."

Holly stood up. "Never mind, I'm going out for a walk. I'm tired and upset and I don't want to talk about this for a while. I'll be back later, I suppose."

"Holly, I'm sorry."

"Sort out your own mess, Qwyrk, so I don't have to clean up after you." She picked up her jacket and threw it on, turned her back, and left without saying anything else.

CHAPTER SEVEN

Qwyrk ran to answer the knock at the door, more than eager to patch things up with Holly. "I'm *so* glad you're back! Huh?"

No one was there.

"Down here, eh?"

She glanced to her feet and saw a peculiar little fellow. He stood about a foot tall, and had a bald head with a bulbous nose, yellow eyes, stubby little horns, and a mottled countenance. "Evenin', love," he said with a little bow, adjusting the ill-fitting sack that barely passed as his clothing.

"Horatio," she sighed in frustration, "what the hell are you doing here? How did you even get here?"

"Now, is that any way to greet your long-time mate and go-to for pertinent information?"

"Yeah, all right, sorry, but seriously: what are you doing here? Our realm isn't exactly all that amenable to you lot."

"This is true. Had to be a bit sneaky gettin' in here. However, when duty calls, we take the appropriate risks and let the cards fall where they may."

"Yeah, because Nighttime Nasties are so damned brave. What's up, really?"

"May I come in?"

She rolled her eyes. "Yeah fine, all right, enter." She made an exaggerated motion with one hand. Horatio bounded into her home and jumped up on the sofa.

"Very comfortable and cozy," he said looking around with a nod. "Can't remember when I was last here, now that I think about it."

"Yeah, that would be because I've never invited you here before." She crossed her arms.

"You wound me, madam." He placed a hand on his chest. "You'll find that I can be as agreeable a house guest as anyone."

"Don't start. Just say what you want to say."

"You're a bit testy tonight, even more than usual. Lady friend problems, I presume?"

"You can presume to mind your own bloody business."

"Ah." He nodded. "A traffic jam on your motorway to love. A detour from the ring road to romantic bliss. A replacement bus service in the…"

"Yeah, all right, I get it. And yes, that's it. Happy now? Goddess, how do you always know these things, anyway? It's infuriating."

"It's what I do, love. Keep me ear to the ground. Keeps me alive, and maybe, just maybe, lets me help a friend in need."

Qwyrk looked around the room, past him, behind herself. "Oh, I'm sorry, you were talking about me? Fair enough, carry on, then."

"You're a right laugh."

"So I'm told. Quite recently, in fact."

"So, a bit of friction with the would-be Mrs., eh?"

"Right, to be clear, we're nowhere near that stage. We're not even in that theater. We're not even on the tube line that goes to that theater. We're not even making plans to go out for the evening to that theater."

"The lady doth protest too much, methinks. But anyway, you're concerned about something, and I suspect it has to do with how she's handling herself in relation to mortals, am I right?"

"No! I mean, not really, I mean, how the hell did you…"

"She has a son, by a human bloke. They're both a big part of her life now, but it's something you can't share in; not really, I mean. No matter what you do, they'll always have something with her that you don't, a family bond, and that bothers you. Makes you a bit jealous, maybe?"

Qwyrk scoffed. "I'm not jealous!"

Horatio shrugged. "Call it what you like, love. But I'm guessing that every time she makes any meaningful connection with a human, you feel a bit of a twinge, am I right? And not just because you're supposed to go about being all secret from mortals and such."

Qwyrk threw her hands up. "Fine! You win. I'm not actually a part of her family, and I never will be. I'm also really insecure, all right? She's amazing, smart, tough as nails, talented at everything, gorgeous, witty, charming, and I honestly feel like a complete prat next to her most of the time. I don't know what she even sees in me. And it's not that I want her all to myself, not at all. I just see how easily she makes friends and charms people, and I feel utterly incompetent in comparison."

"Thing is, love, you got nothing to worry about." Horatio sounded way more calming than he had any right to. "We've all seen the way she looks at you. The only way you could lose her now is by not stepping things up a bit."

"Yeah, well." Qwyrk semi-blushed. "We already did that. Stepping up, I mean, you know."

"Well then, there you have it. I assume you're waiting for her to come back here after some kind of tiff, then?"

"Of course you know that, too."

Horatio rolled *his* eyes. "Come on, love. I know things? Anyway it'll all be fine."

"I wish I had your confidence."

"Well, I was the one that nudged her in your direction to begin with, remember? Because I saw the connection?"

"True. Thanks, mate. For real, I owe you one. Drinks are on me the next time we end up at the Epping Forest Brownie Bar. Look, sorry not to sound more grateful, but you did stop by for some other reason than to offer me relationship advice, I assume?"

"I did indeed. Word on the dirt path is there's a girl out there that can do some snazzy stuff with her voice. Bend reality and maybe more?"

"That's what I've been told. And I'm looking into it, because that kind of power could be very dangerous in the wrong hands."

"Yeah, thing is, it might already be in those wrong hands."

"What do you mean?"

"Something's stirring, or so I've heard."

"Yeah, it is. A banshee from what we've gathered. Any idea which one?"

"Not really." Horatio shrugged.

"Helpful on that front, as usual."

"Again, you wound me, madame. But I am prepared to let it slide. Anyway, it may be that the girl herself *is* the problem. It's not just that she's coveted by some malevolent power, she may already be a part of it, unknowingly."

"Lovely. So what do we do?"

"Keep your eyes open, try to track her down? Get to her first, before whoever's tryin' to sway her over to their side succeeds?"

"Yeah, that's kind of already on the agenda. Any chance that if we make a move, we'll draw out whatever else is interested in her? Like if there's a big bad behind it all?"

"I'd say that's a definite possibility. Eventually, anyway."

"Well, maybe we can stop it before it even gets started and prevent the next big catastrophe."

Horatio jumped down from the sofa and made for the door. "I do admire your optimism," he paused and looked back at her. "It's actually a bit funny."

"Get stuffed."

"And good night to you, too. Your lady'll be back in a bit, I reckon. Get it sorted, all right? We're all rootin' for you two. And I've got some cash ridin' on your success."

"Hang on." Qwyrk loomed over him menacingly. "You bet money on our relationship? That's a thing that folks are actually doing?"

"Oh, there's quite an underground industry; goblin gamblers, pooka poker, bugbear bookies. But it's not just all about you, not even close, so don't flatter yourself. There are pools for just about everything you can imagine. I put up a bit of change on you after asking an ogre oddsmaker about your chances of success in this across-the-magical-order relationship. He rated it about sixty-five/thirty-five in favor of, so it seemed like safe bet."

"Wait, only sixty-five percent? What the hell? Who is he?"

"You don't know him."

"Just as well, or I'd kick his arse."

"And you wonder where the thirty-five percent comes from?"

"What's that supposed to mean?"

"You've got a temper, love, everyone knows that. It's part of your charm, but learn to rein it in a bit, all right? Now if you'll excuse me, I have to sneak back out of your world within getting' me arse kicked."

And with that, he hopped on out the front door.

Qwyrk flopped on her sofa, baffled by the exchange (as usual whenever she talked to him), a mixture of the somewhat profound and the profoundly irritating.

* * *

Moirin had no more sleep-walking episodes, but at some point during the night, she was quite sure that someone else was in the room, watching her. Perhaps watching over her? She was too sleepy to tell. She should have been alarmed, but instead, she just rolled over and drifted back off to the lost land of lovely nothingness (another potential song title!), happy that she still had several more hours of it ahead of her.

* * *

There was another knock at the door shortly after Horatio's exit.

"Oh, what now, Horatio?" Qwyrk grumbled.

Qwyrk opened it, and Holly stood there, looking frazzled, upset, and contrite.

"Hi," she said. "Um, I'm quite sure I just saw Horatio bounding off."

"Unfortunately yes."

"Oh. Well, I've been out wandering, and now I'm tired and don't want to do that anymore and I don't want to go back to my own home tonight because I'm miserable and missing you already. Can I come in?"

Relief washed over Qwyrk. "Yeah, that would be fine. Like, the best thing you could possibly do. Please?"

Holly smiled a little and sidled in, moving to sit down on the sofa, in the same spot where she'd been earlier. "I'd thought to do a dramatic storming out of here when I left, but I suppose it wasn't as impressive as I'd have liked."

"Well," Qwyrk said, "you could have made a bigger scene. Maybe stomped your feet a bit more? Given the door a proper slam?"

"I guess I need more practice."

"Actually, I'd be fine with you never working on that particular skill set at all, if that's all right with you."

Holly looked down and let out a nervous chuckle. "Fair enough." She looked around and sighed, but avoided looking at Qwyrk, until...

"I'm..." They both spoke at once.

"You go first, if you want," Qwyrk offered.

"I'm sorry," Holly sighed again. "So sorry. And you're right. Seeing little Ashanti scared and in danger just melted my heart. It brought up all sorts of guilt that I still have, about failing Lluck, about missing out on doing those same sorts of things with him when he was younger."

Her eyes grew misty.

"I never got to tell him bedtime stories, or see his face light up with joy when he opened holiday presents, or hold him when he had a bad dream, or when he was ill, or dozens of other things. I missed it all, and I can never get it back. And humans live for such a short time. It's like if you blink, you miss most of their important moments."

Qwyrk reached out and took her hands. "But he's also half Fae. Doesn't that give him some longevity?"

"No one really knows. I suppose it's possible, but so far, he's aged just as any typical human would. And it bothers me. No, it terrifies me. I don't want him being fifty years old and introducing me and saying: 'This is my mum; she looks twenty-eight, but she's actually over fifteen hundred years old.'"

"Actually, you don't look a day over twenty-seven, as humans go," Qwyrk smiled, trying to comfort her.

Holly managed a slight teary-eyed chuckle. "You could have said twenty-six, you know."

"I could indeed. But darling, you can't keep beating yourself up about the choice you made. You did what you had to do, to save his life. There was no other option."

"I know. But that doesn't mean I have to like it."

"No, but you're making up for it now, and I know he appreciates it. And if a scared little girl tugs at your heartstrings, you're more than justified in feeling whatever you feel and doing what you think is best to help her. I know I get a bit antsy about inviting mortals into our sphere, but in this case, you did the right thing. I'm so sorry if I suggested otherwise. Honestly, Adjua already knows what we are, anyway, and I'm the one that asked Qwyzz to protect her home, so she may as well be in touch with us if she needs us. To hell with the council and their stupid rules. It's not like I follow their orders to the letter, anyway."

"You are a bit of a rebel," Holly said, wiping at one eye.

"I prefer the term 'pain in the arse.'"

"That works, too. In fact, it's much more appropriate."

"You know, you really weren't supposed to agree with me quite so quickly."

Holly chuckled, and squeezed Qwyrk's hand.

"We got lucky tonight," Qwyrk said. "We can't be so careless from now on."

"No, we can't, and we won't." Holly caressed her arm. "And you're right about us: you, me. This whole thing with you makes me feel like I'm seventy-five again, and I'm loving every minute of it. But I know how important your tasks are. Now that we know something awful might be out there, we have to commit ourselves to being more conscientious. And we can do that. It's quite possible to be giddy sweethearts and still take our duties seriously. I'd never want you to do anything that could get you into trouble, or leave others at risk. Let's try to be more mindful in future, all right? And maybe a bit less impulsive?"

Qwyrk reached out to trace a finger along Holly's jaw line and down to her chin. "Have I told you how much I fancy you when you're being all responsible?"

"Careful now, Ms. Qwyrk, or we're going to risk getting ourselves in trouble again."

"Well, I think the danger's over for now; Qwyzz saw to that. I'll check in with the council later, and I can tell them what we know, what I saw. Maybe they'll be so concerned about it, they won't even be bothered by my little scheduling slip-up. In the meantime," she said as she leaned in for a kiss, "are you up for indulging in a bit more of that giddy, adolescent, responsibly irresponsible behavior?"

"As long as we're being appropriately inappropriate, I'm all for it."

* * *

The next morning, Qwyrk flashed into Jilly's living room to find her alone on the sofa, looking at her laptop. Qwyrk admired the girl's commitment to learning and research; it reminded her of Qwyzz. Jilly was the perfect heir to Granny, indeed.

"Good morning!" Qwyrk announced with a happy smile.

"Hiya!" Jilly set her computer aside, stood up, and came over for a hug. Jilly hugs were the best.

"Where's Blip?" Qwyrk looked around, seeing only squinty-eyed Odin, the family bulldog, sleeping peacefully on his heated dog bed in the corner of the room.

"He said he had some things to do and would be along later. What do you suppose he does when he's not here, boring me with philosophy this and that?"

"I honestly have no idea. I'm sure he must have other responsibilities, but I couldn't guess what they are. Don't really want to, actually."

"You haven't asked him? After all the time you've known him?"

"I try not to speak to him unless I have no choice," Qwyrk answered, amused.

"At least you *have* a choice," Jilly sighed.

"Anyway!" Qwyrk changed the subject. "How was your evening?"

"Not bad, I guess," Jilly said. "I spent some time looking online for more information on the Weasels and Chantz. I found a few things, and then I studied a bit from a grimoire Granny gave me, made a snack, watched some videos, and went to bed early. Pretty boring, actually. How about you?"

"Oh, um, well... I almost forgot to go on patrol in Richmond, and it turns out there was a creepy other-dimensional shapeshifter up there looking for prey, who almost kidnapped a small child, but Holly and I chased it off and I cornered it, but when I was about to find out what it was really up to, it blew up and burned to ash in an alley, and when I got back to the child's house, Holly'd got the girl back to sleep, but her mum found us, and it turns out she comes from a long line of magic-working wise women from Ghana, and her daughter may well have magic super powers, but she doesn't want her to meet you just yet—even though I suggested it—because she's only seven years old, so Qwyzz stopped by and put some protections around their home to ward off any potential Darkfae abductions for a good bit, and then Holly and I had our first fight, but it's fine and we're all good now, so no worries there, and here I am."

"Um, what?" Jilly's jaw dropped.

"Oh." Qwyrk gazed out the window with a silly grin on her face. "And I'd completely forgotten just how brilliant make-up shagging can be..."

"Woah, all right! La la la!" Jilly put her fingers in her ears. "I don't need to know about that. Start over and give me the details, except about the last bit. I'm good there, thank you very much."

Qwyrk filled her in on all the specifics of the previous night's strange twists and pyrotechnic turns, minus her enthusiastic reconciliation with Holly, and she took more than one breath to do it this time around.

"Wow," Jilly said when she'd finished, "that's, um, amazing. Do you think this all might have something to do with Chantz and whatever's going on with her?"

"I don't know. I suppose it's possible, but I don't really see a connection. Then again, we've missed some important clues in the past, so who knows? Speaking of Chantz, you said you learned some things? Did you find out where her band is playing next?"

"Oh right! Yes! Over in York—tonight, in fact—at a place called the Grave Rave. It's a goth club."

"Brilliant! We should go and check it out, see what she's really doing. I'm kind of curious to hear her sing, to be honest."

"There's a problem, though." Jilly frowned. "The club is eighteen and over, so I can't get in."

"Well, I'll just whisk you in by teleporting. No one will even notice."

"No one will even notice a shadow with glowing red eyes appearing out of thin air with a twelve-year-old in hand? Yeah, not sure that's a great plan."

"No, we'll wait until the band starts their set and everyone has their eyes on them, and then poof! In we go. Nobody can see Blip, and Holly can blend in well enough. I'll keep to the shadows; it's what I do. And we'll put some make up and dark sunglasses on you. Just wear whatever you have that's black, and it'll be fine. Maybe you can even use a bit of magic to make yourself look older, or something."

Jilly looked skeptical. "Do you know that spell? Or where I can find it? Because I'm very sure I don't. And like, every underage teenager in the country would pay good money for a copy of that. I could retire by fourteen."

"Yeah well, spells won't matter, anyway. Honestly, how difficult will it be? We're checking out Chantz in secret to see if anything odd happens. If not, then we'll just sneak away and call it a night, and if so, at least we're ready. Sort of."

"Yeah, but what if something really does pop up," Jilly protested, "like when I saw her at the uni?"

"We'll improvise something. It's what we do best, right?" Qwyrk tried to sound encouraging.

"I wouldn't exactly call it our 'best' but I guess it's the only choice we have. Can I just say that I have a bad feeling that something's probably going to go horribly wrong?"

"Oh, come on, you're such a worrier! It'll be fine."

Jilly looked even more skeptical.

"What will be fine?" Blip emerged from a wall across the room.

"Blip, how long have you been eavesdropping?" Qwyrk's annoyance with him returned in full. It felt good. It felt natural. It felt right.

"Obviously, not for very long, since I'm asking you what you're prattling on about."

"Well, for your information, Jilly found out where Chantz is singing next. In York, tonight, and we're all going to see her and her band so we can figure out what's going on."

"I see. And what is the nature of the venue for this concert?"

"The Grave Rave," Jilly said. "It's a goth club."

"Good heavens, are we back to dealing with those barbarians, again? You mean to say there is a location in this day and age where they can gather and plot their nefarious deeds?"

"Not that kind of goth, Blip," Qwyrk answered with a roll of her eyes. "They haven't been too active for the last, oh, twelve hundred years or so."

"Then why in damnation do you both keep bringing them up?"

"It's 'gothic.' You know: Mary Shelley, Byron, Victorian vampires, family ghosts and haunted mansions, that sort of thing."

"Oh, I see!" Blip's expression brightened. "Yes, of course! So, what novel will they be discussing tonight, then? That could indeed make for some stimulating and chilling discourse. A good literary scare is as welcome at Beltane as it is at Samhain."

"No novels, probably," Jilly said. "Just music."

"It's a gathering of a group of enthusiasts who share in interest in gothic imagery, and want to hear some original music based on those dark themes," Qwyrk said, to placate him.

"Hmm, well I suppose that doesn't sound too appalling. Very well. Since I cannot be seen, I surmise that it shall not be overly disgraceful for me to attend, assuming the whole affair does not become too garish or decadent."

"That's the spirit!" Jilly said.

"Really, it's just another covert mission," Qwyrk said, "and you're quite keen on those, right?"

"I have been known to undertake a bit of espionage once in a while for the greater good," he replied with a smugness. "You'd be surprised at how many I've fooled in my time. Right under their noses, and they never suspected me. I think I shall rather enjoy it!"

Qwyrk shook her head and looked back to Jilly. "You said you learned some other things?"

"Oh, right, yeah. I wanted to wait until Blip was here."

"It's Mr. Blippingstone."

"It's not so much what I could find out," Jilly went on, ignoring him, "more like what's not there. It looks like her real name is Moirin Moeran, and she's definitely Irish, but there's literally no trace of her from more than about two years ago. It's like she didn't exist before then. She just showed up one day and auditioned for the Weasels, and has been singing with them ever since. It's really odd."

"That is strange," Qwyrk agreed. "One more piece of the puzzle, I suppose. Maybe we can chat with her after the gig tonight, try to learn a bit more?"

"Is that wise?" Blip asked. "It might put her on the defensive. And if she can call up destructive magic with her voice, we don't want to be making an enemy of her before we have to."

"Yes, Blip," Qwyrk snarked, "that was my plan. Walk right up to her and ask her who she really is and where she really comes from, because we think she's a danger to herself and others and we're going to put a stop to it. What could go wrong?"

"I'm merely advising caution, something that this ragtag band seems frequently to be in short supply of."

"We'll be fine." Qwyrk's patience was evaporating. Again. "We're not going to do anything impulsive or give our hand away. We're on her turf, so we'll just have to react to whatever happens."

"I remain to be convinced."

"And I look forward to proving you wrong. Let's meet again in Jilly's room at seven-thirty tonight? We can all pop over to York together."

Jilly nodded. "My parents won't even notice I'm gone. What else is new?"

The neglect her poor young friend endured at the hands of those so-called parental figures saddened Qwyrk. "In the meantime," she said, "I have the great fun of going and talking with the Shadow council about last night's grand adventure."

"Oh? Did something go awry with you?" Blip asked. "How do the young people say it: 'this is my flabbergasted face.'"

"Do you mean 'shocked'?" Jilly asked.

"Thanks for the support," Qwyrk sneered. "But no, Holly and I encountered a buggane in Richmond, and it may well be a sign of something else going on behind the scenes."

"A buggane?" Blip flinched. "What was one of those vile creatures doing in Richmond, of all places?"

"Jilly can fill you in on the details," Qwyrk answered, stepping back to pop away. "Just wish me luck with the pompous bastards at the meeting."

"I don't envy you, that's for certain," Blip said.

"I don't envy me, either. Bye for now!" And she was off.

* * *

Traces of sunlight filtered in through the closed curtains, which meant Moirin might have to face up to the fact that morning had arrived in earnest. She reached over to grab her phone and check the time. 10:45 am.

"Not bad. Not noon, but not bad."

She'd missed a text from Sam, inquiring about having a breakfast that was surely over by now, but she phoned him back anyway.

"Hey Sam."

"Moirin! You're finally up! Lots of sleep, then?"

"Well, yeah, but it was odd at times. I had this dream that I was in a dark, scary, rocky place, full of mist..."

"So, Wales, then?"

"Heh, not quite. Good one, though. And this strange woman was talking to me, but I can't remember what she said. And the next thing I knew, I was dreaming that I was standing outside, on the old wall across from the B&B, at like, two in the morning! Just standing there, all by myself, in my night clothes."

"Woah. That's a bit mad!"

"I know, right? So, then I dreamed I ran back in here before I froze my bum off and crawled back into bed. Then, I think there was someone standing next to the bed, maybe keeping an eye on me, or something, I don't know. But it all faded away and I don't remember anything else."

"Must've been the Indian food, or the beer."

"That's what I was thinking."

"Well you're up now, so it's all good. We want to be at the venue by 2:30 to load in. Sound check is at 5:00, and it looks like they've got lighting we can use, too."

"Brilliant. I always prefer when we can make it all moody and spooky."

Moirin slid out of bed to sit on the side of it, and crossed her ankle over her knee. She looked at the bottom of her foot and almost dropped her phone in shock.

"Moirin? You still there?"

"Um, yeah, I'll phone you back in a bit. Um, 2:30's fine, we'll sound check and do light stuff and whatever. Talk in a bit, bye!"

She turned her foot closer, picking at a bit of dirt, a blade of grass, and a small dry leaf stuck to the sole. A quick inspection of her other foot revealed the same kind of outdoor detritus, exactly what she might have stepped on, if she had walked down the wet, grassy slope from the wall and back to the B&B.

"What the hell?"

* * *

"The council will come to order," Qworum said. "As I call your names, please answer whether you are present or otherwise."

"Otherwise?" Qwyrk shook her head as she stood in front of the Shadows tasked with protecting the realm from all manner of magical adversaries. They sat before her in the marble hall where they met to discuss matters of importance.

"Look," she added, "if they're not here, they're not actually going to be able to *tell* you they're not here. Right? Also, you're all literally sitting at the table. In a semi-circle. You can all see each other, and you're all here. Like, right in front of each other."

"Your lack of respect for tradition and precedent is not our concern," her most detested councilman, Qwalm, sneered.

"And your annoying insistence on following it isn't mine." Qwyrk rolled her eyes.

Ignoring her, Qworum read out the list as was his duty as head of the council, to which each raised their hand and affirmed their presence. "Qwalm, Qwery, Qwote, Qwyll, Qwire."

Qwyrk stood in silence, shaking her head while staring at the ground. When they'd finished, she looked up and raised her eyebrows. "Oh, are we all here? Brilliant! I was so worried that someone might not have shown up. I'm really glad you took roll, just to be sure. It was a bit touch and go there for a while, wasn't it?"

"Be quiet, Qwyrk," Qworum admonished. "We all know why we are here. You neglected your duties last night, to an astonishing degree of carelessness, and as a result, a mortal child could have been harmed, or worse."

"But she wasn't, and also, I didn't 'neglect my duties.' I was a bit late because I was busy... with something else."

"And what, pray tell, was that?" Qwalm pressed.

"None of your business, Qweasy," Qwyrk snipped.

"You know what my name is," he snapped.

"Silence, both of you!" Qworum snapped.

"Look," Qwyrk continued, ignoring his admonishment, "I was a bit late, and I'm sorry for that, but I chased off the buggane. It was after a child, but it didn't get a hold of her. I went in pursuit of it, while Holly stayed behind and made sure the girl was safe. And she was."

"Holly?" Qwyll asked, a concerned look on her face.

Bollocks! Qwyrk shook her head and swore to herself. "She's a... friend, a Yakshi. She came along to help me out, just in case things got bad. Which they did not, I must point out again."

"It is most irregular to have a non-Shadow accompany you on special assignments," Qwote noted. "Especially someone from so far away, and from a different order of beings."

"Yeah, well, she happened to be there, and we both thought it would be a good idea, all right? Or do I now need to fill out a request in triplicate before I can make in-the-field decisions?"

"Your arrogance is uncalled for," Qwalm grumped.

"Sorry, Qwack, but I'd imagine you don't get many calls of any kind."

Qwalm scowled.

"Qwyrk..." Qworum warned.

"Fine, sorry!" Qwyrk rolled her eyes and made a little mock bow with her hands outstretched and palms face up. "I only did what I thought was best in the moment. And the thing I chased, that buggane? Yeah, it wanted that child for some reason. It even offered to tell me why—which was a bit of a shock, I must say—but then it went all Bonfire Night on me and died screaming as it crumbled to ash. That tells me that someone didn't want it saying anything at all. That's the part that worries me."

"You learned nothing else from it?" Qwote inquired.

"Other than we can't stop what's coming, whatever the hell that means. And I've heard that one enough times over the centuries to know it's usually bollocks, but also that we can't afford to ignore it, just in case it's not."

"Agreed," Qworum said with a nod. "This may be nothing, but it could be the beginning of a new threat. In the wake of de Soulis and the Erlking, we cannot be too careful. Every situation has the potential to portend something worse."

Qwyrk held her tongue and said nothing about the whole Chantz business, or what Horatio had told her. Best not to tip her hand too early. "I asked Qwyzz to place some protective wards around the girl's home, just in case," she said instead. "Nothing should be able to get in there for quite a while."

"A wise precaution," Qworum agreed. "Who is the child?"

"I don't really know. Her mother is human. She calls herself a dream-seer, from a family line of human African magic-workers, apparently. But she thinks her daughter might have special gifts that could make her a target."

"Gifts like what?" Qwery queried.

Qwyrk shrugged. "She didn't say, and I didn't ask."

"Well, you should have found out, and insisted on it if she held her tongue," Qwalm pestered.

"Part of this work is being able to read the tone of the situation, Qwagmire," Qwyrk quipped, "and being sensitive to the needs of others. Not your strong point, I know."

"Cease your contention, both of you!" Qworum ordered. "I agree that this merits more investigation. Qwyrk, look into this further and see if there is anything of interest. And see to it that you are timely in your future assignments. Lateness could lead to human injury or worse, and that must not be allowed. Consider this a warning. You will not have the luxury of another."

Qwyrk nodded. "I know, and I really am sorry. I'll see what else I can find out. Fair enough?"

She turned to leave, but not before tossing a sneering grin at Qwalm that made him bristle even more. Good.

CHAPTER EIGHT

Qwyrk flashed back to her home, and was delighted to find Holly there, already waiting for her. Holly had made the effort to blend in for the evening's activities, with stylish black eyeliner, smoky eye shadow and a dark maroon lip gloss, which Qwyrk was reluctant to kiss, lest she smudge it up. So a light peck had to suffice.

But damn, she looks good!

"So, how did it go?" Holly asked.

"I got a bit of a mild rebuke..."

"Mild?" Holly looked skeptical.

"Well, more of a 'don't ever let it happen again' kind of rebuke. But, as I thought, they're more interested in the buggane and whatever the hell it wanted, so that should keep them occupied."

"Did they ask about Ashanti and Adjua?"

"Kind of, but I didn't give them much info, and once I deflected, they seemed content to move on. I mentioned that Adjua is a seer, but I don't think they made any connection between her daughter being special and the creature choosing her." Qwyrk kept quiet about accidentally mentioning Holly.

"Good, I'd much rather they not be involved."

"Me too, but I think it'll be fine. Qwyzz has their home well protected, and now we can check in with her any time we like."

"I'm glad. So," Holly said as she threw on her black leather jacket, "on to the matter at hand?"

"Yeah, and by the way, you're looking a bit smashing, I must say, all spooky and mysterious!"

"Do you like it?" Holly asked with a proud twirl.

"I do! You'll fit in just fine."

"I thought about painting little spider webs at the corners of my eyes, but maybe that's a bit too much?"

"You know, Jilly would love that for herself! Maybe you could draw some on her?"

"Happily!"

"Right then, let's go." Qwyrk took her hand. "This is going to be one of the stranger things we've done—you know, waiting to see if reality goes bonkers—so we'd best get on with it."

* * *

In dazzling display of purple refulgence, Qwyrk and Holly stepped into Jilly's living room. Blip was situated on the couch, once again immersed in a book. He looked up and nodded at them, but went back to whatever was engrossing him. Jilly came down the stairs, dressed all in black (or as black as she could find), though her attempts at decorating her face left something to be desired.

"Hiya, ladies... oh, Holly, you look brilliant!" Jilly's eyes went wide as she gave each of them a hug in turn. "I'm a bit of a mess, I'm afraid. Makeup's not really something I'm all that good at. I look like a piss poor try at a Halloween costume."

"Well," Holly said as she put a hand on Jilly's shoulder, "why don't we go back upstairs and give it another go? I could even paint some webs at the corner of your eyes?"

"Could you? Oh, that would be amazing!"

And off they went.

Qwyrk smiled as she watched them charge up the stairs together, the two she cared about most. That thought was an odd one in and of itself. Who knew she could get so attached? She wandered over to the couch and sat down near Blip, which made for an odd juxtaposition in her sentiments.

"What are you reading?" She tried to engage him, knowing she'd likely regret it.

"You wouldn't be interested," he said, not looking up.

"Try me."

He sighed. *"Méditations cartésiennes: Introduction à la phénoménologie.* Translated, that's *The Cartesian Meditations: An Introduction to Phenomenology* by Edmund Husserl."

"Yeah, all right, you win."

"I thought as much. I merely wished to indulge in a bit of light reading before tonight's mission. The concept of 'Transcendental Being as Monadological Intersubjectivity' holds endless fascination, whilst being light enough that it goes down like a rather lovely Armagnac before a fine meal. It's not even necessary to hold all of the concepts in one's mind, you see. In fact, I find that even if they vanish from one's thought—a philosophical *part des anges*, if you will, to continue with the liquor metaphor—one may return to them at a later point for renewed stimulation."

Qwyrk nodded. And that was about all she was prepared to do.

She gazed out the window and quite literally twiddled her thumbs for a minute or so, pleased that Blip was back to being enraptured with his Edmund Whosit book and wasn't trying to make small talk, which he was even worse at than she was. She was all the more thankful when Holly and Jilly popped back down the stairs, Jilly sporting proper makeup and sure enough, little webs on both temples.

"What do you think?" Holly asked with a proud smile.

"It's brilliant, isn't it?" Jilly said, grinning from ear to ear.

"You look amazing!" Qwyrk agreed. "And you," she looked at Holly, "are an artist!" *Add that to the list of things you're brilliant at.*

"Thank you! It's hardly a masterpiece, but it will do." Holly sat down next to Qwyrk and ran her fingers through Qwyrk's short hair along the back of her head, "So, what have you two been up to?"

"Oh, Blip's just been telling me about how he's going to be stimulating himself later on."

"Oh, how risible." He didn't look up from his given *Meditation*.

"Do I want to know what you actually mean?" Holly gave her a look that seemed to beg for her not to elaborate.

"Not really, no. Let's just leave it at that."

"So, are we ready then?" Jilly said, taking the cue to change the subject.

"We should head on over," Qwyrk agreed. "Fine city, York; haven't visited it properly in ages. It's changed a lot over the centuries. I mean, I remember when the Vikings were there the first time!"

"Now it's just goths, apparently," Blip said, looking back up.

"You know, that was actually rather clever!" Qwyrk chuckled. "Wrong kind of goths, though."

"Yes, yes I know: Lady Caroline Lamb, Edgar Allan Poe, Bram Stoker, and so on, not Theodoric, Euric, and Alaric. And then there's the whole business with 'Gothic' architecture, and such, which York has aplenty and to marvelous effect. Some splendid erections there, you know, many of which have lasted for centuries, far longer than anyone could have imagined."

Qwyrk slapped a hand over her mouth to stifle a guffaw. She saw Holly and Jilly struggling similarly, which made her want to laugh more.

"I mean, I'm not very familiar with such things," Holly managed to say, "but I suspect that would be rather painful."

Qwyrk lost it and sputtered a burst of uproarious laughter, followed right away by the others, while Blip looked back and forth between them.

"I've no idea why you've all suddenly lost your wits, when we have a task to take in hand."

Another round of hilarity ensued.

"What's so damned funny?" Blip demanded. "Get a firm grip on yourselves!"

"Oh Goddess, stop!" Qwyrk cried. "My sides hurt!" She leaned on Holly for support, and they clasped hands in a tight squeeze.

"Bah, I've had it with all of you." He went back to perusing his book. "I'll be here if you actually want to prepare for the evening."

It took a while for Qwyrk, Holly, and Jilly to calm down, but the seriousness of the situation brought Qwyrk back to the moment. "I hate to say it, but Blip's right. We really should be on our way."

"Oh, so you're finally prepared to be responsible?" He looked up again. "Might we go now, or is there some other random subject that requires your inane giggling?"

"No, I'm good. Anyone else?" Qwyrk asked. A quick shake of heads followed, though not without more grins all around. They all joined hands.

"But it's not like it's anything too serious," she added. "We're just trying to prevent the possible end of the world. Again. Maybe."

"Charming," Blip said as they vanished from Jilly's home in a violet flash and sparkle of magical scintillation.

* * *

"Hey Moirin?" Sam called from the side entrance to the club, as she was leaving the stage after a successful final sound check.

"Yeah?"

"There's someone here who wants to talk to you for a minute. Says she's a friend of yours?"

"I don't have any friends in York," Moirin said to herself, under her breath. "I mean, I don't have any friends anywhere." She raised her voice. "Fine, I'll be there in a second."

She adjusted her microphone stand, and then wandered to the side door. She pushed it open and looked out. The grey skies darkened with a bit of light rain and she beheld something she wasn't expecting. Aileen strode up, dressed in a long, black, velvet, Regency Era-like gown, hair hanging loose and makeup expertly applied, and holding an equally impressive black parasol.

"Good evening, my lady." She curtsied a little. "I thought I'd make a bit of an effort, you know, at least try to blend in." She smiled as she moved to embrace Moirin in a hug that Moirin didn't know to respond to. So she just gave Aileen a perfunctory pat on the back with her hands.

"I'm honestly amazed you showed up," Moirin blurted out, before realizing she sounded a bit rude and adding, "I mean, I'm glad you're here and all, but where did you find this outfit?" She motioned up and down with her hands. "I'm guessing you're not traveling around with that stuffed in your rucksack?"

Aileen laughed. "No, no, I borrowed from the friend I'm stayin' with here. She's into historical recreations and all that, so she has a pile of different outfits. We're about the same size, so it worked out just fine. Not bad, eh?" She spun, looking all the more elegant with the parasol in one hand and the other arm outstretched.

"Yeah, it's all right. I mean, you look really nice."

"Nice?"

"Well yeah, you do want to look nice, or cool, or beautiful, or whatever."

"And do I? Do I look nice and cool and beautiful?"

"Um, yeah, I'd say so. You carry it off well, actually."

Aileen beamed. "Good! Oh, I'm not supposed to laugh, or smile, or anything like that am I, sorry!"

"Well, I won't tell anyone, but you need to watch it for the rest of the evening."

Aileen shot her a concerned look. Moirin tried to keep a straight face. She failed. "I'm joking, silly! Of course, you can laugh. In fact, you're allowed to laugh up to three times at every one of our shows, but any more than that and you risk being forcefully ejected if we find out about it."

Aileen looked at her again, clearly not believing her.

"Yeah, all right, I'm joking about that too! Jokes are fine. Fun is fine. Really! Enjoy yourself. Look, I should probably get back in and get ready, but I've put your name on the guest list, like I said. Go on in, have a drink, have a great time. We'll chat afterwards, yeah?"

Aileen chuckled and took her hand. "I'm so looking forward

to this, you have no idea!" She squeezed Moirin's hand and with another twirl, headed back out to the main street to join the queue.

Moirin watched her with some disbelief. "That girl is way too cheerful for her own good."

* * *

In a flickering glow, Qwyrk and the others found themselves outside in an empty alley, next to the club in question. The air smelled damp, and it had just rained, as the wet flagstones showed. Just the same as the night before in Richmond, which made Qwyrk uneasy.

"Wait," Jilly said. "We're outside. Weren't you going to just pop us inside the club?"

"Too risky," Qwyrk said. "If all four of us just suddenly showed up in there, someone would have noticed, and even with the whole open-minded, alternative thing going on in a place like that, it would have caused quite the stir. We want to be as inconspicuous as possible. I don't want Chantz knowing we're here. Plus, the club's not open yet, so that would've been even more obvious."

"So what's the plan?" Holly asked.

"You and Blip go in through the front door, and Jilly and I will sneak inside, namely by me teleporting us in after the show starts. We'll meet up with you once we're all in there."

"And am I expected to purchase my own ticket for admission to this potentially garish freak show, or are we just going to break the law and have me take advantage of my invisibility and cheat, which would be decidedly illicit, I must point out," Blip protested.

"Blip, do you want to find out what's going on, or not?" Qwyrk asked, getting annoyed. "I doubt that one invisible, imaginary child-hood friend getting an unplanned comp is going to make much of a difference to the overall take at the door. It's not like we're going to be staying around all night, anyway. We just want to see if Chantz's powers make an unplanned guest appearance, or if it's something she's deliberately trying to do. Then we'll be off and no one will know we've even been here. We're just trying to gather information, all right?"

"Hmph! I simply don't like the underhanded nature of the plan, that's all."

"And just how would you propose we do it, otherwise?" Qwyrk asked, getting annoyed. "No one's even going to see you, so what difference does it make? And aren't you the one who's always wanting to be Mr. Sherlock-Solve-the-Mystery-Sleuth, anyway? How are you going to do that without a little trickery? It's a spy mission, for Goddess' sake! So go in there and spy!"

"Fine," Blip harrumphed. "I shall accompany Ms. Vishala through the main entrance on the sly, but let's not make this scene any more crude than it needs to be."

"That's entirely up to you," Qwyrk said, "but I always say a little crudeness brightens up the day!"

"Yes, you would, wouldn't you?" Blip grumbled.

"Jilly and I will wait here until the show starts," Qwyrk said.

"Out here?" Jilly looked at her in alarm. "In the cold and damp? You do know that not all of us are immune to the weather, like you, right?"

"Qwyrk doesn't even have to wear clothes," Holly quipped.

"Yeah, so maybe it'd be nice if we could wait somewhere a bit warmer?" Jilly implored.

"Should we go back to your house, then?" Qwyrk asked. "Have some hot cocoa while we wait?"

"Can we?" Jilly's face lit up.

"No."

"Bugger."

"Language, young lady."

"You're one to talk."

"I'm two thousand years old. I can say whatever I bloody well like."

"Stimulating as this conversation is, we'll be off then, shall we?" Blip turned and walked toward the main street.

"I suppose I'm with him?" Holly said with raised eyebrows.

"Yeah, sorry about that," Qwyrk said.

"Oh not at all. I think it'll be quite the challenge!"

* * *

Moirin sat alone backstage, turning over the crazy events of the past few days for the hundredth time. "It has to be good tonight." She stood up and paced about. "All right, um, hello? I don't know who you are, or what you are, if you're just in my head or if something really weird is happening to me, but in case you're listening, I need to do a good show tonight, all right? This is a chance to prove ourselves to a proper crowd, and if we do a solid one, it'll give us a good reputation. Maybe a few reviews? Other gig offers? So, you can either flow through me or not, but just don't let me feck things up, okay? Or make the power go out, or whatever. We need this one, *I* need this. Oh, crap!" She stopped and closed her eyes. "Now I'm talking to myself, hoping thin air will grant me wishes; that's literally where I'm at right now. I am so pathetic!"

"Who's pathetic?" She turned to see Sam stroll by, a pair of drum sticks in hand.

"Oh, nothing, just me thinking out loud," she lied.

"Who's your friend?"

"Hm? Oh, she's, um, just someone I know. We're just kind of, casual acquaintances, I suppose."

"Well, to hear her talk, it sounded like you two go back a fair way."

"Huh, that's odd. I think I'd remember her better if we were old friends."

"Moirin, are you all right? You seem kind of distracted and a bit more solitary than usual, if you don't mind me sayin'." He looked at her with concern. And, she feared, maybe a bit more than that.

"Really, I'm fine," she lied again. "I'd not had enough sleep before last night, and I think it's all catching up with me. You know, life on the road and all that. But don't worry, we're gonna kill it tonight!" She flashed a vague smile that she was sure wasn't very sincere. "Best audience we've ever had, yeah? So, let's make sure we give them a damned good show!"

Sam nodded and returned her weak smile with a bigger one, before turning and walking away. She knew he didn't believe her, and she felt bad for not telling him what was going on, but what could she do? This gig was huge and her personal issues were not important. He seemed willing to go along with her lie and for the moment, that was all that mattered.

* * *

"So," Holly said, as they wandered out to the club's entrance, happy to see that the queue hadn't grown too long yet. "I'll pay my own way in, and you just follow close behind. No one will be any the wiser."

"Dishonest at best, but we seem to have no better option," Blip said. "At least you seem to be dressed for the part." He looked at the assembled group of young black-clad people waiting in the queue.

"I'm very glad not to be seen, as I'm quite sure I'd not fit in at all with this highly suspect lot."

"Oh, I don't know," Holly quipped, "I think you'd look rather fetching in a black corset and nylon stockings. Perhaps some smoky eyeliner."

"Oh, how very amusing." Blip rolled his eyes.

"It is, isn't it?"

"No, it jolly well is not."

"A comic genius is never appreciated in her own time, I suppose." Holly sighed. "I keep telling Qwyrk that."

"And does she agree?"

"I'm not sure. I think my brand of humor is rather lost on her."

"I can't imagine why," Blip muttered.

"What?"

"Nothing. I said let's see what we can spy."

They took their place at the end of the queue, and Holly kept quiet so as not to seem to be talking to herself about nonsensical things. Having a mobile phone would have been useful, she thought. She could pretend to speak into it while actually chatting with Blip.

"You are special," a young woman in a dark red, hooded, velvet cloak said to Holly as she walked by. She was pale, with black eyeliner and dark red lips.

"Excuse me?"

"Very special." The woman stopped in front of her and stared.

"I... don't think I am."

"I see your essence."

Holly shifted her stance. "You do?"

The stranger nodded once. "There is more to you than meets the eye."

"Well, I suppose that's true of everyone, if you think about it. Look, I'm flattered, I suppose, but if you're chatting me up, I'm spoken for and—"

The woman shook her head once and just stared. She was making Holly uncomfortable.

"Can I help you with anything else?"

A split second of darkness descended around them. Holly squinted, struggling to see. When her vision returned, the woman's features had changed. Her skin had become grey and her expressionless lips had darkened into a hue of charcoal. The hood now covered her eyes.

"A time of death is coming," this new visage of the woman said in a deep but whispery voice. "A time of endings, of change. You will not survive it for long, and everything you have had will be lost. So it was foretold before, so it shall remain. Wyrd unfolds as it will."

"What? Who are you? What are you talking about? How dare you?" Holly shook her head and closed her eyes hard. She heard what sounded like a distant rumble of thunder and when she opened her eyes again, her mysterious interlocutor was gone. She looked up and down the street, but there was no sign of her.

"Did you see that?" she whispered to Blip, trying to be inconspicuous.

"Hmm? See what?"

"The young woman in the red robe. The one who was just talking to me." She tried to pretend she had an earpiece, or something, and put one hand to the side of her head.

"I've no idea what you're talking about, I'm afraid. I admit I was a bit distracted by the notion of feeling in all its unrestricted subjectivity. A fascinating concept, don't you think?"

"Um, I suppose. Never mind. But you really didn't see anyone else right here?"

"Other than these oddly-dressed miscreants in the queue, no."

"So odd." Holly shook her head again and stepped into the street to try one more look in both directions. No sign of her bizarre visitor. "I could have sworn someone was here and she spoke to me. Said something ominous, I think. But maybe I just imagined it. I'm probably overly tired."

"Fatigue can play tricks on the mind, even ours. It looks like you have a headache, or some such, holding your head and all?"

"Hm? Oh, no, I'm trying to make it appear as if I'm talking on a Forkbeard. You know, an ear phone device."

"Why ever for?"

"Because," she said, rolling her eyes. "I'm actually talking to you, and I don't want it to seem as if I'm babbling to myself. No one else can see you, correct? So I'm pretending I'm on a phone connection using my non-existent earpiece, hidden under my hair, like my ears. Got it?"

"Yes, yes, of course. A sound plan. Heh, 'sound' plan! How is the reception?"

"What?"

"The reception. That's a thing with these wretched mobile contraptions, apparently. Do you need to move back and forth, jump up and down, invoke the god Hermes, whatever it is one does to make those... connections work."

"I don't have a real phone! I'm just acting like I do. I can hear you just fine, because I'm standing right next to you!" She'd lowered her voice to a whisper, in inverse proportion to her rising level of irritation.

"Yes, but for the sake of believability, should we not try to add a bit of realism? Is there static? Does the line go dead from time to time? I feel I should say something in the tradition of Mr. Bell, like: 'Ms. Vishala—come here—I want to see you.'"

"Oh Goddess, everything Qwyrk says is true." Holly shook her head in exasperation.

"What? What does she say? You mean about me? I demand to know this instant what she has said!"

"Sorry!" Holly let her hand fall from her ear. "The queue's moving. We'll talk later... goodbye!"

"I'll find out, you know. My sleuthing skills are second to none. Which, may I point out, is why she wanted me to come on this accursed outing to begin with!" He jogged along behind her as they made their way to the entrance, but she ignored him.

She paid her way in and strode through the door, Blip following close behind. He was nearly trod on a couple of times by people wearing platform boots, but of course, his indignant swearing was heard by no one except Holly, who did her best to stifle her laughter.

"Looks like a rather interesting place," she said, taking in the layout of the venue.

"Oh yes, charming," Blip retorted. "A bunch of wayward youths living out their fantasies of being tragically vampiric Lord Byrons or some such rubbish is not my idea of interesting. Though, I grant you that some of the velvet topcoats are rather splendid."

"I fear you have no real sense of adventure at all, Mr. Blippingstone. Tonight should be quite the experience."

"That's precisely what worries me."

* * *

"You've heard about them, you're here for them, you know it's going to be a brilliant show. So put your hands together for The Mystic Wedding Weasels!"

The crowd gave an enthusiastic cheer as the band took the stage. Qwyrk watched from the shadows, while Jilly ventured forward to get an up-close view. The four musicians settled in to their places with barely more than a nod to their potential fans, which was apparently the way of doing things here. No one in the audience seemed put out by it. The band began the first song with no introductions, a mid-tempo piece in a minor key. Moirin stepped up to the microphone and started to sing somber lyrics about dark subject matters. Just like Jilly said, she had a splendid voice: smooth, inviting, emotional, a real natural.

Jilly happened to glance back at Qwyrk, and she nodded and smiled in approval. A moment later, Holly moseyed up to her side and took her arm.

"Rather nice, isn't it?" She leaned in and spoke close to Qwyrk's ear.

"It's very good. I see why Jilly likes them, and why Moirin might be so special."

"I must say, I like her fashion sense and overall aesthetic. And the music... sort of puts one in the mood, doesn't it?"

Qwyrk gave her a side glance. "I'm beginning to think everything puts you in the mood."

"Is that a problem?"

"Not particularly, as long as we're 'responsible' and all that."

"Well," Holly said, slipping an arm around Qwyrk, "until we can do something about it, do you want to dance?"

"What?"

"Dance. You know, that moving bodies thing that people do to music. See all those others out there?" She pointed to the swirly arm motions, cobweb clearing hand grasps, and foot stomping unfolding in front of them.

Qwyrk winced. "Um, thing is, I'm not very good."

"And the amazing thing is, that's not a problem at all." Holly whirled Qwyrk to face her and placed her arms around Qwyrk's neck. Qwyrk wrapped her own arms around Holly's waist, almost on instinct.

"What if someone sees us?" Qwyrk asked, glancing around, still trying to make excuses. It'll look right odd if you seem like you're dancing with a ghost."

"First of all, I don't care. Second, we're back here in the dark. Third, everyone's looking the other direction. And fourth, me dancing with a ghost fits the mood perfectly, don't you think?"

"I cannot argue with your impeccable logic."

"Brilliant!"

"But I'm still crap at dancing."

"Just follow me. It'll be fun!"

"I'm not convinced, but for you, I'll have a go."

Qwyrk did her best and found that, despite her misgivings, and treading on Holly's feet more than a few times, dancing with her girlfriend to moody live music was, in fact, quite enjoyable. She made sure to tear herself away from Holly's gaze from time to time to keep an eye on Moirin, but the first song ended without anything bizarre or supernatural taking hold. The crowd erupted into applause and cheers.

Holly stepped back and gave Qwyrk a little curtsy. "A lovely dance, my dear."

"Oh, stop."

Holly stepped in and took Qwyrk's hand. "May I be so presumptuous as to ask for another before the night is over?"

"You may presume all you wish; I am yours for the evening, and beyond."

The next tune began, a mid-tempo piece in a minor key, still with no introductions or "good evenings" from any member of the band. Moirin stepped back up to the microphone and started to sing somber lyrics about dark subject matters.

This time, Qwyrk and Holly stood together, holding hands and listening. Qwyrk scanned the stage and the dance floor, trying to sense anything untoward, but it all seemed very normal. Irritatingly so. She didn't catch so much as a whiff of magic beyond hers and Holly's. She had no idea where Blip had gone off to, which was not a bad problem to have.

The band played song after song, not all of them mid-tempo pieces, but all in minor keys, and rightly so. Morin sounded lovely throughout and the crowd seemed to enjoy the music more and more as the show progressed. Qwyrk had no doubt the band was very good, but through it all, nothing overtly outré happened.

"If Moirin really has abilities, they're on holiday tonight," Qwyrk said before the final song.

As the Weasels took a bow and made to leave the stage, Moirin spoke her first words of the night. "Thank you all, every one of you. If you'd like to know more, sign up on our mailing list. We have some merch for sale in the back there, an EP and some other things, so if you want to take us home with you, but don't want to have to cook breakfast for us in the morning, that's your next best option. You're brilliant. We hope to see you again soon. Good night."

The crowd gave the band one last cheer as they left the stage and the house lights came up. Qwyrk dissolved into a darker part of the venue, with Holly and Jilly following her.

"Well it was lovely, if a bit anticlimactic," Qwyrk said. "I didn't sense anything at all. Did either of you?"

Both shook their heads.

"This is totally different from Sunday's gig," Jilly said. "I mean, whatever happened there didn't happen here. Like, not even a little."

"So, it must not always come out just because she's singing," Qwyrk said.

"Maybe she doesn't control it," Holly offered. "Maybe the banshee does."

"That's exactly what I'm thinking," Qwyrk said with nod. "If you two can go talk with her, maybe we can tell if something's off."

"You want me to meet her?" Jilly's eyes grew wide. "I mean, that's brilliant, but now I'm really nervous." She looked behind her. "I'm not even supposed to be in here."

"Not to worry," Qwyrk smiled. "I'll pop you outside to the alley by the side door. The band's got to go out that way eventually. Their van's parked nearby."

"Where's Mr. Blippingstone?" Holly asked, looking around for their diminutive foil.

"I'd happily forgotten about him," Qwyrk said.

"Qwyrk..." Jilly glared at her.

"Yeah, all right. I'm sure he's around somewhere."

"I'm here, in fact," he announced, materializing, as he often did, out of nowhere. "So, am I the only one who detected not the slightest whiff of magic about the girl?"

"No," Qwyrk said. "We're all pretty much on that same page."

"Yes, so I thought. However, despite the dreadful name, I found some of the music to be surprisingly pleasant, and the young lady does indeed have a remarkable voice. Should a supernatural entity wish to have a host for its nefarious deeds, young Ms. Moeran would be a most suitable candidate, methinks."

"Blip." Qwyrk stared at him. "You're not helping."

"In any case," he continued, "Ms. Vishala, may I ask a boon of you?"

"Of course."

"The table whereon they are selling various wares, does have a nice black silk kerchief that I think would make a lovely cravat. Would you be so good as to purchase one of these on my behalf? I will, of course, reimburse you in whatever manner you deem suitable."

Holly smiled. "I'd be delighted. And please, it's on me." She wandered off to the table to procure said neckerchief for him.

"A fine lady, indeed," Blip said to Qwyrk. "She is, as the young folks say, a 'keeper.' Just remember that."

"Blip's buying band merch," Qwyrk said to no one in particular. "I think the world really may be ending this time."

As Qwyrk moved out of view into the shadows, she slipped past a young man, whose voice sounded over the general excited post-gig chit-chat: "You ever hear of a band from Liverpool called 'Electric Lemon Collective'? Yeah, that was me and me mates!"

* * *

"You've found her again? Are you sure?"

"Yeah, quite."

"What's she doing up in the north?"

"Singing with a rock and roll band, or some rubbish like that."

"So, will this plan really work?"

"Using them to find her and bring her to us? Yeah, Why not? Who better to recognize her? They almost did it the other night, until that other one showed up."

"It's risky."

"Of course it is! But do we want her back or not? This is a one-time deal, then we'll never have to summon those things again."

"You'd better be right."

"Or else what?"

"Or else, we might end up dead, if... the others find out what we're doing and who we're doing it to."

"Shut up! We kept her all those years before, didn't we? She only got away because of a fluke. They both did. It won't happen again."

"Just do it."

"Calm yourself. She'll never know what hit her. And then she'll be ours again, forever."

CHAPTER NINE

Qwyrk and the others waited in the back end of the alley, far enough from the club's side entrance not to be conspicuous, but close enough to keep a sharp set of eyes out for their target. Blip had tied his black silk kerchief into a proper cravat, but displaying its logo: MWW in silver, gothic calligraphy. Qwyrk couldn't decide if it suited him, or if he just looked ridiculous. Both, actually.

A few minutes into their watch, a fetching young lady in an antiquated black dress came walking down the alley from the opposite direction. She had an impressive mane of curly red hair and carried an old-timey parasol. She strolled up to the side entrance and knocked. A moment later the door opened, and Moirin answered.

Qwyrk listened in, but it seemed to be nothing of consequence, just some small talk about the concert and how much the flame-haired young lady enjoyed it. She handed Moirin a business card, took her hands and held them for a moment, and then kissed her cheek before strolling off again in the direction she'd come from.

"A groupie, perhaps?" Holly suggested.

"Perk of the job, I suppose," Qwyrk said. "But hey, Moirin's out there right now. Why don't you and Jilly go and get her attention while you can?"

"You mean, like *right* now?" Jilly said, trembling. "I have to go and... talk to her?"

"What's the problem?" Qwyrk asked. "She's only human. All right, maybe she's a bit more than that, but she just talked to that other girl, right? So she must be nice."

"But she's famous and brilliant, and I'll just look like a stupid fangirl, and—"

"Come on, Jilly," Holly said with a smile and a pat on her back. "Let's go. I'll be right there with you, and we can congratulate her on a lovely show!"

Jilly gave Qwyrk one more reluctant look before setting off to meet her new hero. Qwyrk smiled and urged her on.

* * *

"Um, Ms. Chantz?"

Moirin had just stepped back into the doorway when she heard a voice behind her. She turned to see a blonde girl of about twelve and a dazzling-looking Indian woman, waiting outside.

"So sorry to um, bother you," the girl said, "but I just wanted to thank you for an, um, amazing show. The Weasels are my, um, new favorite band, right? So it was brilliant to get to see you, in person, I mean."

Normally, these kinds of awkward interactions made Moirin positively cringe, but there was something very sweet and genuine about this girl, so she turned around and stepped back out to greet her.

"Thank you, that's very kind. Call me Moirin. Chantz is just a stage name." She extended her hand and managed a weak smile, which was about all she was capable of at the moment. At most moments, to be honest. The girl took her hand and shook it timidly.

"I'm, um... Jilly. Oh! And this is Holly. She's my best friend's um, other best friend?" The Indian woman smirked and nodded, but Moirin couldn't guess why.

"So, Jilly," Moirin said, looking her up and down, "you look a bit young to be coming to a place like this, yeah?"

"Well, um, that is, uh..."

"Let's just say," the Indian woman's posh voice interrupted the girl's stammering, "we may have broken the rules a bit and smuggled her in, so she could have the opportunity to see you."

"You've got a bit of an anarchist streak," Moirin said, pleased at their subterfuge. "I like it!"

Jilly blushed. "Well, I'm not a real rebel or anything, but... my parents don't even know I'm here."

"Even better!"

The girl smiled. "It *is* kind of cool, isn't it?"

"Absolutely!" She looked at Holly. "So, are you contributing to the delinquency of a minor, then?"

"Something like that," Holly said. "Though I do need to get her home soon. But she really wanted to meet you."

"And now you have." Moirin managed another half-smile and found it almost exhausting.

"Um, would you... would you sign my EP?" Jilly held up a copy of the newly-acquired recording, still in its packaging.

"I'd be happy to." Moirin reached into her coat pocket and produced a pen, tearing off the plastic, and offering up her stage name in a flourish of ink strokes. "If you'd like, we can take a selfie?"

"I don't have a phone." Jilly face fell.

"No worries." Moirin declared, producing her phone from another pocket. "We'll use mine, and I'll send it to you."

"I'd be delighted to take the photo," Holly offered. Moirin gave her the mobile and huddled up with Jilly (far closer than she would normally do, but again, for some reason, she liked this girl) for their portrait.

"Right then," Holly said. "Smile, or lour, whatever you prefer..."

She took two shots, which on inspection, proved to be very good, more than adequate to give Jilly bragging rights about having met her idol.

"Now, give me your email address," Moirin told Jilly, "and I'll send them to you right away, while I'm thinking about it."

Jilly happily offered up the required information. "I can't wait to see them when I get home! Can I... can I post them online?"

"You meant to like on Instantgraph and Twitface? Yeah, sure, if you wouldn't mind linking to our website. It's good publicity for us, too."

"Fantastic! I'll do that. Thank you again so much, for the show, the autograph, the photos, everything!"

"Not at all."

A moment of awkward silence ensued.

"So, uh," Moirin continued, "I should probably get back in. We still have gear to bring out and all that. But it was nice to meet you, Jilly. I hope we're still playin' when you're old enough to see us without sneaking in!"

"Me too! Thanks again ever so much!" She motioned to Holly that they should go, and they started back off down the alley. Moirin watched them for a few seconds, still a bit surprised that she had actual fans, especially ones that were willing to break the law to see her perform.

"That's cool, though. Can't wait to tell the lads!"

But before she could head back in, she noticed something happening at her feet. Something very unpleasant.

*　*　*

As Jilly fairly skipped away, elated at meeting her new hero, but frustrated at not learning much more about her, she happened to glance back, perhaps on instinct. A shadowy form seemed to take shape and grow up around Moirin. No, not a form. More like a whirlwind, a miniature tornado in the alley, centered around her. Moirin looked back and forth at the swirling darkness, an alarmed expression on her face.

"Holly!" Jilly whispered, grabbing her hand. "Look!"

Holly whipped around to see the dark substance rising out of the ground. "Qwyrk!" she whispered loudly.

Qwyrk appeared out of a nearby shadowy corner. "What the hell?"

"What is it?" Jilly asked, still gripping Holly's hand.

"I don't know," Qwyrk said, "but it's definitely not good."

"Is she doing this?" Holly asked.

"I don't think so," Qwyrk answered.

"She looks scared." Jilly looked back at both of them. "We have to help her!"

With those words, the whirlwind transformed. Out of its misty, eddying tendrils, ugly sounds emerged. Then came dark shapes with wings. In a rush, dozens of crow-like creatures materialized, cackling, screeching, and flying in a circle around the now-terrified young singer. Their eyes glowed, and they seemed not to be alive, more like reanimated corpses. Moirin screamed, and swatting at them with her arms, she forced her way through the tangle of rotting feathers and beaks and took off in a frantic run in the opposite direction from Qwyrk, Holly, and Jilly. The birds broke their circle and tore through the air in pursuit.

"Damn it!" Qwyrk swore. "I'm going after her."

"I'll come with you," Holly offered.

"No, stay here. I can keep up with them better on my own. But go back inside the club, both of you. Make sure everyone else is safe. If those things show up in there, do whatever you have to do to take them down. I mean it. If this is more Darkfae crap, they're not playing around. Terminate with extreme prejudice and all that. I'll be back."

She leaned in and gave Holly a quick kiss, a nod to Jilly, and then sped off after the foul fowls.

* * *

Qwyrk leaped up to the chimney of an old rooftop to try to get a better view. York's fabled historic structures spread out in front of her in random and sprawling ways, offering little help in her search. Only the lit-up Minster in the distance presented any sense of place or bearing.

"Damn it! These old streets are a bloody maze, especially at night."

She closed her eyes and tuned in to her surroundings. Sure enough, she heard the cackles, the caws, the crow-cries. After a gentle descent down to the cobblestone street below, she darted off in their direction. She couldn't risk teleportation, not knowing exactly where she was or where she would end up. So, by foot it had to be.

Fortunately, she soon caught up with the appalling avians as they rushed down a long street, closing in on their intended prey. The handful of folk out for night strolls didn't seem to notice the hellish flock, so perhaps they were manifesting in a manner unseen to most mortal eyes. Good. The fewer panicked people the better.

But that meant Moirin was more than a typical human. Just as Qwyrk suspected.

Now that she had more room and could see her desired destination down the street, she waved a hand and vanished, reappearing in front of the oncoming beasties, offering Moirin a chance to get away, while she drew their attention.

"You know, I've met some strange things in my centuries," she announced as they loomed in front of her, "but zombie birds? That's a new one, I must admit. You lot have seen better days, that's for sure. I have no idea what you really are, but instead of terrorizing that young lady, why don't you try me out, and we'll see if you're really as scary as you look?"

One of the creatures flew by and pecked at her before darting behind her and back up into the sky.

"Hey! Watch your beak, mister, ma'am, whatever. Oh crap, if you bite me, I'm not going to turn into a sodding zombie crow am I? Like, shrink down and sprout nasty, wilty wings? The flying dead? That would be a really stupid way to go. I don't fancy flitting about with you lot for eternity!"

She crouched down and jumped into the air, shooting straight up as the monstrous murder bore down on her. As she hoped, the zombirds took the bait and soared up in pursuit. She came to a stop about thirty feet up in the air, and waited for them to fly in a circle around her. Which they did. Anti-clockwise. Good. Spinning herself in the opposite direction, she launched her fists into the tangle of beaks, claws, and scruffy feathers, connecting with several and sending them sailing through the air in all directions, to the sound of much surprised squawking.

"Didn't see that coming, did you?"

After thinning out the corvid cluster, she realized that only some of them returned.

"So, you can be hurt and sent packing. Brilliant. Shall we go for round two?" She lashed out again and connected with several more. A few disappeared into the night. A few others fell to the ground, where they vanished in a flash of sickly green light. The remaining dozen or so hovered just out of reach, cawing with menace, but clearly unwilling to attempt another attack.

"My advice to you lot?" Qwyrk announced. "Bugger off, now. Go back to whoever sent you and tell them to leave the one you're chasing alone. Forever. The more of you that come back, the more I'll destroy, and I'll bring friends to help, got it? And then we'll take out whoever sent you!" Her eyes glowed red to show them she meant it.

They hesitated for a bit, skeletal wings flapping in the air, the occasional rotted feather falling out and drifting randomly downward. They glanced back and forth among each other, as if understanding her threat. With a unison shriek of defiance, they turned and flew off. As they fled, Qwyrk noticed a loose section of roof tile on the building next to her and, snapping off a small piece, she hurled it at the bird closest to her. It hit its mark, and the thing let out an angry and unearthly yelp before hastening its pace to catch up with the others.

"That was petty. And very satisfying."

She watched until they'd all disappeared into another flash of sickly green light. She waited for a bit, to make sure they didn't try to sneak back into this world.

"Well, that could have gone far worse," she said, descending to the ground and glancing around her. "Now, where would Moirin have gone?"

* * *

Moirin ran through the almost-deserted streets, ignored by the few people who were out, barely keeping herself upright on the slippery flagstones, which were not designed for running from undead crows. She didn't dare look back, even though she could no longer hear them. The sound of her breathing and rushing blood filled her ears, and all she could do was keep moving, get away, disappear. Somehow, she knew this wasn't the first time she'd fled for her life. She could see the lighted cathedral in the distance, towering over the town, a useful marker in this ancient maze of lanes and "gates."

Fatigue began to set in, and she had to slow her pace. If something were still after her, she'd either have to face it, or just give in and let it take her. She made an abrupt stop at the next corner, clutching its old stone wall with one hand, bent over and gasping for breath. The world started to come back into focus a bit, as each lungful of cool night air brought her down from the rush of adrenaline and fear that had taken hold. Maybe everything would be all right now, maybe...

"Moirin?"

Morin looked up to see a familiar face, a young lady in a black Regency dress with a shock of coppery red hair, holding a parasol.

"Aileen? What are you doing here?"

"I'd ask ya the same question? What are ya doin' running about the streets of York in the dark, ya daft girl?"

Moirin took another deep breath and hauled herself back up. "It's kind of a long story. Well, not that long, but it's dead crazy, and I don't want to get into it right now."

"Is someone chasin' you? Should we go to the police?"

"No! I mean, no, it's not that. No one's chasing me," she lied. "I'm not in any danger or anything. I just, I had a bit of a panic after the show, what with all the fans and everyone loving it so much, you know? I don't quite know what happened, but one minute I was fine, and the next, I just felt like I had to get out of there, get away. And here I am, I guess. Wherever here is." She actually lied quite a bit. "But I'm better now, thanks. I think I can head back, go face everyone again. Some 'star' I am, having a panic attack in front of the audience. What a loser, eh?"

"I don't think you're a loser at all." Aileen smiled. "I think you're brilliant and talented, and like I said, I love your singing. But I think you're tired, and maybe a wee bit overwhelmed, and maybe ya just need a break? A little time off?"

"Maybe, but that's not really an option right now. We're in the middle of a tour. We've a few more shows to do, so I have to just tough my way through it. Figure out how to cope. And not completely flip out."

Aileen looked at her sadly, with care and concern. "I wish I could help, do something," she said, taking Moirin's hand. "But, I can't. I don't know what to say, but I'll walk back with you to the club, if you like. Or, we can get a taxi. That might be even better."

"No, I'm fine." Moirin held up her free hand, palm outward, as if to push her back. "I'll be all right now. Some fresh air and alone time would do me good, I think. I need to clear me head a bit."

"Are you sure? It's no bother for me at all. It's not like I have anywhere else to be."

"I'm sure, thanks."

"Why don't I come, just to be—"

"I said I'm fine!" She let go of Aileen's hand with a jerking motion and turned to walk away.

"I'm sorry, Moirin, I didn't meant to upset you."

Moirin closed her eyes, sighed again and turned around to look at her would-be helper.

"You didn't. Honest. And I'm sorry, too. That was rude of me and you didn't deserve that. Look, it's not you. It's me, it really is. I'm... complicated. Actually, I'm a complete mess. But that's not your problem. You're kind and thoughtful, and that's lovely, but I'm not worth your time. I'm not worth anyone's time. Thanks for coming out tonight, though. I do appreciate it."

She reached up and held out the pendant. "And thanks for this. I'll... see you round sometime, yeah?"

She turned her back again and started off, feeling terrible that she might have upset Aileen, but deciding she had no other option. She was glad that Aileen didn't follow her or even say anything else as she walked away.

✳ ✳ ✳

Qwyrk stepped out from a narrow side street and waited. "This may be a bad idea, but what else is new?"

She heard the footsteps approaching, and sure enough, Moirin came into view, no doubt wandering back to the club now that the flock of evils was gone. Qwyrk was surprised that she didn't seem scared, but more sad and introspective.

"So," Qwyrk called out, "this has been quite a night, hasn't it?"

"Who the hell are you?" Moirin snapped out of her doldrums and stopped abruptly, scowling at this new intruder.

"Well, that's kind of a long story, but the same question could be asked of you."

"Look, to be honest, I don't really care who you are." Moirin started walking again. "Tonight's been insane, to put it mildly, and I'm in no mood for jokes, conversations with strangers, or anything else. Just leave me alone."

"You seem really good at walking away from people," Qwyrk prodded. "Your red-haired friend back there, my friends by the side door after the show—"

"What, the kid and the supermodel? Interesting company you keep there."

"The kid's one of my best friends, actually. She's amazing. Oh, and the 'supermodel' is my girlfriend, thank you very much. She's also amazing."

"Ah, so you're the 'other best friend'. Well, you've done all right for yourself there."

"Thanks, I think so, too." Qwyrk stepped into the light. "So, here's an odd question for you: what do I look like?"

"Do you really need me to tell you? You could just go find a feckin' mirror."

"Humor me."

"White girl, blonde, blue-green-ish eyes, quite attractive."

"Oh, thank you!" Qwyrk grinned and mock-played with her hair.

"But what's with the ears?" Moirin squinted and stared. "Are you cosplaying an elf for a local fantasy convention, or something?"

"Oh, for crap's sake!" Qwyrk rolled her eyes. "I'm not a flipping elf, all right? Elves are just... silly! Even the big, bad, scary ones in the Wild Hunt."

"I've no idea what you're on about, but if you're taking some kind of new designer drugs, or something, I don't want any, really. Just leave me alone."

"Here's the thing," Qwyrk said. "The ears are real. It's true. And you shouldn't be able to see me as I am, unless you're special, like magic-special. And the fact that a flock of super angry death birds was just chasing you through the streets of old York tells me that there's more to you than even you're willing to admit."

"I... I have no idea what you're on about."

"Oh! Sorry, my mistake." Qwyrk threw her hands up. "So, you weren't just running for your life from a pack of undead crows with glowing eyes and quite the homicidal attitude? They were bearing down on you, like really fast? Because when I chased them off, I was sure that's what they looked like to me. But I might be wrong, maybe I imagined them, and you just like going out for a vigorous out-of-breath sprint in the dark after every gig? I mean, I guess that's believable, sort of."

Moirin glared at her. "Look, I don't know who you are, and I don't really care about you or your gorgeous girlfriend, so you and your shower of gosbshites can piss off and leave me be!" She brushed past Qwyrk and stormed off down the street.

Qwyrk rolled her eyes and circled her hand in the air. She vanished from where she stood and reappeared with her usual illuminated flourish about five feet in front of Moirin, who stared at her in total shock, to the point of dropping her jaw and coming to a complete stop.

"Yeah, it's a nice trick, isn't it?" Qwyrk asked in a matter-of-fact manner, rubbing her fingernails against her shirt. "I'm quite proud of it. Not exactly something a 'cosplaying elf' could do, though, you have to admit."

"This is nuts! How did..."

"Great show, by the way. Your band is really good, and you've got a brilliant voice. Only, it's not just *your* voice, is it? I've heard that you can do some amazing things with it when you start singing. I was hoping to see a bit of that myself tonight, we all were, but nothing happened. I was a bit disappointed, I must say, at least as far as that goes. But if you want to give me a demonstration right now, I'd be more than happy to listen."

Moirin fumed. She squirmed, she looked around like she might try to run away, but then she just sighed and gave in. "Look, I don't know how you know about this, but I don't... I don't control it. At least not completely. I wish I could. Sometimes it's there, and sometimes, like tonight, nothing happens. I was just glad we did a good show. I don't really care about it all that much, and if it goes away for good, that's fine, too. In fact, maybe it already has. That'd be a blessing, to be honest."

"I don't think it's that simple, sorry to say. What happens when it does show up?"

Moirin squirmed. "It's hard to describe. It's like, it takes me over. I'm still there, but I'm sort of watching me, like on a television screen or something. I sing, and this power comes in from somewhere else and just kind of 'rides' the sound of my voice, if that makes any sense at all. And then, things happen."

"What kind of things?"

"I don't know. It's a bit different every time, but it's like the sound bends reality somehow? I don't know what it's doing, or if it's all just in my mind. But when it happens, I feel strong, like I'm on top of the world. It's like I'm connected to something super old, something that goes way back, and it feels good. Really good."

"Yeah, I'm not sure how good it is, sorry to say."

"What do you mean?"

"It's a bit of a story. Look, can you trust me? Me and my friends, my 'shower of gobshites' as you so lovingly called them?"

"No, I can't. I don't even know you. You're some teleporting elf that's going on about magic and zombie birds, and I'm just a singer trying to make a name, with a great band that took me on when I had nowhere else to go, and—"

"Why didn't you have anywhere else to go?" Qwyrk tried to ignore that Moirin had just called her an elf.

"Um, it's kind of none of your business, stranger who I don't know."

"You don't remember, do you?"

"Remember what?"

"Anything. Anything about your life before you joined the Weasels."

"That's daft! Of course I do!"

"Where were you born?"

"Oh, not you, too! Ireland, of course! You may have noticed my accent, or don't they have those in elf-land?"

"Bloody hell. Where in Ireland? What year? When's your birthday? What do your parents do? Where did you go to school?"

"I... I don't have to answer those questions." She put a hand to her head, shielding her eyes.

"Do you have a sister?"

Moirin rubbed her temple. "Just stop. Please."

"A brother?"

She cried out and doubled over, holding her head and swaying back and forth. She collapsed to one knee.

"What happened?" Qwyrk put a hand on her shoulder. "Are you all—"

"Get back!" Moirin screamed as she jerked up with a sudden lurch, spreading her arms wide. Her voice delivered a crushing blow, its force throwing Qwyrk across the street and into the side of an old brick building. She gasped and fell to the ground in a slump. Clutching her midsection, she looked up to see Moirin running down the street and making a hasty turn at the next intersection.

She roused herself, grunted in pain, and stood up.

"Right," she said. "I could go after her and make this whole thing even worse, or I could just go back to the others and tell them I completely cocked it up. Not a great choice either way, really."

But she knew that trying to reach out to Moirin now would be a very bad, even dangerous, idea, so she waved her hand in a circle and willed herself to go back to where her companions were.

"Let's just hope they're not in the middle of their own battle with a hoard of undead hedgehogs or something."

CHAPTER TEN

Qwyrk flashed back to the alley beside the club, where she found Holly, Jilly, and Blip standing about and looking rather bored.

"So, everything's all right?" she asked, glancing between them.

"Fine," Holly answered, a bit curtly. "Better than fine. Literally nothing has happened at all. Everyone left the venue and headed off to the pubs or home, and now we're standing around here, waiting for you to come back. And here you are."

"Well, I'm glad it's all good," Qwyrk said, sensing tension, but not wanting to get into it in front of Blip and Jilly. "I wasn't so lucky."

"Is she all right?" Jilly asked with a concerned expression.

"Yeah, she's fine. I chased off those bird thingies, sent them back to wherever they came from, so they never even got to her. But then she ran into someone, almost literally, that young lady she was talking to earlier.

"The red-haired one?" Holly's tone softened. "That's strange."

"Yeah, I thought so, too. Moirin just happened to run into her on the other side of the old town after chatting with her, and right after those crows showed up. That's more than a little suspicious."

"Perhaps she's behind the attack?" Holly pondered.

"Maybe, but it's really odd." Qwyrk answered. "I mean, she seemed friendly enough with Moirin, so it wouldn't exactly be the best way to prove they got on: 'here, have a flock of zombie death birds to hunt you down, it's a gift.'"

"I agree," Blip interjected. "Something seems off, but I don't think the red-haired lass is behind the attack."

"We could try to find out more about her. Her name, who she is, or something?" Jilly suggested.

"It'd be helpful, but how?" Qwyrk was at a loss for ideas. "I could go out looking for her, I suppose, but even if I found her, I have no idea if she could even see me, and scaring her half to death isn't going to help up us."

"We could both go," Holly suggested. "If we find her, I could talk to her. She's already met me."

"No, I doubt we'd find her now, anyway," Qwyrk sighed and shook her head. "There's probably nothing we can do about it for the moment." Holly glared at her, but Qwyrk averted her gaze and looked at the others.

"Agreed," Blip added. "This is one mystery that shall have to elude us for the time being."

"It does seem to be a night for mysterious women," Holly said, changing the subject. "Moirin, her friend, and that bizarre encounter I had in the queue before."

Qwyrk finally looked at her. "What do you mean?"

Holly relayed the story, with Blip again stressing that had neither seen nor heard anything.

"That's... really bizarre," Qwyrk said, "and more than a bit creepy. Are you sure it wasn't just someone pulling a prank?"

"Possibly. But to what end?" Holly asked. "And she just vanished. There was something about her that was familiar, but I can't place it. It's like my memory is clouded, like I'm trying to remember a dream."

"Yeah, well, when memories start getting tampered with, that's usually a bad sign," Qwyrk said.

"Honestly, I'm not going to fret about it too much," Holly answered. "It's entirely possible that I'm just tired and someone at the show was winding me up."

But Qwyrk remained unconvinced. "Anyway, this evening's a bit of a bust," she said with a frustrated sigh. "Jilly, I'll take you and Blip back to your house and we'll call it a night, yeah? We'll meet up at some point tomorrow?"

"Yeah, my school has half-days the rest of this week, a sort of break for teacher-training business, or something," Jilly said, "so I'll be home by 1:00."

"Brilliant, but we should leave. I'd rather be gone before Moirin gets back. She'll be in no mood to see me again."

So they joined hands and Qwyrk had them back home in two ticks.

*　*　*

"Hey Moirin, where'd you go? You disappeared after the gig, and a lot of people still wanted to meet ya." She didn't want Sam's concern.

She'd wandered back into the club sometime after her encounter with the elf lady. The whole exchange had been surreal, and she thought she might have just hallucinated it. All of it, in fact, including the birds and seeing Aileen again.

Maybe I am really losing my grip?

"Yeah, sorry about that," she answered, walking past him. "All of a sudden, I felt a bit sick and just needed some fresh air, and before I knew it, I ended up wandering a bit too far away. But I did have a chance to talk to a few fans outside afterward, and they really liked it, so I think we did great!" That part, at least, was true.

"We really did," Sam said. "In fact, the club is already talking about having us back, and not just that. They want us to headline a Saturday night gig in a few months!"

"Sam, that's brilliant!"

"See? I knew when we found our audience, we'd click with them. We also sold a ton of merch, so we actually made money on this one. I think this is it, Moi. I think we're gonna be onto some bigger things really soon. We're finally gettin' a reputation; a good one, I mean!"

"I hope so," she sighed. "I could use some happy news right about now."

"Why's that?" He moved in a bit closer.

Oh gods! Please don't try to touch me! She thought. "Oh, no real reason. I've just been frustrated with everything so far, and I'm tired. You know, mid-tour crankiness. But yeah, top billing here would be fantastic. Look, I'll help load up the van, and then I'm goin' back to my B&B for an early-ish night. I'm still a bit off, and the show wore me out."

With that, she had the perfect excuse to back away from him and go off to do post-gig chores. Anything to avoid having to face what she feared he was hoping for.

* * *

Jilly flopped onto her bed in frustration, not even bothering to wash the webs off her face. "Well that was annoying! We didn't get to see her do her magic, and then we just sat around after. I mean, it was brilliant to see her and the band again, and oh my gosh! I got to meet her and we chatted and she's actually really nice and she took photos with me and she sent them to me so now I have her email address, but I suppose I shouldn't write back to her, but no, I should, to at least say 'thank you' because it'd be rude not to, but I shouldn't write to her regularly or anything, because that would be odd and she might think I was creepy, but what if we became like pen pals and she wanted me to write her? Not every day, of course, but sometimes at least... oh that would be so brilliant, and I don't know if I could handle it, but first we still need to figure out what's going on with her, right? I mean, if she's in trouble we need to help her, right, Mr. Blip?"

"I'm sorry child, you lost me at something about not getting to see her work her magic." He jumped up on the bed and sat himself down.

Jilly gave him an embarrassed chuckle. "Yeah, fine, sorry, I was just fangirling over her, that's all."

"I'm sorry, doing what?"

"Fangirling."

"I don't recall you bringing a fan with you, much less using it for her benefit. And it's hardly the time of year when such a device would be necessary."

"No, not fanning her, silly! Though, I'd totally do that for her if she wanted me to! No, it means being a fan, you know, really liking someone, like a band or an actor, or whatever. Being a fangirl or a fanboy just means that."

"Oh I see, yes, being a 'fanatic' as some people like to indulge in. It seems a bit over the top, don't you think?"

"And you've never really admired someone?"

"Of course I have, but I've always conducted myself with all the appropriate respect and decorum that goes with such admiration. I was very taken with the work of Botticelli during the Italian Renaissance, but I did not turn into a gibbering fool over it. In fact, I simply showed my appreciation by having some food prepared for him: some—wait for it—pasta 'Primavera.' Heh!"

Jilly knew he was trying to make an art joke, but she had no idea what he was talking about. And honestly, didn't want to.

"I was the same with a certain famous German composer residing in eighteenth-century London," he went on, ignoring her obliviousness. "I once congratulated him on the completion of his quite splendid *Music for the Royal Fireworks*, but there was a bit of a problem, I'm afraid."

"He... couldn't see you?"

"Not only that, he was very bad at taking compliments. He could not, shall we say, 'Handel' them! Ha!" He slapped his knees.

Jilly gave him a blank look bordering on a glare. This time she got the joke. Not that it made it any better.

"Oh dear, that was rather dreadful," he admitted. "I do apologize."

"I'll just pretend you didn't say it, thank you. But, he couldn't hear you, anyway, right? No adult can sense you?"

"Yes, yes, quite true. The point is, I did not scream, or giggle, or embarrass myself, or do anything untoward, unlike those self-styled fanatics who throw themselves at rock and roll bands and make ludicrous fools of themselves. Please, Miss Pleeth, promise me that you will not lower yourself to that level of mortifying comportment. Ms. Moirin Moeran, while certainly a gifted vocalist, does not warrant such behavior, and I'd wager she has no interest in being the object of such unruly affections."

"Yeah, you're right. I think it'd just wind her up. But she still sent me those pictures, and I have to see how they look on a bigger screen!"

She reached for her laptop and checked her email, excitement coursing through her. Sure enough, the two photos waited for her. The note that came with them read: "Hi Jilly, here u are. Looks good, stay a rebel. Luv, Chantz/Moirin." She squealed a little, in spite of Blip's cautionary admonishment, and opened up the photos to take them in.

"Ooh, they look great!" she said with joy, "I still can't believe I got to have photos with her!"

Blip peered over her shoulder. "They are adequate enough, I suppose, taking into account the lighting, the position, and the fact that they were obtained on one of those blasted mobile contraptions instead of a proper photographic device. Why it seems like only yesterday that Joseph Nicéphore Niépce first took the bold steps to capture images by—"

"Sir, look at this!" Jilly gasped.

"What? What is it, child?"

She pointed to the right-hand side of the photo, behind Moirin and a shadowy figure that seemed to hover nearby. "That's not Qwyrk, is it?"

"Highly doubtful. But it's a very dim image, so we can't be sure."

"Maybe I can enhance it," she said. She opened the picture in her photo program and played around with contrast, brightness, and other settings, and in a moment, the figure popped out a bit more.

"It looks like a face," she said. The ghostly visage revealed itself as that of a woman with long, unkempt hair, a leering grin, and eyes that seemed to be sunken in darkness.

"It's faint, but it's most definitely present," Blip agreed.

"Who is she? What is she? She's not another Shadow. What's she doing hanging about Moirin? That's creepy! She doesn't look very friendly."

"My dear, I think your shelfie—"

"Selfie. But Holly actually took the photo."

"No matter. I believe that the image has quite possibly captured the likeness of the entity, the very banshee that is for some reason working her magic into Moirin's voice."

"And that's not good, is it?"

Blip's expression darkened. "If it is who I think it is, then not only Moirin, but all of us could be in grave danger."

*　*　*

Qwyrk and Holly materialized back in front of her home. It was dark and quiet, the very epitome of peaceful, but Qwyrk already feared that peace wouldn't last very long.

"Right, well that was quite a night, wasn't it?" she said as she started toward the house, hoping to deflect away any impending conflict. But she noticed right away that Holly walked behind her. She turned around, a knot in her stomach. "Hey, are you all right? What's wrong?"

Holly didn't answer but stared at the ground.

"Holly?" Qwyrk knew something was up. *Crap.*

"I don't want to seem overly testy, especially after last night," Holly said, looking up, "but I need to get something off my chest."

"Of course, what is it?" Qwyrk swallowed hard.

Holly hesitated. She stammered. She himmed. She hawed. "Damn it! Fine, here it is: I don't like being ordered about, Qwyrk. I don't want to be treated like your foot soldier."

Qwyrk looked down, now a bundle of nerves. "What?" she managed to say.

"Whenever a situation happens, you immediately take charge and start giving orders for who does what and when. I get it, I suppose. You've a lot of experience in these things, but you're not the only one with fighting skills, remember? Earlier tonight, you basically ordered me to stay put, with no thought for my opinion, or how I might have helped."

"I'm sorry. I was... I was just trying to make the best use of everyone, and it was like a split-second decision, you know? Those things showed up and took off after her. I had no time to plan." Qwyrk tried to be understanding, but feared she just came off as defensive.

"Yes, I know, and you were right. You can teleport, and you stood a better chance of catching up with those creatures, but it's not about those birds, or the buggane, or any one thing. It's a pattern, and it bothers me. I'm your girlfriend, not your assistant, not your servant. I know you wanted us to make sure that everyone in the club was safe, and they were, but that's the whole problem. Literally nothing happened, because whatever was after Moirin was only after her. And my skills were wasted tonight, when I might have been of help. Instead, I stood there outside the club, twiddling my thumbs and doing nothing, while we waited for news from you."

Qwyrk tried to protest. "But Jilly might have needed—"

"Jilly's very good at handling herself, and she has Mr. Blippingstone, who at the very least could whisk her back here if things become dangerous. She's immune to this world's effects now, right?"

"I suppose." Qwyrk answered, feeling sheepish.

"Look, I'm not trying to be unreasonable. There were good reasons for you to go after those creatures and for me to stay behind. But this 'Sergeant Qwyrk and Private Holly' business is not on. At least not every time. You even shut me down when I proposed that we go back out and look for Moirin's red-haired friend. I was only trying to help, and you made it seem like my suggestion was a waste of time." She took a few steps back and turned away.

Qwyrk's stomach tightened. "I'm so sorry, I really am. I never meant to downplay your skills, or make you feel lesser. I think you're absolutely amazing, and there's no one else I'd rather have by my side in a fight."

Holly turned to regard her. "I know, but sometimes it doesn't feel like that, if I'm being honest. It feels more like you're trying to protect me, the way you protect Jilly. But I don't need that, Qwyrk, and I don't want it. I'm more than capable of taking care of myself."

"I know, and if *I'm* being honest, I think I'm just in absolute awe of you all the time, and I feel like I need to prove to myself that I'm not useless." She found surprising relief in this confession.

Holly's expression softened. "What? Why ever for?"

"Are you kidding me? Look at you!" Qwyrk gestured at her with both hands. "Everything about you is incredible! It's like there's nothing you can't do brilliantly: fighting, dancing, knowing languages, being charming, making friends. I feel like a complete pillock next to you a lot of the time, and honestly, I can't even begin to imagine why you'd... why you'd want to be with me." She looked away, fearful that tears might come.

Holly she reached out to take Qwyrk's hands. "Why I'd want to be with you? Do you know who you are?"

Qwyrk looked back at her. "Um, I think so... unless I'm mistaken. Am I... someone else and no one's ever told me?"

"Silly. You're brave, caring, kind, funny, lovely, a genuine hero, and I adore you. Even when you *are* a bossy pain in the arse."

Relief washed over Qywrk like a spring rain. "Thank you. Really. These are my own hang-ups, and I admit that. After all this time, I'm still a bit rubbish at this. You know, the whole 'relationship' thing. If that's, you know, what this is. Us, I mean."

"It most definitely is. And you think I'm not, too? Rubbish at this, I mean? I'm far from perfect!"

"Are you? Really? I mean, seriously, is there anything you're not good at? Other than footie and cricket, which I don't care about in the slightest."

"Let's see: I'm punctual to the point of being annoying. I have a singing voice like a harpy with a migraine. I'm absolutely terrible when it comes to learning most human technologies. I feel like I'll never live up to my mother's expectations... oh, and my cooking is crap."

"Just as well I don't eat, then."

"No, for real. My mother makes food to positively swoon for, but, try as I might, I can't get the hang of it. I'm far more likely to make someone sick or burn the house down, I'm afraid."

"I think you're exaggerating."

"I'm not! I'm dreadful. In any case, you'll see how lovely her meals are when you meet her."

"When I... meet her?"

"We talked about it the other night, remember?"

"We did?"

"Yes, after we, you know, made things 'official' for the first time?" She chuckled and looked down. "I said I'd like you to meet her, and you said of course, you'd be delighted."

"Honestly, I... don't remember that. I was a bit, well, preoccupied, blissed out."

"I promise you it's true." Holly glanced up.

"Maybe I was in Reverie?"

"I'm sure you weren't." Holly caressed Qwyrk's arm.

"Um, all right. Must have been the joy of the moment. Yeah, I suppose we could do that, um, sometime?"

"Brilliant! She's free tomorrow just after mid-day."

"Tomorrow? As in, *tomorrow* tomorrow?"

"That's generally what 'tomorrow' means."

"Uh, great, yeah, all right, fine. Brilliant, actually. Can't wait!"

"Excellent! I'll stop by and take you to our home."

"Oh. So, you're not staying over here tonight, then?"

Holly sighed. "I'm sorry, darling, but I'm exhausted. I need a good night's sleep for a change."

"Shall I take that as a compliment?"

"You shall." Holly bit her lower lip teasingly.

Qwyrk felt all tingly. "Look: I'm really sorry about the whole giving orders thing; it's an old habit, but when I'm stuck with sidekicks like Blip and Star Tao, or Qwypp and Qwykk, you can understand why. But you're right, we're a team; we're different, and that's important. We need to work together. So if I do it again, feel free to give me a smack on the head with your stick. But, I mean, not too hard, or anything."

"I don't think that will be necessary. Well, at least after the first few times."

"Oh, thank you for your confidence."

"Not at all. Goodnight and adieu, then?"

"Parting is such sweet sorrow, and all that." Qwyrk leaned in and kissed Holly's lips. Only, something happened. Something unexpected. She was jolted by a shock, rather like a static spark from too-dry clothing. She recoiled. "Ah! Did you feel that?"

"Yes!" Holly reached up to rub her lips. "What was it? It was rather unpleasant."

"I have no idea. I mean, it's not terribly dry here. Hang on..." She kissed Holly again. Nothing this time, beyond the usual delicious feeling that such kisses brought her.

"How odd," Holly said. "Could it be some kind of magical residue or some such, floating about? Is that a thing that could happen here?"

"You know, it's entirely possible. In fact, nothing would surprise me. Maybe it's something in the air left over from Qwyzz's booby-trapped book. Honestly, I'm sure it's nothing to worry about." She kissed Holly again, and again. All was well. "See? It's fine."

"Splendid! So, I'll collect you tomorrow, then? Shall we say, just before midday? My mother will be ever so delighted to meet you at last! And you'll love her food, even if you don't need it."

"Looking forward to it!" Qwyrk smiled what she was certain was the most insincere smile she had ever insincerely smiled. But if Holly picked up on it, she didn't let on. And that made her all the more special. With another non-electrified kiss, Qwyrk bid her girlfriend goodnight, watched as Holly located a nearby tree to use as a portal, and waved as she vanished into it. She turned and walked toward her own home. And nearly tripped over a boulder embedded deep in the ground that she was quite sure had not been there a minute or two before.

"What the bloody hell?"

* * *

Moirin was lying in her bed, in her warm, comfy B&B, but she couldn't sleep, couldn't even relax. She'd had a great show, the band sounded great, she'd met some adoring fans, and nothing had derailed her performance. And then, of course, everything had to go to blazes.

"Crows. Freakin' death crows. Chasing me through the streets. I mean, I've seen some weird shite in the last week or two, but that takes the flipping cake. Maybe I should have listened to the elf lady. The elf lady, who's apparently not an elf and gets wound up about it." She rolled over and buried her face in a pillow.

"Oh, shite, Moirin, listen to yourself! Death crows and elves. Elves, for feck's sake. You're not the full shilling, are ya? There *has* to be a logical explanation for it, for all of it." She looked up and sighed. "At least the girl and her gorgeous friend were nice enough, even if they do know the elf. The elf who's dating her, or whatever. Oh, this is ridiculous!" She buried her face again, feeling frustrated and stupid.

"And then there's Sam. Poor, sweet Sam," she went on, remembering her other problem. "He's a gem, and he wants to help me all the time, and he's so genuine about it, but no... just no. I can't. And Aileen, bollocks, Aileen. She's also right sweet, like a puppy following me around. Gah, why does everyone want to be so damned nice? Why can't they just bugger off, leave me alone, and be nice from a distance? Send me postcards, or encouraging emails, or bottles of whiskey, or something?"

"Is that what you really want?" the voice echoed in her head, startling her. "To be left alone? Or is there something else? Something more?"

"Who are you?" Moirin demanded, sitting up at once.

"You've been abandoned enough in your young life. You really want to belong for a change, don't you? To feel truly accepted. To know where you come from and who you are."

"Why're you messing with my head, my voice? I have a life to live, and things are looking up, so why are you here, ruining it?"

"The life you are meant to live is far beyond the small dream you have now, little one," the voice tempted and taunted. "If you will let me, I will show you a destiny much greater than you could possibly hope for."

"Did you send those crow things after me tonight?"

"The Sluagh? Most definitely not. Why would I do that?"

"I don't know, but if it wasn't you, then who did? And what are they?"

"The restless dead. Come to collect the living."

"Oh, that's charming. I feel so much better now." Moirin grabbed her pillow and slammed it on the mattress.

"I didn't create them, nor did I set them upon you."

"Then who did?"

"I do not know."

"Why do I have a feeling you're lyin' to me?"

"There is no need for me to do so."

"And why am I speakin' to an imaginary voice in my head?"

"That's not what I am, and you know it."

"So, what are you, then?"

"Search within. You know the answer."

"Great, so not only am I going insane, my crazy inside voice is giving me riddles to solve. You know, you could just bugger off and leave me alone, too."

"That is not your fate."

"Oh, and you know my fate, I suppose."

"After a fashion."

"You know what, I'm sick of this: magic, dead crows, voices

buzzing in my brain, elves, the whole damned lot of it. I don't know what any of it is or what it means, but I'm done with it, you hear me? We have a few days until the next gig, so tomorrow I'm pissin' off to the Dales and parking my arse in the country to clear my head. And then with any luck, all of you will be gone from my life forever!"

There was no response.

"Good." Moirin looked around, as if trying to see her visitor. "Maybe I convinced her to feck off at last. Yeah, a few days in the fresh air will do me good. I'll text the lads and let 'em know." She reached for her mobile. "I'll get a taxi out to somewhere, another B&B or a farm or something, and meet up with them again in Newcastle. Hang out with some sheep and cows; at least those make sense. Yeah, this'll fix everything!"

* * *

Far away, in another world, a barren land of twilight and shadow, the banshee watched Moirin and chuckled with satisfaction.

CHAPTER ELEVEN

At the sound of the knock, Qwyrk opened her door. There stood Holly, looking radiant and dressed in an elegant ensemble, black leggings and stylish boots, with a lovely, flowing long purple shirt-coat thing. A black scarf completed the look. Qwyrk looked down at her own blue jeans (though new), black boots, and grey collared shirt, charcoal waistcoat; at least the boots were a little dressier than normal.

"Um, hi," Qwyrk said, "Also, you look stunning!"

"Thank you, darling." Holly kissed her. "See? Sprucing can be smashing!"

"Yeah, I'm definitely getting that. Feel free to spruce any time you like around me, by the way."

"I'll keep that in mind. Come on, then, mother is expecting us." Holly took her hand and off they went.

"So," Qwyrk said, "how was your evening?"

"To be honest, a bit odd. I have the distinct impression of having had some disturbing dreams, but I can't for the life of me remember them. It's probably just as well."

"I'm sorry, I hope it wasn't because we quarreled before you left."

"Honestly, it was more likely because you weren't there."

Qwyrk melted for at least the twenty-seventh time in the last few days, but she was reminded of her own encounter.

"I had a strange experience last night, too," she said. "Right after you left, I turned to go inside and tripped over a big rock that shouldn't have been there."

"Is this another of those changes, like the tree that wandered up to your house?"

"Exactly the same. I have no explanation for it. If there is some magic about, whether it's Qwyzz's book's residue, or something else, I really need to look into it, especially if it's happening where I live. I don't want to answer my door some night and find out that an army of stinging nettles is laying siege or something. Crap, I just sounded like Gargula."

"Minus the swearing in French. Will you ask the council?"

"Oh Goddess, no! I'll talk with Qwyzz when I can. He keeps that enormous library and all, and that means that someone, somewhere, has probably had this experience before and written about it."

They found themselves in a clump of oak trees a moment later. Holly strode to one nearby and examined it.

"So, how do we get there?" Qwyrk asked.

Holly closed her eyes and placed her palm on the tree in question. "Only certain trees are portals back to our home, and those change all the time," she explained. "I'm checking to see if this one is a conduit, and if so, I'll ask permission to let us pass through."

"That's very polite of you."

"They're living beings, Qwyrk, deserving of far more respect than they're usually given, by mortals or Fae. Even if they *are* sending a tree and a rock as scouts in advance of an all-out attack." She winked.

"You're right, I'm sorry." Qwyrk wanted to ignore Holly's joke. "So, will this one work?"

Holly nodded. "Yes, and we're fine to pass through. Take my hand."

Qwyrk did as she was told. "So, what happens next?"

"We walk straight into it."

"Of course we do. And we don't just slam right into the bark because?"

"Because we're passing through it, silly. It's not unlike your teleporting, though less flashy."

"My teleporting's not that flashy!"

"It is rather! With the lights and sparkles and lavender and all."

"What's wrong with that?"

"Nothing at all. It's just a bit, well, grandiose."

"I prefer 'impressive,' thank you very much."

"Please don't misunderstand me. I think it's all rather remarkable. You always look smashing when you emerge from your shower of lights."

"Oh, I do, do I?"

"I think so. Come on, then."

Qwyrk let herself be led, and to her astonishment, the tree opened up before them, creating a tunnel to another world. She was dazzled by deep greenery a short distance beyond, and sensed the familiar shimmer of magic that imbued every molecule of Symphinity and its overlapping and adjacent realms. After a few more steps, they were through. Qwyrk glanced back to see what looked like the opposite side of the tree, only now she was in this other place.

She marveled that she had just stepped through a tree, when she turned around and almost gasped as she beheld lovely and lavish home of wood and stone situated in a wooded glade. Golden sunlight shining through the leaves gave it a glowing quality. It blended in, seeming to be both separate from the trees and growing out of them.

"Wow, this is lovely!"

Holly beamed. "It has its charms, to be sure."

"And you grew up here? It's still your home?"

Holly nodded. "It's more elaborate now than it was back in the day, but I like to think that we brought a fair bit of our homeland with us—on the inside at least—and made it more appealing as the centuries rolled on. To other Fae, it looks like a modest faery dwelling; nothing special about it at all."

"This is 'modest' and 'nothing special'?"

"Well, to us it is. It was smaller when we first settled here. We didn't want to attract attention in a dangerous time. And most humans aren't able to see it. It's designed to never be in quite the same place twice. That way, if some clever mortal did manage to pierce the enchantment and walk through a given marker tree, they'd never find it again once they went back and told all their mates about it, assuming they ever got back at all. It keeps us safe and makes them look foolish, or drunk, or both.

"I wonder what it's like to actually be drunk?" Qwyrk asked.

Holly shrugged. "I've no idea. I'm sure we'll never find out, which is probably for the best."

"Yeah, from what I've seen of how it makes humans and some

faeries behave, and the side-effects, I'm not sure I'd want to go through all that."

"Thankfully I can enjoy all the single malt scotch I wish, with no consequences. Except for that one time." She looked away as if embarrassed.

"Yeah well." Qwyrk squeezed her hand. "There's no chance of any more unexpected offspring as long as you're with me!"

"Thank goodness. Can you imagine what a terror a child of ours would be like?"

"What, a brilliant, powerful, beautiful, athletic, genius, posh, smart-arse girl who doesn't take crap from anyone and saves the world on regular basis?" Qwyrk punched the air.

"Exactly! It doesn't bear thinking about; there's already two of us like that, and that's more than enough!" Holly looked back to the front entrance. "Joking aside, we should probably go in. Um, also, you should prepare yourself for something a bit... odd."

"Well, that will be new."

"Ha! Well, you presented me with the gargoyles at your mentor's home, so let's just say that now it's my turn."

"Is this something I'm meant to look forward to?"

"You'll see. Ah, here he comes!"

A fluffy and regal, if somewhat chubby, tabby cat strode toward them and let out a meow. A handsome and tawny creature, he sported white patches and black stripes in all the appropriate places.

"Hello Mango." Holly held out welcoming arms.

"I'd just like you to know that I'm starving. Terribly so," the cat said in a high-pitched voice with a fairly posh accent, oblivious to her greeting.

Qwyrk looked at Holly with a raised eyebrow.

"And you thought talking gargoyles were bizarre," she whispered. "Really." She turned her attention back down to her diminutive feline visitor. "Are you quite certain?"

"Indeed," the cat said. "I'll have you know that it's been nearly thirty-five hours since I last had a proper meal."

"I suspect it's rather more like thirty-five minutes," Holly retorted.

"Minutes seem like hours to cats," Mango answered defiantly. "Days seem like weeks, months seem like years, years seem like centuries or even millennia."

"Only to cats in the mortal world, love, which you are most definitely not. You have at least nine hundred and ninety-nine lives, if not more, and just as much time as the rest of us to contemplate them in."

With that, she motioned to Qwyrk to follow her inside, leaving Mango to his self-imposed misery.

"Will you not feed me? I am the hungriest cat ever to have hungered," Mango called out behind them. "Fine then. Let my suffering be on your conscience!"

"I'll sleep quite well tonight, I should think," Holly called back. She stopped and turned around. "Where's your brother, by the way?"

"How should I know?" Mango replied, obviously still trying to sound pathetic. "Am I his keeper? He's most likely complaining about something or other to the lady of the house. It's what he does best. I'm too weak from malnourishment to think about it any further; I'm fairly wasting away, as you can plainly see!"

Holly rolled her eyes.

"So... your mum has talking cats that whine and complain?" Qwyrk asked, "which... isn't all that different from cats in the mortal world, it must be said. Except for the whole talking bit."

"How is that different?" Holly looked confused.

"Wait, you can understand what those cats say? You speak 'cat'?"

"Don't you?"

"Um, no, actually."

"How odd. Anyway, he's quite charming, isn't he?"

Qwyrk looked past her to Mango. "I honestly don't know how to answer that question."

"Really, they are very sweet. They're loyal and loving, even if they are a bit dramatic at times."

"I heard that!" Mango called out. "As I'm fading into nothingness, you'll be sorry that you ever said such slanderous things about me."

Ignoring him, they entered the house proper. Qwyrk took a deep breath and prepared herself for something that made her more nervous than the idea of a rematch with de Soulis and the Erlking combined.

Meeting her girlfriend's mother.

* * *

Moirin breathed in the fresh air of the country surrounding Fogram Farm and knew she'd made the right choice. This fine rural establishment in the Dales welcomed visitors who needed their own space. And they'd taken her last-minute booking and let her come early, just as morning gave way to noon. She felt bad about bailing on the band on such short notice and was quite sure they now saw her as a diva worthy only of being dumped, but she knew she had to take the risk.

"I'll make it to Newcastle on time, and everything'll be fine. It's not like we need to rehearse much before the next show, anyway."

She wandered up to the top of a hill near the barn and paddocks and took in the green landscape. This was what she wanted.

"Reminds me of home."

Home? Ireland, presumably.

But why was everything so fuzzy? Why couldn't she remember her past? The elf woman asked questions, questions that made her uncomfortable. Not just emotionally, but in her body, too. When she asked about a brother, Moirin had lost it. She went crazy, like the words burned into her head. Was she hiding something from herself? Something important was missing. It had to be.

She realized she was clutching the pendant Aileen had given her. She looked down at it. "With a bit of luck, I'll figure things out and find a way to put this whole mess behind me."

But how she was going to do that, she still had no idea.

* * *

Inside, Holly's home looked nothing like its exterior. It was simple, yet decorated in a beautiful, almost timeless, Indian style. The air smelled of fresh perfumes and spicy curry, wafting in to the greeting room from some undetermined direction. Holly closed her eyes, took a deep breath, and smiled.

"They say that humans associate smells the most with memory, but I think it's true for us, as well. Being here makes me feel safe. It's still home."

Qwyrk smiled and took her hand. "It's lovely to see you in such a good space, emotionally, I mean. It's important to have that kind of connection to your own history." She was acutely aware of not having her own connections, though she held back the thought. "So, when do I get to meet her?" Despite her nerves, she wanted to put on a brave show.

"Don't worry, she shouldn't be too long," Holly said with confidence. She motioned to some comfortable-looking cushions, which were more like bean bags. "Why don't we sit there while we wait?"

Qwyrk nodded and plopped herself down on one rather unceremoniously, which she regretted at once, feeling like quite the slob. But if Holly noticed, she said nothing, bless her. This was the perfect way to relax, and soon it would be underway, a genuine meet-the-parent occasion.

Crap. Qwyrk took a deep breath.

A quarter of an hour went by, and then an agonizing ten more minutes. Qwyrk grew ever more restless and tempted to stand up and pace back and forth to combat her nervousness, but she settled for fidgeting in place instead.

"Are you sure this was a good idea?" she asked. "I'm getting the feeling that she's stalling and doesn't want to meet me."

"Shhhh!" Holly whispered. "Here she comes."

The ornately-carved wooden door at one end of the chamber opened, and in she walked.

"Mother!" Holly said with a smile as she stood up, though she didn't go straight for hugs and kisses, Qwyrk noted. She followed Holly's lead and rose to her feet, trying not to seem like a clumsy fool.

The elder Vishala was an imposing and lovely woman, who very much looked like a more mature Holly, though Qwyrk didn't know if that was because her kind indeed aged, or if she chose to adopt that look as someone who had earned the right to the respect that came with her station in life. She wore a sari of golden yellow with an exquisite red choli. Her black hair was tied back and adorned with jewels and gold, though it still hid her pointed ears. She was every bit as magnificent as Qwyrk expected her to be, and even more impressive in person. Qwyrk felt underdressed and wished she'd taken Holly's advice to "spruce up" a bit more.

So much for first impressions. She was just relieved she hadn't tripped and fallen flat on her face. Though, the afternoon was young.

Vishala approached them in a steady but confident manner, with an expression that betrayed neither friendliness nor antagonism.

When she was about ten feet away, Qwyrk put her palms together and bowed slightly.

"Shrimati Vishala, it's an honor to finally meet you and..."

Vishala held up one hand, as if gesturing for Qwyrk to be silent, but her face betrayed no emotion.

Qwyrk took the hint and said nothing else, but she managed to cast a quick questioning glance at Holly, who only responded with a shrug, which was not helpful in the slightest.

She's enjoying this. Qwyrk endeavored to keep as calm an expression as possible.

Vishala approached and looked at Qwyrk with a stern, but not confrontational, gaze. She crouched a bit in front of Qwyrk and stared at her, with a squint and a scowl.

Is she looking up my nose? Qwyrk felt the sudden urge to sneeze, an uncommon Shadow problem, like so many other unusual bodily complaints that had greeted her at the worst possible times during the past year.

Vishala stood back up and walked to Qwyrk's left side, where she paused again.

Now she's inspecting my ear, isn't she? Qwyrk was convinced that said ear was ringing, but she remained still as Vishala walked behind her and paused again.

Hang on, is she checking out my arse? Qwyrk was completely confused.

In a moment, Vishala strode back around to face her again. "You are a warrior, my beti Vishala says?" Her voice was soft as velvet, her accent was Indian and regal.

"Beti Vishala?" Qwyrk asked.

"Beti... daughter," Holly explained in a hushed voice.

"Oh, right. Well, I don't know if 'warrior' is the best term. I mean, I've won a fair number of fights in my time, it must be said." She blushed a bit and tried to hide it. "Some of them rather convincingly, thank you very much, but—"

"You are so slight," Vishala cut her off.

"What?"

"You are strong, yes? You can fight, I am told, but there is so little to you. How do I know that can you protect my daughter when you are so sparse?"

"Mother," Holly objected, rolling her eyes. "Qwyrk is strong as a tank, and besides, I don't need anyone to defend me. You've trained me for centuries, as you always like to remind me?"

"I've seen her in action. She's amazing," Qwyrk offered in a quiet voice, trying to defend Holly, but be respectful at the same time; Vishala rather terrified her. Regardless, Holly smiled, and her eyes said "thank you," which made everything better.

"Eh," Vishala waved her hand in mild dismissal. "You both must train, become more skilled, grow stronger. These are dangerous times."

"Qwyrk was the main reason we defeated the Erlking last winter, mother," Holly said, a defense that Qwyrk knew would have an emotional impact on the older woman. But for good or bad?

"I know." Vishala's expression softened as she nodded, somewhere between grateful and sad. She turned back to look at Qwyrk. She paused for a moment, as if thinking of something. Perhaps a "thank you." Perhaps a compliment. Perhaps a "welcome to the family" speech. She seemed to be thawing, and Qwyrk was more than ready to meet her halfway, embrace, and be fast friends. Yes, there was no doubt that things were looking up...

"What do you eat?" Vishala's voice became stern and commanding again.

"Uh, sorry?"

"What do you eat?"

"Well, the thing is, um, I don't really... eat much of anything, at all, to be honest."

"I can tell! Just look at you!" She stood and motioned to Qwyrk. "Follow me. I have a feast prepared; you'll soon gain strength. This not eating is foolish! You young people and your fads."

"I'm... two thousand years old," Qwyrk tried to protest, but Vishala would have none of it.

"My beti needs more than just a suitor or a lover. She needs a warrior at her side, yes? And I think it may be you, but you must be strong. I'll see to it."

Qwyrk shook her head and cast another helpless glance at Holly, who responded with a "just go with it because you're not getting out of this" look, and off they all went.

*　*　*

Jilly sat on the living room couch, scrolling through Twitface on her laptop, but nothing interested her and she couldn't concentrate. She waited for Blip, whose unexplained absences seemed more and more common these days. She shut her laptop, sighed in frustration, and got up to go stare out the living room window at Granny's house. As she expected, there was no sign of anyone home.

"Damn it and bollocks!" she said.

"Now, now, my dear, there's no need for someone of your young age to resort to profanity."

"I'm glad you're back, sir." She turned around, ignoring Blip's admonishment.

He hopped up on the sofa. "While our situation is indeed frustrating and somewhat worrying, we have yet to ascertain whether or not it merits anything bordering on panic, or whether it is much ado about nothing and we shall once again be triumphant."

"Did you learn anything? About the mystery woman, I mean." She sat down next to him.

"Yes, I believe so. Her name is Aeval, which may be derived from the proto-Celtic 'Oibel-ā,' which means 'burning fire.' Tradition ascribes that she was something of a protector for the Dalcassians of Munster in Ireland, and…"

"Excuse me, but did you learn anything about what she's doing?"

"Oh yes, of course, forgive me. I do get a bit carried away with the excitement of good research, you know. There is nothing quite like opening a tome in a venerable library, breathing in the rich scent of an ancient book, the accumulation of centuries of wear and tear, and the accompanying energy of knowledge that has been deposited into it. Why it reminds me of the time when—"

"Um, sir?"

"Yes, yes, sorry, I was spirited off again by the thrill of scholarship. My apologies. Aoibheall, or Aeval, is indeed a keening woman, a wailer, a ben síde, or banshee, if you will. She is among the eldest of her kind and very powerful. Though seen by some as a protector, her true motives throughout history remain somewhat occluded."

Jilly shifted about, anxious for him to get to the point. "What does that all mean?"

"Her allegiances are unclear. She has seemed both good and evil at various times, but on balance, she exudes a strong sense of amoral self-interest. In short, she wants what she wants, when she wants it, with little concern for the consequences, or the effect on others."

"So, what does she want with Chantz… Moirin?"

"I don't know. It could be that the young lady's vocal talents are useful to the creature, for reasons that we have not yet ascertained. She seems to be hovering around her and manifesting her eldritch magic through Moirin's voice when it pleases her."

"Do you think Moirin knows about her? I mean, who she is?"

"Doubtful. It seems to me that the banshee wishes to keep her true motives hidden, even while revealing herself. Perhaps she's told Moirin that she is a supernatural benefactor, or some such lie."

"So, this banshee comes and goes as she pleases, and might be using Moirin for something that's not good for her, or any of us?"

"That seems a reasonable hypothesis."

"So, how do we get rid of her? Can we even do that?"

"That, my dear, remains to be seen."

Jilly opened her laptop to look for more on their mysterious nemesis, but something stirred her to check her email instead.

"Oh! Sir!"

"What? What is it? Has that confounded technology finally collapsed in on itself? Oh, that will be the happiest of days!"

"No, I just got an email from Star Tao! I'm glad I texted him."

"Ah! Splendid! Fine young lad. The very best!"

"Well, it turns out he's on his way up north and wants to stop by and visit. Oh, this is brilliant! I've missed him."

"As have I. A good fellow, despite his shortcomings and that dreadful hair. When does he arrive?"

"He says later today. I hope Qwyrk stops by, too! We'll all be together again!"

Blip nodded. "An experience most satisfying, methinks! However, I may be a bit late to the reunion, as I have matters to attend to presently."

Jilly eyed him with suspicion. "Where are you going these days? You seem terribly busy."

"Nothing you need concern yourself with, my dear. All mundane affairs, I assure you."

But for some reason, Jilly didn't believe him.

* * *

"That was really satisfying, delicious, I have to admit," Qwyrk said, polishing off her fifth samosa and third plate of chana masala. *That's more than enough.*

"You see? I told you!" Vishala said triumphantly, looking confident that she had won over a convert to her culinary masterpieces. "There is no need for this 'not eating' that you do. A silly trend."

"It's not a trend, I promise," Qwyrk countered. "Shadows don't need to eat. It's just the way we're made."

"What a ridiculous situation!" Vishala shook her head.

"Mother!" Holly looked exasperated and a bit embarrassed.

"How could you go through the long years of your lives and not enjoy one of the greatest pleasures there is?" Vishala protested. "It makes no sense! Whatever god or goddess decreed this nonsense, I would like to have words with him, or her. Many words. And make them try my chana masala."

"I don't think anyone knows why, it just is," Qwyrk said with a shrug.

"No matter," Vishala said. "You will come here and partake of proper nourishment, at least once a week. And you and my beti will train, harder than ever. I sense danger since the return of that vile Erlking, and you must be ready should another menace arise."

"Honestly, I have no problem with that." Qwyrk looked to Holly. "If that's good with you?"

"I'd relish the chance to knock you on your arse on a regular basis!" Holly taunted with a grin.

"Language, beti!" Vishala reprimanded.

Holly rolled her eyes. "On that note, we should probably get going."

"Right," Qwyrk said with a nod. "We did tell Jilly we'd stop by at some point. If you'll excuse us, and thank you again." She stood up and bowed. "It was a delight to meet you and dine with you."

Vishala gave her a slight nod in response, but her expression remained blank. "It was agreeable to meet you, Qwyrk of the Shadows. I believe you have potential, both as a warrior, and for my daughter."

Agreeable? Potential? Qwyrk could think of nothing worthwhile to say in response, so she just nodded again.

Vishala and Holly embraced and exchanged pecks on the cheeks.

"Beti."

"Mother."

Qwyrk found it all rather cold and formal but knew it wasn't her place to say anything, at least not here. With another farewell, the two of them returned to the entrance chamber.

As they made for the front door, a thinner and slinkier tabby sauntered toward them, his pretty, pointy face hinting at some sort of dissatisfaction.

"Hello, Minty, how have you been keeping yourself?" Holly said, but gave Qwyrk a "wait for it" look.

"Appalling," Minty answered with an exaggerated sigh, a roll of his eyes, and one paw going to his forehead.

"Oh you poor thing," Holly quipped. "It must be ever so dreadful for you here, living in the lap of luxury, getting fed the finest foods, sleeping all day, never wanting for anything." She leaned into Qwyrk and whispered in her ear. "We have this conversation several times a week."

Qwyrk bit back a smile.

"It's far worse than usual, thank you very much," Minty declared. "Everything that could possibly go wrong does so, with alarming frequency. Just this morning, a door was closed. A door! It was blocking my way to the sitting room. It took nearly ten minutes of pleading with the lady of the house for her to open it."

"It does sound rather appalling." Holly nodded.

"Indeed, it was. I'll have you know that because of this and many other similar predicaments, I've been moved to compose a series of songs about my ongoing plight."

"Songs?" Holly raised an eyebrow.

"Yes, I foresee a Broadway show as a distinct possibility. It's all coming along quite nicely!"

"Is it, now?"

"Indeed. It will serve as a rallying cry for oppressed felines across all the worlds. The story of one cat's triumph over the depths of despair and deprivation. I shall call it: 'Minty: the Musical.'"

Holly shrugged. "An inspiring title, I suppose?"

"It is. Shall I sing you an aria from it? It features a melodic theme that recurs throughout the program. It's quite poignant."

"Um... tempting, and I'm sure it's artistically sumptuous, but we should probably be on our way. Perhaps some other time?"

"Oh, it won't take long." He raised himself up on his hind legs and cleared his throat. Thankfully without producing a hairball.

"Uh..." Holly gave Qwyrk an apologetic glance. But it was too late to escape, and so he began:

"Da dum, dum dum,
Everything is terrible | Everything is horrible
Everything's detestable | And everything sucks."

"Charming, but we do need to get on..."

"Everything is miserable | Everything's despicable
Everything is execrable | And everything sucks..."

"Really, we should go..."

"It's the worst thing ever | the door is closed right now..."

"I'm so terribly sorry we can't stay longer..."

"I have no clue of what I'll do | and I just want to meow—here comes the big modulation up a half-step—MEOWWWWW!"

"Gorgeous, really. You have a true gift. Or something..."

"It's incomprehensible | And it's reprehensible..."

"Sorry, someone's calling to me on my ring and I do have to run. Ta for now, darling, I'll see you soon." And with that, she grabbed Qwyrk by the hand and fairly ran from the scene.

"An artist is never appreciated in his own time," Minty called out as they fled to less obnoxious environs. "You'll see; there are Tonys and Oliviers in my future!"

"Well, Tunas and olive oils, perhaps," Holly said as they dashed outside. She located a tree and bounced them back to Qwyrk's home in haste.

"Nice save," Qwyrk said with a smile. "I'm not sure how much more of that I could stand."

"My pleasure. To say he's a bit dramatic is putting it mildly. I wasn't lying, though," Holly answered. "Someone really is calling me."

"Who is it? Not me, obviously."

Holly closed her eyes and placed her other hand over the ring. "It's Adjua."

Qwyrk tensed. "Look, 1 know we agreed it was the right thing to do, letting her contact you and all, but we still have to be careful here. We can't be at random humans' beck and call whenever they need us for something."

"1 know," Holly said with a nod. "But she's hardly random, and she doesn't strike me as the kind to make frivolous calls, especially after what almost happened to Ashanti."

"You're right," Qwyrk conceded. "Fair enough, let's go see what she wants. But 1 have a bad feeling that we're not going to be happy about it."

CHAPTER TWELVE

Moirin wandered the countryside around the farm, reveling in being out in the open, away from civilization, and even better, away from people. She'd turned her phone off to avoid Sam or anyone else, and just let herself be in the moment.

"I should have done this ages ago," she said, reaching the summit of a hill that afforded some spectacular views over the area: green knolls dotted with trees, dry stone walls that somehow didn't fall over (she'd never understood how that worked), a few sheep going about their business, the smell of earth and air and flowers and probably some sheep deposits. It was all idyllic and perfect. Even the sheep deposits.

"If only all those fans from last night could see me now, all country girl, basking in the sunlight; I'd lose my morbid cred straight away!" She laughed, something that seemed harder to do these days.

"Whatever the hell's happening can wait. This is all I need right now."

She found herself once again holding the pendant, and feeling guilty for pushing Aileen away last night and storming off, but it was the right thing to do.

"She'd never understand any of this. And it's a damned good thing she didn't see those zombie bird crows, or the elf lady." She shook her head. "Anyway, I don't need some fangirl... fangirling over me. It's bad enough that Sam's been making eyes at me lately. How do I tell him that I'm not interested in him? Maybe I'm just a freak."

"No, you are focused." The voice returned.

"Oh, for crap's sake, not you again!" The creepy woman was the last thing Moirin wanted to hear.

"You don't need them, any of them. You are different, you are strong, you are better."

"Look," Moirin said, making fists in anger, "just because I'm still figuring myself out doesn't mean I don't need friends, all right? I just want them to like me for *me* and not for what they think I can give them."

"But they will never like you just for you, my darling. They will hate you for it when they come to realize what you really are."

"And what am I, really? Huh?" Moirin demanded. "A singer with super powers? A stark raving loony who talks to voices in her head? A victim of undead crows who chats with elves? I'm starting to think that me being mad is the only sensible answer!"

"Oh, but you are mad: mad to discover your real nature, to learn of your true life."

"Fine, so what is that life? Who am I? Who are you?"

There was no reply.

"Answer me, damn it! Arrrghgh!"

She kicked at the ground, stomping and punching her arms in the air.

"I hate you!" she shouted. "I hate all of this! Whatever it is you think I am, I don't want it, any of it! Just leave me the hell alone!"

For a moment, she thought she heard a faint sound of laughter, mingled with the wind, but then it was gone. She was alone again with no more answers than before.

*　*　*

"Thank you for answering my call," Adjua said as she opened her front door. "I hope I did not intrude."

"Not at all," Holly answered.

Qwyrk suppressed a smile. *Saved us from the cat opera.*

Adjua motioned to them. "Please, come in."

They entered, and she led them to her front room, where they both took seats on her sofa.

"May I offer you coffee? Tea? Chocolate?"

"Ooh, chocolate does sound lovely, especially after all those samosas." Holly winked at Qwyrk, who did her best to ignore her. "But we're fine, thank you."

"So, what can we help you with?" Qwyrk asked, deciding this sounded less rude than "Why did you call us?"

"The protections are working, I hope?" Holly added.

Adjua nodded. "Yes, thank you again. I'm keeping Ashanti home from school for a few days, just to be sure. She is upstairs having a nap right now. All is well, but I saw something this morning that worried me."

Qwyrk leaned forward, now concerned. "Please, tell us."

"I wake up early most mornings, usually at half past five," Adjua continued.

Now that's just unrealistic, Qwyrk thought.

"I sit, I meditate, I commune with my ancestors, whatever

seems best. But this morning, I saw something alarming after I completed my morning devotions. I noticed two figures standing outside in the alley behind my home. They wore dark cloaks, but their clothing looked old, like centuries old, and it was rough, as if well worn. I did not want them to realize that I had seen them, so I stood back from the window, but I did get a good view of them."

"What did they look like?" Holly asked.

"Strange, not of this world. They were short, no taller than my shoulder, with yellow, bumpy skin on their faces, and they had pointed noses and ears. Their eyes unnerved me: all black, like a malevolent obsidian. They whispered to each other, and kept staring up at the window of Ashanti's bedroom. They scared me, so I prepared some defensive magic. They tried to come closer, but retreated at once, which tells me the protections work, thank Asase Ya. They seemed surprised, but they soon left and did not return."

"Sounds like kobolds," Qwyrk said without missing a beat. "Nasty little buggers who enjoy pranks more than anything else. Sometimes, though, one of them gets the idea that they really want to give being bad a go, and they can cause real headaches."

"But why are they here? What do they want with Ashanti?" Adjua looked distressed. Holly reached out and took hold of her hand.

"That's the real question, isn't it?" Qwyrk said. "And I'm sorry to say, I don't have an answer. Maybe whatever sent them also sent the buggane, but given how many factions of Darkfae there are, these two gits might represent someone else entirely."

"Are you sure they're kobolds and not some other creatures?" Holly asked, looking at both Qwyrk and Adjua.

"Did you notice anything else about them?" Qwyrk asked as a response.

"I went outside sometime later," Adjua said. I noticed an odor in the air, like burnt rubber and boiled cabbage."

"Yep, kobolds," Qwyrk answered with a definitive nod.

"But why would they, and the buggane, be interested in Ashanti? Even if she has the gifts you say she has?" Holly asked. "A seven-year-old girl can't possibly be of any use to them. Most young mortals with magical gifts don't start coming into them until they're adolescents, or nearly so." She looked at Qwyrk. "Like Jilly and Lluck."

Qwyrk nodded. "Yeah, that's odd. Look, we'll to try to find out what's going on. Keep her close to you for a few days, all right? Nothing's going to get in here, and she should be safe enough outside, as long as she's with you. Darkfae don't like being out in the daytime; they hate being seen, and they probably won't try anything stupid."

"I will do as you ask." Adjua nodded. "Thank you."

"Our pleasure," Holly said as they rose to leave. "Please call on me any time. If there's any worry at all. We'll come to you as soon as we can."

Qwyrk nodded. "This is important. If anything else decides to hold a stake-out near your house, contact us right away."

"Before you go," Adjua said, "take this." She handed Qwyrk a small, dark, wooden dowel with a face carved on it.

"What is it?" Qwyrk asked, turning it round and looking it over.

"An abosom wand. Give it to your young friend, the one you would have meet my daughter. I had a seer-dream last night, and I presented it to her, though I have not yet seen her in the wakening world." She proceeded to describe Jilly's appearance so well that Qwyrk was unnerved.

"What does it do?" Holly asked, taking it from Qwyrk and also giving it a look-over.

"In the right hands, it will turn back the power of an adversary against them. But only once."

"How?"

"The rightful user will know."

"And Jilly is the rightful user?"

"My dream says so."

"Then we'll trust your judgement, thank you," Holly said, handing it back to Qwyrk.

They made their farewells, and Qwyrk sped them back to her home.

*　*　*

"I don't understand what they want with her, those kobolds," Holly said, as they once again flopped down on Qwyrk's couch.

"Yeah, it's odd." Qwyrk tried to make sense of it. "Ashanti might be useful to them when she's older, like Jilly or Lluck, but the only other thing that kobolds are really into is changelings, you know, swapping out human babies with imperfect copies."

"That's utterly horrid!" Holly grew angry. "Do they still do that?"

"How do you think the world keeps getting so many awful politicians, billionaires, and tech CEOs? But interest in a girl who's in between being a baby and a teenager? That's really strange. I just don't... hang on. Hang on one minute!" She snapped her fingers for dramatic effect as an idea took shape.

"What? What is it?"

Qwyrk shook her head. "It's not about Ashanti, but something just clicked in my head. Moirin can't remember anything earlier in her life than from around two years ago. She couldn't even tell me the most basic information about her family or where she came from. This is kind of a wild guess, but what if those kobolds did the baby swap thing with her?"

"What are you saying? You think she's a changeling?"

"No, no, I think she might have been the human baby, and something stole her away from her family, kept her for years. And now somehow she's gotten free of it, but can't remember what happened. She wouldn't know anything about her real family, and maybe even her memory of her other life with her captors has been messed with."

"All right, but what about her power? And the keening woman that seems to be attached to her?"

"That's just it. What if she's human, but special? What if these creeps abducted her years ago because they knew she was important somehow and they wanted to take her before whatever is special about her finally bloomed? Like, before the whole keening woman business happened? Maybe they wanted to use her for some other purpose."

"It's an intriguing theory, but it doesn't tell us why they were at Adjua's this morning. Assuming it is the same creatures."

"It's a long shot, but if it *is* the same ones, maybe they're eying up Ashanti as a possible replacement, you know, in case they can't get Moirin back? Maybe they need a magical mortal for something?"

"That is quite the stretch. But if I've learned anything in my time with you, it's also crazy enough that it might be true."

Qwyrk stood up. "I like this idea. Well, I don't *like* any of it, but you know what I mean. It feels like at least a few puzzle pieces could fit in the right place. I think we should check in with Jilly and Blip, see if they've learned anything else, any more about Moirin, or who the red-haired girl is."

Holly stood, and reached out to stroke Qwyrk's arm. "I'd love to, darling, but I promised Lluck that I'd pop by to see him this afternoon. I'm really trying to keep my promises to him."

"No, of course, it's fine." Qwyrk wanted to be especially reassuring and supportive after their previous tension. "I'll take you there now, before I pop on back to Knettles."

"That's very kind, thank you."

"Not at all. Just let me know if you want another thrilling ride on the Qwyrk highway afterward. Right, that... came out decidedly more naughty than I intended."

"Sounds quite enticing, honestly." Holly sidled up next to her. "Something to look forward to!"

Qwyrk nuzzled her cheek as she whisked them away to Leeds in a shower of violet radiance.

✳ ✳ ✳

After dropping off Holly at her son's home, Qwyrk headed back to Knettles and into Jilly's living room to be met with a surprise, though she couldn't decide if it was a welcome one, or not. Star Tao was sitting on the couch, holding a mug of tea. He looked the same as always—scraggly beard, long brown hair in plats, neo-hippy clothing—and he likely smelled of patchouli, too.

"Wow, um, hey there. All right, mate?" she said. "Didn't know you'd be in town."

"All right, Qwyrk!" He stood up to hug her, an embrace she made sure was brief. She caught the full-on scent. *Yep, still patchouli.*

"Yeah, well, I wanted it to be a bit of a surprise," he said, sitting back down and taking his tea in hand once again. "I let Jilly know earlier, to make sure it was a good time to pop by, but I thought I'd keep it a secret otherwise, you know, just for fun."

"And what fun it is!" Qwyrk fake-smiled.

"Now that you're both here," Jilly said, "I need to step out. I'll be back in a minute or two. Granny emailed me and told me she's left something for me on her back porch. I have a key to the gate, so I'll just go in and get it." With that, she dashed out her front door.

"So," Star Tao said, holding up his hands as if in prayer, "will the Divine Lord Blippingstone be gracing us with his holy presence this afternoon? I know that I've fallen short in my duties as a devoted servant, so I'd like to apologize in person and see what penance he would have me do."

"Um... honestly? I don't know." Qwyrk held back from shuddering, just barely. "He's really busy right now, apparently. No idea doing what, though. He seems more occupied than usual these days. I don't see him much." *Thank Goddess for that.*

"Yeah well, a god's work is never done, I suppose," Star Tao lowered his arms. "We mustn't place too many demands on those of the higher celestial order, those who bestow their blessings upon us and give our lives meaning. It's not for us to question their ways."

"Uh, yeah, something like that..."

"Anyway, how's the Mrs.?"

"What? Not you, too. Oh, good flipping Goddess on a baked baguette, we're nowhere near that stage! And she's fine, thank you for asking."

"Well, it's just a matter of time, I reckon."

"A matter of time until what?" Qwyrk glared.

"You know... you and her, Mrs. and Mrs. It's brilliant, by the way. You two seem really right for each other."

Qwyrk's mood softened, and she even smiled a little. "Yeah, we are, actually. Cheers for noticing. So, what brings you to town this time?" She was not entirely sure she wanted to know the answer, but she wanted to change the subject to something less personal.

"Right, well I've got an incredible opportunity to do a new weekend-long workshop in Edinburgh, right? Twenty-seven seekers have already signed on for it! Amazing, innit? I'm driving on up, and Freedom Rainbow's joining me there..."

"Freedom Rainbow? Oh, right. That." Qwyrk had a headache thinking about her friend Qwypp's newfound New-Age identity, or rather, just what the hell she was doing dating this (admittedly likeable) weirdo, and participating in his cringe-worthy odes to enlightenment.

"Well yeah, that's her professional name and all, but don't worry, we still call her Qwypp behind the scenes. I think Qwykk's tagging along this time, too, but we don't have an alternative name for her yet. If you happen to think up something, let me know, eh?"

"How about: 'Sweet-but-dim-who-dances-with-pillocks?'" Qwyrk muttered to herself.

"What?"

"Nothing, never mind. Are they here with you, by any chance? I'd actually love to see them." Qwyrk couldn't believe her words, but she did miss them. "We've been best mates for ages, but we've drifted apart lately. It's all this saving the world nonsense, I suppose." *And Holly, of course.*

"Nah, they said they'll meet me up there. They're still hopping around Majorca or Ibiza or some place at the moment."

"Of course they are."

"But yeah, Qwypp talks about you, and says she keeps meaning to pop by and have a good chat and catch-up. I think she's also been right busy lately, what with policing bad faeries and the like. Sounds right mental to me."

"It's that time of year." Qwyrk nodded. "Trust me, it's a bit of a nightmare."

"Fair enough. Anyway," he said, clasping his hands together, "we have a new collaborative spiritual program we've put together that explores all kinds of eastern energies. We're giving it the first go up there. Sort of a test run, really."

"Eastern energies. So what, like power stations out by Hull?"

"You're a good laugh," Star Tao chuckled.

"See, I think so," Qwyrk said with a wave of her hands. "You'd be amazed at how many people fail to realize what a smashing wit I have."

"Actually, we're gonna be working with the wisdom of Asia, especially the feminine forces, which seems like a good idea since Freedom's taking the lead on this one," he elaborated. "It's going to be all about Shakti and the divine feminine, which I think is brilliant. We have a whole range of Shaktivities lined up for participants on both days."

"Shaktivities?"

"Yeah, groovy name, eh? Freedom came up with it. It's mainly meditations and chanting and so on, but it's got quite a ring to it, don't you think?"

"Kind of like tinnitus," Qwyrk mumbled.

"What?"

"Nothing, nothing, just clearing my throat. So." She knew she was going to regret asking. "What sorts of classes do you have planned?" She expected him to thrust a flyer toward her with a whole list of the weekend's inspirational idiocies, all thoughtfully laid out in a rigid timeline, commencing at 6:37 am, or some such horrifically early hour, and offering a smorgasbord of the spiritually silly for the cosmically confused.

"Well, we're trying something a bit different this time," he said, and she didn't know whether to be relieved or a bit disappointed.

"We're calling the workshop 'Shaktivate Your Life'!"

"Of course you are." She braced herself

"See, instead of having a planned class structure," he went on, "we want it all to be a bit more loose, to let those energies flow where they will and see what rises up to the surface. Gives us a bit more freedom—heh, no pun intended. That being said, I do have a few topics I came up with that I want to make sure we cover. They'll be sort of mini-classes spread throughout the weekend, mostly on some of the common problems that can arise on the path, like: How do you Tao?; Dharma Drama, Darn It; Flakey Reiki: Sussing Out the Dodgy and the Dubious in Energy Healing; and Don't be a Meanie to your Kundalini. I really like that last one, actually."

"I don't doubt it." Qwyrk *really* wanted Jilly to return.

"Oh yeah," he went on. "Freedom's doing a special class on devotion to the yoni, which I reckon, you know, you might be a bit interested in?"

"Yeah... I'm kind of good with that one already at the moment, thanks anyway."

"Well, if you change your mind and want to drop by, you and your lady friend would be most welcome. You could even be our special guest speakers, if you want."

"Actually, I might tell Holly about it."

"Oh, right! Do you think she'd be interested in giving a talk? Being from the culture and all..."

Qwyrk suppressed a guffaw. "Not really, I just want to see the look on her face. Say, do you ever worry that maybe you're putting a few too many subjects into these workshops."

"Nah," he answered with confidence. "They're like spiritual smoothies."

"Spiritual... smoothies."

"Yeah, I like to toss everything I have into a blender, metaphorically speaking, and mix it all up into one big, cosmically nutritious and delicious meal that can be more easily digested."

"Yeah, maybe not the best metaphor, mate."

The front door opened and Jilly returned.

Thank Goddess. "Did you find what you were looking for?"

"I did, actually," Jilly said as she strode into the living room holding an old book, "and I think it's going to be useful. It's a one-volume encyclopedia of Irish legends and such. And Granny's left little sticky bookmarks on a bunch of pages, which I guess means she wants us to read those first."

"So what's going on now?" Star Tao asked. "Seems like every time I come round, there's some new bad supernatural hoosiewhatsit out there."

"You're right." Qwyrk narrowed her eyes at him. "Maybe... you're the one behind them all."

"Wait, what?" He looked confused.

"I'm kidding, mate," Qwyrk assured him. "Jilly, why don't you fill him in on the latest bizarro urban fantasy we find ourselves in, as it stands so far?"

She did, starting with her own weird experience at Leeds Uni and ending with the flock of undead birds flying about in York.

"Crikey," Star Tao said. "Things don't happen by halves around here, do they?"

"Yeah well," Qwyrk said, "we like to try out a new apocalypse every few months. You know, just to keep things interesting."

"Well, can stay around for a couple of days. Maybe I could reach out to the celestial otherworld for some help?"

Qwyrk was about to tell him not to bother in the politest way possible, but a glare from Jilly made her rethink her response. "Sure, why not? What have we got to lose?" *Except our dignity, any hope of being taken seriously, and our sanity.*

"Well, whatever Moirin is, the band's brilliant," Jilly offered up, once again excelling at changing the subject. She looked back at Star Tao. "Have you heard them?"

"No, sorry. I'm more of space rock fancier meself. My mate's in a group called Olmec Barnacles. They're super groovy. Made quite a name for themselves at the festivals. If you want, I'll play some of their music for you."

"I'd like that!" Jilly said eagerly. "And I'll introduce you to the Weasels."

"As enriching as this cultural exchange no doubt is," Blip said as he emerged from the living room wall, "we should probably focus on the matter at hand. Good to see you again, my boy, by the way."

"My lord!" Star Tao fell to his knees, hands touching the floor in worshipful supplication. Blip beamed.

Qwyrk face-palmed.

* * *

Moirin meandered down the side of the hill. Any hope of avoiding that miserable old woman seemed to be gone. But at least she could enjoy the bliss of no one else being around. No one outside of her head, anyway.

"Hello there!" a man's voice sounded in the distance.

"Crap."

George, the farm's owner, came wandering up the path toward her.

"Hi," she said with the fakest smile she could fake.

"Settlin' in all right, are ya?"

"I think so, yeah. Just wanted to get my bearings and see the area. Lovely view back up there." She pointed to where she'd been, but said nothing about the argument she'd just had with her own mind.

"Aye, it is indeed. I'm just out for a short stroll mi'sen, before headin' back down to finish up chores for the day. But ey up on thy way down, luv. The path gets a bit slippy in spots, what with the rain we've had and all."

"I'll keep that in mind, thanks." She hurried away, eager not to be drawn into an agonizing and long conversation consisting of small talk.

"Oh, by the way, there was a phone message for ya, just before I went out."

"Wait, someone phoned me here?" Was it Sam or one of the others? Why didn't he just ring her mobile if he needed to get in touch?

"Aye luv. I wrote it down for you. Left it taped to your door. Anyway, have a nice rest of yer afternoon, tarra!" And with that, he wandered on up the hill.

Moirin looked after him for a moment then turned and fairly ran back down to the farm, minding the "slippy" bits.

Taking off her muddy boots at the front door and dashing up the stairs, she found that yes indeed, a small piece of paper was folded over and taped to her bedroom door. Yanking it off, she opened it and read the handwriting aloud to herself: "Hey Moirin, hope you have a great time relaxing out there. Turns out I can be in Newcastle in a few days, so I'll be able to see your next gig. Hooray! Take care for now, and we'll chat soon. xx Aileen."

She folded the paper, now very confused. "How the hell did she know I was going to be here?"

*   *   *

Qwyrk cringed, as Star Tao seemed over the moon at the opportunity to bask in the presence of his god incarnate again.

"So, you're doing another of these instructional gatherings, are you?" Blip sat on the couch and polished his monocle.

"Yeah, I think everyone's going to have some real interesting and life-affirming Shaksperiences."

"I'm sorry, what?" Blip asked. "Am I to understand that this is a course about the works of the Bard of Avon? Now that could be most rousing and educational. Well done, young man, a much better choice of material than your previous offerings."

"Um, what?" Star Tao looked lost.

"You made a rather mundane play on words—good heavens, now *that* was quite the marvelous pun, I must say!" Blip beamed. "'Play'... on words! A pun within a pun, in fact!"

Qwyrk's face went to her palm. Again. And stayed there.

"You said something about 'Shakespeariences,'" Blip explained to his disciple, "which I presume was a deliberate attempt to incite humor through the use of a *bon mot* to entice the masses into attending your assemblage for a weekend of sixteenth-century literary and dramatic enrichment."

"Oh! No, my lord, it ain't about Bill..."

"I'm sorry, to whom are you referring?"

"Shakespeare! You know: William, Will, Willie, Bill?"

"Seems a tad irreverent, if you ask me."

"Well, anyway, the workshop's actually all about the great goddess Shakti, and working with her energy."

"A distinguished deity, to be sure," Blip said with haughty confirmation, "though I confess I've not met her. We divinities hold one another in mutual admiration, of course, regardless of personal acquaintance and affiliation. There are many to whom I've never been properly introduced, but I suppose that cannot be avoided, given our many duties. I can only hope to remedy that at some future point."

Qwyrk sighed into her palm. Or more like whimpered.

"But are you sure you wouldn't rather focus your attention on the energies of the *First Folio*?" Blip pressed.

"Nah, that's a bit outside my area of expertise, I'm afraid."

"A shame. You could make quite the impression." He cocked a slight smile. "*Shake* things up a bit, heh."

Qwyrk looked up from her face palm in semi-disbelief.

Blip grinned. "Bring in students from around the... *Globe*, ha ha!"

Qwyrk's eye twitched.

"However," Blip mercilessly continued, "we wouldn't want to *Mar* his name. That would be—wait for it—*low*. Ha, ha, ha!"

Qwyrk worried that her eyes might roll backwards and just stay there.

"Still, if you serve refreshments at such an assemblage, you must make them available in half-pints, pints, and... *quartos*! Bwa ha ha!" He slapped his knee.

Qwyrk wondered if it was possible to die from cringing. And he just wouldn't stop.

"After all—"

"Blip, will you stop being such a complete Coriolanus." Qwyrk had most decidedly had enough.

"Oh, how crudely clever and lewdly witty," Blip snorted.

"Yeah, well, at least one of us is," she answered.

"I'm just gonna stick with what I know, actually," Star Tao offered, diffusing their bickering. "And yeah, we will have food and drinks there. It's necessary for proper grounding after astral voyages and so on."

"Well then," Blip said, "Since your theme is Shakti, the real issue will be your cooking and preparation methods. To ghee, or not to ghee, that is the question! HA!"

"Oh, for crap's sake, what on earth is wrong with you?!" Qwyrk said. "For real, who the hell are you, and what have you done with Blip? Not that I mind if he's gone missing, by the way."

"Am I not entitled to make a jest or two on a topic of which I am fond?" Blip asked defiantly.

"Yeah, I suppose," Qwyrk said, "when you actually get around to making one, let us know, all right?"

"At least I'm trying to bring a small bit of levity to the situation, unlike you, who prefers to wallow in sarcasm and self-pity."

"Wallow in... are you bloody kidding me? Have you not seen how over-the-moon happy I've been since yesterday? I'm practically exploding with joy, damn it!"

"I've seen that you have been acting like a giggling tomfool, no doubt due to Ms. Vishala's presence and affections, and if she has the fortitude to tolerate you and make you the better for it, then more power to her, I suppose."

"Tolerate?"

"That's what I said, yes." He folded his arms in defiance.

"You know, I should smack you to the rail station and back."

"I'd like to see you try," Blip snorted, unfolding his arms, and standing up to assume his ridiculous martial arts crane pose, his monocle flying halfway across the room.

"Um, this is all interesting, as usual," Jilly interrupted, to no avail.

"Don't tempt me, you annoying amphibian," Qwyrk snapped, ignoring her.

"Oh, so that's how it is, is it, you pragging pea-witted pignut?" Blip shook one fist while still holding his pose, one foot raised in the air.

"What?"

"I'm still in Shakespearean mode. Just go along with it."

"Um," Jilly tried to interject, "maybe we could have a look at the book Granny left me? You know, and learn more about what we're facing, maybe help Moirin?" She held up the book, almost as if threatening to smack them both.

"A splendid notion, my dear," Blip said, dropping back to a standing position. "Anything to divert attention away from this humorless killjoy."

"Oh, you're a fine one to talk," Qwyrk growled.

"Qwyrk…" Jilly glared.

"All right, yes, I agree," Qwyrk said. "Let's see what she left for you." She wandered to the window. "I'll just be over here, being a joyless grump who needs to be tolerated, apparently."

"Far more than apparent, I would say," Blip snipped.

Qwyrk opened her mouth to fire off another insulting retort, but thought better of it, and stayed silent, lest she find herself dueling in a battle of absurd Elizabethan insults, which wouldn't even be the strangest thing that had happened in the last twenty-four hours.

"In any case," Blip said, "if we're done with the current riposte, I've some new information, which I suspect is echoed in Jilly's Granny's book. Er, that came out wrong, but you know what I mean. Jilly," he said, pointing up the stairs towards her room, "go fetch your computer contraption and show her these two the photographs."

"Photographs?" Qwyrk asked.

He turned back to her. "It's all rather distressing, I'm afraid."

CHAPTER THIRTEEN

Qwyrk examined the photos on Jilly's laptop with a mixture of interest and concern. "So, the thing that's latched itself onto Moirin is actually showing up in photographs of her? That's not going to do her public image any good!"

"We think she may only be visible because Holly took the photos, and I'm magical," Jilly offered as an explanation. "But who knows?"

"Or, it could simply be that the banshee is getting braver," Blip added.

"All right, so who is she?" Qwyrk asked.

"I believe her name is Aeval, which may be derived from the proto-Celtic 'Oibel-ā,' which means 'burning fire.' Tradition ascribes that she was something of a protector for the Dalcassians of Munster in Ireland, and—"

"I'm not bothered about all that right now." Qwyrk mercifully cut him off. "What's so special about her?"

"I believe she is among the first of her kind. That makes her exceedingly powerful, and exceptionally dangerous. It's no wonder her image is bleeding through in those photographs. It's possible that the poor young lady is channeling her spirit, even if unintentionally."

"Except, it ain't the same, is it?" Star Tao interjected.

"What do you mean?" Jilly asked.

"Well, like with channeling, you're a conduit of the entity, right, but once you've done the work, or whatever you set out to do, it buggers off. That's the usual agreement. But this is different. That scary lady is renting permanent accommodation in Moirin's mind, just usin' her instead of cooperating. I guess the less nice way of putting it is, this is more like a possession."

"So, we've got to find a way to get her out of Moirin," Jilly said.

"It might not be so simple," Blip said. "I fear that the young lady is not a random target, rather that she was chosen for a reason, though what that could be I cannot yet say."

"Let's look at Granny's book," Jilly said. She picked it up and opened to one of the marked pages. As she skimmed through the flagged entry, a chill went down her back. "Oh, this isn't good. Like, not good at all."

"What is it?" Qwyrk asked.

"It's about those horrid bird things last night. You didn't get rid of them, Qwyrk. They'll be back, even more of them, and they'll keep coming until they get what they want."

"And what do they want? To kill Moirin?"

"No, I think they want to take her away from this world and back to wherever they came from, like forever."

* * *

"Should I phone her? Text her? Send smoke signals? Call the police?"

Moirin sat on the edge of her bed, looking at Aileen's message for the umpteenth time and turning over events in her head, like she'd done for every bit of weirdness that had recently stopped by and introduced itself in a not-so-welcome manner.

"There's no way she could've known I'd be here. I only told the band, but really just Sam. This is nuts. It makes no sense. She's spyin' on me. But how? Who is she? What does she want?"

She stood and paced about the room, which somehow made her feel less helpless, less useless. Until it didn't.

"Sod it, I'm going for another walk."

Grabbing her small handbag, she left her room and decided to wander off in the opposite direction of her previous sojourn, figuring there was enough countryside out there that she couldn't possibly have exhausted it all yet. And with sunset still awhile away, she needn't worry about getting lost. Also, lots of greenery and no people. And with luck, no voice in her head, either.

* * *

"So what are those damned birds, really?" Qwyrk pressed, ever more concerned.

"It says they're called, um, Sluagh? I'm not sure how to pronounce it." Jilly looked over the entry in Granny's book again.

"Allow me," Blip said, striding up to her side to have a look. "Ah, yes, you should say it as 'SLOO-ahgh,' with an emphasis on the first syllable, and the 'gh' forming a soft sound at the back of the throat, rather like the Parisian 'r' in proper French, an important sound not often heard in the English language, but common in Celtic languages—"

"Yes, thank you, Blip," Qwyrk said, heading him off at the linguistic pass. "Go on, Jilly."

"This says they're the spirits of the hateful and vengeful who can't rest in death. No place in the afterlife will accept them, so they roam the world at night in packs in the form of decaying birds, and try to capture people, or at least their souls. They can also be caught and made to do the bidding of others."

"Which is exactly what we saw last night," Qwyrk pointed out. "Someone sent those creatures after Moirin."

"Do you think it was the banshee, this Aeval person?" Jilly asked.

"Aeval is not a person, my dear," Blip corrected. "She is more like a force of nature, and not a pleasant one. But no, I don't think she is behind the Sluagh attack."

"It doesn't make sense that Aeval would send these spirits for Moirin, when she's already 'possessing' her, anyway." Qwyrk hated agreeing with Blip, and seeing that Star Tao was right. But she conceded the point, just this once, and only to herself.

"So, we can assume that someone else may be after the girl," Blip said. "There is a magical tug-of-war going on to which we are not yet privy."

Qwyrk nodded. "I think I saw some of those birds in the Erlking's hordes back in December, so I'm guessing more than one faction uses them. Obviously, there's more to Moirin that meets the eye." She explained her theory about what might be happening, the kobolds showing up at Adjua's house that morning, and how they might have held Moirin against her will if she was a changeling child.

"Oh, Qwyrk, how awful." Jilly looked horrified. "She's so nice and talented, and if that's true, we have to help her!"

"We will, I promise," Qwyrk assured Jilly with a comforting hand on her shoulder.

"How?"

"I don't know yet, but that's what we do isn't it? We figure things out. Sometimes at the last minute."

"According to the book," Blip said, having taken it from Jilly to read further, "these bird creatures are fairly relentless, and will not stop until they have achieved the goal set for them, which, we may presume, is the apprehension of Ms. Moeran. That being the case, it is safe to assume that they will return for her at or after sunset again tonight. Do we know her current whereabouts?"

"Isn't she still in York?" Qwyrk asked. "Can we find out where the band is staying? They might be there for another night."

"I think she said they were off to Newcastle for their next show," Jilly remembered, "but I'm not sure when it is. I can look it up." She picked up her laptop and searched for a moment. "Not until the day after tomorrow, so they could literally be anywhere between York and Newcastle until then."

"I could, maybe, you know, reach out to the cosmic multiweb," Star Tao said in a quiet voice, as if he knew what Qwyrk's reaction would be, "and see if I can find out." He was right. She gritted her teeth, but held her tongue.

"Maybe I could just email her and ask?" Jilly said. "I could say that a friend wants to come see the show up here, and just sort of happen to ask, 'Hey, where are you now?' or something."

"It's worth a shot." Qwyrk nodded, eager for anything that didn't involve having to talk to Star Tao's loopy channeling buddies on the other side, or wherever the blazes they came from. If they were even real. And she was sort of worried that they were.

"Right, I'm on it!" Jilly set herself to typing a message. When she was finished, she looked up with a triumphant smile. "Done! I can't believe I can just write to her like that! So, now what?"

"We'll have to wait and see if she gets back to you, I suppose," Qwyrk said. "Yep, just sit around and do nothing. Won't that be brilliant?"

"But hey, at least we're all here!" Star Tao offered. "That's pretty groovy. It's been a while, but the team's back together again!"

The team... bloody hell. But Qwyrk kept her thoughts to herself, knowing how Jilly liked having him around.

"A splendid observation, young man," Blip said. "We have accomplished much in our time, we few, tasted splendid victory and bitter defeat, we happy few, we band of brothers—and sisters, of course—and gentlemen in England now a-bed shall think themselves accursed they were not here—"

"Blip, just can the Shakespeare, all right?" Qwyrk snapped.

"Well excuse me for trying to muster up some enthusiasm, boost morale, and infuse the proceedings with a smattering of culture!" Blip folded his arms and sulked.

"Ooh, she just sent me a reply! That was quick!" Jilly snatched up her phone at the sound of a new text.

"Well?" Blip said, not sounding impressed, and mired in his sulk.

"'Dear Jilly, thanks for your message. It was nice to meet you, too. Yeah, we're playing in Newcastle next, and it would be brilliant if you could tell any friends up there about us. In the meantime, I'm taking a little break at Fogram Farm in the Dales. Just getting some fresh air and peace and quiet. Hope all's well with you. Love, Moirin.'"

"Well, it's helpful that she gave us her location," Qwyrk said. "Now we just need to find this place on a map so I can get a fix on it, and we can stake it out and keep watch."

"Excuse me," Blip said, "do you mean sitting out in the elements, possibly for hours, waiting for a supernatural attack that we are ill-prepared to face, one that may not even happen?"

"Yes, exactly!" Qwyrk said. It'll be fun. Where's your sense of adventure, Blip?"

"I'd much rather have the adventure of a fine glass of Armagnac while being soothed by Purcell's *Trio Sonatas*, thank you very much."

"What?" Qwyrk fairly oozed sarcasm. "Mr. Blippingstone, international jirry-jirry of mystery, master martial artist, and self-styled sleuth, can't handle the high-stakes assignment of sitting out at a lonely farm in the Dales? Are the cows armed with throwing stars? Are there ninja sheep hiding in the darkness? Are pig double agents in trench coats waiting to betray you at any moment? The danger is non-stop!"

"I see you're still undertaking the same un-funny excursion you've been on for the last few days."

"Just never missing a chance to wind you up," Qwyrk needled. "Anyway, we'll bring Holly, too, and I'll ask around about how we can gain an advantage over these things."

"You may not have to," Jilly said, recovering the book from Blip and thumbing through it to Granny's marked entries. "It says here that the Sluagh are fearsome, but not invulnerable."

"Well, I know that; I kicked some of their feathered arses in York, quite literally. Sent them packing," Qwyrk said with a bit of pride.

"Yes, but you only chased them off for a bit. They'll keep coming back. It says here that to send them away forever, we can use weapons made of iron."

"Those would be kind of heavy," Qwyrk said, "and wouldn't they be dangerous to Holly?"

"Oh no, that's just a silly story someone dreamed up," Blip said, one froggy finger extended as if preparing a lecture. "Thus faeries could hide their presence among humans when circumstances dictated. If they could be seen wielding iron, they obviously weren't Fae. A clever ruse."

"So clever that I didn't even know about it," Qwyrk said.

Jilly scanned another page. "Oh, brilliant! There's a banishment spell right here! If I can get these ingredients together, we might be able to send the Sluagh away for good!"

"What do you need?"

"Dragon's Blood incense, an iron horseshoe at least a hundred years old, a raven feather, some dirt from Avebury, and an oak leaf... from Sherwood Forest. Oh come on!" Jilly's face fell.

"I actually might have most of those things in my van." Star Tao perked up.

"Of course you might," Qwyrk said flatly.

"I'll go and check. Back in a mo!" He got up and dashed out the door.

"Does he really have all those things?" Jilly wondered.

"Nothing would surprise me, anymore. Do you really think this'll work?" Qwyrk asked her.

"Well, Granny left this book for me, so I trust she knows what she's doing."

"But how on earth would she know to mark out those particular pages in that particular book when she's not even here?" Blip posited.

"I kind of stopped worrying about stuff like that early on," Jilly said. "She's been around a long time, so I just go with it."

"It is quite fortuitous," Blip conceded.

"Well, we need all the help we can get," Qwyrk added. "I'm not going to worry about odd coincidences and convenient plot twists."

"It is almost as if there is a guiding hand in all this," Blip mused, "as if some author is actually writing this story, rather than we actually living it."

"Now that's just silly!" Qwyrk said.

"Be that as it may, Grandmother Boatford's assistance is always appreciated. Do you think you can concoct the enchantment, Ms. Pleeth?"

"I'll give it my best shot," she answered. "Looks like I need to put all those things together and speak the right words to create a magical powder. But we won't know for sure until we see those creatures again."

"Well, I suppose we must try," Blip admitted. "I suspect that young Ms. Moeran is not at fault here, and she needs whatever supernatural aid we can provide. Very well, off to the farm it is."

"Just keep an eye out for those samurai chickens," Qwyrk teased.

"Sorry, you're still not funny."

"Come on Blip, you could ride Snickerwocky into glory out there. I'd pay faery gold to see that!"

"Where is she, anyway?" Jilly asked. "You haven't mentioned her much since last winter."

"My dear mount has moved on to greener pastures," Blip answered.

"Oh, sir, I'm so sorry! I didn't know she'd passed away." Jilly put one hand on her chest.

"Hm? Oh, no. I mean, she's literally out in greener pastures, eating and lounging and enjoying a life of leisure, still resting on her laurels after her splendid performance during the battle against the Erlking."

"I'm just glad you moved her away from my home," Qwyrk said.

"Oh, you mean the home that absolutely nothing happened to because my dragon is well trained and respectable and would never have unleashed her flame upon it? That home?"

"Yes, Blip, *that* home. Anyway, I have enough problems with trees and rocks moving about near my house, anyway."

"Eh what?" Jilly looked lost.

Qwyrk sighed. She hadn't intended to bring up the unusual wanderings, but since she let it slip, she went ahead and told them about the foliage and strata that had been displacing themselves for the past few days.

"That's... really odd. What do you suppose is causing it?" Jilly asked.

"At the moment, I have no idea, and honestly, I'm not worrying about it as long as a fully grown oak tree doesn't pop up in my bedroom."

"Why do you have one?" Blip eyed her.

"What, an oak tree?"

"A bedroom, you gormless goof. You don't sleep, so what purpose could it serve?"

"Uh, I do like to have a place for nice, quiet Reverie, all right? Also, guests? It happens. Especially recently, and it's none of your bloody business, so can we talk about the wanderings around my home, instead?

"It is very curious, I grant you." Blip stroked his chin. "Such a phenomenon would imply that some magical disturbance has occurred somewhere else, that this is some kind of ripple effect."

"Hm, hadn't really thought of it like that," Qwyrk admitted.

"Has anyone else noticed?" Blip inquired.

"I haven't asked. I told Holly about it, but she's as baffled as me."

"What kind of magical disturbance?" Jilly said.

Blip shook his head. "It could be someone innocently fooling about. Perhaps some eccentric Shadow is trying to perfect a new spell or some such. There are more than a few of those." He glared at

Qwyrk. "However, we cannot rule out the possibility that something more nefarious is going on. An attempted attack, perhaps, or a test to see how well Symphinity's defenses are arrayed."

"That seems pretty far-fetched," Qwyrk said. "I mean, we're talking about a few inanimate objects wandering around."

"For now," Blip countered. "But we still don't have all the answers as to who else helped de Soulis. Perhaps there is more occurring than we know."

"Honestly, I'm not losing Reverie over it," Qwyrk said, "but I'll keep an eye on things. In the meantime, let's just focus on how to help Moirin."

"Got it all!" Star Tao said as he stepped back in to the living room and eagerly handed everything to Jilly.

"You really had all that crap just stored in your van?" Qwyrk was baffled.

"Yeah, well, you gotta be prepared for anything, don't you?" He seemed chuffed with himself.

"Thanks!" Jilly said. "It might take me a bit to put it together, but I think I can do it."

"Brilliant." Qwyrk rolled her eyes at Star Tao but was impressed at the same time. "Whenever you're ready, let's go visit a farm!"

* * *

Moirin wandered over hill and dale. She'd traveled a good distance from the farm and needed to head back soon, but the peace and quiet of the springtime Dales landscape was too appealing to abandon until the last possible moment. Also, no people. At some point, she made the reluctant decision to turn around and head back.

"Not a problem, I know the way. I think."

Looking about, she realized she hadn't been paying that much attention to her route on the outward journey, instead getting lost in her own thoughts about all the recent craziness.

"How the hell did Aileen know I'd be here? I'm not sure if I should be flattered or creeped out."

She reached the bottom of a hill and despaired as she looked up at the next one. "I wish I could just snap my fingers and be back. Why can't this magical shite in my head actually be useful?"

As she began the climb, she heard something in the distance, or rather, felt it, an odd sensation that she perceived more as being inside of her than outside. But it was definitely the latter, too.

"What the hell, now? Can I not just have one day when this craziness leaves me be?"

The sound of fluttering disrupted the quiet of the country air. Many flutterings, in fact. Just like...

"A flock of birds. A murder of undead crows. Great. So I'm gonna get pecked and clawed to death out in the middle of nowhere and probably not found for weeks. Pictures of my decaying corpse will be all over the nightly news, and I won't even get any benefit from it. Damn, this is a good idea for a song!"

The festering flock flew nearer, and for a moment, she had the thought just to give up and let them do with her as they would, but self-preservation and fear kicked in and she bolted up the side of the hill, gasping for breath by the time she reached the top. Turning in every direction, she at last caught sight of them, those infernal creatures from the night before.

She scrambled down the other side of said hill as fast as she dared and started into a full sprint at the bottom. She knew she couldn't outrun them, so she searched in desperation for a place to hide: a clump of trees, an old stone barn, something, anything. Scanning the darkening landscape in front of her, she saw a dry stone wall that might work, if she could get to it in time and hop over and hide behind it.

The malicious caws of the phantom birds pierced into earshot.

Ignoring the burning in her lungs, she reached the wall and scrambled over it, falling to the ground. Catching her breath, she closed her eyes and tried to focus on something inside her, anything that might connect her with her power. She even tried to reach out to the old woman again.

"Please," she heaved, "help me!"

The birds drew nearer. Nothing answered her call.

"Damn it!" She looked around, hoping for greater cover, but everything before her was just open land and another wall too far away to be of use. She started to panic, and tears filled her eyes. "I don't want to go, not like this. I know I joke about it, but this isn't fair. Please, gods, goddesses, if you're real, if anything is out there, please help me now."

The crows descended upon her, their eerie cackles and squawks stinging her ears. The wind kicked up all about her as they flew overhead. And so they circled around her as they'd done in York. She feared they were going to fly straight into the ground and drag her with them, never to be seen again.

They dove.

She screamed and covered her face with her arms.

This was it. This was her end.

She was at once aware of a bright purple flash nearby, of voices yelling. When she dared to open her eyes again, she saw the elf woman from last night with her model girlfriend in the thick of the creatures, slugging at them and fighting them off. In the distance was a girl; was it Jilly? She was doing something with two others, a hippy with plats and... a bullfrog walking upright?

"What the hell?"

* * *

"Argh! These things are so annoying!" Qwyrk swatted several of them away in one go.

Holly bashed the beasts left and right with her stick, which left trails of sparks and light. She swung her elegant weapon about her, connecting with some that were behind and out of her line of sight. Even in the midst of a good scrap, Qwyrk couldn't help but be impressed. For her part, Qwyrk kicked and punched, but this just sent the creatures fluttering away and coming back madder than ever.

"Jilly!" she called out. "How's that spell coming?"

"Working on it!" Jilly called back.

"Work faster!"

Qwyrk ducked down to avoid a swoop from a particularly enraged avian zombie and happened to glance over to Moirin, who was inching herself away from the chaos, back toward the stone wall. Good. She had no business being involved.

Qwyrk gasped as one of the creatures slammed into her and she grabbed for it, but it flew away too soon. No matter. She and Holly were keeping the things away from Moirin while Jilly worked on banishing them, so she'd suck it up and do the proverbial heavy lifting until her friend had the spell ready. Which really could be any time, now. Any time at all.

"Jilly?"

"Yeah, almost there!"

"Yuck!" Holly yelled. "They just keep coming!"

"Well, they're dead," Qwyrk shouted back. "It's not like they need to take a breather or anything." Another batch of corvid corpses swooped down on her and pecked at her head. "Ow! Jilly! Come on!"

"Got it!" Jilly yelled with excitement.

Qwyrk nodded to Holly and they fell back.

Jilly strode toward the flock. Qwyrk hated seeing her do this, but the needs of the moment outweighed her overprotectiveness. Qwyrk's heart raced as she watched the birds turn their attention to her young friend.

"Damn it!" She found Holly's free hand and gripped it. "This had better work."

The creatures regrouped and seemed to ignore Moirin, focusing their ill intent on Jilly, who held out her hands, palms up, as if making an offering. They flew right toward her, but that brave young lady didn't even flinch.

Qwyrk's admiration blended with a profound terror for her friend's safety.

As the first of the creatures opened their beaks to attack, Jilly blew into her palms and a red dust flew up and enveloped them. They screeched in a hideous cacophony of unearthly tones and began to dissolve away into nothingness.

"Yes!" Qwyrk cheered, pumping her fist. "She did it. She damned well did it!"

Jilly blew again, and a second burst of her power powder showered the next wave, with the same shimmering results. Those birds still farther away slowed their descent and hesitated, dead though they were.

"You've got them, Jilly!" Qwyrk shouted, elation taking her as she glanced over at a smiling Holly. "Keep giving them hell, keep—"

The birds in the back line flew up and into a new, denser

formation. As if acting as one, they formed a kind of phalanx and turned their attention back to their young foe. With a surprising swiftness, they launched themselves down toward her, catching her off guard. Jilly wavered, and in a moment of panic, put her hands up to cover her face, spilling what magic dust she had left all over the ground.

"No!" Qwyrk shouted.

She and Holly took off in an instant, racing to reach Jilly in time. She saw Blip do the same. But what if they couldn't get to her? What if they were too late?

* * *

Moirin pressed her back against the dry stone wall, watching in shock as Jilly dispersed the first wave of birds with what looked like some kind of powder. She couldn't understand how these freaks she'd met last night were here or how they did what they were doing.

"She really is some kind of elf."

Moirin was grateful to whatever deity had answered her plea, and wouldn't sit by and be rescued like some clichéd damsel in distress. "Feck that nonsense! If they're fighting these bastards, I'm gonna do it, too!"

She jumped up and started toward them, seeing that young Jilly had panicked and lost the rest of her magic powder. Clearly, things hadn't going according to plan. The elf lady and her companion sprinted toward the girl. The bullfrog also raced toward her and seemed to be... cursing in a posh accent?

"I can do this, I can help her, I can stop them!" she told herself as she also broke into a run. "They're not going to hurt her!"

Her mind went back inside of herself then, and she could feel it: the power, raw, unbound, untamed, hers to use in this moment. She took a few deep breaths and could see the creatures, as if watching a film, almost as if seeing them from their perspective.

"Come to me, flow through me, help me!" She muttered some other words in a language that might have been ancient Irish. Heat rose up from within her, but even as it concentrated in her throat, it felt far away. She opened her mouth and began a low-pitched hum. She saw nothing, but somehow she saw it all. Her voice rose in pitch and volume and the heat in her throat became so intense it should have burned her, but somehow, it didn't. It joined with her voice, now a high pitched wailing that erupted into the air. A beam of sound shot out from her throat and hit the creatures full force.

* * *

Qwyrk and Holly stopped short as an astonishing sight unfolded in front of them: Moirin dashed into the fray, arms open wide. Qwyrk had no idea what to do. She could only stare in astonishment as time seemed to slow down. Moirin came to an abrupt stop. Her eyes glazed over and became solid white as she thrust her arms forward. She opened her mouth and a blinding light shot forth from inside of it, followed by an unbearably loud scream. Qwyrk and the others clutched their ears in a desperate attempt to keep out the deafening noise.

Moirin's light expanded and struck the creatures as they hurled themselves toward Jilly. But they didn't just dissolve back to another plane. The force of her voice collided with them, incinerating them in the heat and light and sound that flowed through her. They screeched in agony and terror, if they could indeed feel those things. In an instant, every last one of them was gone, only waves of smoke and ash (and a few stray feathers) falling to the ground showed that they had ever been there at all.

~ 249 ~

Qwyrk looked to Holly and then the others in astonishment. Moirin buckled to her hands and knees and vomited. Qwyrk had no idea what just happened, or what would happen next.

CHAPTER FOURTEEN

As the smoke cleared and the light faded, Qwyrk got a better view of the scene. Red dust still trailed from Jilly's hands. Star Tao swayed back and forth in the distance. Holly brandished her stick, looking for any remaining creatures. Blip brushed feathers off of himself, cursing mildly.

Moirin stood up with some effort, gasping for breath. After a few more gulps, she looked up at all of them. "Are they gone? Are they dead?"

"Yeah," Qwyrk said, still in shock. "Yeah, I think they are. What you did... that was beyond amazing, by the way!"

"Astonishing, even," Blip said.

"Fine, thanks, whatever. But just who the hell *are* you people?" Moirin stammered, demanding anger in her tone.

"Um, we're the good guys, honest!" But Qwyrk didn't think she was making much of a case.

"The good guys?" Moirin looked them over, back and forth and forth and back as they drew near. "So, a not-elf, a faery from India, a girl-wizard-something, a talking bullfrog, and..." She looked at Star Tao again. "Whoever the hell you are."

"Oh, I'm a channeler," Star Tao answered as he ambled up to the rest of them, his swaying complete. "I'm plugged into the cosmic multi-web to receive communications from beyond the astral skies, and I'm a representative in good standing of the Council of 27."

"Of course you are." Moirin winced. "That's fits with how the last few days have gone. Oh, that and getting chased by a flock of scruffy, undead birds, who want to steal my soul. That's my life, now. Grand."

"You are, if I may, oversimplifying things," Blip countered, "however—"

"Blip," Qwyrk interrupted, then turned to Moirin. "Look, I know it all seems crazy. Honestly, I live in it and a lot of times, it's nuts to me too. But if you'll trust us, we can help you. Those birds, the Sluagh? They're not going to stop trying to get you. You destroyed this lot, but I'm guessing more will come."

"Yeah, I figured. I don't suppose if I asked them nicely, they'd bugger off for good?"

"Afraid not," Qwyrk said. "Sorry."

"So what do they want? Seems like someone's goin' to a lot of work to kill me."

"They're not trying to kill you," Jilly said, "they're trying to take you somewhere."

"Where?" Moirin asked.

"I don't know." Jilly shrugged, looking apologetic.

"But it's all right," Qwyrk added, "we can protect you until we figure out how to really get rid of them."

"And how're you gonna do that, not-elf lady?"

"I'm not a not-elf! I mean, I'm a Shadow! We're different."

"Real easy to confuse the two, looks like."

"No, it damned well isn't," Qwyrk countered, her defensiveness on the rise. "It's just a human perception thanks to endless fantasy novels and role-playing games, and it's one of the reasons I'm glad most people can't see us as we really are!"

"But she's a faery, right?" Moirin pointed to Holly. "The South Asian version. And that's just fine, apparently, but gods forbid that someone mistake *you* for an elf!"

"I'm a Yakshi, actually," Holly added, "though faery is close enough."

"I'll keep that in mind," Moirin said, "in case there's a pop quiz later."

"Look, this is really not important right now." Qwyrk fumed. "What *is* important, is that we get you out of here, and some place safe."

"Oh, and just where is that going to be, eh? Seems like I can't get away from those things. What are you going to do, hide me away in one of those secret military bases around here that everyone denies exists?"

"I think some of those are fronts for extraterrestrial star ports, actually," Star Tao said.

"Not now," Qwyrk sighed.

"Or, are we going on a trip to faery land, or maybe I'll get to see the marvelous city of the talking bullfrogs? That's always been a bucket list one for me." Moirin leaned into the sarcasm.

"Now just a minute, young lady." Blip pointed an angry finger at her.

"What *are* we going to do, Qwyrk?" Jilly asked, mercifully cutting him off.

"Not to worry." Qwyrk appreciated Jilly's well-timed verbal feint. "I've got the perfect solution." She reached out to Moirin. "Take my hand."

Moirin eyed her with suspicion. "Why?"

"Trust me," Qwyrk insisted. "There's one place where you'll be totally safe."

* * *

"Aaalooooooo!"

They all stood at the entrance to Qwyzz's castle of the curious, as a small shower of pebbles rained down on them.

"Are you certain this is the best idea?" Holly asked, brushing away some stony debris from her black leather jacket.

"Safest place of all, love," Qwyrk assured her. "We just have to get past the built-in guard-goyle up there, which shouldn't be too difficult."

"Are you sure? It was rather touch and go last time. I know I was quite intimidated." She winked at Qwyrk, which did nothing to alleviate her exasperation at knowing they faced an imminent lengthy interrogation.

"Well," Qwyrk said, "we're probably going to have to explain that we aren't really fifteenth-century Landsknechte mercenaries, or a mini-horde of Hunnish warriors, or some such."

"Much irritation will inevitably ensue," Holly agreed. "I look forward to being entertained by your efforts."

"Thanks for the support, love."

"Always."

"Who goes there?" a little stony voice called out.

"Gargula!" Qwyrk called back, "you know damned well who we are. We need to see Qwyzz right now, and if you don't go and fetch him, I'll make sure that Babewin hears about it and gets to have some fun thumping you. And I'll watch and laugh."

The miniature monument scowled and was quiet for a moment. "You know, you take all of zee fun out of being my master's guard."

"Yeah, apparently, I'm quite the killjoy." Qwyrk glared at Blip, who responded with a look of mock offense. "So, are we agreed?"

"Fine." The piffling creature scowled and scuttled away from view.

"Was that a—" Moirin started.

"Gargoyle?" Qwyrk finished the sentence. "Yeah, things just keep getting stranger, don't they? And that's not even the last of it."

Shortly thereafter, the main door opened. Qwyzz stood before them wearing another colorful robe from his endless collection, this one a vibrant violet velvet featuring medieval snails made of golden thread, meandering very slowly all over the garment.

"Oh ace," Moirin said. "So, a real wizard wearing a robe that's... alive."

"Told you." Qwyrk grinned and then turned to give Qwyzz a quick hug.

"What brings you here so urgently, my dear... oh. Oh?" He looked at Moirin.

"What? What?" She said looking around and then at the ground, as if trying to avoid his gaze.

"This is most unusual," Qwyzz continued.

"What?" Moirin blurted out again. "What's unusual?"

"Yeah, Qwyzz, what is it?" Qwyrk looked back and forth between them.

"You've brought me some extraordinary guests over the centuries, dear Qwyrk," he said, "but I can honestly say this is the first time you've brought me a mortal descended from the first banshee."

* * *

From far away in her cold and dim dwelling, she perceived, and she hated what she sensed.

"This must not happen, it *will* not! They will not take her. They will not rob me of my prize, not when I am so close!"

She closed her eyes and formulated her plan. "It will be risky, it will be painful. If the great one discovers it, I might be severely punished. But I must try. If my existence is forfeit, then at least she will be ready, and I will live on through her."

She prepared to attempt what for many of her folk was unthinkable.

* * *

"What do you mean, 'directly descended' from the first feckin' banshee?" Moirin demanded as they entered Qwyzz's abode and filtered into the sitting room. Her shock at the weird and wonderful goings-on in the sitting room made Qwyrk feel a bit bad for her. This was a lot for a young human to take in all at once, even someone like Moirin.

"It's true, my dear," Qwyzz assured her. "You have the air of the Fomorian about you."

"The For-what?" Moirin furrowed her brow and looked confused.

"Fomorians," Blip said. "Primal rulers of the Western Celtic lands, mainly Ireland. If the histories are to be believed, those were decidedly unpleasant times."

Qwyzz nodded. "They were formidable beings in all shapes and sizes, some quite beautiful, others most grotesque and monstrous. That mixture of many different orders of enchanted creatures breeding with one another made them quite varied, utterly bizarre, and terribly dangerous. They ruled Ireland with the proverbial iron fist, and might have spread their tyranny and evil much farther if they had not been stopped, banished from the Earthly realm to planes of the dead by Lugh and the Tuatha Dé Danann. They have remained outside of these worlds for thousands of years now, but their legacy in the mortal realm was a curious one."

"Curious how?" Now Moirin just looked annoyed.

"Well, they bred with some humans, you see, and so their magical legacy passed on into humanity. A good number of the humans who practice magic these days have a drop or two of Fomorian blood in them."

"Wait," Jilly interrupted, "does that mean that Granny and I might have some of this Fomorian blood in us, too?"

"It's quite possible, my dear," Qwyzz confirmed. "But in the case of Moirin, the bloodline is stronger, more direct, as efforts were made to keep it from straying too far, in order to preserve the lineage and keep the magic strong."

"Oh, so my ancestors were a bunch of inbred, evil sorcerers? Brilliant! My day keeps on getting better. Maybe it's just as well that I don't know anything about my real parents!"

"It's a bit more complicated than that," Qwyzz said, "but the important thing is that you have a powerful streak of very ancient magic in you. Um, pardon my asking, but do you sing?"

"Uh, yeah, it's basically my full-time job these days."

"Splendid, I knew it!" Qwyzz clapped his hands together. "As I'm sure you're aware, banshees are known for their beautiful, though often terrifying and deadly voices. This only further proves your heritage."

"She's really brilliant," Jilly piped in. "One of the best singers I've ever heard!"

"Oh, please!" Moirin blushed, looked down, and tried to deflect. "I'm not all that."

"It's true!" Jilly continued. "She's amazing, and I've felt the magic in her voice, when she sang at Leeds University. It was powerful, like it could change reality."

"You noticed that?" Moirin looked surprised.

"Uh, yeah. 'Wizard girl' here, remember? Knows all and sees all? That's how this all started, actually. That show was really strange to me, especially how it ended with the power going out and all, so when I got home, I told Blip about it—"

"It's Mr. Blippingstone..."

"And then I told Qwyrk, and she wanted to figure it out, and now here we are. I hope you're not mad at me?"

Moirin shook her head. "As peculiar as you lot all are, I appreciate your interest in what's going on. Um, what *is* going on, by the way?"

"That's what we're trying to figure out," Qwyrk said.

"In the meantime," Holly spoke up, "it seemed like a good idea to bring you here, where you'll be safe."

"And where exactly are we, if I may ask?" Moirin finally looked around in wonder at the curiosities dotting the sitting room.

"It's my world, and it's complicated," Qwyrk answered. "But we have the best magical resources available to help you. Qwyzz is a top-notch scholar. He'll find out everything he can, and we'll do whatever it takes to help you."

"Thank you," Moirin drew her attention back to them. "I was starting to feel like I was nuts, you know? None of this makes any sense. Not my voice, not the magical whatever, not the woman in my head, not the ginger girl I keep running into—"

"I'm sorry, what did you say?" Qwyzz interrupted her.

"Um, none of this makes any sense?"

"No, no, the part about a woman in your head, and a girl you keep meeting?"

"Well, I'm just guessing it's all related, but yeah, you see... hang on, do you hear that?"

A rushing sound, like a whirlwind, grew out of nowhere, and became louder with each passing second. Darkness formed in the middle of the sitting room, a spinning whirl of grey mist, black smoke, and white dust.

"What's happening?" Qwyrk raised her fists and Holly sprang to her feet, her stick at the ready. Blip assumed his karate stance with one foot raised and both arms out.

In an instant, the mists parted and Qwyrk saw someone emerge: a short old woman with a wild shock of long hair, streaked with white. Her sickly grey blotchy skin was further marred by dark circles under her milk white eyes, while her black, tattered robe flapped in the whirlwinds. Her presence both repulsed and alarmed Qwyrk.

Before anyone could act, the woman muttered some unintelligible words and reached out for Moirin's arm, yanking her up from the sofa in a swift, violent, but oddly smooth motion. Moirin screamed and tried to fight her off, punching and thrashing about, but the woman's grip was too strong. She pulled Moirin into the swirling chaos, into the mini-tornado now pulsing in the room. With a sharp whistle, the whirlwind spun itself out and disappeared, leaving only the desolate, lingering echo of a breeze, and a few wisps of acrid smoke.

No one said a word, until...

"What the blue, bloody hell?" Qwyrk blurted, breaking the

stunned silence, staring in astonishment, while the others did likewise.

The whole horrible thing had taken only a few seconds, but now, somehow, Moirin was gone.

* * *

"This... is an interesting development."

"You have quite the way with words. How do we know she'll really be there?"

"We don't, but isn't it worth the risk?"

"It depends on what we are risking."

"Everything. To get back everything. We've already lost one; if we can at least bring her back, we stand to regain our advantage, move on to the next stage."

"And if we fail?"

"Then there isn't much left for either us, is there?"

"True enough. Let us go, and hope she can be persuaded."

"And if she can't?"

"Then we take that choice away from her."

* * *

Moirin gasped and opened her eyes.

"What the fecking hell?" she blurted out in a loud whisper.

She sat alone, on grass, out in the open. The wide open, to be exact, in the middle of a stone circle under a night sky. The smallish stones made a wide oval, while a low range of mountains (or what passed for them in these islands) ringed the site. The air was crisp and cold, and rain clouds blew in and out overhead.

She shivered in the cold and felt sick to her stomach again as panic overtook her.

"Well, I couldn't leave you there," the woman's voice echoed in her head, "not with them. Miserable lot of false heroes. You deserve better than their company."

"You!" Morin hissed. "I saw you, like for real. You grabbed me and dragged me away!"

"I did, and it was terribly painful, I'll have you know. I risked my life to retrieve you, but I could not leave you in their company, cut off from me, cut off from yourself. You should be grateful."

"You had no right!"

"I had every right."

"What is this place? Why the hell did you bring me here?"

"This is the ancient stone circle of Castlerigg, my dear, in what these human creatures call the Lake District. Magic is strong here, for those with eyes to see it. And I did it to facilitate a reunion of sorts. You see, you need to remember who you are before you can become who you were meant to be. I brought you here so that you could make a choice: to return to your old life, or to embrace a new, but even older and truer, life that is already yours by right. I know what I would prefer for you, but even I cannot force you to join me. So, I had word sent out to some little beings who have as much of a vested interest in you as I do, but for different, even opposing reasons."

"What are you talking about? What beings?"

"The ones that raised you, of course, the ones that stole you and your brother away from your real parents and kept you in captivity for so many years before you escaped them. The ones who never allowed you to live your original life."

"What? Escaped? My brother?"

The woman chuckled. "It's all a bit much to take in, isn't it? Perhaps it's best for them to explain."

"Explain what? Who?" The woman didn't answer. Two small, dark figures made their way into the circle. They waddled a bit in their stride. One circled its clawed hand in the air and, muttering some words in an elder, unintelligible tongue, a yellow light appeared around them, revealing creatures with pointed faces and yellow, bumpy skin. Their jet black eyes fixed on her, and a vague recollection of past cruelties stirred in her mind. As they lumbered toward her, she stood up and put her hands out, like a warning.

"Moirin," one said in a thin voice, "we are glad to see you, after so long."

"After so long?" Moirin snapped. "I have no idea who you are. Or what you are, for that matter."

"You do not remember, because you have been slumbering under an enchantment of forgetfulness," the other creature said in a higher pitched voice, possibly female.

"And why would I do that, exactly?" She refused to believe them.

"It was your choice," the first one answered, "a way to distance yourself from us, from your family."

"You are *not* my family, you freaks!" she yelled.

"Only because you do not yet remember us," the second one said. "But we can remedy that. We can give you back your memories, if you will return with us."

"Return where?"

"Back to your home, of course."

"I have a home; it's here, with my band, with what we're building."

"An illusion that robs you of your higher purpose," the male said.

"And what would that be?" she sassed.

"Come with us and we will reveal all."

"No. No feckin' way. I'm not taking one step unless you tell me everything."

"If we restore your memories, will you consider our offer?" the female asked.

"Maybe. So, give them back to me, or it's no deal and I walk away from you. And don't even try to stop me!"

"Agreed," the male said. "Hold still for a moment." He approached and reached out to touch the side of her head.

"Wait, what are you..."

A white flash exploded in her vision, and somehow, unbidden images and thoughts began to flood her mind, not new ones, but old ones, as if they'd been hidden behind locked doors. She reeled at the onslaught of memories, events spanning her entire life, things that she shouldn't have been able to remember: that tune she liked, sung to her by her mother as a newborn, being taken from her crib with her brother—her fraternal twin—when they were only weeks old, being raised by these two creatures, these kobolds, kindly at first but more sternly later on, being trained for some task they never understood, seeing their magical powers manifest as teenagers, deciding at last that they needed to be free of their captors.

She saw him, her brother. What was his name? Colm? Yes, that was it! He had long dark hair like hers; he looked a bit intimidating, but he was kind, and she adored him. They were best friends, they relied on each other, they survived together. And they made a pact: they would escape, return to Earth somehow, and they would hide.

"One of us had to remember," she said out loud. "He said it would be him. He said that I needed to forget, for my own safety, and that he would find me when the time was right. He said we should adopt new names, so we could be anonymous. I agreed to go with 'Chantz.' It was kind of silly, a play on words, like good luck, but also because I was a singer, a 'chanter' with a magic voice. But he didn't sing, he could... fly? That's crazy, but yeah, he could fly! I remember now. And he was tall, so he came up with a new name. It was... Longwing? That was it!"

"Chantz and Longwing," the male kobold confirmed. "New identities to help you hide in this mortal world. And it worked. For two years, you hid yourself away, only vaguely aware of the potent magic you have inside you."

"So well have you kept yourself secret from us," the female added, "that at times we despaired of ever finding you, even to the point of seeking others to take your place. Only just this morning, we observed the home of a child with great potential power, greater than yours to be honest, but we could not enter into the domicile. Some vile Shadow magic blocked us, forced us away. No matter, we heard that you would be here tonight, and here you are! So you'll have to do. Now you know the truth, now you remember. It is time to come home with us, Moirin. You have a great task ahead of you, and only we can help you accomplish it."

"What task? What the hell are you on about? Where is my brother? Where is Colm?"

"They won't tell you," the banshee answered in her mind. "They dare not. You see, your brother lost his way, so to speak, though in another sense, he found it."

"What?" Moirin whispered.

"He fell in with a delightfully insidious creature, the Erlking," the banshee continued, "an ancient Germanic forest spirit, who, while useful, had delusional aspirations of ruling this world. Your poor brother probably thought that alliance would make him strong, give him power. But, sadly for him, it did not end happily."

"What are you saying?" she demanded.

"We haven't said anything," the male kobold answered, looking confused.

"I'm not talking to you, piss off!" she yelled.

"Your brother thought he was on the winning side, but alas, it was not so," the old woman continued. "You see, those folk you were with earlier, they fought the Erlking last winter and drove him away from this world, but in doing so, they killed your brother."

"No, you're lying!"

"Um, we still haven't said anything," the female kobold said, looking around.

"You can deny it," the head-voice continued, "but if you search your heart, you'll find it's true. Your brother is no longer on this mortal plane. Admit it, you two had a special connection and you can't feel that now, can you?"

"No, damn it, you're lying!" Tears formed in Moirin's eyes. But she knew, just as the woman insisted, she knew that he was dead. Colm was gone.

"I assure you, I'm not," the voice confirmed. "And while those fools who took you to their realm earlier played their part in his death, it is fair to say that these two vile creatures in front of you are even more guilty. They stole you both as infants, they kept you away from your parents, tried to control your power. Their cruelty led to you running away, and Colm running right into the embrace of the evil spirit that eventually got him killed. I mean, these two are the ones who sent the Sluagh after you, you know."

"Did you send those dead birds after me?" she demanded of the kobolds.

"Moirin," the female pleaded, hands held out, "please understand that they would never have hurt you. We thought it best to have them transport you away from this realm in haste, so as not to cause further problems for anyone. Humans go missing all the time in this world. But we didn't count on that wretched Shadow woman and her companions being able to send them away, nor your own powers. Believe us: the Sluagh would not kill you, they would simply have brought you back to us."

"Brought me back? You sent those zombies after me—twice— scaring the crap out of me, and I'm supposed to just believe they were going to gently air lift me off to goblin town? And my brother *is* dead, isn't he?"

"Moirin…" the male said.

"Answer me!"

"Yes, he's dead! I am sorry. We both are. We never wanted that."

"And what did you want?" Tears streamed from her eyes now as rage built up inside of her.

"Your gifts, to help us achieve something of greatness for all of us."

"I don't want your stupid greatness, I don't want your home, and I don't want you! I only want what I don't have, what I can never have now, thanks to you: my *real* family. My parents who I'll never know, and my brother, who's dead!"

"Moirin, please listen."

But Moirin was done hearing them. The only voice she heard now, the only voice she wanted to hear, was her own. She started to hum, a low, persistent tone. It grew louder, more powerful; was the old woman empowering it? Was it her magic feeding into it? Moirin didn't know and didn't care. An energy pulsed inside her, weaving in and around the sound of her voice. The ancient connection was being forged again, as it had been near the farm. The sound intensified, and she opened her eyes to see the kobolds backing away, but she had no intention of letting them go. She started toward them, deliberate, calm, determined, fierce. She opened her mouth so that the tone changed again. She barely needed to breathe as the ancient forces within her coalesced into audible power.

The kobolds panicked, turning from her and breaking into a run, but it wouldn't save them. Her voice grew into a full scream, and she stopped and flung her hands out to her sides. A beam of hot, raw energy shot from her mouth, flew across the range of the circle, and struck the kobolds full-on. They cried out and collapsed to the wet ground.

But Moirin wasn't finished.

Striding up to their writhing forms, she kept the sound focused on them, a single note without beginning or end. It pinned them to the ground, and they twisted in agony. If they pleaded with her, she no longer heard them.

And still her voice intensified. Its volume did nothing to her, but had a horrid effect on her prey. Blood, thick viscous brown blood, begin to ooze from their pointed noses, their pointed ears, and even from their dark eyes. They screamed and clutched at their heads with clawed fingers, but there was no relief. She would give them none.

Her cry reached a breaking point, but not for her. For them. With shrieks of terror, their heads expanded like balloons and exploded, leaving not piles of gore, but darkness and ash.

She let her voice subside, the energy within it dissipating, until there was only the quiet hum of her own very mortal sound. The primal magic that had fueled her rage now seemed long gone, far away. But the headless bodies of her former captors were still sprawled on that wet grass, very real, and very dead. In her mind, she heard the old woman laugh.

CHAPTER FIFTEEN

"Can somebody please explain to me what the hell just happened?" Qwyrk's voice broke the stunned silence yet again.

"Um, it looks like that banshee lady popped round and grabbed Moirin and took her away?" Star Tao said in a quiet voice.

Yes, thank you, captain obvious. But Qwyrk held her tongue.

"This is most peculiar," Qwyzz said after another bit of awkward silence. "Oh, decidedly that, this is thoroughly worrying. She should not have been able to do that. This realm is protected against Fomorians and their kin and allies, and has been for thousands of years. It is utterly unassailable."

"Apparently not," Blip said in a tone more sarcastic than Qwyrk had heard him use before with her venerable mentor.

"We must inform the council at once," Qwyzz said, seemingly ignoring Blip's borderline rudeness.

"Um, can we *not* do that? Not just yet?" Qwyrk asked. "I mean, of course we'll tell them, but I want us to follow up on this first." She looked at Holly. "All of us. That way, we'll have more useful informa-tion to bring to them when the time is right." She lied about that last bit. *Something about those idiots has felt really off recently.*

"As you wish, but we must speak to them soon," Qwyzz replied.

"But where did Moirin go?" Jilly asked, looking very upset as Holly put a comforting arm around her.

"I can probably find out," Qwyrk answered, trying to calm Jilly's fear and be encouraging. "Since all magic leaves a trail, those of us who use it to shoot across the planes can basically follow its bread crumbs. Either the banshee doesn't know we can do that, or she doesn't care. But if she's using any kind of sorcery, I can track her."

"But what then?" Blip asked. "If she has the power to breach the enchanted barriers to Symphinity, she might well have more power than any of us could muster to counter her."

"No, I don't think so," Qwyrk shook her head. "She was in a damned hurry to get in, grab Moirin, and get out. I'm guessing she couldn't stay here long, and that she hurt herself pulling that little stunt. If she's still on the other side of wherever they went, she'll be a bit roughed up. Maybe we can trap her and question her."

She knelt down, closed her eyes, and put her hands on the floor where Moirin had been whisked away. "It's going to take me a bit to get a fix on it." She ran her palms over the hard wood, thankful that Qwyzz kept his home clean to an immaculate degree.

"I definitely sense something," she said. "It's a magical energy, but it's like the opposite of energy. It's almost cold."

"If she's using Formorian magic, then it will feel very odd, very out of sorts," Qwyzz confirmed. "Their ways are so ancient that we can barely understand them now, so I'm not at all surprised that their magic would seem off-putting."

"Off-putting, yeah, that's it!" Qwyrk said. "There's something ugly about it." She traced her hands over the panels again. "Moirin's back on earth, somewhere in the north of England."

"You can tell that just by feeling the floor?" Jilly asked.

"Yeah, I know it sounds crazy," Qwyrk answered, "but trust me, I know what I'm looking for."

Qwyrk closed her eyes and spent a short time moving her hands across the wooden flooring, parts of it warmer than others. At one spot, she felt a ripple and its vibration opened her inner eye to a vision of a new place.

"They went to Castlerigg, in the Lake District."

"An unusual choice," Blip said.

"Not if the banshee is planning to use Moirin for some not-so-nice magical shenanigans," Qwyrk said, opening her eyes. "Being in a power center like that will give Moirin's voice an extra boost. And if that's the case, we need to get over there, right now."

She stood up. "All right, everyone join hands. Qwyzz, I think you should come, too. We could really use you."

"Well, yes, all right, I suppose, but I haven't engaged in a battle in quite some time, you know."

"You'll be just fine."

They all linked hands.

"Right, be ready, everyone. Teleporting this many people at once is at the limit of my ability, so it might take me a minute or two to recover, and all of you need to be on guard for whatever might be waiting there for us." She looked at Holly. "Keep them safe if I need a moment?"

"Of course," Holly assured her.

With a nod, Qwyrk closed her eyes and concentrated on pulling all of them across the worlds to that one stone circle. "Bloody hell," she said, "this is going to hurt."

* * *

Moirin wandered the slick streets at the edge of the town of Keswick, west of the stones. Had she walked here? No, someone had given her a lift. Maybe. She had nothing with her, not even her handbag; it was still at Qwyzz's crazy home, wherever the hell that was. The drizzly and cold air stung her face, and she didn't know what to do. The woman in her head was gone again, apparently satisfied that she could kill. Kill?

"What the hell happened back there?" She plopped down on a sheltered bench at a bus stop. "It was an illusion or something, it had to be."

But memories—vivid, hazy, jumbled, and clear—competed for space in her aching head. It was true, all of it. Her stolen life, her power, the brother she loved and had forgotten. She didn't know how to feel, or how to process it; she didn't even know if she could. She rubbed her throbbing temples. This was the worst "banshee" headache yet, but then, she'd never done anything like that before. Whatever the hell "that" was.

The old woman seemed very pleased the kobolds were dead. "Your initiation has begun," she'd said, "and will be complete when next you perform."

The words echoed in Moirin's mind, haunting her. "Maybe I'm finally just losing it."

She looked out again at her quaint, yet touristy surroundings. "Lovely little town, I suppose. Great if you have money to stay somewhere, which, of course, I don't. Because all of my money is in my bag, back in not-elf land. Maybe Qwyrk and her gang of weirdos will find me. But what if it's true that they... killed Colm? They don't seem like murderers, but everyone lies about everything these days, so maybe their friendliness was just a big con. Maybe they were just trying to get me away from my mates, so I'd end up staying at that nutty mansion, and then they'd kill me in my sleep, or lock me away in a dungeon. Oh, I don't know!"

She buried her face in her hands and wanted to cry, but no tears came; she was drained. With a sigh, she stood up and wandered toward the town center. It was early enough that some pubs were still open.

"Maybe one of them has a guest room, and I can trade labor for a place to sleep. Worth a try, anyway; better than sleeping at the bus stop."

A few minutes later, she found herself in the middle of town, amid a scattering of other folks, both tourists and locals, but they ignored her. She probably scared them, and that thought amused her.

"Which one of these pubs would be likely to put up a scraggly, scary-looking goth girl resembling a soaked rat, on the promise of deferred payment? And maybe a pint and a hot veggie pie of some kind?" She stopped and looked around. "Oh, who am I kidding, no one's gonna do that! I may as well find a rubbish bin somewhere and just climb inside."

"Moirin?"

She almost jumped and turned about with a start. "What? No! No way! Aileen?"

* * *

Qwyrk and the others stood in the middle of a dark and misty Castlerigg stone circle. Thankfully, the place was abandoned for the night, but a gruesome sight confronted them.

"Damn it!" Qwyrk swore as they circled around the kobold's headless bodies. Black ash was all that remained of the thick-skulled heads that once topped their shoulders.

"Cor, this is grim!" Star Tao gasped.

"I think it's them," Holly said. "The two kobolds that Adjua told us about earlier. That means you were right. There is a connection between them and Moirin, and maybe Ashanti."

Qwyrk nodded, a knot of worry tightening in her stomach.

"Were they after your friends, Adjua and Ashanti?" Jilly asked, still gripping Qwyrk's hand.

"Maybe, probably," Qwyrk said. "The bigger question right now is what actually happened here. How did these two end up in the Lake District, and who blasted them into oblivion?"

"What a horrible way to go," Jilly said with a disgusted face, looking at the remains, but keeping her distance.

"Honestly, don't feel too bad for them," Holly said in an icy tone. "They kidnap babies from their real human parents and leave fakes—changelings—behind, while bringing up the children to do terrible things on their behalf. We think Moirin may have been one of their victims and might have been raised by them before she escaped. That would explain why she only showed up on Earth a couple of years ago."

"Well," Blip said, "if she was raised by them, that is dire. It makes me wonder if she did this to these creatures to exact revenge of a sort."

"It's possible," Qwyrk nodded. "We need to find out if the banshee just dropped her here and buggered off back to her own world?"

"I'd wager that is the best explanation," Qwyzz suggested. "Just as Aeval could not stand to be in Symphinity for long, she wouldn't fare very well here, either. My guess is that once she had taken young Moirin away from us, she fled. This is a place of great power. Perhaps these kobolds were waiting for her. I doubt young Moirin would have enjoyed seeing them again. If so, we can plainly see the results."

"Whatever the cause," Holly knelt and looked at the bodies, "it can't have happened long ago. These explosive wounds are fresh."

"So, Moirin might still be close," Jilly offered, sounding optimistic.

"She might." Qwyrk didn't want to dash her young friend's hopes. "But it's just as possible that once whatever happened here… happened, the banshee whisked Moirin away again. For all we know, she could be in the Outer Hebrides, or on Skellig Michael, or at flipping Camelot."

"She wouldn't really be at Camelot, would she?" Jilly nudged her with a skeptical look.

"What? No, I was being sarcastic to make a point."

"I figured, but I just wanted to be sure, because pretty much everything I thought was fake has turned out to be real. I mean, the whole Father Christmas thing?"

"Scoundrel!" Blip muttered.

"Well, Camelot *was* real, but—"

"Hang on, not that too!" Though Jilly looked less shocked than she should have been.

"Yeah, it was quite the scene back in the day," Qwyrk said. "I mean, some modern versions of the story are good, but others get it completely wrong, and they've all left out the bit about Arthur's troupe of magic dancing snails."

"Dancing snails?" Jilly scrunched up her nose.

"Yeah, like the ones on Qwyzz's robe?" Qwyrk pointed. "It was quite a thing at banquets. Their shows took a long time, though. You can see knights fighting them in medieval manuscripts, probably irritated because they took forever to get to the point. Anyway, we're getting way off topic here, so can we—"

"How did they dance?" Star Tao perked up.

"What?" Qwyrk already dreaded where the conversation was going.

"They only have one foot, right," he went on, "or they wouldn't be snails. So how did they dance? Was it sort of a wiggling inside their shells?"

"I don't know," Qwyrk sighed. "I never saw them. I just heard about them."

"They might have engaged in something akin to a *pavane* or a Baroque French *courante*, with all due stateliness," Blip suggested.

"You are wise, my lord." Star Tao bowed in reverence.

"Thank you, my boy. However, since neither of those dance forms existed in fifth-century post-Roman Britain, nor would they for well over a thousand years, we shall have to conclude that they engaged in another type of rhythmic movement that allowed said curious creatures to successfully entertain Arthur and his court."

"I would hazard a guess that they might have utilized some kind of back-and-forth rocking motion, perhaps using their heads only, but swaying in unison in a simple but satisfying choreography." Qwyzz stroked his bearded chin.

"A plausible theory," Blip concurred, "given their obvious physiological limitations. The music no doubt would have been slow-paced to accommodate them."

"This is that thing you told me about, isn't it?" Holly whispered to Qwyrk. "Where everyone just goes off on their own little absurd journey right in the middle of a crisis?"

"See? And thank you for noticing!" Qwyrk waved her hands in their general direction. "Right, everyone shut up about the sodding snails! I don't care if they were dancing gastropod galliards, waltzing to the bloody 'Blue Danube,' or twisting like they did last summer. That's not why we're here, all right, so can we please focus and get back to the very disturbing topic at hand? Which is that there are two headless kobolds in the middle of a stone circle, we don't know exactly how they got to be headless or why, but we need to find out. Oh, and move the bodies so that tourists coming out here tomorrow morning don't get the flipping fright of their lives, fair enough?"

Everyone fell silent. Star Tao and Blip stared at the ground.

"Good! Thank you! Now, Moirin might have been here just a little while ago, but she could be literally anywhere now, so I'm not sure it's a good idea to spend a lot of energy trying to find her."

"But Qwyrk!" Jilly protested.

"We're not abandoning her, I promise. She's going to have to resurface at some point. Her band's doing another show in Newcastle, right?"

"Yeah, but, what if the woman who took her tries to keep her just like these kobolds did?" Jilly's voice betrayed her upset about her idol and new friend.

"I don't think that's why she took Moirin." Qwyrk put a hand on Jilly's shoulder. "If all that banshee wanted was to make Moirin a prisoner, she could have waited for a much better time to try to do it than grabbing her out from under our noses in one of the most protected of all the realms."

"You think she wanted to get her away from us?" Holly asked.

Qwyrk nodded. "That's exactly what I think."

"That would make sense," Qwyzz agreed. "Snatch her away before we could make that task too difficult, and then return her to England somewhere that we wouldn't likely find her, at least not for a few days."

"And we need to figure out what's happening during these few days that Moirin needs to be hidden away," Qwyrk said.

"She could be undergoing some transformation," Holly posited. "Or being trained to do something specific, something horrible."

"It is possible, I fear," Qwyzz said.

"So we just have to wait and hope she shows up for her next show, and that nothing awful happens between now and then?" Jilly sounded annoyed.

"Not necessarily," Qwyrk said. "There *are* those who keep their ears and noses and other appendages to the ground and know things. Lots more things than they should."

"Wait," Holly said, an alarmed look on her face. "Are you suggesting what I think you are?"

Qwyrk nodded. "Yep, unfortunately, it might be time for me to go see Bogtrotter and the Nighttime Nasties."

* * *

"What're ya doin' here, ya daft girl? Out in the rain with nothin' to protect you?" Aileen, by contrast, was wearing a long coat and held a sizeable umbrella, one that was sturdier than her gothic parasol from the night before.

"With nothing to protect me? What the fresh hell are *you* doing in Keswick? How is it remotely possible that I'd run into you again all the way out here? I'm not even supposed to be here, I was in the Dales a little while ago... it's a long story. I mean, what are the odds?"

"Well, fate works in mysterious ways, don't it? Look, I'm stayin' here for a wee bit, house sittin' for a friend, just up the way there and down a side street. And you're comin' back there with me, and gettin' warm and sleepin' for the night. Unless you have a better offer?"

"Not really, no."

"Din't think so. Off we go, then!"

"Um, I was actually going to stop into a pub, or something. Have a bite to eat?"

"Not a problem at all. Pick whichever one ya like. Get you good and stuffed."

"Um, well there's actually just one problem."

"You've no money?"

Moirin shook her head, embarrassed. "I mean, I *do*, just not on me. It got left behind in a hurry. Like I said, it's a really long and super strange story."

"That's all right. You don't have to tell me. Supper's on me. Come on, then!"

They found a suitable warm and cozy establishment, and Moirin ate and drank her fill. Properly sated, she left with Aileen, who true to her word, was staying at a charming little home far enough away from the bustle of the main town to be quiet and inviting.

"My friend has loads of clothes and she's about your size," Aileen told her after they were safely inside. "Pick some comfy sleep things and you can wash and dry out what you've got on."

After warming up the place and settling in, they chatted in the sitting room over mugs of tea and chocolate biscuits.

"This is all just too much," Moirin said. "I don't even understand how we could possibly run into each other in a random town nowhere near York. It makes no sense. Oh, and I'm sorry for how I acted after the show last night. You were just trying to be helpful, and I was really rude."

"Oh, think nothin' of it. I figured you were probably just tired. It's fine."

"No, Aileen, it isn't fine. Not at all. You didn't deserve that, and I'm really sorry. Look, my life has taken a turn for the freakish lately, and I still don't know how to process it all. I feel like I want to tell you all about it, but I'm also kind of afraid to."

"Why?"

Moirin rubbed her forehead. "Because it will make me look completely mad and I don't want to do that to you after you've been so kind, more than once."

"I don't think you could. I mean, how crazy can it be?"

"Um, really crazy, like the most insane, unbelievable things you've ever heard. You'll probably think I'm a menace to myself and society. Or just delusional."

Aileen leaned in and looked her straight in the eye. "All right, now you've piqued my interest. If you want to tell me, of course. You don't have to."

"No, I want to. It's burning me up inside and I really need to get it out, no matter how ridiculous it sounds."

"I'm all ears."

Moirin let out a nervous sigh. "All right then. Hold on, and maybe consider swapping out your tea for some whisky?"

"Ooh, I like it already!"

* * *

"There has to be another way," Holly said in an exasperated tone (though Qwyrk couldn't quite tell if she was being serious or just winding her up), sipping a glass of Qwyzz's magnificent port, and leaning on Qwyrk as they sat on the plushy sofa back in his ever-unusual sitting room. Blip, Jilly, and Star Tao had all been safely returned to Jilly's.

"I hate to say it, I mean, I really do." Qwyrk interlaced her fingers with Holly's, convinced that Holly was already internally laughing about it. "But the NN's know lots of things. And the more we find out about everything, the less I like it. I mean, even though Horatio stopped by last night."

"Oh, right. I recall."

"Yeah. Seems like news about Moirin is spreading among the enchanted folk, and I have a feeling Boggie might know more."

Holly raised a teasing eyebrow. "You realize that you may have to do the dance this time?"

Qwyrk restrained from wincing. "It's a risk I'll have to take. Maybe I can just bribe him with a rhubarb pie topped with candied cockroaches, or something."

"That sounds revolting." Holly's mirth vanished in an instant.

"No one ever said the job was easy, love." Qwyrk drained her glass. "I'll reach out and try to set up a meeting for tomorrow. It's usually easy enough, it's not like he has a lot to do except parade around with his sycophants, anyway."

"Well, I'll make myself available for whenever it's scheduled." Holly finished her own port.

"Are you sure you want to come along? Remember the bombs last time?"

"You *are* joking, right? I mean, honestly, you might have to do the dance. I wouldn't miss that for all the samosas in the world!"

"Thanks for the support, darling."

The little wyvern breezed into the room, leaving a trail of smoke as it exited thought the opposite door.

"Where is Qwyzz, anyway?" Holly said, as she watched the diminutive dragon disappear.

"I think he went to the library; wanted to look up something about the kind of magic that could tear off someone's head."

Holly laid her head on Qwyrk's shoulder. "That was horrid, even for them."

"Yeah, this just keeps getting grimmer. Must be Tuesday, as Jilly would say."

"Shouldn't we be looking for Moirin? If she's being used, she might do something really terrible."

"She might, but unless the banshee is still working magic through her, there won't be any trails to follow, and it's not like you can just go up to random humans and say, 'Pardon me, but have you happened to see a young, gothy Irish woman wandering around tonight who can change reality by singing? She might have a millennia-old supernatural force clinging to her, and they may be doing terrible things.' I mean, we *could*, but it'd probably cause way more upset than we'd want."

Holly gave her a mock-exasperated look. "You always have such a lovely way of phrasing things."

Qwyrk beamed and poured herself some more port. "It's a gift!"

* * *

"Wow. That's... that is quite a story," Aileen said, having finished her tea and moved on to whisky.

"You see?" Moirin threw her hands up. "I told you it was mental! And now you probably just think I'm nuts."

"No, I don't, actually."

"Fine, but you can't possibly believe it. *I* don't even believe it!"

"Ya know, I've seen some fair strange stuff in my time, so I can't say for sure what you're goin' through, but ya seem honest and sincere, and if you think this is all real, I'm not gonna say otherwise. There's a lot out there we don't understand."

"Don't I know it. I think after telling you all that, I could use a drink, too."

"Help yourself!" Aileen handed her the bottle, and Moirin poured a bit too much into her now-empty tea mug.

"What I don't get," Moirin said between sips, "is, assuming this is in any way true and I'm not completely delusional, why now? It's bowled me over in the past few weeks like a gale force wind." She took a generous swig. "Just be glad your life is boring by comparison."

"Oh, I don't know that it's that boring."

"What, are you secretly a dragon, or something? Because nothing would surprise me anymore."

"I don't think so, but that would be brilliant!"

"Hey, how is it that you're here? I mean, I've seen some crazy shite in the last few days, but honestly, running into you out here has got to be the most unbelievable of all of it. I mean, the odds on something like that have to be almost impossible, don't they?"

Aileen shrugged. "Weird things do happen. If all that stuff you're tellin' me is true, then maybe fate just brought us together again. Ya know, so I could keep an eye on you and make sure you're not gettin' into any more trouble!" She wagged a good-natured finger at Moirin and cracked a smile.

"That's as good an explanation as any, I suppose," Moirin emptied her mug and poured some more. She offered the bottle back to Aileen, who shook her head and waved it away.

"Thanks," she said, "but I'm actually knackered myself. I think I'm gonna turn in for the night. Please, make yourself as comfortable here as you like, stay up till you get tired, and stay in bed for as long as you like tomorrow."

"Thanks. And then tomorrow, I have to get myself back over to the farm. The blokes'll be wondering where I've gone off to."

"I'll let ya sleep."

Aileen smiled and stood up. "Night." She placed a hand on Moirin's shoulder and walked past her toward the door.

"Good night. And thank you, really. This is a better end to the evening than I could've possibly hoped for."

"Ah, you're most welcome," Aileen turned around and smiled. "I'm just glad to be of service. Kith and kin, and all that. It's what we do for each other."

Aileen was long gone upstairs and Moirin had taken a few more sips of whisky before it hit her. What did she mean "kin"? And do what for each other?

CHAPTER SIXTEEN

"This has been a hell of a few days," Qwyrk sighed as they lounged again on her sofa, having opened another bottle of gift port from Qwyzz's prized collection. Their lack of success seemed as good a reason to imbibe it as any.

"It's all been rather horrid," Holly agreed, swirling her glass and savoring the enticing aromas of butterscotch, wood, and sugar wafting upward, before finishing it off. "Is it always like this when a world-shattering crisis come up?"

"Oh, no. It's usually much worse."

"That's encouraging. Anyway, you know I'd love to stay up with you all night, darling, but I'm exhausted." Holly put down her empty glass. "I think I'll go home and turn in, if that's all right? We can get a fresh start tomorrow if we're both rested."

"Of course. I'll walk you to your tree. I can't believe I just said that!"

They left Qwyrk's home and wandered into a nearby copse, where Holly located a suitable oak.

"Right then, love, I'm off," she said. "Have a good rest in your Reverie."

"I will. And I'll send a Faegram out to Horatio to set up a time for... that thing we have to do. I can let you know by your ring in the morning, yeah?"

"Always," Holly smiled. She leaned in for a kiss. Their lips touched and Qwyrk was nearly jolted backward by the force of a powerful shock.

"Ow, bloody hell!" Qwyrk blurted.

Holly had reacted the way same and was rubbing her mouth. "Qwyrk?" She looked worried. "What's going on?"

"I don't know, love. I wish I did." She reached out to take Holly's hand, kissed her again, and... nothing. Everything was fine. "That was worse than before. Something's wrong. I have a feeling it's just the stupid after-effects of some careless twat dabbling with spells they can't control, but we'll get to the bottom of it, I promise."

"We could ask Qwyzz," Holly suggested.

"One more thing to burden the poor fellow with. At least it doesn't seem to linger. Come here." She kissed Holly again. And again.

"Not that I'm complaining," Holly said, "but what are you doing, exactly?"

"I'm conducting an experiment," Qwyrk answered, between kisses, "for science."

"How positively rigorous of you," Holly answered, between kisses.

"I believe in being thorough, and I can happily conclude that whatever it was is gone now."

"I accept your findings. Shall I see you tomorrow then?"

"Without a doubt. Good night."

"Good night."

A few more parting kisses and Holly turned and melted into the tree with a smile, leaving Qwyrk to wander with some giddiness back home. And to behold something new.

"Why is there a birch tree right in front of my door?"

* * *

Moirin sat with Aileen at a little breakfast table in the nook off the kitchen, sipping coffee and nibbling on toast as they looked out on a grey and misty Lake District morning. She was grateful for the bliss of a long sleep, but her situation still nagged, and she couldn't let it go, no matter how much she told herself to.

"So, there's something else I've been meaning to ask you," Moirin said.

"Sure, anything."

"How did you know I'd be out at that farm in the Dales, to phone and leave me a message?"

"Oh, um, you must've told me you were goin' there when we chatted after the show."

"No, I couldn't have. I only decided to book a room after I'd gotten back to my B&B, after I, you know, stormed off and left you. Uh, sorry about that again."

"Are you sure? I'm certain you mentioned somethin' about it to me. I mean, how could I have known, otherwise? That would be really creepy, right? Maybe you just don't remember it?"

"Honestly, I don't know what I know right now. I might well be hallucinating everything that's happening, for all I can figure out. But I'm absolutely sure that I made up my mind to take a break after I got back to my room. So, what's going on?"

"I don't know what you're talkin' about, don't be daft!" Aileen snapped.

"Look, Aileen. I'm very grateful for your help over the last few days, and especially last night when I was stuck out in the elements. But I'm not stupid; I know something's up and I want to know what the hell's goin' on, so level with me, or I'm walking away. If you know something, you've no right to keep it from me, and if you're spyin' on me, then that's not even remotely okay, so what is it?"

Aileen sighed. "You're a clever girl, Moirin. And I suppose it's all a bit obvious, in't it?"

"What? What's obvious? What are you talking about?"

Aileen stood up. "Finish up your coffee and get dressed. I'm takin' ya back to the farm."

* * *

"So," Qwyrk said as she met Holly the next morning. "Something else really odd happened last night."

"Oh?" Holly asked.

"Yeah, I walked back to the house, and out of nowhere, there was a large birch right in front of my door, almost blocking the entrance."

"You're sure?"

"I mean, I admit I'm not always as observant as I could be, but I would have noticed a ginormous tree making it impossible to get in or out before now."

"What did you do? I mean to get back in?"

"Oh, I called on a dryad friend of mine, who came over and convinced it to wander off."

"Convinced it... to wander off. You know, you really should have contacted me. I'd have paid good faery gold to see that! Maybe it's related to our shocking kisses, all part of some enchantment gone wrong?"

"Yeah, might be."

"In which case, we really should tell Qwyzz about it."

Qwyrk sighed. "You're right, but first things first. Horatio got back to me and has arranged the meeting before noon, so let's head on over there and get it over with."

"I can't wait to see what he has in store for you," Holly playfully taunted.

Qwyrk grimaced as they prepared to poof away to somewhere remote and unseen in North Yorkshire.

* * *

Jilly sat on her sofa and sketched, the first time she'd had the inclination to do so in a while. It comforted her, like seeing an old friend, and it helped take her mind off of Moirin.

"Just me and some lovely peace and quiet, just..."

"Good morning, Ms. Pleeth," Blip announced as he materialized from the corner of the living room, which caused Odin to raise his head and ears in alarm, but only for a moment, before settling down on his bed again and lapsing back into slumber.

"Good morning!" She was actually happy to see him today. "I didn't expect to see you here so early. You've not been around much lately."

"I know, I know," he said, hopping up to sit next to her. "I have been frooncing quite heavily of late, and it has weighed on my conscience, I assure you. I fear that I am growing most neglectful of my duties, but on my word, I am not the proverbial whiffle-whaffler that I might at first appear to be."

"I don't think you're a... whiffler at all." Jilly had no idea what he meant, as usual.

"You're too kind, my dear. But in view of the rather distressing events of the past few evenings, I thought it only proper that I be here to provide some comfort and support, should you need it."

"That's very kind of you, sir. I think I'm all right, though. So, no word on where she is?"

"I made some inquiries, but so far, nothing. Not even a smattering of a clue."

"That lady who took her was quite scary."

"It's not a lady, as I've said. Those creatures are more like elemental forces of nature, with all of the unpredictability and chaos that such forces contain. They are very dangerous and not to be taken lightly. That one of them has emerged from its dark and forbidding realms for purposes of which we are not yet aware is a worrying sign. I do not mean to alarm you, but it is something most serious."

"No, I understand. To be honest, I've gotten kind of used to supernatural threats of all sorts."

"And therein lies a problem. We cannot become complacent, and we must strive to comprehend why these things occur. To that end, I would like to devote a lesson to the philosophy of conflict, contrasting two fascinating views, those of von Clausewitz and Tolstoy. It shall be, I hope, an illuminating examination of the intricacies of the subject, showing that there is no one clear answer to the problem, even when we are faced with such extraordinary circumstances. So, note pad and pen at the ready, and we shall delve in."

So much for a quiet morning.

"On second thought," Blip said, "I, um... I just remembered something."

"Sir?"

"I have a meeting I need to attend, and so will have to take my leave of you. My sincere apologies. It slipped my mind."

"A meeting about what? With who?"

"It's of no real concern, I assure you, but my presence is necessary. You know how meetings are: boring, pretentious things that everyone despises. Alas, duty calls, but I shan't be more than an hour or two. Should you wish to study on your own until my return, feel free to do so. Cheerio!"

And with no further explanation, he hopped off the sofa and wandered away to the opposite wall in haste, where he disappeared, leaving Jilly feeling confused and even a little offended.

* * *

Qwyrk and Holly waited for their unusual host next to a remote, rocky outcropping on the Yorkshire Moors, while assorted and sundry Nighttime Nasties fussed and scurried about, as if anticipating the most important of royalty to arrive. Time seemed to pass extra slowly this morning, and Qwyrk found herself ready to start picking up random NNs and throwing them in equally random directions if things didn't speed up soon.

"How much longer is this going to be?" she grumped.

"His eminence will see you now," the diminutive trumpet-nosed herald proclaimed in his tooty voice. Qwyrk always wondered how his sickly yellow coloring and brassy-shaped schnozzle were both disconcerting and somehow quite funny at the same time.

"His eminence?" Qwyrk repeated, giving the little Nasty a nasty look of her own.

"This is going to go very well, I see," Holly whispered.

Qwyrk shot her an irritated glance, which seemed to amuse Holly very much, and they set off following the herald's lead. After a short trek they found themselves in the presence of their pompous host. He looked the same. He always looked the same: a bipedal Highland cow with shaggy red fur, wearing a dark blue doublet and a kilt. He was seated on an impressive wooden stool, surrounded by a score of pixies, nixies, pookahs, and pucks, who all looked as if they were ready to cheer for him. Some of them even held banners ready to wave at a moment's notice.

"Lovely to see you both again." Bogtrotter remarked with a bovine grin. "And nice to see that my observation about you two, romantically speaking, was one hundred percent accurate." He bowed his head a little, as if in egotistical acknowledgement of his own achievement.

"Yeah, all right, fine," Qwyrk said. "You were right, and I'm not complaining."

"Nor I," Holly added, obviously far too amused about this whole nonsense.

"Look, we don't have a whole lot of time, as usual, and we didn't come here for you to gloat about being a matchmaker." Qwyrk already wanted to smack him. "We need to know a bit more about the big picture, if there's anything we should look out for. And I probably don't need to give you the background, because you lot already know everything, so just give it to us straight up, fair enough?"

Bogtrotter held up his clawed hand. "In a moment. Before I disclose such sensitive and potentially classified information, I do need a short tribute to prove that you are worthy of receiving the news I am about to impart."

"Oh good, I can't wait." Holly elbowed Qwyrk, who refused to acknowledge her.

"Bloody hell, Boggy, I'm not singing all nine hundred verses of your stupid song!"

"No need." He shook his horned head. "Nor will I require you to do the dance."

"Oh. That's a pity." Holly made a mock sad frown.

"However," he continued, "there is a poem you must recite. We have a copy, so you only need to read it out."

"Right, fine," Qwyrk shook her head.

"It's in the style of an Elizabethan sonnet."

"Why's everything about Shakespeare all of a sudden? Whatever, just hand it over."

"And," He leaned forward, "you have to speak it in appropriate period costume."

"Wait, what?"

"Oh, please tell me it's a tavern barmaid in a tight bodice, because I'm all in for that!" Holly cracked.

"No, forget it! Sod off! I'm not wearing a flipping costume for your personal twisted Renaissance Faire!"

Holly pulled her to one side. "I'm sure it's just a silly costume, and only for a minute or two. Just long enough to read his wretched poem. It could even be fun. Go on, what say you?"

Qwyrk gritted her teeth. She looked back at Bogtrotter, grinning his toothy grin, no doubt knowing he had her over a barrel if she wanted any information at all.

"Gah! All right, fine!"

"That's my girl." Holly gave her a quick peck on the cheek.

Qwyrk turned to face Bogtrotter. "Right, let's get this over with!"

*　*　*

"I've not had my second coffee and I was going to put jam on my toast, and now we're already on our way," Moirin complained as they drove in a hired car along a wet country road, morning mists partially occluding their view.

"Shush, ya daft girl! Once you're back at the farm, ya can have all the coffee you want! And jam, I suppose. Gettin' out on the road is a great way to clear your head. Why don't you show me what you can do?"

"What, here? I don't know how."

"I'll pull over if you need."

"Don't think that'll make any difference," Moirin protested.

"Well, what's happened when it worked before?"

"Usually, I'm in some kind of state. Afraid, angry, in the music zone, something."

"So, try gettin' one of those, then."

"It's not something I can just turn on or off. Especially without more coffee."

"Yeah, all right, Ms. Addict. We'll have ya back to your beloved caffeine soon enough."

Suspicion still tugged at Moirin. "Before I try anything, I want you to be honest with me, Aileen. How did you know I'd be at the farm? The truth."

Aileen sighed. "I had a chat with your band mates after the York show, and to be honest, they're worried about ya. I told 'em we'd shared a hostel room and kinda connected, so they asked me if I could keep an eye on ya. I said sure. So when you decided to get away for a few days, one of them texted me and let me know. I said, sure, I'd phone the farm and check in on ya, because I din't know if you'd get reception out there. And that's all it was. They're worried, so I thought I'd help 'em out. I'm sorry if that seems out of order or whatnot."

"No, it's a nice gesture, thanks." Moirin wrestled with guilt over pressing the issue. "I suppose I'm a bit mad at them for goin' behind my back, but then, I have been acting like a tosser lately, so I can't really blame them for thinking I might be crackin' up."

"I don't think you're crackin' up. I think you have gifts that you can't control, not yet, but you'll figure it out."

"Maybe, but I can't just turn them on and off, sorry to say. If you were hoping for a show out here, it's probably not gonna happen."

"No worries," Aileen assured her. "Just thought I'd try. See if a change of scenery would be inspirational."

"But if I get the sudden urge to burst into song, I'll let you know."

"I'm all ears!"

* * *

Holly paced back and forth, waiting with considerable impatience to see exactly what outfit Bogtrotter was making Qwyrk wear. She imagined many possibilities, some of them enticing, nearly all of them amusing.

"Right, I'm coming out!" Qwyrk yelled from behind an outcropping, clearly less than enthused. "Let's get this the hell over with."

"I can't wait!" Holly yelled back, barely holding back her amusement.

Qwyrk emerged, wearing only a white, pleated, sleeveless, belted toga-ish garment that ended at her knees, with sandals laced up over her shins. A long, curly black wig perched atop her head, like an inebriated sheep struggling to stay standing.

Holly pressed her hands over her mouth to hide her guffaw.

"Not. One. Word," Qwyrk grumbled. Holly shook her head as an answer, not daring to release her hands.

"I'm failing to see how my being dressed for a bad toga party in any way relates to English sonnets," Qwyrk growled at Bogtrotter.

"I like to fancy that there's a connection between ancient Greek greatness and Renaissance Shakespearean greatness," he explained. "Like in the Bard's Greek plays. They're all prancing about in Athens or Rome or what have you, but still speaking the English of his day. So a sonnet with Greco-Roman themes but married to the artistry of Elizabethan language seems an entirely appropriate vehicle for a classical praise to my esteemed personage, don't you think? It's in iambic pentameter, of course."

"I think it's rather splendid." Holly couldn't help herself, bringing a glare from Qwyrk. "I told you I'd get you into a little dress sooner or later. Mind you, it's not quite what I had in mind, but I must, say, it's growing on me."

"Just give me the damned poem," Qwyrk snapped, thrusting out her hand.

One of Bogtrotter's sycophants marched up with pride and offered up a roll of parchment, tied with a red ribbon. Qwyrk undid the bow, and let the paper uncurl. She scanned it, closed her eyes, sighed, and opened them again as if hoping it would be different somehow. No such luck, apparently. She stepped forward and cleared her throat:

"If I couldst ask the gods whom they adore..."

"Um, excuse me," the herald interrupted. "A bit louder, if you don't mind. And with a little more drama, more oomph! Also, if you could strike a bit of a theatrical pose, that'd be lovely, thank you; you know, arm held out in declaration... that sort of thing."

Qwyrk scowled. She rolled her eyes. She took a deep breath, and extended one arm as if to make a dramatic gesture.

Holly almost felt sorry for her. Almost.

Qwyrk started again:

"If I couldst ask the gods whom they adore

On land, or air, or e'en in the water

Betwixt them there shouldst be a great uproar

Divine proclaim that it is the Bog-trotter... this is complete crap."

"Shhh!" the herald hissed. "You're doing fine. Go on."

Holly struggled to hold back giggles as her eyes watered. She was quite afraid she'd need to make a run for it and unleash her hysterics out of earshot. But she really wanted to hear the rest of this iambic atrocity.

Qwyrk struggled on:

"O starry night, to blazing sun above

Apollo's golden light illuminate

His folk declare their everlasting love

And raise their pints to say, 'Ey up there, mate!' Are you kidding me?"

"Stop stopping, already! You're spoiling the mood!" The herald demanded. "It's brilliant! It's transcendent!"

Qwyrk glanced over at Holly, so she raised one hand as if holding a pint glass and said, "Ey up!" She enjoyed this far too much.

"I know not where such brilliance can be found

If not this place, this Nighttime Nasty's cottage

And who beholds him as this boss so crown'd

Shall honour him with roasted cricket pottage..."

Qwyrk sighed. She clenched her jaw and rolled her eyes again.

"And if we Nighttime Nasties do offend

Go bugger off and get stuff'd, you bellend."

The herald jumped to his feet and started applauding, joined in an instant by the other sycophants, whose whoops and cheers seemed all out of proportion to the work and its delivery.

"That was lovely, that was." Bogtrotter stood up and gave her a little nod. "Almost brings a tear to the eye. You got a knack for theatrical presentation, I must admit. I'm writing a play, by the way, a neo-Tudor work, *The Evisceration of Prometheus: A Comedy*. If you'd like, I'd be happy to put a role for you in it."

"Tempting, really." Qwyrk scowled. "But I think I'll pass, if it's all the same."

Bogtrotter shrugged. "Suit yerself. Now then, what did you want to ask me?"

"You know what we're here for: what's going on? I mean, beyond the obvious, it's clear that this Irish singer and her banshee whatever-the-hell aren't the whole story."

"They ain't even half of the story, luv," he said in a somber voice. "If what we're hearin' is true, we've all got a much bigger flipping problem than some singer that can warp reality with her voice."

"What are you hearing?" Holly asked, her amusement blunted by his serious answer.

His tone grew even more ominous. "There's some kind of big bad out there, like a *really* big bad, that ain't been seen in so long, folks've forgotten about it. A thing that may as well be a myth, only it ain't. And whatever it is, it can't be beat, not even by Shadow folk or faeries. There may be nothing at all that *can* beat it. It's angry, it's coming back, and it's almost ready to get on with it. And if that happens, we're all farked."

"Well that's comforting," Qwyrk said.

"On the other hand," he continued in a lighter tone, "it may all just be a load of bollocks, a scary story invented by someone who's having a laugh, or wants to mess with everyone's heads. Wouldn't be the first time."

"Do we want to take that chance?" Holly asked, more to herself than anyone else.

Bogtrotter shrugged again. "It's up to you, luv. Personally, I ain't taking any chances. The NNs will be lying low, very low, should the need arise."

"Brave, as always," Qwyrk quipped.

"May I remind you of who came to your rescue when the Erlking was trying to make a right mess of everything last winter?" He stared down at her.

"Yeah, all right, fair enough. Cheers again."

"Oh, one other thing," Bogtrotter cautioned. "The girl singer? She may not be the main problem, but she's still a problem. She's gonna be serenading a crowd again soon, am I correct? And if she unleashes all the power she has runnin' through her now, accidentally or deliberately, it's likely a lot of folks are gonna end up dead. So, you might want to stop her."

"That's horrible, but helpful, thank you," Holly said.

"Yeah, cheers, mate," Qwyrk added. "We appreciate the heads-up. So, can I get out of this stupid outfit now, and maybe burn it?"

"Oh, I rather was hoping you could hold onto it for a while," Holly interjected with delight. "You know, wear it from time to time and feed me grapes and figs and dolmas? We could drink little glasses of piney Retsina together. Maybe read poetry by Sappho? I'm sure I can rustle up a gown to match. It could make for some smashing summer evenings!"

Bogtrotter chuckled. "Your wish, luv, is my command. Now bugger off, both of ya!"

He snapped his fingers and they were at once beset by his flashy fireworks and sparkly bombs exploding around them.

"Are you joking?" Holly yelled. "This again?"

"Oh, sod you, Boggy!" Qwyrk swore, as she grabbed Holly around her waist and popped them out of the danger zone to the first place that came to mind.

CHAPTER SEVENTEEN

In a flash of purple light, Qwyrk and Holly jumped into Jilly's living room, leaving the exploding bombardment of Bogtrotter's pyrotechnic puerility far behind. Jilly was sitting on the couch, laptop on lap, an old book open next to her, and a sketch pad next to that.

"Holly! Qwyrk? Uh, what are you wearing?"

"Long story," Qwyrk said, trying to deflect. "No actually, it's a short story, but it's a really stupid one." She saw Holly once again stifling giggles. "You're not helping, you know."

"Sorry darling," Holly said with obvious glee, "but you were ever so good and inspiring back there, I think I feel a poem of my own coming on. An Elizabethan ode, if you will."

"Don't." Qwyrk glared.

Holly cleared her throat and held out a dramatic hand. "My Qwyrk, she is a most delightsome thespian. She makes a lady glad to be a les—"

"Yeah, all right, that'll do, thank you."

"Um," Jilly started, confused.

"She's having all kinds of fun at my expense; just ignore her," Qwyrk advised, pulling that wretched wig off and throwing it to the floor. She ran her hands through her own hair in an act of defiance and to smooth out the "wig head" that was no doubt making her look even sillier. She flopped herself down on the couch with a big, exaggerated sigh. "I never want to go through that again."

"Oh come on, it wasn't that bad," Holly said in a reassuring voice, settling down next to her and running her own hand through Qwyrk's mussed-up hair. She looked around. "Mr. Blip's not here again, I see?"

"He was for a while this morning," Jilly said, "then gone, then back again, for another of his philosophy lessons. Just when I think there can't be any more of them, he comes up with something new, and worse! And I still have no idea where he's going these days. It bothers me."

"Is it something we need to know?" Holly asked. "I mean, I'm sure if it were important, he'd tell you. And keep on telling you in excruciating detail."

"He'd keep on telling us even if it was completely vapid," Qwyrk said, "which is what makes it a bit strange, I agree. It's not like him not to toot his own horn. Speaking of horn tooting, where's Star Tao?" She cringed to ask.

"Oh, he said he was off to visit some mates, or something, and would stop back by later."

"I'm gutted, as you can plainly see," Qwyrk said. Actually, she was thrilled he was absent; if word of her enforced Grecian get-up ever got back to Qwypp and Qwykk, she'd never hear the end of it.

"Anyway, what did you find out?" Jilly set her laptop to one side.

Qwyrk relayed the new bits of information, but refrained from going into detail about why she was dressed the way she was. She knew Jilly was curious, but appreciated that she didn't ask, at least for now.

"Qwyrk, we have to help her," Jilly said in a worried plea. "She doesn't know what she's doing when magic's flowing through her, and that banshee is what's really causing all the trouble. We should go out and find her, right? Like today?"

Qwyrk shook her head. "No, I don't think so."

"Why not? She needs us!"

"Where would we even start to look? And if we did find her again after that whole business of taking her to Qwyzz, telling her it was safe, and her getting abducted, she'd be even more angry and suspicious and rightly just tell us to sod off. Honestly, I don't think she's in danger right now. That creature needs her alive and healthy, and I'll bet it's more than happy that she's performing again soon. So I say we wait until the Newcastle concert and be there to stop anything bad from happening, however we have to."

"We're not going to hurt her," Jilly said in a stern and determined tone.

"No, we're not. But we might have to neutralize her for her own safety and everyone else's. And that doesn't mean we have to knock her silly. If we can figure out what kind of magic she's channeling, maybe we can shut it down. Try to figure out how that totem that Adjua gave us works?"

"I don't know if that's even possible," Jilly said.

"It must be," Holly suggested, "what with Granny's library at your disposal and the entire internet at your fingertips, surely you can discover something. Plus, there's that book she gave you."

"I meant to," Jilly said, "but I kind of got distracted, you know, with the zombie crows and everything else. But I'll have a look in her book. It might tell me how to use the little statue. Maybe there's even something in there on how to stop a banshee."

"Good," Qwyrk said. "The banshee's magic is old, older than anything we've seen before, but that doesn't mean that somebody, somewhere hasn't said something about it, maybe a whole lot of somethings. Let's try to come up with a solution that will stop that magic without hurting Moirin at all."

* * *

"I'm so glad you can drive," Moirin said as she and Aileen cruised back toward the farm through rolling green hills.

"Ah, there's nothin' to it," Aileen said. "And you never know when you'll need to."

"Like driving a girl back to a farm she was whisked away from by some supernatural weirdos after being attacked by dead crows, and then getting kidnapped again by a banshee and dropped off across the country in a random stone circle with no money and no place to stay?"

"Exactly! It pays to be prepared!" Aileen flashed a cheesy grin.

"I really am grateful. You don't have to do this."

"I want to. And how else are ya gonna get back? Anyway, want to try usin' your powers again?"

"Oh, I don't know." Moirin squirmed.

"Come on!" She sped up. "Maybe some danger'll do ya good!"

"Aileen, no! I really don't think that's a good idea."

"What, are ya scared?" She pressed her foot down on the pedal again.

"Come on, stop," Moirin protested, "I don't want to. Please!"

"Go on, give it a... crap!" Aileen swore, looking in her rear-view mirror.

"What now?"

"There's a police car behind us with the lights flashing. I doubt he wants a friendly chat."

Morin's stomach knotted. This was bad.

Aileen slowed down, pulled over, and rolled down the window. She bore a sour, sulky, angry expression, unlike any that Moirin had seen before; it was quite unsettling.

The officer, forty-something and clearly out of shape, approached the right side of the car and peered into the window. "Good morning, miss, or perhaps it's afternoon?"

"Hello officer." Aileen kept her hands on the wheel and stared straight ahead.

"I say that because at the speed you were going, you could probably race from one time zone into another without even noticing."

"I don't think I was going *that* fast... sir."

"Probably not, but it were fast enough to get my attention. And that means it were fast enough to be breaking the law."

"Look, I'm really sorry. I was chattin' with me friend here, and it just got away from me, but it won't happen again, I promise. Can ya just let me off with a warnin' this time?"

"Now, if I did that, I'd have to do it for everyone, and that would negate the whole purpose of the pulling-over, wouldn't it?"

"But how would anyone else know? Come on..."

"I'd know, and that's all that matters, young lady. Asking me to break the law for you is not doing yourself any favors. I might just increase the fine for that."

Aileen exhaled sharply and rolled her eyes. Moirin's stomach clenched as the conversation became more strained.

"So, am I gettin' a write-up, or what? Can we just get this crap over with?"

"It's gonna get worse if you keep up with that attitude, missy."

"I've a better idea," Aileen shot back. "Why don't you get stuffed, and I'll drive away like nothin' happened."

Morin's heart raced. *Aileen, no!*

"Right, that's it, step out of the car."

"What if I don't want to?"

"Step out, or I will use force to make you!"

"Yeah, I'd like to see ya try, ya pathetic little man."

"Aileen, stop!" Moirin blurted out.

Aileen ignored her, but with a sneer, she held up her left hand as if grabbing for his throat. The officer's eyes went wide and he lurched backward, clutching at his neck.

"What's happening?" Moirin yelled. "He's choking!"

But Aileen said nothing, increasing the tension in her imaginary grip.

Moirin panicked. "Aileen, stop! Please! You're killing him!"

Much to Moirin's relief, Aileen waved her hand away, and he stumbled and fell to his knees, gasping for air.

"Now, then," she said, "how about you bugger the hell off and never bother us again?"

The officer shook his head and, struggling back to his feet, managed to croak, "What the hell did you do? I'm calling for backup."

Aileen glared. "Bollocks to that. No, you're not!"

Moirin's opened her mouth in shock as Aileen's pupils vanished into pure white. She glanced at Moirin with a sinister smile and turned her attention back to the hapless officer. She emitted a harsh wail that sounded not even remotely human. The sonic wave struck the poor man, disorienting him. As it faded, she followed up in a haunting voice: "You're gonna get back in your paddy wagon and drive your ugly arse away from here, and you're gonna forget that you ever saw this car, or me, or her. Got it?"

The officer jerked to and fro. Staggering back to his car, he got in, pulled out, and drove off.

Light-headedness, nausea, and pretty much everything in between engulfed Moirin. She fumbled for the car door handle, and pushing open the door, she almost fell out. Picking herself up, she turned around in panic to look back at Aileen, who now stepped out of the car on her own side. Her features had returned to normal, but that offered no comfort.

"S-stay back," Moirin whispered.

"Moirin, it's all right, let me explain."

"No. I don't want to know. Whatever you are, just keep your distance, all right? You nearly killed that bloke."

"I wasn't gonna kill him. I just wanted to scare him off. He's fine, and he doesn't remember a thing. No harm, no foul."

"Oh, so that makes it all right, then?"

"Moirin, please. It's not what you think."

"Oh, and what do you think I think it is, eh? Do you have any idea what's goin' on in my head? Or if you do, do you even care? Am I just some pet project? Something you find funny? You're just like those kobolds and all the others, aren't you? Well, sod off, the lot of you!"

"If you'll just let me explain—"

"Shut up! Stay back! Stay away from me!" Moirin backed away in terror from the car and stumbled across the narrow road onto a grassy slope. A muddy path nearby offered a way to get up the closest hill in a hurry. Gasping and trying to hold back a scream, she climbed as fast as she could. Anywhere was better than this nightmare that wouldn't leave her alone.

* * *

"I can't believe that bastard cheated me out of my clothes. Those were my favorite boots!" Qwyrk fumed.

"I'm sure you can retrieve them at some point," Holly offered.

"Damn right I will, if I have to throw every one of his stupid sycophants in every direction in a field of his stupid fireworks to get them back."

They'd flashed back to Qwyrk's home, minus the terrible wig, which she was happy to have left in a heap on Jilly's living room floor.

"Right, let's figure what's next," Qwyrk said. "But first, I need to get out of this thing."

"Really? I think it's rather fetching," Holly teased as she sat on the sofa. "Gives you a sort of super hero look, you wondrous woman!"

"You're so funny, as usual."

"You will hang on to it, though, won't you? Pretty please?"

Qwyrk gave in. "Yeah, all right, fine. I'll keep it and we can play amazon and lady Trojan warrior some other time. Fair enough?"

"Oh, now *that* sounds fun!"

Qwyrk disappeared into her bedroom.

She soon emerged, sporting a more familiar look.

"Hm," Holly observed, folding her arms and resting her chin on one hand.

"Hm? Hm what? What does 'hm' mean?"

"So you've traded brown boots, blue jeans, and a white collared shirt for black boots, black jeans, and a grey collared shirt. Is this your formal evening wear, then?"

"You continue to be hilarious."

"It's just that I can see all sorts of things that we could do with this look. A nice scarf, a long, tailored coat."

"Do we have to talk about this whole sprucing thing right now? We have work to do. We need to stop that damned banshee from possessing Moirin at her next concert. The girl could accidentally kill someone, or a lot of someones." Qwyrk tensed at the thought.

"Well, thankfully, we have Jilly and Qwyzz, our resident genius scholars. I'm sure between them they'll come up with something."

"It's more than that, though. I'm worried because she's already killed those kobolds. If she goes further and kills any of her fellow human beings, she'll cross over to a really dark place and there won't be any coming back. We'll lose her to the banshee, and maybe whatever else is behind it all."

"You're right, we have to stop her." Holly stood up.

"Not just that, we have to help her."

* * *

Moirin raced up the hillside, slipping several times in the mud and cursing.

Aileen hurried up the path behind her. "Wait! I have to help you!"

Moirin stopped and turned to confront her. "I told you," she growled. "Stay away from me!"

"Moirin."

"Stay away from me!" she screamed, stumbling back, desperate to put distance between them. "You said you wanted to see my power? Well, keep coming toward me and you will, I swear it. I disintegrated those dead crows. I tore the kobold's heads off. Do you really want to risk it with me?"

"I don't want to risk anything, Moirin. I'm on your side." Aileen held up her hands in surrender.

"Ha! Yeah, sure you are. Lyin' about yourself this whole time. What are you? Another shadow elf freak, or some ghost in human form? Is that how you keep finding me?"

"I'm as human as you are, and I can help you, Moirin, *we* can help."

"What do you mean 'we'?"

"Haven't ya seen, girl? It's been right in front of ya the whole time! Why d'ya think I keep turnin' up? The world doesn't have those kinds of crazy coincidences. It's the amulet, silly."

"The amulet?"

"The one I gave ya that's hangin' about your neck! It's a connection, it lets me keep an eye on ya and know where you'll be. I charged it when I painted that magic spiral over your head at the hostel, and it's guided me ever since. I can find you, even project an astral form to your side, to watch over you. I mean, yeah, I was in Keswick, anyway. I really am lookin' after me mate's home, but our ancestor knew that, so she brought ya to the closest ancient power center, which was those stones just outside of town."

"Ancestor?"

"It worked brilliantly and got you away from those meddlers."

"Qwyrk and the others?"

"You don't need them. You only need us."

"Us? Us who?"

"Like I said, I'm human, but I'm just like you. I'm her descendant, too!"

A chill rippled down Moirin's back. "You've got banshee blood, too? So we're sort of related?"

"Kind of, very distantly, I suppose."

"I don't even know what that means." Moirin's anger faded, replaced by confusion.

"It means that maybe it's time to accept all these strange things about yourself, to embrace them, and stop runnin' from who you really are. Literally, in this case." She waved her arms about, pointing to the slope they were perched on.

"I don't even know what I am, what *we* are," Moirin countered. "I mean, I know about the Fomorians and all that, but it still doesn't make any sense."

"It's complicated, but I can help ya figure it all out. I didn't have anyone to help me, so it's the least I can do."

"How long have you known?" She took a hesitant step forward.

"Four years and a bit, since I was seventeen. I always knew I was different, but not how. I never had any real friends, and things at home were not good. But then, she came into my life. When I was hiking at Rannoch Moor on a school trip, she called to me and I don't know, I guess I just answered. She understood me, showed me how I was special, different in a really important way. Just like you, I was scared of her at first, but when I learned about my power, *her* power, and what it meant, everything finally made sense. I felt like I belonged somewhere for the first time in my life. And I don't want that feeling ever to go away, just because a bunch of wankers get in my way, or try to make me into something I'm not."

"What are you saying?"

"I can't stand to see special folk like us held back, by that bloody police officer, or anyone else. I'm tired of everything bein' so difficult for the likes of us, and sometimes I get so mad I just want to break things, tear them apart!"

"Aileen, I don't understand." Moirin started to feel bad for her. "You're so angry. What's wrong?"

"You can't tell? Like you haven't felt the same your whole life?"

"Well, no, because I was stolen as a baby. I told you, my brother and I both were. Kobolds took us away from this world and tried to make us into their tools, weapons. So I never grew up around other kids."

"I know, and I'm sorry." Aileen sounded sympathetic. "But she can be there for us now."

"Who is she? I mean really?"

"The woman in your head? In mine? She's everything! And she'll make you feel more complete than you ever have."

"Complete how?"

"Look, you must've felt awkward sometimes, like an outcast, especially since you've been singin' with your band."

Moirin nodded. "Pretty much every day."

"See? That's what I'm talking about. And you know why. We're misfits *because* we're her descendants. We're like her great-great grandchildren a hundred generations on, but we still have her power inside of us after all that time, and we can use it!"

"But I don't know if I want to. Something terrible happened when I faced those kobolds last night. I think she wanted me to meet them. And this rage took over inside of me." Her eyes teared up. "It was like I wasn't there anymore, but she still was, in my head, I mean. And this power, this ancient, primal energy just welled up inside me. I opened my mouth and sang, and it all just rushed out. All the anger, the hurt, the disappointment, the hate, the sorrow, everything I was holding back just flowed into my voice in that moment. It hit them and just sort of melted their brains inside. I killed them both, Aileen, and I did it with no effort and not even much thought."

"And how did it make you feel?"

"Honestly? I don't know. Odd at first, but now, I just feel bad, guilty. Like it's a power I shouldn't have. No one should."

"Are ya serious? Well, feeling weak all the time may not've been a problem for *you*, since you were abducted by those things, but—"

"No! I felt weak and scared every day, exactly because of what happened to me."

"Well, let me tell you a bit about me, and then maybe you'll understand. Me mam died when I was a baby, so I never knew her. And me da's just a worthless, ragin' alcoholic. He never hit me, but when he was drunk, he was always yellin', always on about how I was never good enough, about how disappointed in me my mother would be, how maybe I was the one that killed her. Do you know what that does to a little girl? Years of that crap?"

"I have a good idea."

"So you can imagine how I was around other kids. Oh, it was so funny when I was a wee lass." She scowled. "Aileen, the hen with the wild coppery hair. The awkward one, the bairn they all made fun of and din't want anything to do with. And then, I grew up and filled out and suddenly, all the lads wanted to get with me, din't they? The same ones who'd laughed at me a few years before were now just a bunch of randy wallopers tryin' to get in me knickers. They disgusted me, the lot of them. I wasn't havin' it, and told 'em to sod off. Kicked the crap out of a few of 'em and enjoyed it." She sighed and her expression changed from anger to something calmer.

"But all that's in the past," she went on. "None of it matters. This is what counts. This is real, Moirin, *this* is power!" She gestured back and forth between them. "We're not like them, other human folk. We have ancient blood in our veins. Magic blood. This is our gift, our birthright! Don't ya see? We can have everything we want but never had, everything we deserve. This is our time." She reached out her hand. "We're special, you and me, and together, the world can be ours!"

"I don't... I don't know. It bothers me. I don't feel like I have a choice in this. It's like I'm being forced down a path I don't know if I even want to go down."

"But that's only because you haven't truly seen what we can do. Let me show you."

"No, I have. I've seen what *I* can do. It scares me. And that, whoever she is, in my head—"

"Her name is Aeval. She's the first of us. The greatest. The most ancient banshee in Ireland."

"Fine, but it sounds like she wants us to do bad things. To hurt people."

"No, she just wants us to come into our own and be who we were meant to be. And if others try to stop us, even after we've warned them to stay away and not cross us, then that's their fault, in't it?"

"It just doesn't seem right. What she made me do to the kobolds."

"Is exactly what they deserved. They stole your life, Moirin, yours and your brother's. She din't make you kill them, you did it because you wanted to. Because you could. And yeah, I know it's not my place to say anything, but your brother'd probably be alive now if it weren't for them. You had every right to do what you did. They had it comin', nasty little baby-stealin' buggers!"

"I know, but I still don't understand."

"You will, trust me." She held out her hand.

Moirin hesitated. She looked at Aileen's smiling freckled face, looked at her hand. "I want to. I feel like you're the first person other than my brother who actually gets me. That emptiness never left me, even when he was hidden from my mind by whatever magic shite we came up with. I always knew I was missing something. And now he's gone and you're here, to help with that emptiness. It's confusing and tempting and brilliant and scary all at once."

"Yes, Moirin, I can be that for you, and you can be it for me. We can have what we never had in our own crap lives." She held her hand out a little farther. "Please, let me help you. In return, you'll be helpin' me." A calm settled over Moirin. Whether it was a true peace, like a return to a long-lost home, or just wishful thinking on her part, she didn't know. But she didn't care. She wanted to belong, she craved it. She reached out and took Aileen's hand.

CHAPTER EIGHTEEN

Jilly ate on the sofa, laptop at hand, Odin sleeping in the corner. She flipped though the book Granny had left for her, taking a bite of her cheese sandwich (gourmet food was not on offer tonight, alas).

She'd spent the day at Granny's looking for any information about how to use Adjua's small object to neutralize Moirin without hurting her. Granny's impressive library contained such classics as *Encyclopedia Paradoxica* and *The Wand in the Willows* and *The BiblioBabbleBible*, which Jilly reasoned must have been what Qwyrk was trying to remember while she was making up excuses to sneak off with Holly. She half-despaired at seeing so many books spread throughout several rooms and not as well organized as one might hope for England's most impressive seven-hundred-year-old mystic.

Alas, hunger set in, and since her parents were nowhere to be found, she went home to scrounge up what she could in the kitchen. There was always food there of course, but it'd be nice if her mum or dad were actually home to *make* dinner once in a while. Now nibbling, she turned to a bookmarked page to see: "How to disentangle an ancient spirit from its victim. Wait, what?" She almost dropped said sandwich. "This is it! It's just an incantation and scattering some crushed sage leaves. This is easy! This is... hang on." She scanned the paragraph with a bit more intent, reading aloud: "'The victim must be willing to have the spirit take leave of it. For if the two are in accord, no such sundering can occur.' Are you kidding me? I have to get her permission for it to work? Bollocks, that's never going to happen!"

She slammed the book down in frustration and took a big bite of bread and cheese. "Why is witching so difficult?"

* * *

Qwyrk and Holly had a much-needed night together, and everyone else spent the next day in preparation for the coming evening's concert, which is really just a convenient narrative device to skip over having to peer into their lives and eavesdrop on hours of conversations and activities irrelevant to our story. The day progressed without much incident, except for an afternoon assignment that sent Qwyrk to go and break up a brawl outside of Bolton Castle between a Monopod (a surly bloke with only one large leg, who hopped his way to England from some unknown land) and a Blemee (a somewhat less surly bloke with no head, but rather with his face on his chest). Qwyrk was half-tempted to let them duke it out to the finish, it being a once-in-a-lifetime match-up. But she stopped it, sent them on their way, and scolded everyone who had gathered to go find better things to waste their coins on. Horatio was particularly annoyed, as he'd bet some very nice antique doubloons on the Monopod, with the promise of doublooning, er, doubling his wager.

Despite such distractions, the day passed well enough for all concerned. Moirin returned to the farm and prepared to head up to Newcastle to sound check before the show. Aileen was eager to accompany her, her own motivations not yet completely evident. Jilly worked at Granny's house, though without much success. Holly trained at home, with considerable success. Star Tao meditated in his van to the music of Olmec Barnacles for several hours to sharpen his mind for the channeling that he'd likely be doing later. Blip... well, no one knew where he was; off doing something very important, no doubt, at least as far as he was concerned.

And with that little interlude finished, we now rejoin the story, already in progress.

* * *

Qwyrk, having prevented a Monopod arse-kicking, went home. Nothing was out of place; no trees or hedgerows or rock formations had seen fit to saunter their way into new and unexpected locations, so that was something. Relieved, she was about to enter her house when she heard, or rather, sensed, a sparkle in the air.

"Bloody hell, what now?"

Two little pink creatures—female, cute, sweet, and to be honest, rather insipid—popped out of an iridescent, glittery shimmer, floating in mid-air.

"Pixies. Lovely. What can I do for you?" Qwyrk asked, not really wanting to know.

"Faegram for Qwyrk!" they said in unison.

"Fine, thanks. Give it here, and I'll have a look at it later."

"Oh no! It's far too important to deliver a written copy!" one said.

"We were told to memorize it and repeat it only to you," the other added.

"So, it's important, secure, need-to-know info for my ears only, and the sender chose you two to deliver it?"

They looked at her and blinked, as if they didn't understand.

"Fine, whatever," she went on. "Lay it on me. What's so important?"

One cleared her throat, the other hummed a quick musical scale.

"Wait, you're going to *sing* it to me?"

"Of course!" one answered. "And in harmony!"

Qwyrk contemplated face-palming, but just nodded. "Fine. What does it say? Or sound like?"

They began their tune in a hum, a jaunty little piece reminiscent of a 1940s swing or boogie-woogie song:

"Qwyrk, if you receive this, can you come right away?"

"It's really quite important, but just why I can't say.

"I'll tell you all just when I see you, and explain the moving tree, too

"But you have to come to me too, there's more than this melody, ooo...

"Qwyrk if you receive this can you come right along

"There isn't much more, now we've reached the end of our song

"Keep it secret, this is Qworum, meet me now, outside the forum,

"Qwyrk come see me, please, right awaaaaaay!"

Qwyrk gave them a blank stare. A blanker-than-blank stare, really. Plus, there were only two of them, but somehow they'd sung in three-part harmony. She didn't want to know how.

"He gave us the message, but we put it into rhyme and song!" one said. "It was lovely, wasn't it?" the other boasted.

"Um, amazing, really, thanks. Tell him I'll be right there."

They giggled, bid her adieu, and disappeared in a puff of pink mist that smelled like strawberry candy and bubblegum.

She walked back into her home, still bewildered. And almost slammed face-first into an oak tree just inside the door.

* * *

"You really don't have to take me all the way to Newcastle," Moirin protested, as she packed up her clothes. Aileen had stayed the night, and Moirin had kept her hidden.

"How else are ya gonna get there, you daft girl?" Aileen said. "It's not like your powers let you fly! Gonna try drivin' on your own? Now that would be scary!"

"Yeah, that's a shame. About the flying, I mean. But honestly, are you sure you want to go all that way?"

"Of course, I want to see you perform again, silly. Plus, the only way you're ever gonna figure out about your true power is to explore it where you shine the most, on stage, singin' your heart out. Your gifts are more subtle than mine, and you've got to use them where they'll work best."

"But what if things go wrong? What if I can't control it? I don't want to hurt anyone; they're just fans comin' to see us."

"Nothin's gonna go wrong. This is a way for you to get rid of your inhibitions about your true nature and really be you. I'll be there in the audience for you, and she's gonna be there, too."

"What? How do you know?" Moirin remembered with uneasiness Aeval's promise of a completed "initiation."

"She told me, put the thought in me head. I dinnae know how she'll do it, but I believe her. So I have to go along, see? It'll be a glorious night, and afterward, you'll be changed forever. You'll really be home, and we'll be there to welcome you."

"I don't even know what I'm supposed to be doing."

"Just sing and let it flow, and let the magic come as it will, let her work through you as she will. Now come on, get your stuff together and let's be off, eh? You've got sound checks and all that to do, right?"

Moirin managed a meager smile, but she had none of Aileen's confidence. Despite the pep talk, a sense of foreboding about the evening haunted her, even as she tried to push it away.

＊　＊　＊

Qwyrk flashed into a small ante-chamber, where Qworum stood waiting, arms folded in his voluminous sleeves, his shoulder-length grey hair neatly combed back.

"Seriously," Qwyrk said, "do you even own any other clothes? I mean, I think I'm bad! Anyway, I'm kind of in the middle of something, so if we could speed this up?"

"Thank you for meeting me alone," he said, ignoring her joking.

"A Faegram, really? Sung by pixies?"

"Yes, the Annwn Sisters. It seemed the most innocuous way of reaching out to you."

"Not sure that's how I'd describe it. Anyway, what's so important that you couldn't say it in front of the others? Is this some embarrassing personal problem? Because I'm not sure I'm the best one to talk to."

He motioned with a quick turn of his head. "Come with me."

She shrugged, and followed him from the council room area and into a side alcove, where he motioned to her again.

"Seriously?" she said, louder than he probably wanted her to.

He led her into a darkened hall and pointed to a door on their right.

"In here," he said in a hushed tone.

"Why are we chatting in private?" she asked. "What's with the whispers? Are we supposed to be wearing trench coats and fedora hats or something?"

He looked behind him before turning again to face her.

"Come on, what is it?" Qwyrk had half a mind to storm out and leave.

He shut the door and turned to face her. "I am sorry to have to broach this subject with you, Qwyrk. It concerns the Yakshi."

"What about her?" Qwyrk glowered. "Also, she has a name. Holly Vishala, but you know that already, don't you?"

"Yes, my apologies. What I'm telling you is, shall we say, off the record, but..." He paused and looked pained at the thought of continuing.

"But what? Come on, say it!" She pondered grabbing his robe and shaking him, but held off.

"It might be in your best interest not to see her for a while," he said. "You two have formed an intimate relationship?"

"Not that it's in any way your business, but yes we have, and what the hell are you talking about, not seeing her for a while? What's going on? And how do you even know about it?"

"It's not an official pronouncement. It's more of a hunch on my part, and on the part of a few others."

"A hunch? A hunch about what?"

"I really cannot say, not just yet. But I would advise you not to see her, and maybe not to be seen with her, at least for a while."

"Or else what?" Though well past angry at this point, she managed to keep her eyes from glowing bright red. Just. "You'll haul me in front of the council and accuse me of 'neglecting my duties' again? Trying to shame me isn't going to get you very far, just so you know."

"I told you, this is merely something I am saying off the record, as your friend."

"Look mate, thanks, but I'm not taking any crap suggestions unless you tell me what's actually going on!"

"I don't know, not yet. Honestly. But there could be danger in associating too closely with her. Just be careful, please?"

And with that he turned, opened the door and hastened away, leaving Qwyrk furious, and completely confused.

*　*　*

Jilly had given up on trying to separate Aeval from Moirin, and instead stared at the talisman for the hundredth time. She turned it upside down, right-side up, sideways, and every way in between. Other than the carved face on it, there was nothing: no markings, instructions, warranty notices, expiration dates, nothing. A good night's sleep hadn't given her any new ideas.

"That lady, Adjua, said something about using it to turn power on itself. Hmm, I wonder. If I use it against Moirin, maybe it will make everything silent, so she can't sing? That'd be a good way of stopping things without hurting her."

She held the object out in front of her, both hands gripping it. She closed her eyes.

"Focus, Jilly, focus... I will that all sound be drained from this room for the time being, and only return when I so choose. So may it be!"

She waited. She intended. She visualized. Yes! That was it! It was happening, maybe? Everything seemed so quiet... was it working? Yes, yes, it most certainly was... perhaps?

I think I'm doing it! she thought. *I think I've cracked it, I—*

A loud snort from Odin startled her and she dropped the talisman on the carpet, jolting her eyes open. The dog adjusted in his bed, turned over, and went back to sleep.

"Crap!" She reached down and picked the little object up.

"Maybe it will let me sing just as well as she does and I can beat her that way!"

She held the talisman and concentrated on being the best singer she possibly could be. The strands of enchantment wove their way into the room, wrapping themselves around her.

"Yes, this is it!"

She opened her mouth and sang the first lines from her favorite Weasels song, proudly belting out her newfound talent...

Odin looked up, whined, and buried his head in his bed, one paw over his exposed ear.

"Yeah, all right, fine! That didn't work, either. Everyone's such a critic."

She tossed the object on the couch next to her and sat back in frustration, glancing at the time on her laptop.

"May as well go and get ready. Not like I'm going to be very useful, though."

Leaving Odin to recover from the shock of her horrid singing, she trudged upstairs. "I may not be much of a witch, but at least I can look like one!"

*   *   *

Back home, Qwyrk edged around the unexpected arboreal intrusion in her entryway, and found that Holly was already there, getting herself ready for the evening's adventure.

"Hello darling! Lovely tree, by the way; really adds to the décor."

"Yeah, I was thinking of changing things up a bit, and I thought, why not have a forest in my sitting room?" Qwyrk replied without a hint of humor. "You do realize I need this out of here? Whatever's happening is now happening in my house!"

"It seems fairly innocuous."

"You know, you're the second person to use that word with me in the last hour. And I must say, in both cases, I'm not convinced it's the right choice."

"Well, have your dryad friend take care of it." Holly kissed her. "Right now, we have to get ready for tonight. You're a bit late, where were you?"

"Oh, I got a Faegram from Qworum, had to dash over there for a bit."

"Nothing serious, I hope?"

"No, no, not really," Qwyrk fibbed. "Look, I'm going to get changed, so carry on and I'll be out in two ticks."

"The evening formal wear tonight, then, is it?"

"Something like that. Goddess, you're lucky you're adorable!"

"And that I use it to my advantage."

"That you do."

"So, what did the council want?" Holly applied her gothy makeup while Qwyrk went to change.

"Not the council," Qwyrk said from her bedroom, "just Qworum. Some administrative stuff. I had to... break up another gambling match today, and he just wanted the details."

"Oh. Who won?"

"No one. I broke it up. Oh, don't tell me you go around betting on these pillocks, too."

"No, not at all, but this time of year is rather amusing, what with everyone riled up, wound up, turned on, and such."

"Yeah, it's quite the spectacle."

She emerged wearing black jeans, short black boots, and a black long-sleeved collared shirt.

"See? You're getting there," Holly said with admiration. "My sense of spruce is rubbing off on you. Now we just need to accessorize you, and you'll be smashing!"

"You *do* realize that this is a mission tonight, right? Not a date?"

Holly shrugged. "Why not both? I love the idea of us kicking arse and looking smashing doing it together. I scrounged up some things for you. Here, try this on."

She offered Qwyrk a long, thin, form-fitting coat, as black as the rest of her garb. It fit well, and looked quite good, Qwyrk admitted, in spite of herself.

"It's light-weight, won't interfere with your punching and kicking, and absolutely lets you get your spruce on, you goth girl, you."

"It's not bad, I must admit." She looked at it admiringly. "I could take to this."

"It gives you that mysterious, trench coat look, but still suits you."

The word "trench coat" reminded Qwyrk's of her unpleasant conversation with Qworum, which just made her start worrying all over again, but she pushed it away. "Right, so, if you're ready?"

Holly threw on a similar coat. "Let's go save the world again!"

* * *

Qwyrk and Holly waited in Jilly's living room. Jilly sported a long black dress and wore the black wig that Qwyrk had found so humiliating yesterday.

"I don't know why," Qwyrk said, "but it actually works on you. I'm so sorry."

"I thought it might help me hide my face, so Moirin doesn't recognize me," Jilly explained. "Also, it might make me look a bit older. I mean, we *are* sneaking me into another over-eighteen club, right?"

"That's the plan. Oh here, this is Moirin's handbag. She left it at Qwyzz's. Maybe you can give it back to her later? That is, if she doesn't destroy us all." Qwyrk handed the black satchel over to her young friend for safe-keeping.

"Thanks. I'm sure she'll be glad to get it back, unless she's turned into some malefic creature of the night by now."

"Malefic? You've clearly been spending too much time with Blip."

"Not like I can actually do anything, though." She told them about her lack of progress.

"Hey, you're very resourceful, especially under pressure," Qwyrk assured her.

"Absolutely," Holly agreed. "You still have time to figure out what to do."

"I guess, I just wish it wasn't always so complicated," Jilly sighed.

"That's part of what makes it worth doing, I suppose," Qwyrk said. "If it were easy, everyone would be doing it, and it wouldn't be special."

Jilly just shrugged. "I suppose."

"Speaking of being more difficult than need be, where's Blip?" Qwyrk looked around.

"Right here," he announced, wandering out of a wall. He wore his monogramed Weasels scarf as a cravat, carried his sword cane and sported a top hat, along with his monocle. "I trust I am attired appropriately for the festivities?"

"Considering that no one will see you, I'd say so," Qwyrk quipped.

"I think you look spiffing, Mr. Blippingstone," Holly offered. Qwyrk admired her ability to make even fools feel good about themselves. It was a talent she didn't possess and to be honest, didn't want.

"Thank you, my dear, I did try to be a tad sprauncy, I must admit. I'm glad to see that at least one of the two of you has some sartorial savvy and appreciation. Though, you've dressed her up quite well, I must say, given what you had to work with."

Qwyrk clenched her jaw.

Blip looked around. "Where is our excerebrose lad?"

"Oh," Jilly answered, before Qwyrk could come back with some form of sarcasm, "he said he'd be here soon. He just had to find a place to park his van and such."

"Well I hope he doesn't take too long." Blip sniffed and polished his monocle. "We've a night on the town to attend to."

"Yeah," Qwyrk sneered, "and also, not letting Moirin lose control of herself and, I don't know, accidentally kill a bunch of people and go over to the dark side from which she might never escape. Like, the whole, actual reason for this mission? But please, don't let us interrupt your fabulous evening out."

"I'm merely pointing out that as long as we have to make the journey, we might as well enjoy ourselves a bit. Maintaining a relaxed state is crucial to being prepared for conflict. Be as the water, be utterly yielding and yet contain the power to wear down the mountain." He waved one hand about in some pseudo-martial arts gesture.

"Oh splendid," Qwyrk shot back, "Ninja Blip is back in full force. I feel a lot safer."

"One of these days I will demonstrate the full capacity of my abilities, and then you shall have proverbial egg on your face. My weapon is ever at the ready, prepared to deliver good hard thrusts at a moment's notice!"

Qwyrk stifled a laugh and saw Holly do the same. She looked away to try to gain back her composure, but that didn't work well, and the moment she spied Holly also trying not to lose it, she lost it. The fact that Jilly was also giggling made it that much worse.

"What is so damned funny?" Blip demanded. "If I didn't know that liquor has no effect on either of you, I'd suspect a bit of over-indulgence, which incidentally would jeopardize our mission. And you, young lady," he said, pointing an accusatory froggy finger at Jilly, "would do far better to avoid the undue influence of these stultiloquent inamoratas."

A knock at the door dispelled their mirth and Jilly ran to answer it. Sure enough, Star Tao strolled into the living room behind her, dressed a bit more dark than usual.

"Evenin' all," he said with a wave. "You're all looking dapper, especially you, my lord." He bowed to Blip.

Qwyrk rolled her eyes. She would never stop rolling her eyes at these two.

"Sorry I'm not a bit more formal," he went on, "but I don't have too much in the way of black clothes, sorry to say. Black tends to sap me energies and makes channeling more difficult. You really need bright hues to attract positive vibes. But my coat's charcoal, yeah?" He held out the sides. "So it'll be all right, and I'll blend in well enough. And I've got me special rainbow tie-dye underpants on, so

I'll still be able to achieve the desired multiversal outcome, regardless of my gloomy outer wear."

"You have rainbow colored tie-dye underpants?" Qwyrk echoed. "Never mind." She closed her eyes and held up one hand, as if to push the thought away. "I don't want to know any more than that. I don't even want to know that. We'd best get a move on if we're going to sneak in properly. Come on, then."

They joined hands and in another second, they were on their way.

* * *

"And here we are," Qwyrk declared as they blinked into yet another empty side alley. "What's this club called again?"

"Philisophi-ghoul," Jilly said.

"Where do they come up with these sophomoric names?" Blip said.

"I kind of like this one," Qwyrk said, "Makes your favorite subject sound a little less tedious."

"How rebarbative of you. Color me shocked."

"Let's not waste time paying to get in," Qwyrk said, ignoring his invitation to another round of verbal sparring, tempting though it was. "I'll pop inside, get the lay of the land, so to speak, then come back and get you all."

"I'll see to it that the club comes up with £100 extra, quietly placed in the cash box, in case anyone is worried about the ethics of it all," Holly assured.

"Very good of you my dear," Blip said with a nod. "You are a shining example of excellence that your lady companion would do well to learn from."

Qwyrk ignored him and darted inside for a quick look around. "More velvet than I've seen since the eighteenth century," she mused.

Indeed, she spied a sizeable number of Stygian-hued people already milling about. Good for the box office take, but not so great if paranormal things started happening, as she feared they might. She spotted a good, shadowy corner and returned to the others, bringing them in one by one, so as not to draw attention.

"Now," Qwyrk said, "we wait and see what happens, and hope the whole place doesn't fall down around our heads." Qwyrk was being metaphorical, but she wasn't so sure that a more literal meaning wasn't also appropriate.

* * *

"This is gonna be a good one, eh?" Sam said.

Moirin heard his voice as if it were far off. "What? Oh, yeah, absolutely. It'll be the best show we've done, yeah?"

"It's a big crowd tonight. Maybe the biggest we've had. I've heard tell that there's at least one record company rep out there, too, but no pressure, eh?"

"No, none at all. We'll just, um, we'll just go out there and kill it like we always do." She gave him a weak and insincere smile. Somehow, the show mattered much less now. "It'll be grand!" She didn't know if he believed her or not, but her mind quickly wandered off again to Aileen's words.

"It's all inside of you," Aileen had said. "Just let yourself be the channel and it will come through. Don't fight it; the power is almost limitless if you let it be."

"Easier said than done," she said out loud.

"What is?" Sam asked.

"What?"

"What's easier said than done?"

"Um, oh, you know, playin' a show without a few little cock ups here and there, not that we'll do that, but you know, it happens."

"You all right, there? You seem a bit far off."

"Yeah, fine. Just still a bit tired, you know. I guess my couple of days in the country weren't as restful as I'd hoped. Ah well, some stage fright could do me good tonight, I think." She offered him another fake smile. "Come on, then, they're waiting for us, and it's almost time."

They found their band mates at the edge of backstage, as the lights dimmed.

"You've heard about them," a voice announced over the PA. "You've fantasized about them, maybe you've been lucky enough to have nightmares about them. But the time for lucid flights of darkest fancy is past, darlings. They are fire and ice, they are roses and thorns, they will break your hearts and you'll thank them for it. They are... the Mystic Wedding Weasels!"

The crowd roared its approval and the band made their way to the stage. The power would flow tonight, Aileen had promised. The ancestor would manifest herself, to complete the circle and bring her descendants back to their true home.

"If these folks want to see the real Chantz magic," Aileen had told her, "let's show them tonight what you can do!"

The cheers increased as Moirin took her place on stage. Without a smile, she gave a nod to the crowd, just enough to acknowledge them without being friendly, because who would want to do that? The music began.

Moirin moved in time to the melancholy melody, closing and

opening her eyes in a long rhythmic pattern. She glanced off to her right and saw Aileen standing in the shadows, adorned in the same black dress, her antique parasol firmly in hand. She blew Moirin a kiss and flashed a smile, though there seemed to be something more behind it, something knowing, something almost sinister. But this was an evening for magic and for reclaiming her birthright. Wasn't it?

Moirin took a deep breath, and another. The moment had arrived. Feeling the stirring of ancient forces somewhere deep within her, she opened her mouth and began to sing.

CHAPTER NINETEEN

"Here we go," Qwyrk said as the first song began. She and the others kept to the shadows' edge, easy enough once the house lights went down. "Right, everyone knows what to do. At the first sign of anything going weird, we don't wait. We act."

"I'm still not sure what I'm supposed to do," Jilly said. "And how am I supposed to get Moirin's permission to block Aeval? Walk up to her between songs and just ask? Yeah, me in an over-eighteen club interrupting the show. That should go over well. They'll toss me out on my arse!"

"I have faith in you." Qwyrk smiled.

"I'm glad one of us thinks this isn't completely impossible," Jilly sighed.

"Just be ready. You may have a chance we don't even see yet."

"I'm going to mingle a bit," Holly said. "I'll come back if anything gets out of hand."

Qwyrk nodded, pleased that Holly was making her own

decisions instead of taking directions. It was a far better way for them to work together. And it was kind of hot.

"I'll stay back here and plug in to the cosmic multi-web," Star Tao announced, "see who's out there. Could be a galactic directive on this kind of thing."

"Yeah, you do that," Qwyrk replied, unconvinced.

"I shall also mingle," Blip declared. "I can't be seen, and my sword cane is ever at the ready to defend the defenseless in a melee, and riposte against, er, the riposteless."

"I feel so much better knowing that you and Star Tao are on the team," Qwyrk faked grinned.

"I came through for us in a rather large way last winter, in case you've forgotten."

"Did you bring your dragon along? Have I missed her somehow?"

"It wouldn't do to set her loose in such close quarters. There could be unexpected consequences." "Well, I'm glad you realized that. I guess we'll just have to settle for your ripostey, hard thrusty, swordy skills. Goddess help us."

Blip sniffed and wandered off without another word.

For once, Qwyrk took no comfort in their pre-battle banter.

* * *

Moirin sang like she'd never sung before, maybe giving her best performance of her life.

Whatever happens, just let it flow. Aileen's here for you, and the old woman, too.

As one song ended and the crowd offered up enthusiastic cheers, she glanced again over to Aileen, hiding in the shadows off to the right side near the stage.

"Let it happen, Moirin," Aileen said in no more than a whisper. Somehow Moirin heard her over the din of the crowd. "Let yourself be free."

The word "free" trailed off in Moirin's ears as the next song began. She glanced back at Aileen again; her eyes had turned white and her smile had distorted into a sinister grin.

A chill ran down Moirin's back, but it was time to begin the next song.

* * *

After an unnervingly uneventful five songs, Qwyrk's intuition told her that they were right on the edge. Surely everything would go to blazes. She hoped she was wrong.

She glanced at Star Tao, who swayed back and forth, his head rolled back and eyes closed. He looked like he was really stuck into it, but she worried he couldn't control whatever it was he was opening himself up to. She wondered why she trusted him at all.

The Weasels' current song became even more morose. They hadn't played it at the previous show. Moirin seemed to be giving it her all, but something felt off.

Holly wandered back to the side-shadows. "I'm not seeing anything out of the ordinary, but I'm worried."

Qwyrk nodded. "Me too."

"Is that a good sign?" Holly asked, looking behind them at Star Tao.

"I guess he's really going for it. Whoever the hell he's channeling, I hope it's someone useful, and not his make-believe council of babbling idiots that can't speak in anything like normal sentences."

"He hasn't let you down before, has he?" Holly asked.

"Technically, no, but that's not saying much. As cool as he thinks it is, he's opening himself up to all kinds of not-great things out there."

As Qwyrk spoke, she heard the current song become ever more morose. Moirin seemed to be focused on her delivery now, giving it her all. That was good from an artistic standpoint, but maybe not so good for other outcomes, especially of the "ancient banshee wants to decimate the nightclub" variety.

"I don't like this," Qwyrk said. "If anything's going to happen, I think it'll be soon."

She sensed a change in the air around her, spreading out into the whole club, like the feeling just before a thunderstorm breaks. She clenched her fists, fearing the worst.

Moirin seemed lost in her performance. Her eyes closed as she gripped the mic stand with both hands. She looked like she was slipping away to somewhere dangerous.

Qwyrk shot Holly a nervous look. "Get ready."

Swirls of colored light appeared around the club, just a few at first, followed by dark vortices of mist.

"Those look like..." Holly said, clutching her stick.

"Portals," Qwyrk finished. "Bollocks, she's trying to bring things from outside this world into here. Or, the banshee is."

She glanced back at Star Tao, whose upper body had gone limp, like marionette without strings. "Hey, sorry to be pushy mate, but if you're going to connect with someone, can you speed it up? Things are about to get a whole lot hotter in here, and we need all the help we can get!"

Star Tao jerked his head up and thrust out his arms. His completely white eyes contrasted with a curious blank expression on his face. But almost at once, his mouth twisted into a tortured smile.

"That's... not a happy look," Holly said, taking a few steps away from him.

"But why wouldn't it be happy, my dear?" an old woman's voice sounded through his mouth. "This little man-fool is the perfect vehicle for me to manifest on this mortal plane, and to ensure that my descendant comes into her own this night, with all the power and terror that she should rightfully wield. Oh, there will be many here who are unhappy with that, but if a few sacrifices have to be made, that is a small price to pay."

She laughed, a cackling, bitter mockery that sent chills down Qwyrk's back. Holly inched in close to Qwyrk and grasped her hand.

* * *

Moirin slipped backward inside her own mind. The power was upon her, and she was relinquishing control to let it flow. Aileen's words still echoed in her mind: "Be free." That was all she wanted, freedom. But was this it? Was giving up her body and mind to this elder being the path to that liberation?

She brought her attention back to the song, to the words she was singing. She wouldn't allow herself to forget them, to make a mistake, but now it seemed as if someone else was singing them and she was just a spectator.

She saw swirling lights above the room—doors to other worlds opening—and the fearsome shapes that were inside them. She knew this was wrong, that these creatures mustn't be allowed through. She knew they wanted to hurt. To kill. And yet, she sang on, her voice providing the power needed to open those doors. She couldn't stop herself, and she started to like it. Aileen's smile twisted into a hideous grin. And she heard the laughter of her ancestor.

* * *

Jilly watched from the crowd as dark mists and multi-colored spirals began to appear at the edges of the club. It reminded her of the same disturbing magic she felt in Leeds. Ancient, but tainted. And just like at the uni, no one else in the audience seemed to notice.

She pulled out the talisman and stared at it, turning it round and round, hoping to see something she hadn't before. But that little face carved on the wooden stick gave no hint of power or magical properties, nothing to show that it was anything more than a nicely-carved trinket.

"Come on," she demanded, "what do you do?"

She looked up at Moirin, who swayed to the music, her eyes closed, lost in the power of the sounds that came from the band and the mesmerizing vocal line she was singing. It was the same swept-away look Jilly had seen before, and it meant that at any moment...

Misshapen beings, large and small, creatures of a baleful heritage long banished from this Earth, began to form in those rainbow swirls. And still the crowd danced and moved to the intoxicating music and the increasing intensity of the melancholy song, oblivious to the danger manifesting right on top of them, to the pulsing of a magic that no one but she could hear.

She had to do something.

* * *

"How nice of you to join us." Qwyrk readied her fists as Holly raised her stick. "After that stunt you pulled back at Qwyzz's, I've been eager to see you again."

"I thought you would be," Aeval snarled back, her voice projecting through Star Tao's mouth. He—or was it her?—approached them with slow steps. "My child will be born tonight, on Beltane eve, into her real life, her true destiny. It's likely that you will all die, but at least you can know that you served some purpose."

"Yeah, funny that, because no one is actually dying tonight," Qwyrk shot back, her confidence finding its footing again. "See? I've heard this same kind of crap from a whole lot of you types, so I just don't buy it anymore. You're all mouth, but when you're actually faced with any real challenge, you just—"

Star Tao's right arm lashed out at Qwyrk's belly with shocking swiftness, sending her sprawling to the ground. At the same time, his left arm swiped at Holly's shoulder, flinging her to one side.

"You were saying?" Aeval's voice taunted.

Qwyrk dragged herself up and shook off the effects of the blow. She offered a hand to Holly. They kept their eyes on the possessed Star Tao. "That all you've got?"

"Not at all, but I have no time to be distracted by fools," Aeval scoffed. "While this boy's body is useful, it won't survive long if I expend all my energy humiliating you. I'll discard it when I am ready, so I'd advise you against taking any more action against me, unless you want me to burn him alive from the inside."

Qwyrk hesitated. "How do we know you're telling the truth, eh, banshee?"

"You won't risk it." Aeval warned. "Now stand aside, both of you, unless you want to see this little form explode in front of you. It will make those dead kobolds look tame by comparison!"

Cursing, Qwyrk and Holly backed away. Aeval sneered and shoved past them, entering the crowd and approaching the stage.

A swirl of color above them caught Qwyrk's attention.

Then another.

And another.

"Um, love?" she said to Holly. "I think we may have more immediate problems."

* * *

"Gah! I have no idea what to do!" Jilly despaired.

Twisted shapes hovered in the swirls and shadows, unnatural beings clambered to invade the gathering. And still, no one saw them but her.

She held up the talisman and stared at it. "What do you *do*? Come on, I need some help here!"

"Ms. Pleeth! May I be of assistance?" Blip strode up to her, sword drawn.

"I'm sorry sir, but not unless you know how the activate the magic in this ancient African totem."

"I'm afraid not, but I have faith in you, we all do. You continue to be a shining beacon of excellence in sharp contrast to far too many of the youth of today, well removed from the uncouth and uncultured plebes that make me weep for the next generation, those who—"

"Sir, we need to stay focused on—"

A gangly creature lurched towards them, covered in mottled green fur. It opened its maw and squawked. Jilly shuddered and almost fell backwards.

"Gaaah!" Blip aimlessly thrust his sword at it.

"Jilly! Stay behind me, girl," Blip commanded, but she could see that his efforts to hold off the beast did little. It lumbered toward them, oblivious to Blip's hapless feints and swings. It cried out again and took a swipe at Blip's sword.

"Back, you varlet, back O wretched foe, lest I smite thee with the full force of my blade!"

Jilly and Blip retreated, trying to draw it away from the oblivious dancing crowd. Her hands trembled as she tried to concentrate on a spell.

What were the words? Bollocks! I can't remember, I'm useless! No, wait, I've got it!

She started reciting an incantation out loud, barely hearing herself over the music. Four simple lines, that was all. Four lines said three times.

The creature lunged again. Blip stumbled to avoid it and bumped into her, just as she recited the final line. In the ensuing collision, she said... something? But it wasn't the right set of words. It was something she garbled.

At that same moment, a white light flashed around their enemy, and as the glow disappeared, a strange sight confronted them. Where the gangly green beast had menaced them, a strange hybrid animal with a pig's head and front feet, and the back legs of a chicken now stood. It oinked at them, snorted, turned, and wandered off.

"Ms. Pleeth, Jilly!" Blip looked at her in astonishment. "That was extraordinary! You made a veritable living Cockentrice. What did you do?"

"I have absolutely no idea at all," Jilly said, confused. "I think I made a mistake, actually."

"A very providential one, in that case. Just remember what you did when the next one comes along."

"The thing is, I don't even know what I said. I kind of mangled some of the words."

"In that case, perhaps a variation will yield similar results?"

"But what if it does something bad? What if it..."

"Argh! Jilly!"

"Sir!"

A gnarled, bat-winged horror swept out of the gloom and grabbed Blip by the arms, dragging him into the air and back into the darkness from whence it came. Still no one else noticed. The swirling portals grew larger and multiplied.

"Mr. Blip!" Jilly shouted. "Where are you?"

* * *

"Qwyrk, look out!" Holly warned.

Qwyrk ducked, just as an Unseelie something-or-other with sharp teeth and claws lashed out at her from behind. She jumped to her feet, turned around, and gave the thing a good walloping backhand, sending it crashing to the floor.

"Let's see if these portals work both ways, shall we?" she said as she grabbed the creature and heaved it straight up into a swirling vortex directly above them. It shrieked as the magical entryway caught it and sucked it in, like an upside-down whirlpool.

Holly slammed her stick into the noses of a goblinoid monster with two faces residing on one head. Both of them grunted as it slumped down, out cold. She took hold of it and flung it upwards, where the whirlpool hoovered it back to wherever it came from.

"So, we know how to get rid of them," she said.

"But how do we get to them all?" Qwyrk said, looking around as ever more twisted shapes began appearing in the swirls. "They could kill a lot of people before we can send them all back. These folks can't even see them."

"That must be the banshee's magic weaving its way through the song," Holly said, slamming another two-face goblinoid in the nose with a remarkable air of casualness before tossing it upward. "But I don't think we can stop it. It has to be Jilly."

"Let's just hope she does in time." Qwyrk stepped to one side as another beastie swung an old club at her. She caught the crude implement, yanked it out of the creature's hands, hit him over the head with it, and then shoved him through another portal that just opened up to their left. She heard him slam into something else on the other side and both yelped.

"That should slow them down for a bit. Come on, we have to get out into the crowd and protect people from any more of these tossers. Those bedazzled fans are sitting ducks!"

They waded into the thicket of undulating concert-goers, a sea of black and blacker that moved in an eerie unison, like puppets controlled by Aeval through Moirin's mesmerizing voice. The crowd seemed hypnotized.

"Stand back to back and move in a circle with me!" Holly shouted over the music. "We can see more that way."

They rotated together, keeping their eyes on as many portals around them as they could. It was like some odd dance; not the best romantic night out, it must be said.

Qwyrk happened to glance to the left side of the stage. "Look over there," she leaned back and said in Holly's ear, "behind me, in the shadows."

They rotated around so Holly could see. "It's the red-haired young lady from York, isn't it?"

"Yeah, and I'm guessing her being here isn't a coincidence."

"Another banshee? A human servant?"

"I doubt she's here for anything good."

"We could try to capture her, make her talk."

"If we grab her, Star Tao could be toast, like literally. As much as he annoys me, I couldn't live with that."

"I know, but it's a moot point anyway, look!" She turned to face Qwyrk and pointed above them.

The swirls near the ceiling lit up for a brief moment and then faded back to darkness.

"Crap!" Qwyrk swore. "Incoming!"

A swarm of flying, bipedal, bat-like creatures emerged, screeching as they began to circle above. They could strike at anyone in the club at any moment, and Qwyrk and Holly wouldn't have time to stop them.

* * *

Jilly watched Moirin sing, her exquisite voice a bizarre contrast to this surreal scene, like a Bosch painting come to life. Foot-tall, toad-visaged beasties, like caricatures of Blip, hopped about on their hind legs and croaked in their secret language. Haddock-faced critters carrying little swords eyed the club-goers with menace, as if ready to pay back a lifetime of human consumption of fish and chips. Goblins with maces skipped about in glee, growling, while floating eyeballs with teeth (oh, not those wretched things again!) hovered in the shadows, waiting to do goodness-knows-what.

The band played on, a sinister soundtrack to this macabre show. They were oblivious to what was happening, just as they'd been in Leeds.

Improbable creatures of all sorts emerged from the mists for short durations and faded back into them, as if they could only be here in this world for a moment and then had to depart. Whatever was happening, Jilly surmised, they couldn't remain here, not just yet. But some of them did stay behind, and these hissed and sputtered, giggled and snorted, flashing teeth and claws. Some swayed absurdly in time to the music, while moving with menace toward a human crowd that had no idea they were even there.

A scream tore through the club.

Jilly panicked, realizing that the audience was starting to see the monsters all around them.

She caught a glimpse of Qwyrk and Holly trying to fend them off, with limited success. These creatures clearly feared them, but there was only so much the two of them could do. Qwyrk pushed, punched, and shoved back whatever monsters got too close to the concert-goers or too bold in encroaching into their space.

Holly took every opportunity to smack anything and everything with her stick, eliciting loud squeals and shouts that sounded like curse words in some ancient tongue. Sparks flew in every direction in the wake of her attacks.

More vortices opened, and the howls of the strange things beyond them tore into the main hall. Many fans screamed again, and scrambled to get out of the way of the encircling creatures closing in on them. And still the band played on.

"Jilly, whatever you're going to do, you need to do it now!" Qwyrk kicked at a snake-like creature coiling around her ankles. It slithered away into the misty shadows. Holly managed to stomp on it, but it was gone before she could strike again.

"I'm working on it!" Jilly tried another incantation, but she messed up the words and had to start over. "Gah! I'm rubbish at this!" She clutched the talisman in frustration and shook it, but nothing happened, no matter how much she willed it.

A winged, furry, goblin-beastie-thing with sharp teeth soared by her head, screeching and breaking her concentration. And then another did the same. Several more of them appeared from another smoky vortex, their cackling joining together into a macabre chorus. Fans crushed against each other, surrounded on all sides. They started to panic, pushing against each other and strugglling against being penned in.

And still the band played, lost in a daze. Only Moirin and Aileen seemed aware of what was happening. And why was Star Tao now hovering near the stage, arms raised up?

Jilly could only hope he was channeling someone to help.

"Jilly!" Qwyrk yelled as she swung punches in every direction, even as the creatures overwhelmed her. "We're out of time!"

"Time," Jilly repeated. "Time! That's it!" In Leeds, Moirin's voice slowed down time. That's why everything seemed so strange, that's why no one else but Jilly noticed. She held up the talisman and concentrated on it. "So you turn things back on their users, eh? Let's just see if this works..."

And all at once, everything stopped.

CHAPTER TWENTY

Reality wasn't what it used to be.

All was silent, frozen in time.

She'd done it!

Jilly stared past the multitudes of unmoving fans and assorted beasties to the stage. The singer she so admired glanced about in bewilderment, pulled from the grips of her ancestor's spell. The two of them were the only ones unaffected.

"Moirin!" Jilly shouted. "Please, listen to me! I need to talk to you."

"What did you do?" Moirin demanded, stepping to the side of her mic stand.

Jilly looked at the talisman in her hand. "I slowed down time. Or, I pulled us both out of it, just for a bit. When I put us back, it'll be like we were never gone."

"I don't know what your game is, but stop it now. I mean it! I don't want to hurt you, I really don't."

"Then don't! Don't hurt me. Stop all of this. Please. You know it's wrong."

Moirin scowled. "I'm tired of people tellin' me what I should do. Manipulating me, using me. I lived for years under the thumb of those horrible creatures that just wanted me and my brother for whatever the crap they had planned. Now they're dead, he's dead, but I'm free. It's time I took back my power."

"But it's not your power, not really," Jilly implored. "It's hers; she's just using you, making you do what she wants you to, making you do her dirty work. And now she's forced her way into my friend's mind so she can mess with us in this world. Do you know how violating that is? She wants to harm people and cause trouble."

"It's not like that. You don't understand. She's my ancestor, we're bonded by blood. I'm a—"

"A Fomorian? Most of the humans who can do magic have a bit of Fomorian blood in them, me too. It's why I could do this," she gestured around her. "But that doesn't mean you have to be like them, Moirin. They're evil. They were awful tyrants in Ireland in ancient times. So whatever she's up to now, it's not good. It won't help anyone but herself and them. She'll drop you when she's used you up."

"No, you're wrong." Moirin pointed an angry finger at Jilly. "She's helped me. She's helped Aileen. She freed us from the crap we were stuck in and showed us who we really are."

"But who you are is up to you, not someone else. I don't know about your friend, but you're kind and you care, even if you hide it and act like you hate everyone. Believe me, I feel like that sometimes, too. But you're not bad. You're just scared. You want to be a singer, not some banshee that wails at the dying, not a killer that massacres innocent people. What good is any of that going to do? You're amazing! You're my favorite singer, and your band is brilliant, and I want you to come back and do that. You have so many gifts to share. That's what we want to see and hear. Stop this, please?"

Moirin glanced away. "It's not that easy, Jilly. Aeval... it's like she's got hooks in me. She's there, in my head, and I couldn't get rid of her even if I wanted to. Honestly, I'm not sure I want to."

"But you don't want to hurt anyone."

"Maybe. But I don't want anyone to hurt me ever again, either."

"No one will, not if you let me help you."

Moirin hesitated, but then her expression darkened. "I don't need to listen to you. Because of you lot, my brother is dead!"

"Your... brother?"

"Colm. You knew him as Longwing."

Jilly froze. "Longwing? He was your brother?"

"Yeah, and Qwyrk killed him, so shut the hell up!"

"No, no! Qwyrk had nothing to do with that. It was the Erlking."

"You're lying." Moirin crossed her arms, as if to block Jilly's words.

"No, I'm not, I promise." Jilly took a step forward. "Look, take my hand, I can show you my memories, you can see for real what happened, if you want to."

"Yeah, right. How do I know you're not tricking me, wizard girl?"

"You'll know. It's a simple spell. Just close your eyes and try it. Please?"

Moirin reached out a trembling hand and clasped Jilly's. Jilly let her own memories flood into Moirin's mind. She saw Moirin accepting them, but struggling with what she witnessed. Moirin shivered, her grip on Jilly's hand becoming tighter. Realization and grief seemed to overcome her. She let go of Jilly's hand and sank to her knees.

"You're right," Moirin said, looking at her with teary eyes. "And I heard him in my head just now, tellin' me the truth. He spoke to me before, in Leeds, when Aeval tried to take hold of me. He told me to resist her, not to give in. His spirit's still out there, lookin' out for me." She choked back a sob. "Aeval lied to me about the most important thing of all."

"I'm sorry, Moirin. We tried to save him. I think I can stop her. I can keep her power from flowing through you, at least for a good long while. But I need your permission. You have to let me do it."

"Can you help Aileen, too?" Moirin motioned to her.

"I don't know, but I'll try, I promise. By the way, here's your bag. We saved it for you."

"Thanks," Moirin said, taking hold of it. "Thought I'd lost it in not-elf land."

"Come on, we need to get back," Jilly said with a comforting smile.

Moirin nodded as Jilly squeezed the talisman and closed her eyes.

* * *

Jilly opened her eyes. Moirin looked around in confusion from the stage.

Chaos raged all about them. Multi-colored swirls of magic interlaced with shouts of panic and confusion. Qwyrk and Holly struggled to shove back the horrid creatures popping in and out of the mists.

The band continued to play, still under Aeval's spell.

"Aaaahhhh! Unhand me, thou lump of foul deformity!" Blip commanded as he thrashed about with his sword cane. The bat-beast toted him around the upper confines and rafters of the club, before disappearing into darkened mists again.

Moirin was shaking, no longer singing even as the music continued. Jilly rushed toward her. Just as she did, Star Tao and Aileen approached the stage from opposite sides, blocking her way.

"There you are, my darling," Star Tao's body said with Aeval's voice. "I hope that nasty little sorceress didn't keep you too long." He shot a hateful stare back at Jilly. "I'll be sure to snap her neck to prevent any further interference."

"Moirin!" Aileen said. "Where'd ya go, ya daft girl?"

"Don't listen to them, Moirin!" Jilly yelled. "Remember what I said. They don't get to tell you who you are."

"Be silent, you little wretch!" Star Tao's mouth commanded. "You know nothing of her heritage and her birthright. You are an insect compared to her. You carry only a tiny droplet of the noble blood, and it is wasted in your weak little form. Go from my sight while I yet have the mercy to let you live because of it."

"Moirin," Aileen pleaded. "This is your time. This is *our* time. She's here for us right now, in that idiot's body. Look around and see what you can do, what you've done already."

Jilly looked back and forth between all three of them. Her heart raced. "Remember who you are," she implored. "Please."

"Don't listen to that girl and her friends," Aileen hissed. "They're just deceivin' you and tryin' to take you away from your *real* family."

"My real family?" Moirin said in a weak voice to no one in particular, tears again in her eyes. "My real family's gone. My life was stolen from me, and I'll never know my parents." She looked at each of them in turn. "And my brother—Colm, Longwing—was the only family I had left. One of you pieces of magical shite killed him." She glared at Star Tao. "She showed me." She pointed at Jilly.

"Don't listen to her!" Aileen begged as she stepped forward. "She's lying!"

"She isn't!" Moirin insisted. "Our lives were turned upside down as babies by this stupid enchanted world, and it's still after me, never lettin' me be free. That ends now."

"Cease this nonsense, child, or the consequences will be severe," Aeval demanded, as Star Tao's body closed in.

Jilly knew they'd try to take Moirin away again, but she also knew she couldn't face them in a fight, not while her friends were still struggling to hold back the creatures bursting through the veils. So she pressed her one advantage, reaching for the crumbled sage in her small handbag. "Just say the word, Moirin, and I'll do it."

Moirin wiped away tears from her eyes and nodded. "Do it!"

"Do what?" Aileen yelled. "Ancestor, stop this!"

Aeval screeched as Star Tao's body rushed at Moirin.

Jilly flung her hands out, scattering sage on him, and uttering something in an ancient tongue that she didn't even understand. Moirin screamed and fell to her knees, clutching at her head.

"No, no!" Aeval shrieked. "What is this?"

"What's happenin'? What's goin' on?" Aileen panicked.

Star Tao's form looked again at Jilly. "What have you done? What? You vile little creature! I will tear you apart with this idiot's bare hands, I will—"

Qwyrk jumped between them and stood up from a crouched, superhero landing. "I've really had about enough of you for one week."

"You will not harm this little mortal form, Shadow," Aeval spat.

"Well, you don't really have any powers in his body, right? I mean, maybe you could channel some eighth-dimensional aliens singing prog-rock lyrics, or something, but that's a bit of a shite ability, to be honest."

Star Tao lunged at Qwyrk, and she launched a backhand across his face that sent him sprawling, tumbling to the floor, out cold.

"Sorry mate, I held back as much as I could." Qwyrk frowned with regret.

At once, the creatures throughout the venue howled and screeched as they were drawn back into the mists and vortices, which one by one, spun themselves into nothingness until they vanished, leaving only a few tendrils of smoke wafting through the air. And quite a few astonished concert-goers, gasping and looking around in fear and wonder.

"What did you do?" Aileen screamed.

"Oh nothing really," Qwyrk shrugged. "I mean, Jilly cut off Aeval's psychic link to Moirin, and I knocked our mate there for a loop, stopping her from possessing his body and having a vessel on this plane. Closed all the portals, hoovered up all the freaks. Just like that. It's kind of funny, actually."

"You will pay!" Aileen howled. Her eyes faded to pure white and streaks of grey slithered through her flaming curls. She raised her hands and emitted a low moan that grew louder and louder.

"Qwyrk?" Jilly said nervously, "I think we still have a problem."

Aileen's voice exploded, knocking Qwyrk and Jilly on their arses and sending them rolling backward several feet.

"Aileen!" Moirin shouted, pulling herself to her feet. "Don't! Please!"

Aileen ignored her and started toward Qwyrk and Jilly as a half-dozen terrified onlookers scrambled to get out of her way. Dark circles formed under her eyes and her face twisted into something almost unrecognizable, something not human. And still she cried out, still the ancient wail of her bloodline found its terrible, destructive expression.

Qwyrk jumped to her feet and put herself between Aileen and Jilly, fists raised. "Right, banshee 2.0, you want to go a few rounds? I'm game."

But Aileen said nothing as she glided toward them like a ghost. Jilly watched, horrified. "Qwyrk, I don't know, I don't—"

Aileen's wail intensified and struck Qwyrk like a gut punch, sending her stumbling back, and almost tripping over Jilly.

Aileen smiled and pressed her advantage.

"I'll tear the two of ya in half with my bare hands!"

Jilly knew she meant it.

But as she moved in, Jilly heard a thump. Aileen yelped and stumbled, falling to her hands and knees, a shower of sparks and light bursting forth behind her.

"I'm really quite done with you lot for the day," Holly said, brandishing her stick and looking quite satisfied with her critical hit.

"Yes!" Jilly pumped a fist in the air.

Aileen groaned and pushed herself up, her terrifying eldritch features gone entirely.

"Without your granny about," Holly said, "you're not so powerful, eh? Used up the last bit of magic in your little temper tantrum? Are you going to surrender, or do I have to smack you again? Feel free not to. I'd rather enjoy it, I must say."

Aileen opened her mouth, trying to recapture her primal visage, to scream, to wail, but nothing happened. With surprising swiftness, she turned and punched Holly in the stomach. Holly gasped and stumbled backward. Aileen was on her feet in an instant, shoving past Holly and Qwyrk and a few terrified onlookers. She disappeared into the darkness of the club.

"Holly!" Qwyrk ran to her side to help her to her feet.

"I'm all right." Holly sounded more irritated than hurt. She rubbed her belly, grabbed her stick from the floor, and stood up. "It's nothing, just a bit of a surprise. I should go after her."

"Yes, please. I mean, if you're sure you're all right?" Qwyrk said. "Looks like she's not so powerful now, and we could use some more answers. With Aeval out of Star Tao, I don't think she'll be able to draw any more energy, but be careful. That yell packed a wallop; who knows what else she can still do?"

"I'd rather not find out. But you take care of things here. I'll find her."

Qwyrk nodded. "We have to clean up this mess and try to do damage control, somehow. Bollocks, this is a nightmare!"

Qwyrk planted a quick good luck kiss on Holly's lips. "Off you go then."

* * *

Holly dashed out of the club into the side alley and shot a glance in both directions. She didn't see Aileen running away in either of them, but trusted her instinct and started off to her left. She ran for a block until she was faced with a cross street, packed with rubbish bins and old wooden crates. She had three options, none of which revealed the young woman fleeing on foot.

Fearing she'd lost her before the chase had even begun, she turned with a frustrated sigh and looked back toward the club. She lurched forward in pain as something slammed into her head, knocking her to her hands and knees. Stunned and disoriented, she struggled to shake off the pain and wooziness.

"Thought to get the better of me, eh? Just 'cause I can't wail doesn't mean I don't have other talents, like sneakin' up from behind." Aileen stood over her holding a wooden plank from one of the nearby boxes. "Since you lot saw fit to banish my ancestor, I'll just have to use whatever else I've got left."

Holly spun and lashed out with her weapon, catching Aileen's ankle and sending her crashing to the ground in a hail of sparks and lights. "Looks like I'm not so easy to finish off, either!" Aileen cried out and clutched her leg as she dragged herself up. She inched back along the ground, but Holly was still too stunned to pursue her. Aileen struggled to her feet and grabbed the wooden plank she'd used in her cheap shot.

Holly got up on one knee, but Aileen came at her again. She let out a small burst of sound, nothing like before, but enough to cause Holly to drop her stick and cover her ears. Aileen struck again, hitting Holly on the shoulder with the plank and sending her sprawling back to the ground. Aileen kicked her in the mid-section and Holly cried out.

"Not so tough, now, eh, faery?" Aileen taunted through her heavy breathing. She sounded exhausted. "Stay down! Don't follow me, or you'll be the worse for it."

Holly rolled over to see Aileen flee, limping down the left-hand street, dropping the plank in a loud clatter and disappearing into the night. Holly pulled herself up into a sitting position and swore again, retrieving her stick and weighing the wisdom of going after her foe.

As she stood, she grimaced from the pain in her back and side. She took a few deep breaths and tried to calm herself, having every intention of starting off in pursuit once again.

In a heartbeat, her surroundings changed. She found herself standing in a cave, with only a dim light glimmering from somewhere, neither from within this place, nor outside of it. Nothing made sense. She had no idea where she was or what was happening.

Nearby, a figure in a dark red robe stood, silent and unmoving, its arms enfolded in the robe's voluminous sleeves.

"Who are you?" She saw her breath, though the cavern didn't feel cold.

The figure said nothing, but Holly knew it was watching her. She swung her stick around as a threat, only to see that it left no light trails at all.

Something called to her. Not from the cave, but in her mind. A voice, ancient and sonorous, but somehow hollow and brittle at the same time, spoke. "Soon," it said.

"Soon what? Who are you? Answer me!"

"Soon, the end will come. Soon everything will change."

Holly tried to stand, to approach the robed figure. But as she did, it faded and she found herself back on the street, as if she'd never been away. There was no sign that anything unusual had happened. And Aileen was long gone by now.

Her head was cloudy. Surely her odd vision was because of Aileen's attack. She hadn't really just been in a cave, had she? Someone had spoken to her, someone in a robe. The memory of it had already begun to fade. She thought that maybe she'd just imagined it. Maybe she had a concussion.

But she knew that Aileen still had some of her power, even without Aeval. And she had to go back and tell the others the less-than-good news.

* * *

As Qwyrk pulled Star Tao's still unconscious body away from prying eyes, the murmur of the crowd turned excited. Then a few people started clapping. The clapping grew into rounds of applause. Then enthusiastic cheers.

"What the hell?" She looked back.

Leaving Star Tao in the dark, she crept as close to the edge of the light as she dared to see all manner of fans giving a proverbial standing ovation to Moirin and the rest of the band, all of whom seemed confused.

Jilly slipped past them and came to Qwyrk's side. "Uh, I think everyone thinks that was all part of the show," she said.

"Yeah, that's a first," Qwyrk nodded. "On the plus side, we may not have to do anything at all."

"That's a relief, because I really wasn't looking forward to wiping out everyone's memories."

"Wait, you can do that?"

Jilly chuckled. "You're far too easy to fool, you know?"

* * *

Moirin didn't know how to react, or even what to think. She'd been through hell, lost her connection to Aeval, probably to Aileen, and now she was here with the band, getting a damned ovation for something she didn't even do. She was a messy mix of just about everything one could feel, all thrown into a blender and messed up right poorly. She smiled at the fans, bowed, and tried to act like the macabre spectacle was all a part of the show, but her bandmates would have questions, questions she couldn't answer. Or with luck, maybe they never saw anything.

"Excuse me, pardon me." A man's voice brought her out of her confused state of mind and back to reality, or whatever passed for it these days. She looked down to see a middle aged fellow in a black suit with wider lapels on the jacket than were strictly necessary. He probably wore his longish hair loose to try to look younger than he was. Whatever.

"Sorry," she said, "have we met?" It was all she could think of to say.

"Not yet, but the thrill is mine. My name is Auberon Percival of Black Neutron Records. That, my young friend, was stunning, one of the most amazing shows I've ever seen! The music, the effects, the atmosphere... you gave us something truly extraordinary, something quite new, and I want to talk with you all about signing the band. I see big things for you, and believe me, I know how to pick them! You can view my CV on our website; it speaks for itself."

It was all too much and Moirin couldn't take it in. Sam and the others cheered and high-fived, and Sam hugged her, but she ignored all of it and simply smiled. "Thanks, that sounds amazing," she said. "Why don't you talk with the lads here first? I'm a bit wiped out and just need a few minutes backstage."

"Not a problem at all. Take the time you need. So what say you, lads? Shall we convene to a pub in a bit to talk business?"

"Absolutely!" Keegan answered.

As she walked away, she heard a voice over the collective post-concert chatter: "You ever hear of a band from Merseyside called 'Me and Me Mates'? Yeah, that was me and me mates!"

Another, more familiar voice called out to her. "Moirin?" Sam said as she left the stage.

She closed her eyes and sighed. "I'm fine, Sam. I just need a few minutes, yeah? I'll be back out in a bit."

"Yeah, sure, no worries."

She was grateful he didn't try to follow her, to touch her, to anything. She staggered to the dressing room and shut the door, shut out the noise, the talking, the people. She flopped down into a chair and looked at herself the mirror. She was exhausted, her makeup was streaked, and she had nothing left to give. Nothing at all. The sting of tears came to her eyes once more and she just gave in, broke down, and sobbed as she never had in her life.

* * *

Holly returned to the club, wading through the throngs of fans, surprised to see that fear seemed to have been replaced by giddy enthusiasm. She found Qwyrk and Jilly hiding in a dark corner with the still-unconscious Star Tao.

"So, the damage control went fine, I see," she said as she sidled up next to Qwyrk.

"Yeah, they think it was all part of the show, so I guess we're good," Qwyrk said. "The only problem for the band is that it's a performance they'll never be able to repeat. At least I hope they won't! I take it you didn't find Aileen?"

"Oh, I found her, or rather she found me. Managed to get a few cheap shots with a wooden plank. She taunted me and then ran off before I could get my bearings. I figured it wasn't a smart idea to try to face her alone, even if she doesn't have the banshee's full power any more."

"Smart call. Are you all right?" Qwyrk placed a gentle hand on her back.

"I'm a bit sore, but I'll live."

"I could kiss it better later on if you'd like."

"I'd like very much. You still have that Greek costume at hand, I assume?"

"Right, I'm going to check on Moirin," Jilly interrupted, extricating herself from a potentially awkward situation. "Make sure Star

Tao wakes up, all right?" And off she went, that ridiculous wig still on her head.

Holly looked after her and her gaze and thoughts drifted.

Qwyrk waved a hand in front of her eyes. "Are you sure you're all right?"

"Yes, I'm fine, really." She brought her attention back to Qwyrk. "I mean, I think I am."

"What does that mean?"

"I'm sure it's nothing. Do you remember me telling you about how I've had some disturbing dreams of late?"

Qwyrk nodded.

"I feel like… this is silly, but, I feel like I've just had another one of them, even though I was awake the whole time. I know that makes no sense at all, but, that's what it seems like."

"Are you sure you didn't get knocked out?"

"Fairly sure."

"Do you think Aileen could have done something to you? Some kind of Fomorian magic mind mess-up?"

"I don't think so. It's different, but I couldn't tell you why." She shook her head, still trying to clear it. "Oh, I'm probably just tired and imagining things. Let's revive Star Tao and get out of here. Where's Mr. Blippingstone?"

Qwyrk shrugged. "Haven't seen him in quite a bit. I'm sure he'll reappear and tell us how heroic he was soon enough."

"Bloody hell, what happened?" Their mortal companion said in a weak voice.

"It was quite the mess, I'm afraid," Holly answered, helping him sit up.

"Aeval, the banshee, she possessed you, sorry to say," Qwyrk added.

"What? No! No, that can't be right. That can't happen," he protested.

"It did, sorry to say." Qwyrk gave him a brief summary of the evening's paranormal events. "Nothing to worry about, though. It's all good, and you're back. I'm sure you'll do better next time."

But Star Tao didn't answer. He just kept looking down at the floor, seeming distressed, lost in thought.

* * *

Jilly pushed open the dressing room door just a little. "Moirin?"

Her new friend slumped in a chair, holding herself in a hug. She looked up at Jilly, her face streaked with tears.

"Hey," Jilly said, entering the room and closing the door behind her. "It's all right. You're all right, Everything's going to be fine now."

"No, it's not, Jilly. Nothing's ever gonna fine again. I had a family once, and I lost them, all of them. And then, I had a chance at another, and now I've lost them, too."

"But the banshee wasn't a real family. She wanted to use you; make you hurt people." Jilly came close and knelt down.

"Not Aileen," Moirin protested. "I mean, I got to know her, and she's a good person. She's just been under Aeval's spell for a lot longer than I was. Is she all right?"

Jilly shrugged. "She ran away. Holly went after her, but Aileen attacked her and then ran off. She still has some of her powers, I guess."

"See? That's what I'm sayin'. She's alone now, probably afraid. I have to find her. I have to help her."

"You have to help yourself first, and you're in no condition to do anything right now."

Morin sighed. "I never wanted any of this. I just wanted to sing, to have some friends, a band, a bit of a family. Now, it's all gone."

She buried her face in her hands, and Jilly put a comforting hand on her shoulder.

"But doesn't that bloke want to sign you to his record label? That's brilliant! You so deserve it!"

"I can't do that right now." Moirin looked up. "I can't even think about it. I don't want to let the lads down; we've worked really hard for it. We do deserve it, but I think I have to step back, just for a while."

Jilly's heart sank. "You're not leaving the band?"

"No, but I need time for me. Maybe to find Aileen? Try to find myself. But I can't keep singing right now, Jilly. I have to go away."

Jilly swallowed her disappointment. "I'm sure the band will understand."

"Maybe, but they've put up with so much crap from me already."

"You'll just have to trust that things will work out."

"Yeah right," Morin scoffed, "because that's always gone so well before."

"Maybe things will be different this time, if you just let them?"

"Maybe, but I'm not gonna hold my breath."

Jilly smiled and took her hand. "That's fine. I'll hold it for you."

* * *

The happy crowd had dispersed, the band (minus Moirin) had gone to a nearby pub to discuss their impending stardom. Qwyrk, Holly, Jilly, and Star Tao stood just outside the backstage door of the club, enjoying the quiet after the chaos.

"Where *is* Blip?" Qwyrk asked, looking around, eager to be on her way.

"I haven't seen him since one those creatures swooped him up." Jilly frowned and fidgeted. "I'm worried."

"I am right here, thank you very much," he said stepping through the door, sword cane in hand, Weasels cravat in place.

"You're all right!" Jilly exclaimed, holding out her arms.

"Quite, thank you. I was making sure that every one of those damnable beasties had been sent off. The last thing we need is those creatures running amok in this world."

"And is the clean-up complete?" Qwyrk asked with a heavy dose of sarcasm.

"Indeed," Blip retorted. "I'll have you know that at one point, I single-handedly beat off three of those things at once!"

Qwyrk tried to suppress an immediate guffaw, but couldn't manage very well. She saw Holly struggling with the same problem, so she grabbed her hand and squeezed it. They looked at each other again, but that only made things worse. To complicate matters, Qwyrk saw Jilly holding her hands over her mouth, also trying to fight off a raging case of the giggles.

"What?" Blip demanded. "Why is everyone acting the fool lately?"

"No reason," Qwyrk sputtered, "none at all." She glanced again at Holly, who had shut her eyes to fight against the tears forming in them.

"I demand to know what's happening!" Blip exhorted. "You, boy," he spoke to Star Tao, "what's is the cause of this affliction?"

"No idea, my lord, though me head's not in the game tonight, I'm afraid."

"Well, get it in the game, man! We're beset by lunatics!"

"It's nothing sir, nothing at all," Jilly managed to blurt out, before doubling over in a fit of laughter so strong that the wig fell off her head and flopped straight to the ground in a comical thud. Qwyrk and Holly completely lost what small portion of composure they still clutched at, and soon all three were howling in laughter, while a bewildered Blip glared at them.

"Gah! I'm surrounded by miscreants and Bedlamites! Never mind. I'm leaving. I'm late for an appointment as it is."

"Don't forget your walking stick... sword... thing. I'm sure it can take a beating!" Qwyrk chortled, leading to a new round of uncontrolled hysterics.

"I snurl at the lot of you." Blip turned to storm off.

"That sounds a bit indecent," Qwyrk remarked with glee.

* * *

Their amusement subsided and Qwyrk deposited a tired Jilly and a forlorn Star Tao at Jilly's house. Soon after, she and Holly snuggled on Qwyrk's sofa, as ever, sipping Qwyzz's port.

"Well, that was a hell of an evening," Qwyrk sighed, moving on from sipping to gulping.

"At least no humans were hurt." Holly followed Qwyrk's lead and drained her glass, before helping herself to another generous pour.

"Thank Goddess for small favors. Not one of our finest nights, though. Aeval's only been shut out for a while, and Aileen's still out there with an unknown amount of power left in her, ready to do Goddess-knows-what in her anger."

"She was formidable, it must be said."

"Yeah about that: are you sure you're all right?"

"I'm fine. Just a few lucky hits on her part, and we Fae heal quite quickly, so nothing to distress yourself over."

"I know, but I wouldn't be much of a girlfriend if I didn't worry."

"Well, I think you're a smashing girlfriend!"

"Oh you do, do you?" Qwyrk smiled and moved in for a much-needed kiss, which led to another and another.

A scratching sound at the front door interrupted the moment. Alarmed, Qwyrk was up at once, Holly close behind. She opened the door, but no one was there. Only a letter sealed with wax rested on the ground.

"Who the hell would leave me a letter in the middle of the night?" Qwyrk asked.

"Maybe one of the trees dropped it off." Holly joked.

Qwyrk shot her a sarcastic smile and broke the seal to reveal a short message.

"Qwyrk: Castlerigg Stone Circle tomorrow, mid-afternoon. Come alone." Qwyrk read it aloud and looked at Holly. "No signature, and I don't recognize the handwriting."

"Oh, that doesn't sound ominous at all," Holly said. "And who would know to deliver it here? It's worrying."

"True, but it still might be worth me going. Whoever sent it might have important information. NNs aren't the only ones who sneak around, trading secrets, and it can't be a coincidence that whoever it is wants to meet back at the circle."

"It's obviously a trap!" Holly protested. "I don't think you should go. Or at least I need to come with you."

"It says come alone."

"Qwyrk."

"I'll be careful, I promise! First sign of any trouble, I'll teleport right out of there."

"But what if you can't?"

"I've got your ring." She held up her hand. "I'll call for help."

"I still don't like this."

"Nor should you. But taking risks is what we do. This story isn't over yet, and we need any leads we can get to figure out what's going to happen next."

Holly sighed. "Fine. I just wish you weren't so damned heroic sometimes."

"Can't help it, darling. You bring out the best in me." They went back inside and Qwyrk closed the door, tossing the letter aside. "Let's not worry about it tonight." She smiled, leaning in for another kiss. "Now, where were we?"

CHAPTER TWENTY-ONE

Qwyrk stood in the center of Castlerigg circle. She had a good idea of who she'd be meeting, and the last thing she needed were any mortals getting in the way. The dark sky threatened rain at any moment, but at least there were no people about.

"Come on out, banshee!" she shouted. "I can feel your presence here. Not that I really want to deal with you, but apparently, I've got no choice if I'm going to wrap this up. Let's finish this so you can bugger off back to wherever the hell you came from!"

For a short while, there was no response. She grew increasingly irritated and pondered just giving up and leaving, but then, a loud wind whooshed past her and the air distorted around one of the far stones. In a moment, an old lady with sickly grey skin stepped out from behind the stone.

"So, you decided to show up," Qwyrk said. "How nice of you. Let's talk, or whatever. If you want to fight, I'm not especially in the mood, but I'll give it a go if I have to."

"You do not want to test me, my dear," Aeval retorted as she hobbled forth, gripping her ornate walking cane. She pointed it at Qwyrk. "It would not end well for you. There are some of us whom, even you in your bravado, cannot defeat. My kind are among them."

"What exactly are you, anyway, besides a big pain in the arse?" Qwyrk recoiled at her gruesome countenance.

"Think of me as... a demigod? As such, you can barely harm me, not for long anyway, and you certainly cannot kill me, or force me to do anything I do not wish to do."

"Well, that's the funny thing, isn't it? I don't need to kill you. Honestly, I don't even want to. We've already beaten you; Moirin is free of your influence, free to live her own life, do whatever she wants. You've lost."

Aeval cackled. "Oh, this is not the end, naïve Qwyrk. Not at all. I do commend your young witchling, though. She has power, but her spell will not last forever. She has only delayed the inevitable. Moirin will eventually embrace her destiny, and I'm afraid there's nothing you can do to stop it."

"Yeah, we'll see about that, lady," Qwyrk fired back, clenching her fists, spoiling for another fight despite the banshee's warning.

"We will indeed, but if I were you, I'd be far more concerned with what's about to come than worrying about the fate of a wayward Fomorian girl over which you have no say."

"What do you mean?" Qwyrk furrowed her brow.

"You have searched far and wide for answers to the mysteries of de Soulis and the Erlking, but the truth has been right in front of you all along, and you've been too arrogant to even see it, or maybe just too foolish."

Qwyrk bristled. "What are you talking about?"

Aeval chuckled. "A war, Qwyrk. An ancient war that has been

waged for time beyond reckoning, occasionally out in the open, but most often in secret, away from prying eyes."

"What the hell do you mean? What war?"

"A war between the ancients, the primal ones and the innovators, the changeable ones. In short, between the old and the new amongst the factions of darkest magics. The Erlking was supported by hidden partisans of the ancients, de Soulis by secret members of the innovators. Both of them sought to rule the world, but they were merely pawns in an even larger game. Both were in service to an opposing side, though I doubt that they even knew it, foolish and vain creatures that they were. They were merely figureheads for those factions that want control of all magic and the worlds it encompasses."

"So, different groups of villains are battling it out among themselves. Lovely. Sounds like a problem that'll take care of itself. And what about you, then?" Qwyrk asked, hands on hips and not especially impressed with her story.

"I am of the old, whilst the kobolds were of the new. They wanted their stolen children, Longwing and Chantz, to be warriors for the innovators, but the Erlking ensnared Longwing, and I will yet have young Moirin return to her true heritage; I am patient. Know this, Shadow: the ancients now have the upper hand. We have waited a long time and we will soon return to reclaim this world for ourselves. There is nothing you can do to stop us. The Fomhóraigh will walk this earth once more. You'd best be certain that you choose the correct side, for choose you must. A warrior with your strength could do very well in the new-old order that the ancients will bring back. We were quite pleased when you defeated de Soulis for us, less so when that foolish young man channeled the Erlking's daughter and banished him back to their realm, but some battles we win, some we lose. There is a greater goal to be achieved and that is the retaking of this Earth."

"All right, let's get one thing straight," Qwyrk snapped. "I am not working with you ancients, or the damned innovators, or anyone. I've spent most of the last bloody year standing against you pillocks. If there's a bloody war between bad and worse somehow going on under our noses, you can all just wipe each other out and be done with it, as far as I'm concerned. I'll happily stand back and watch that show."

Aeval laughed again. "So be it. Have a great care in these coming months, Qwyrk of the Shadows. You cannot stand against us, or against what is coming. None that are of your magic can. But if you want to achieve some degree of contentment in these last months of your long life, then look to those among your own folk, look for those who have led you astray and set up snares for you. They wish you nothing but misery and will be happy to leave you alone in such a state. Ask yourself if you really want to defend them. Are they worth the cost of your own life? Your own happiness?"

"What the hell are you on about?" Qwyrk's patience was almost worn out, and her eyes started to glow red.

Aeval held up a hand in mock innocence. "You shall learn soon enough. For now, I take my leave from you. We may yet meet again, but whether as allies or foes, that is up to you. Be assured that you are being watched closely. Some believe that you may be the key to everything that is about to unfold, or you may be its undoing. If I knew which, I would deal with you myself."

Qwyrk flung her hands up. "Oh, bloody hell, stop with the cryptic crap! You're making no sense at all, and I'm getting a headache trying to suss out what you're babbling on about. And honestly? I don't want to anymore. Since you're not going to give me any real answers, and I can't beat them out of you, just sod off and leave me alone!"

Aeval made a slight bow, mocking and insincere, then turned and limped away to where she'd appeared. A whirlwind rose up from the ground, encircled her, and then vanished, taking her with it.

Qwyrk exhaled a frustrated sigh and lingered for a while longer, pondering it all. But she had no idea. She held out her hands to shape the air around her and vanished in a subdued flash of violet light.

* * *

Qwyrk reappeared back at her home. Thankfully, no rocks or trees had moved in the time she was gone. Even better, Holly waited for her outside, looking decidedly relieved.

"You're back, thank goodness!" Holly opened her arms wide. Qwyrk ran to her and let herself be wrapped up in her lady's warm and very welcome embrace. She wanted to hold on for dear life and never let go. After a good half an eternity or so, they stood back, gazed at each other, and kissed while Qwyrk stroked Holly's hair.

"It *was* Aeval," said Qwyrk. "She managed to spend a few minutes on the earthly plane, probably tapping into the circle's power."

"Goddess, are you all right?" Holly shivered and took her hand.

"I'm fine," Qwyrk said. "She really did just want to talk."

"Well, that's something, I suppose. So, what did Lady O'Malice have to say?"

"It wasn't great, to be horribly honest," Qwyrk said. "In fact, it was basically awful. In just about every way you can imagine." They went inside and she relayed what Aeval had told her.

"Oh, that's not good," Holly said afterward. "Not at all."

"No, it isn't, but there's more." Qwyrk's stomach tightened.

"I, um... I had some odd news from Qworum, you know, the head Shadow council member. I've... been meaning to tell you."

"What news?" Holly raised a worried eyebrow.

Qwyrk exhaled and debated what to say, wishing she could avoid it altogether. "It's really strange, infuriating. Nonsense, I reckon. He, sort of off the record, well... basically told me that I, um, I should away from you."

Holly stepped back, jaw open. "What? Whatever for?"

"I have no idea, and honestly, I think it's a load of bollocks. I don't even know how they found out about us. I think they're just really not happy with me after the whole buggane incident, and now they're trying to upset me, or at least mess with my head. I wouldn't at all be surprised if Qwalm is behind this. Stupid prat."

"Well, maybe we should go to them and give them a piece of our minds; and our boots. The nerve!" Holly looked angrier than Qwyrk had ever seen her.

"No." Qwyrk laid a sympathetic hand on Holly's arm. "I mean, you know how much I'd love to knock him and few of the others around, but that would only make things worse. I could be locked up for 'insubordination,' or whatever they wanted."

"Fine, but why would they try to separate us?"

"Because you and I are brilliant together, and we aren't taking their crap. Maybe they think that if they can drive a wedge between us, they can weaken me, make me more obedient. I don't know! But honestly, I'm not going to worry about it right now, and I'm certainly not going to let them tell me what to do. We can chat more about it later, but I should probably head on over to Jilly's in a bit and check in on her and Star Tao. They're not used to losing a fight, or how crap it feels afterward. They're both young and still inexperienced. It's the least I can do for dragging them into our world."

"Sounds lovely of you, as always." Holly kissed her. "See you later then?"

"Yes, please," Qwyrk said. "Come back here? Whenever you like. I definitely need you tonight; the council can stuff it!"

"Well, I'll see what I can do." Holly grinned her grinning Holly grin. Qwyrk was happy to behold her resilience and optimism in the face of such a terrible couple of days.

"I'm counting on it." Qwyrk gave her a reassuring hug and kissed her one more time before stepping back, and with a wave of her hand, shooting herself away from the best romantic thing that had happened to her in pretty much forever and off to see the best new friend she'd had in at least as much time.

* * *

Sam and Moirin met in an old cemetery in Newcastle. They sat on a bench near some headstones and Moirin took comfort in her surroundings.

"So, what did you want to tell me?" Sam asked.

"It's not easy to say," she said. She took a deep breath. "I have to go away for a while, a few months, maybe more."

"Wait, what?" Sam looked crestfallen.

"Look, I know it's not fair to you and the lads, but I need this time, Sam. I'm all kinds of messed up right now. I have to clear my head if we're ever gonna make a go of this band, make it the success we want it to be. But that record label bloke really liked us, yeah? And I've chatted with him, and he said it's fine for me to take time to get myself together before we start into a proper recording and really get it going. But when I come back—and I will, I promise—we'll be able to dive right in and do it right."

Sam looked away. "No, I get it. Band-wise, that makes sense, I suppose. I was just, I don't know, hoping I could be there for you, be there in whatever way you, you know, might need me?"

Moirin sighed. She looked down to avoid meeting his gaze. "Sam... you're lovely, you really are, but I just, I can't."

"Is this the part where ya tell me it's you, not me, to make me feel better, which won't work at all, but I'll say it does to make you feel better about me not feeling better?"

She shook her head and looked back at him with a weak smile. "I mean, yeah, all right, it *is* me, but it really is. I don't fancy you that way, but I don't know *what* I fancy. Honestly, it's all a big question for me. I don't know if that makes any sense. I probably seem like a big freak, or something."

"No, you don't. I'm disappointed, obviously, but I get it. You have to be true to yourself."

"Thanks, Sam, that means a lot, really. Uh, you're not just sayin' that to make *me* think we're good when we're really not good and you know we're not good even though we're pretending we're good, are you?"

"Not that I know of, no. Unless I didn't understand a word of what you just said, which I admit, is possible."

"Great, brilliant, thanks, Sam."

She hugged him, which was far less awkward than she feared it would be. Maybe some people weren't so bad after all.

* * *

Jilly met Moirin at the Newcastle coach station, where Qwyrk had surreptitiously taken her.

"Again, I'm so sorry about what happened at the gig, about everything," Moirin said in a guilty voice. "I just, I couldn't control it. Once her magic flowed through me, I was hardly even there in my own head, and it was like all I could do was watch and let it happen. But I also liked it, the power, and what I might do to people, and that really scares me. That's not who I am, Jilly. At least I don't think it is, which is why I have to go away for a bit and try to figure things out."

"I understand. Where will you go?"

"Not sure. Maybe back to Ireland, get in touch with my roots, or something."

"Will you try to find your family?"

Moirin shook her head. "Even if I could, it's been too long. I don't know them and they don't know me. What would we say to each other? Hell, why would they even believe me? They've been living with a fake 'me' for more than twenty years. They'd probably think I was crazy and call the police. And I don't think I could handle meeting my replacement... and Colm's."

Jilly felt bad and wanted to hug her. "What about Aileen?"

Moirin sighed. "I don't know. She's a lot like me. Like I said, she's not a bad person, but she's caught up in it, way deeper than me. I want to help her, but I don't know if she can come back. I've no idea where she is, either. And she can't find me, since I tossed away her amulet and you blocked out Aeval. So I'll just have to be alone for a while, which isn't a bad thing. I'm used to it; I prefer it, to be honest."

Jilly wasn't convinced by her brave front. "How will you get by?"

"Oh, Holly fronted me a good pile of cash. Came from faery gold, she said, whatever that means. I told I'd pay her back every penny and she just waved it off, said not to worry. She's a good one, so kind and generous. Your Qwyrk's a lucky lady."

Jilly smiled. "She knows it."

Moirin looked behind her. "Anyway, my coach is leavin' soon. I'd best be off."

They made their way toward Moirin's coach, working their way through a throng of passengers, rather like salmons swimming upstream. As they arrived at said bus, Jilly felt awkward, unsure of what to do or say. In the next instant, Morin surprised her and gave her a big hug, which she was delighted to return.

"Goodbye, Moirin. Good luck, take care of yourself, eh?"

"Goodbye, Jilly. I will. And you be well, too, okay?"

"Promise me you'll write to me once in a while?"

"I will. I quite fancy the idea of havin' a pen pal to check in with, so I'll email you when I can."

"I can't wait! Go and have some adventures and tell me all about them!"

Moirin took Jilly's hand and gave it a squeeze, and then turned to board her coach. She looked back to give Jilly a final wave. Jilly waved in return and smiled, though she couldn't shake the feeling that they would indeed meet again, but not under happy circumstances.

* * *

"I can't believe that happened," Star Tao said, sitting cross legged on Jilly's living room floor, looking dejected. "And even worse, I could've hurt you, Jilly, and everyone else."

Qwyrk sat on the couch nearby, thinking about how to comfort her young companions, but coming up blank.

"I'm so sorry about it all," Jilly said in a sympathetic voice. "Are you all right?"

"Well, I've had better days," he sighed, "I can promise you that."

"Aw, cheer up!" Jilly patted him on the shoulder. "I mean, you've got your next big workshop coming up, right? That's going to be really special."

He looked up at her, a haunted expression darkening his usually cheerful face. "I don't know if I even should be doin' it. After bein' possessed, I mean. I failed, like totally. I have no idea what happened, how she got in me head. I might've killed someone. I couldn't live with myself if I did that."

"But you didn't," Jilly touched his arm. "And besides, it wasn't you. We all know that. Plus, we got everything back under control, we drove her out, and that's all that matters, right?"

"It's not that simple," he said. "I've thought about it. I'm done, with channeling, anyway, and I need to have a think about all the other things. See if I can redo the workshop a bit. I can't cancel it. Wouldn't want to let everybody down. But if I could get possessed like that, it might happen again, and I don't want to risk it. I sure as hell don't want to be teachin' it to anyone else. I'll talk it over with Qwypp and see what she thinks." He drew himself up with some resolve. "But yeah, for now, I'm done. The Council of 27 will just have to find another conduit on this plane until they can get me a more secure connection. I won't let it be hacked again!"

Jilly looked sad, but said nothing else.

"I'm sorry mate," Qwyrk said after a moment of awkward silence, "I actually really am. You've been right helpful in the past. Thomas, the Erlking's daughter, all that. But maybe right now, it's for the best? Just until you get a better take on what's going on?"

Jilly shot her a look, but Qwyrk didn't acknowledge it.

"Yeah, you're right," Star Tao said with a resigned sigh. "It's time to put it on hold. Anyway, I'm gonna head on out now. Lovely seein' you all again, what even with that whole mess. I'll, um, I'll be in touch, yeah?" He stood up, gave Jilly a hug, and nodded at Qwyrk before slipping out the front door without saying anything else.

"Wasn't that a bit unkind, encouraging him to stop?" Jilly asked after he'd gone.

"No, it wasn't," Qwyrk answered. "He's done some real good, but he's still a young human messing around with powerful magic that he can't control well, at least not yet, so going cold turkey is probably a really good idea at the moment. At least until we figure this all out. That thing that possessed him? She's powerful. She just butted right in and kicked out whatever else he was connecting to like it was nothing. We can't risk that again. And she's strong, really strong. She threatened me at Castlerigg, and honestly, I believed her. It's not often I back down from a fight, but I had a sense she could've laid me out for good if she'd really wanted to. He doesn't need her getting into his head again."

"You're right," Jilly said, looking out the window. "But he looked so sad, like his whole world just got turned upside down."

"It happens," Qwyrk said.

"That's mean, Qwyrk."

"No, it's not. We lost, Jilly. Fine, so we got Aeval and the other girl to back off, but this isn't over. Who knows how long it'll be before Moirin succumbs to her ancestral urges while she's out 'finding' herself? Maybe she can resist it for a while, maybe your spell will hold, but maybe not. And if not, we'll have a big problem. Also, it's not just her. There might be other things happening in the background."

"What are you talking about?"

Qwyrk shook her head. "I don't really know. There's some

rumblings going on about some kind of bigger play. I'm getting warnings."

"Warnings? About what?"

"It's not important, because I don't believe them, but some odd things *are* happening in Symphinity, like little ripples in reality, things being where they shouldn't. Trees, rocks, even buildings showing up in new places, kind of randomly. It's worrying, because it feels like something is probing, testing, looking for a way in, trying to break our magic barrier, the same way Aeval did at Qwyzz's."

"What kind of something?" Jilly looked concerned.

Qwyrk shook her head. "I don't really want to think about what might have the arrogance and the power to do that."

"Could it be more of the banshees? Or someone on their side?"

"Possibly. We don't have enough to go on yet, but yeah, it could be someone with that same kind of power, looking to start a fight. The banshees might be an early sign of something much worse."

"That's not good." Jilly sat back down on the sofa, crossing her arms and hugging herself.

Qwyrk sat down next to her and took her hand. "Hey, don't worry. I'm sure things will be all right. Our world has been around for a really long time, and it's not easy for anyone we don't want to get in to actually get in. All right, Aeval is the exception. But I think that was only because Moirin was there, and they're connected. Whatever happens, *if* something happens, we'll be ready for it. It's nothing you need to worry yourself about."

"Are you sure?"

"Very! Look we've had a bad few days, but it's a good lesson, not just for you, but for me, too. Sometimes the good guys lose, or at least we don't win as well as we want to. We've been really fortunate that those previous crazy outings turned out in our favor, but that doesn't always happen. It's just the way of things. Learning to accept it when you've gotten your arse kicked is an important part of growing up. You've done amazingly well with everything my bonkers world has thrown at you, so don't feel bad. We'll pick ourselves up, do the proverbial dust-off, and get back on the horse tomorrow."

"Or the Komodo dragon?" Jilly managed a weak smile.

"Oh Goddess, don't bring her up! A least she hasn't burned my house down."

Jilly squeezed Qwyrk's hand. "So, what are you doing tonight?"

"Taking a much-needed break, maybe having a hot bath, enjoying some time with my girlfriend, and putting off worrying about anything else until tomorrow."

"Sounds lovely. Makes me wish I had someone to be here."

"I'm sure Blip would be happy to give you a lecture on Kierkegaard."

Jilly elbowed her. "Internet videos, drawing, and a book will be just fine, thank you very much. Though now that you mention it, a bath would be lovely, too."

"Parents not home again?"

"What do you think?"

Qwyrk sighed in frustration. "What the bloody hell is wrong with them? I swear, I want to thump them. Not that I ever would, of course, but you know what I mean."

"I feel that way a lot myself. Strange as it sounds, Blip's actually nice to have around, in a sort of eccentric uncle kind of way."

"Is he off again? Seems like he's gone all the time, now."

Jilly shrugged. "Yeah, he's quite absent these days. His face is always in some book or other, and then he's away far more than usual. He doesn't tell me where he's going, and it seems a bit rude to ask, so I don't. He is rather proud, you know."

"Hadn't noticed," Qwyrk quipped. "But I imagine he'll be back to his old, annoying self soon enough."

"I hope so. I actually miss that."

Qwyrk put her hand on Jilly's forehead. "Are you feeling all right?"

"Oh, stop!" Jilly said with mock irritation, shoving her hand away.

"Don't worry, my dear," Qwyrk smiled, wrapping her arms around her young friend. "Everything's going work out fine."

* * *

Qwyrk opened her eyes and looked out the window into the dark. But why had she opened her eyes at all? Her Reverie normally ended well after dawn.

"That's odd," she whispered to herself. She glanced over to her right, but Holly wasn't there.

"Holly?" she whispered a bit louder, but a quick scan of the bedroom revealed no one.

She slid out of bed and, throwing on her silk robe, she made for the door, which was a bit ajar.

"Holly?" she whispered again, and again there was no answer. But stepping out, she saw a red glow coming from the sitting room. On instinct, she clenched her fists.

This was not good at all. She tried to force back the horrible thoughts clawing to get into her mind, her pessimistic imagination taking over and filling her with dread, especially after all that had happened the past few days.

"Everything's all right." She edged toward the glow, trying to convince herself, but not succeeding. "Everything's fine. There's a perfectly good reason for this. We'll be laughing about it in a minute, we'll be... oh no!"

As she stepped into the sitting room, she unclenched her fists and clasped her hands over her mouth in disbelief. What she saw was unnatural, impossible. Even in this world.

"Holly!"

She stared at the scene in shock. Holly was floating on her back in mid-air above the sofa, dressed only in her nightshirt and seemingly still asleep, or unconscious. A red light swirled, pulsed, and hummed all around her, as if it were alive. Alive and dangerous. And in the distance behind her there was a darkness that was both there and not there, a void that seemed to be reaching out toward her, toward both of them, from somewhere else, from some other plane of existence. Somehow Qwyrk knew that it wanted Holly. Maybe it wanted them both.

She gasped, unsure of what to do. Holly seemed unaware of any of it, her arms hanging by her side and her long hair trailing away beneath her as she drifted up and down in a slow, repeating pattern.

Qwyrk started toward her, only to feel something, some force pushing her back, resisting her, fighting her off. She shoved forward in defiance, but each step seemed to take more effort. The void began to move, too, as if it were now racing against her to reach Holly first. It was trying to take her. And Qwyrk panicked.

"No!" she shouted. "I don't know what the hell you are, but you're not having her. Not tonight, not ever!"

She willed herself forward, determined to reach Holly first, determined not to let this thing anywhere near her. The humming sound grew more intense as she drew closer. Holly stopped rising and falling and began to spin slowly.

"Holly!" Qwyrk shouted, though she could barely hear herself over the rising rumbling. "I'm coming, darling, hold on!"

Each step was agony, like trying to move through a wall of mud. But she pushed forward and ignored the pulsing in her ears that made her head throb.

"Holly, wake up!" she shouted as she reached out. "Please! Hear me! Help me fight this!"

The void yawned nearer to them now, extinguishing the red light little by little. Qwyrk fought against it, not only with her body, but with her mind. It seemed to be calling to her, telling her to retreat, to let Holly fall into the darkness. There was something almost soothing about it, as if by letting it claim Holly, all would be well. It was trying to tempt her. *Give her to me*, it seemed to say.

But Qwyrk was having none of it.

"Get out of my head, you bastard! I don't know what you are, but I'll kick your arse, wherever it is on you!"

She pushed back with her mind, but the void surged, striking at her with the full force of its power, knocking her backward to the floor. And then it moved for Holly, who spun faster. She started to spin into it, to be absorbed by it.

"No!" Qwyrk shouted, jumping to her feet and leaping forward. She propelled herself right into Holly, catching hold of her, but still the void called, still it drew her in. Qwyrk strained to hold her in her arms.

"You are not taking her from me!" Qwyrk yelled, and her words seemed to stir Holly, if only a little.

"Qwyrk?" she said in a weak voice without opening her eyes.

"Yes, love. I'm here. It's me. I've got you."

Holly said nothing more, but brought her arms up and wrapped them around Qwyrk's neck.

"That's it!" Qwyrk yelled. "Fight it! We're a team, you and me, right? Nothing is going to come between us. This thing can't stand up to us." Tears came to her eyes. "And we've still got so much to do. We're just getting started." The ominous words of Aeval echoed in her mind, but she pushed them away. "You can beat this, *we* can beat it. Come on, darling, stay with me. This thing isn't real, it's all in our heads, okay? I've got you, and I'm not letting go. I'm never letting go!"

Holly's grip on Qwyrk tightened. She didn't open her eyes. She didn't even seem like she could hear a word Qwyrk said. But she held on.

Qwyrk cried out as the void attacked her mind again, and she felt Holly stiffen in her grip, but Qwyrk wouldn't let go of her.

"You're not taking her, you hear me? You're *not!*" she yelled out in defiance, knowing that if she were to die, it would be here and she would do so gladly.

And then the pain vanished. The pull, the resistance, the void, the red light, all of it, gone as if it had never been there. Qwyrk collapsed to the sofa with Holly in her arms. There was only the darkness of the sitting room, the blessed natural darkness and the quiet that came with it. They were alone again.

"Qwyrk?" Holly said in a weak voice, opening her eyes a little.

Qwyrk cradled Holy in her arms, stroking her hair and leaning over to kiss her forehead. "Shhhh, it's all right, darling, everything's all right."

"What happened?"

"You just woke up." Qwyrk tried to sound as soothing and calming as she could.

"I had a terrible dream. At least, I think it was a dream. I saw a red light in the sitting room. And then, I was floating somewhere. And there was someone else there. Not you. Someone in the dark, wearing a robe, I think." She shivered, and Qwyrk pulled her in closer.

"It spoke to me. I think the voice was a woman's voice. There was something familiar about her? I couldn't see her eyes under her hood. She knew me, said things to me; I can't remember them."

She opened her eyes a little more and looked up at Qwyrk. She started shaking and looked scared.

"She told me that... that everything is about to change. That my world is ending and that I... I'll die. I think I've met her somewhere else, maybe more than once, and she told me the same things before. And then I felt something terrible pulling at me, trying to take me away. Away from you, from myself. But I heard you, too, far away, calling out for me, trying to pull me back. And then I woke up and now you're here. What was it? Was it a dream?" Her sleep-filled eyes seemed to plead with Qwyrk for words of comfort and assurance.

"Yes, love, it was only a dream. But you're all right now, darling. There's nothing to be worried about. I have you, you're fine, you're safe. I'd never let anything happen to you." Qwyrk stroked her head again.

Holly curled up in Qwyrk's lap and closed her eyes. "I know. I'm glad. It seemed so real, but it's fading already. What did I just say? Something about someone talking to me? Telling me something? I can't remember. I'm so tired. Will you hold me for a bit while I sleep?"

"I'm not leaving you," Qwyrk whispered. "Ever. I'll stay with you all night, and well beyond."

Holly smiled. "Good. That's lovely. Thank you, darling." She spoke no more and soon drifted off into a peaceful sleep, as if nothing had happened.

"Everything's fine," Qwyrk repeated as she held her dearest

close, but she knew in her heart that something was very wrong, and she was very much afraid of finding out what it might be.

*   *   *

Light streamed into a dark, candle-lit stone chamber as the door opened. The shadowy form of a small figure stood in the doorway, in stark contrast to that dim luminance. It walked toward a wooden, circular table at the center of the room. Several figures sat around it, all wearing dark robes, hoods drawn over their heads. The little figure wore the same garb.

"So," one of the seated said in a raspy voice, "all is going as planned?"

The diminutive figure stopped and nodded. "The way is made clear," it said in no more than a whisper. "By the coming of Hallow's Eve, the work will be complete. The Deathly Eye shall finally return and reclaim the mortal world."

"And I take it that those under your watch still remain ignorant of our plans?"

"Trust me," the figure said in a louder and more posh voice as it lifted back its hood, revealing a frog face, with a handlebar mustache and muttonchops. "Qwyrk, her Yakshi lover, the witch girl, and the foolish young man have absolutely no idea what is about to descend upon them."

"Very good, Mr. Blippingstone," the seated figure replied with satisfaction. "Very good, indeed."

ACKNOWLEDGEMENTS

A third trip into the weird and wacky world of Qwyrk and her staunch companions was inevitable, because so much still needs to be told!

There are always people behind the scenes who help when one is writing a book of any kind. I like to think of this novel as a product of "Me and Me Mates." Thanks to my agent, Maryann Karinch, for continuing to believe in this strange and silly series and for wanting to share it with the world. Thanks also to Armin Lear for providing a home for it. The grand finale is on its way!

Special thanks to my ever-wonderful partner, Abigail Keyes, for being willing to take a deep dive into these stories and make suggestions that strengthen the narratives and leave them better than when she found them. And thanks again for her splendid editing skills, taking my draft and fixing all the mistakes I so inconveniently included.

Thanks to my readers and "blurbists," who always provide great feedback and make these books better than I could come up with on my own.

And as always, thanks to Freya for inspiration, guidance, and insight.

COMING IN AUTUMN, 2023
FAYTTE

Well, things turned rather bad, didn't they? After a summer where everything seemed to be going so well, Qwyrk and company are abruptly reminded of just how cocked-up things can get in a terrible hurry. Qwyrk and Holly are literally being driven apart by mystical, magical forces they don't understand, Blip might be involved in some sinister undertakings, Star Tao's lost his mojo, and Jilly, well, she knows everything is going wrong, but doesn't have a clue of how to fix it.

It gets even worse when Holly goes missing and Qwyrk loses something else that's just as important to her. All of the behind-the-scenes scheming and shenanigans come to the fore at last, as Qwyrk and her friends finally learn just what they're up against, and it's not very nice! And who is the mysterious and ancient figure dwelling in an alternate reality that seems to know all and see all, but annoyingly won't talk about it?

Traitors abound, old friends return, armies will form, sides will be picked, and the final battle between good and evil will rage. Well, all right, maybe not the *final*, final battle, but if the good guys don't win this one, things are going to be rather rotten for the foreseeable future. To stop it from happening, Qwyrk might have to make a decision that will change her life forever.

Faytte is the final book in a series of four novels about the comic misadventures of a group of misfits at the edge of normal reality in modern northern England, a world of shadows, Nighttime Nasties in a bakery, a mysterious key, every monster you can imagine, an abundance of sarcasm, and the answers to all the questions. Oh, and a hapless professor who might have accidentally initiated the end of the world. And once and for all, Qwyrk is going to definitively prove that she's not a bloody elf! They're just silly!

AUTHOR BIO

TIM RAYBORN has written an astonishing number of books over the past several years (approaching fifty!). He lived in England for quite some time and has a PhD from the University of Leeds, which he likes to pretend means that he knows what he's talking about. His generous output of written material covers topics such as music, the arts, history, the strange and bizarre, fantasy and sci-fi, and general knowledge. He undoubtedly will write more, whether anyone wants him to or not.

He's also an internationally acclaimed musician. He plays dozens of unusual instruments that quite a few people of have never heard of and often can't pronounce, including medieval instrument reconstructions and folk instruments from Northern Europe, the Balkans, and the Middle East.

He has appeared on over forty recordings, and his musical wanderings and tours have taken him across the US, all over Europe, to Canada and Australia, and to such romantic locations as Marrakech,

Istanbul, Renaissance chateaux, medieval churches, and high school gymnasiums.

He currently lives in Washington state (where it rains a lot), surrounded by many books and instruments, as well as with a some-times-demanding cat. He is rather enthusiastic about good wines, smoky single-malt Scotch, and cooking excellent food.

timrayborn.com
timrayborn.bandcamp.com
@timrayborn@mastodon.social
twitter.com/Tim_Rayborn
facebook.com/TimRaybornMusicandWriting

Ingram Content Group UK Ltd.
Milton Keynes UK
UKHW040846130423
420106UK00004B/129